A powerful blow came out of nowhere like a bolt of lightning, striking her in the middle, doubling her over. Her muscles strained against a force squeezing her chest. She heard snapping and felt her ribs break, sending yet another kind of pain ripping through her.

Magda dropped heavily to her knees.

Her vision narrowed to a dark tunnel. Everything seemed far away. She thought she heard voices but she couldn't make them out over the piercing, painful, high-pitched noise. She recognized that she had only precious moments to live.

With that awareness, she realized how desperately she didn't want to die. Despite how much she wanted the pain to stop, she didn't want to die. She had never felt so strongly about wanting to live. But she could feel herself slipping ever closer to the dark rim of the underworld. Magda remembered then her husband's last words on the note in her pocket.

Be strong now, guard your mind, and live the life that only you can live.

COMPLETE SWORD OF TRUTH SERIES
BY TERRY GOODKIND

TERRY GOODKIND

THE
FIRST
CONFESSOR

THE LEGEND OF MAGDA SEARUS

TOR

Tor Publishing Group
New York

THE FIRST CONFESSOR

Copyright © 2012 by Terry Goodkind

All rights reserved.

A Tor Book
Published by Tom Doherty Associates/Tor Publishing Group
120 Broadway
New York, NY 10271

www.tor-forge.com

Tor® is a registered trademark of Macmillan Publishing Group, LLC.

ISBN 978-0-7653-8307-5

Our books may be purchased in bulk for promotional, educational, or business use. Please contact your local bookseller or the Macmillan Corporate and Premium Sales Department at 1-800-221-7945, ext. 5442, or by email at MacmillanSpecialMarkets@macmillan.com.

First Tor Edition: July 2015
First Mass Market Edition: July 2016

Printed in the United States of America

17   16   15   14   13   12   11   10   9   8

To one of my best friends, Rob Anderson, whose support and encouragement have been invaluable in making this book possible. Besides being one of the smartest people I've ever known, he is also a man of tremendous integrity, scrupulous honesty, and boundless enthusiasm. His considerable talents have brought stunning visual imagery to my words and a beautiful social environment for friends of my books and visitors alike. His deep appreciation for both my work and my readers keeps him working tirelessly behind the scenes to create cool things that bring people closer to me and the books than was ever possible before. We are all indebted to him.

This one's for you, Rob.

THE
FIRST
CONFESSOR

CHAPTER

1

I have heard it told," the old woman confided, "that there be those walking among us who can do more than merely speak with the dead."

Coming out of her distracted thoughts, Magda Searus frowned up at the woman leaning in close over her shoulder. The woman's intent expression drew heavy creases across her broad, flat brow.

"What are you talking about, Tilly?"

The woman's faded blue eyes turned to check the shadowed corners of the gloomy room. "Down in the lower reaches of the Keep, where those with exceptional talents go about their dark work, it is said that there be gifted among them who can speak with souls beyond the veil of life, those souls now in the world of the dead."

Magda placed her trembling fingers on the creases in her own brow. "Tilly, you should know better than to believe such gossip."

Tilly's gaze again lifted to search the somber room lit only by thin streamers of light coming in the slits between the ill-fitting, warped shutters. The narrow slices of light revealed specks of dust floating almost motionless above the heavy wooden worktable set hard up against the stone wall.

The table bore the age-softened evidence of dark stains, cuts, and scars collected over centuries of varied use. The edges of the thick top had been irregularly rounded over and worn smooth by the touch of countless hands that had over the passage of time given the wood a polished, chestnut-colored patina.

Sitting at the table, facing the shuttered windows, Magda stared down into memories held in a small silver box sitting alone before her as she thought of all that was lost to her.

Everything was lost to her.

"Not mere gossip," Tilly said softly, compassionately. "A friend I trust works in the nether reaches of the Keep. She knows things, sees things. She says that some of those whose work it is to know about the world of the dead have not merely spoken to those passed on, but have done more."

"More?" Magda couldn't bring herself to look up from the memories in the box. "What are you saying?"

"My friend says that the gifted down there may even have ways to bring people back from the world of the dead. What I'm saying is that maybe you could have him brought back."

Elbows on the table, Magda pressed her fingertips to her temples as she struggled to keep the tears from springing anew. She stared down at a dried flower he had once given her, a rare white flower he had climbed all day to retrieve. He had called her his young, fierce flower and said that only such a rare and beautiful thing befit her.

So why would he choose to abandon her in this way?

"Brought back? From the dead?" Magda slowly shook her head as she sighed. "Dear spirits, Tilly, what has gotten into you?"

The woman set down her wooden pail and let the washrag she was holding slip into the soapy water. She leaned down a bit more, as if to make sure that no one could hear, even though there was no one else in the cluttered, rarely used storage room.

"You have been kind to me, Mistress," Tilly said as she laid a gentle, wash-wrinkled hand on Magda's shoulder. "More kind than most folk, even when you had no need to be. Most ignore me as I go about my work. Even though I've worked here most of my life, many don't even know my name. Only you have ever asked after me, or offered me a smile, or a bite to eat on occasion when I was looking haggard. You, of all people."

Magda patted the warm, comforting hand on her shoulder. "You're a good woman, Tilly. Most people don't see the simple truth in front of them. I have offered you nothing more than common decency."

Tilly nodded. "Common decency is what most of your standing would offer only a woman born noble."

Magda smiled distantly. "We are all noble, Tilly. Every life is . . ."

Magda had to swallow, fearing that another word would put her over the edge.

"Precious," Tilly finished for her.

Magda managed a smile for the woman. "Precious," she agreed at last. "Maybe I see things differently because I wasn't born noble." She cleared her throat. "But when a life is over, it is over. That is the way of life. We all are born, we live, we die. There is no coming back from beyond the veil."

Magda considered her own words and realized that they weren't entirely accurate.

It occurred to her for the first time that it might have been that he had brought death back with him, that even though he had succeeded in returning from his perilous journey to the world of the dead, perhaps he had never really escaped its grasp. Perhaps he couldn't.

Tilly fussed with the end of her apron strings as she mulled something over for a moment.

"I don't wish to upset you, Mistress," she said at last. "It is only because you have been kind to me and always treated me with respect, that I would tell you that which I would dare not speak of to another. But only if you wish to hear it. If you don't, you have but to say the word and I will never again speak of the matter."

Magda let out a deep breath. "Tell me then."

Tilly ran the side of a finger along her lower lip as she took a final glance around the somber room before speaking.

"Down in the burial vaults, Mistress, down in the tunnels running far underground near where some of the departed are placed and most visitors aren't allowed, my friend says that the wizards working for the war effort have found a way to bring the dead back to life. Though I admit that I have not seen such things with my own eyes, she swears on her soul that it be true.

"If it be true, then perhaps . . . perhaps there be a way to have Master Baraccus brought back." Tilly arched an eyebrow. "You are one with the standing to ask for such indulgences."

"Do you forget so soon exactly who my husband was, Tilly? Take it from me, wizards are masters of deception. They can conjure all sorts of illusions and make them seem real."

"No, Mistress, I have not forgotten who your husband was. He was loved by many people, me included." Tilly picked up her bucket. She paused to consider Magda's words. "It must be as you say. You would know of such illusions far better than I." She dipped her head respectfully. "I must be on to my work, Mistress."

Magda watched the old woman make her way toward the door. She moved with an ever so slight, rocking, hitched stride, the result of a fall the past winter. Apparently, the broken hip had never healed properly.

Tilly turned back before reaching the door. "I didn't mean to upset you, Mistress, with talk of returning a loved one from the dead. I know how you are suffering. I only thought to help."

The woman probably couldn't begin to imagine that Magda's husband, a man of great power and ability, had already returned once from the world of the dead. After others had been lost in the attempt to answer the warning of each night's red moon, a desperate call for help from the Temple of the Winds beyond the veil, her husband had undertaken the unprecedented journey himself.

He had traveled to the world of the dead, and returned.

Magda knew that, this time, he would not be returning.

With nothing left for her in the world of life, Magda wanted only to join him.

She managed another small smile for the woman. "I know, Tilly. It's all right. Thank you for thinking to help."

Tilly pursed her lips, then thought to add something. "Mistress, perhaps you could at least visit a spiritist. Such a woman might be able to contact your husband for you. There be a woman of such ability down there. I believe those wizards consult her in their work."

"And what good could it really do to visit such a woman?"

"Perhaps you could at least speak with her and ask her to help provide the answers that would let you be at peace with what First Wizard Baraccus did. She may be able to bring you his words from beyond the veil, and put your heart at peace."

Magda didn't see how her heart could ever again be at peace.

"You may need help, Mistress," Tilly added. "Maybe

First Wizard Baraccus could still somehow help to protect you."

Magda frowned at the woman across the small room. "Help to protect me? What do you mean?"

Tilly took a moment in answering. "People are cruel, Mistress. Especially to one not born noble. As the beautiful wife of the First Wizard, you are widely respected, despite being so much younger than him." Tilly touched her own short hair, then gestured at Magda. "Your long hair is a mark of your standing. You have used your position of power to speak before the council for those in the Midlands who have no voice. You alone give them voice. You are widely known and respected for that, not just because you were the wife of the First Wizard.

"But with Master Baraccus gone you have no one to protect you, to give you standing before the council or anywhere else for that matter. You may find that the world is an unfriendly place to a widow of a powerful man who herself is not gifted and was not born noble."

Magda had already considered all of that, but it was not going to be a problem she would live to face.

"Perhaps the spiritist could bring you valuable advice from beyond the grave. Perhaps your departed husband could at least explain his reasons and ease your pain as well."

Magda nodded. "Thank you, Tilly. I will think on it."

Her gaze again sank to the silver box of memories. She couldn't imagine why Baraccus had done what he had done, or that he would be able to explain it from beyond the grave. If he had wanted to explain his reasons, he'd had ample opportunities to do so. He would have at least left a letter waiting for her upon her return.

She knew, too, that there was nothing Baraccus could do from beyond the grave to protect her standing. that didn't really matter.

A faint glow of candlelight fell across the floor as Tilly opened the door on the far side of the room.

"Mistress."

Magda looked back over her shoulder to see Tilly standing at the open door, lever in hand.

Men, their faces in shadow, their hands clasped, stood out in the hallway.

"There are . . . visitors come to see you, Mistress."

Magda turned back to the table and carefully closed the silver box of treasured memories. "Please let them in, Tilly."

Magda had known that sooner or later they would come. It appeared that it was to be sooner rather than later. She had planned to be finished with it all before they had a chance to show up. That, too, it seemed, was not to be.

Her spirits would have sunk lower, but they could go no lower. What did it matter anymore? What did any of it matter? It would soon enough be ended.

"Would you like me to stay, Mistress?"

Magda touched her fingers to the long, thick, freshly brushed hair lying over the front of her shoulder.

She had to be strong. Baraccus would want her to be strong.

"No, Tilly," she said after getting a firm command of her voice, "it's all right. Please let them in and then you may go on to your work."

Tilly bowed deeply from the waist and backed away a little as she held the door open wider for the men to enter. As soon as all seven of them had glided into the room, Tilly hurried away, closing the door behind her.

Magda slid the ornately engraved silver box to the side of the table, placing it beside a well-used collection of exquisite metalsmithing tools, semiprecious stones in divided trays, and small books filled with notes that had belonged to her husband. She let her hand rest for a moment on the table where his hands had been when he had sometimes worked at the table, late into the quiet of the night, crafting items like the extraordinary amulet he'd made when the war had begun.

When she had asked its purpose, he had said that it was an ever-present reminder of his calling come to pass, his talent, his duty, and his reason for being. He said that it represented a war wizard's prime directive: to cut the attacker down, to cut them down to their very soul. The ruby red stone in the center of the intricate lines represented the blood of the enemy.

He said that the amulet represented the dance with death.

He had worn it every day since he'd made it, but left it in the First Wizard's enclave, along with his singular black and gold outfit, a war wizard's outfit, a war wizard's battle armor, before he had stepped off the side of the Wizard's Keep and dropped several thousand feet to his death.

Magda lifted her long brown hair back over her shoulder as she turned to the seven men crossing the room. She recognized the familiar faces of six members of the council. Each face was fixed with a stony expression. She suspected that the expressions were a mask for a bit of shame they likely felt at what they had come to see done.

She had known they would come, of course, but not this soon. She had thought that they would have paid her the grace of a bit more time.

There was another man with them, his face shadowed by the hood of his loose brown habit. As they came closer, into the weak light leaking in around the closed shutters, the seventh man pushed the cowl back to rest on his rounded shoulders.

The man's black eyes were fixed on her, the way a vulture's steady gaze fixed on a suffering animal. Men often stared at her, but not in this way.

He had a short, wide, bull neck. The top of his head was covered in closely cropped, wiry black hair. Stubble darkened the lower half of his face. A high hairline made his forehead and the top of his skull look even larger. The lines and folds of his face for the most part tended to all draw in toward the center, giving his expression a pinched, pushed-in look. All his coarse features looked firm and densely packed, as if every part of the man was as hard as his reputation.

He wasn't ugly, really, merely unusual-looking. In a way, his striking visage gave him an intense, commanding air of authority.

There was no mistaking that it was the head prosecutor himself, Lothain, a man of far-reaching authority and the renown to match it. His singular features, punctuated by those black eyes, made him impossible to forget.

Magda didn't know what such a man was doing with the council, carrying out the formality of a miserable little task. It seemed beneath his time.

Lothain's grim expression, fixed with weathered creases lining his leathery face, did not look as if it might be covering the slightest bit of pity, as did the expressions of the others. Magda didn't think the man was capable of uneasiness, much less shame, and certainly not pity. The hard lines of his face bore testimony to the fact that this was a man who went about his work with relentless, iron determination.

Not a full moon before, everyone had been stunned when Lothain had brought charges of treason against the entire Temple team, the men who had, at the direction of the Central Council, gathered dangerous items of magic together into the Temple of the Winds and then sent it all into the underworld for safekeeping until after the war. The trial had been a sensation. In it, Lothain had revealed that the men had gone far beyond their mission and not only locked away more than they were supposed to, but made it all but impossible to recover.

In their defense, some of them said that they believed in the Old World's efforts to save mankind from the tyranny of magic.

The convictions had ensured that Lothain's reputation had an edge to it that was as razor-sharp as the axes that had beheaded the hundred convicted wizards of the Temple team.

In a bold effort to try to undo the damage done by the traitors, Lothain himself had on his own authority then gone beyond the veil, into the underworld itself, to the Temple of the Winds. Everyone feared for him on such a journey. Everyone feared to lose a man of such ability and powers.

To everyone's relief, Lothain had returned alive, if

shaken by the journey. Unfortunately, the damage done by the Temple team had proven to be greater than even he had suspected, and he had not found a way in, so he had returned without being able to repair the damage done by the Temple team he had convicted.

Lothain strolled in closer to Magda and gestured, indicating the formality of his preamble.

"Lady Searus, may I offer my condolences on the unfortunate and untimely death of your husband."

One of the council members leaned in. "He was a great man."

Lothain's sidelong glance moved the man back in line with the others.

"Thank you, Prosecutor Lothain." She glanced at the councilman who had spoken. "My husband was indeed a great man."

Lothain lifted a dark eyebrow. "And why do you suppose that such a great man, a man beloved by his people as well as his alluring young wife, would throw himself over the Keep wall to drop several thousand feet down the side of the mountain to meet his death on the rocks below?"

Magda kept her voice steady and spoke the simple truth. "I wouldn't know, Prosecutor. He sent me away for the day on an errand. When I returned, he was dead."

"Really," Lothain said in a drawl as he touched his chin and gazed off in thought. "Are you saying that you suspect that he didn't wish you to be here, to see the terrible damage a fall from that height to the rocks below would do to him?"

Magda swallowed. She had been unable to prevent herself from imagining it a thousand times in her mind's eye. By the time she had returned, people had already seen to having him sealed in a stately coffin.

That morning, scant hours after she had learned of his

death, the ornately carved maple coffin with her husband's remains had been placed on a funeral pyre on the rampart outside the First Wizard's enclave. Because his body had been sealed in the coffin, she wasn't able to look upon his face one last time. She didn't ask to have it opened. She knew why the coffin was sealed.

The pyre burned for most of the day as hundreds of solemn people stood silently watching the flames consume their beloved leader, and for many, their last hope.

Instead of answering such a tasteless question, Magda changed the subject. "May I inquire as to your business here, Prosecutor Lothain?"

"If you don't mind, Lady Searus, I will be the one to ask the questions."

His tone had an edge to it that took her by surprise.

Seeing the shocked expression on her face, he offered a brief, insincere smile. "I didn't mean to interrupt your grieving, but you see, with the war threatening our very existence, there are matters of pressing concern to all of us that I'm afraid I must ask about. That's all I meant."

Magda was not in the mood to answer questions. She had her own pressing concern. But she knew this man well enough to know that he wouldn't leave her to her own business until he saw to his.

She saw no choice but to answer his questions.

CHAPTER
3

Magda smoothed the front of her dress as she gathered her composure. "And what pressing concerns would you need to ask me about?"

He flicked a finger out toward the shutters. "Well, there is the matter of the moon turning red." Lothain strolled off a few paces and then turned back. "After I failed to gain access to the Temple of the Winds, others, presumably with abilities more effective for such a specialized undertaking than I, also made the journey. None of them returned."

Magda was baffled as to what he was getting at. "They were good men, talented men, valuable men. It was a great loss."

Lothain strolled back close to her. His black-eyed gaze glided over items on the table, like the eyes of a vulture looking among bones for scraps. He turned a notebook with a finger to see what was written on the spine before addressing her again.

"Your husband selected those men."

"They were volunteers."

He smiled politely. "Yes of course. I meant to say that your husband selected the men who were to go to the

Temple and ultimately their death from among a group of volunteers."

"My husband was First Wizard." Her brow tightened. "Who would you expect to select men for such a dangerous mission? The council? You?"

"No, no, of course not." He gestured offhandedly. "It was clearly First Wizard Baraccus's responsibility to select the men who would go."

"Then what is your point?"

He smiled down at her. That smile might have been on his lips, but it was not in his eyes.

"My point," Lothain finally said, "is that he selected men who failed."

Hard as she could, Magda slapped the man across his face. The six council members gasped as they drew back. Her hand probably stung more than Lothain's solid face, but she didn't care. The sound of the slap seemed to hang in the air for a moment before fading.

Lothain dismissed the slap with a polite bow of his head. "Please accept my apology if it sounded like I was making an accusation."

"If it was not an accusation, then what was it?"

"I am simply trying to get to the truth."

"The truth? The truth is," she growled, "that while you were in the underworld, attempting to gain entrance into the Temple, the moon each night and each night since turned red in a warning, the most serious warning possible from the Temple, that there is some sort of grave trouble—"

He cut her off, dismissing the issue with a flick of his hand. "The appearance of repeated red moons was probably because of the damage done by the Temple team."

"And when you returned, after failing in your attempt to undo that damage, the First Wizard had the terrible duty to select a volunteer to answer the Temple's nightly call of a red moon. And when the first man failed to return, the First Wizard had to send another, more experienced wizard, and when that one failed to return, he had the grim duty to select yet another, even more skilled man, all of them friends and close associates.

"I stood beside him at the rampart each night as he stared off at the red moon, inconsolable, as one friend after another failed to return from the underworld. Inconsolable that he had sent valuable men, his friends, men who were husbands and fathers, to their death.

"Finally, when no one else had succeeded, my husband undertook the journey himself, and in the end paid for it with his life."

Lothain let the ringing silence go on for a moment before speaking softly. "Actually, he did not pay for it with his life. He took his own life after returning."

Magda glared at him. "What is your point?"

Lothain tapped his fingertips together for a moment as he studied her wet eyes. "My point, Lady Searus, is that he took his own life before we learned what had happened on his journey to the Temple of the Winds. Perhaps you can tell us?" He cocked his head. "Did he make it in?"

"I don't know," Magda said. But she did know. Baraccus had told her that he had, and told her a lot more. "I was his wife, not a member of the council or—"

"Ah," Lothain said as he tipped his head back. "His young, exquisitely beautiful, but so very ungifted wife. Of course. So obviously a wizard of such great ability would not discuss matters of profound power with someone who had none."

Magda swallowed. "That's right."

"You know, I've always been curious. Why would . . ." His frown returned as his black eyes again fixed on her.

"Well, why would a man of such extraordinary ability, a gifted war wizard, a man whose talents included everything from combat to prophecy, why would a man like that marry a woman who had no ability at all? I mean, other than . . ." He let his gaze wander down her body.

He was fishing, accusing her of being nothing but a pretty bauble, the shallow possession of a powerful man. Prosecutor Lothain was making the bold charge that she was simply sexual entertainment and nothing more— repeating what contemptible gossip took for granted—in an attempt to get her to admit that she was indeed more, and that she knew more, than would the mere attractive status symbol of an older man.

Magda didn't take the bait. She didn't want to trust this man with anything she knew. Her instincts told her not to tell him what she knew about Baraccus's journey to the Temple of the Winds.

She felt tears begin to run down her cheek and drip off her chin.

"Because he loved me," she whispered.

"Ah, yes, of course. Love."

Magda was not about to explain her relationship with Baraccus to this man. Prosecutor Lothain was too cynical to begin to understand what she and Baraccus had meant to each other. Lothain saw her the way so many men saw her, as an object of desire, not as a person, the way Baraccus had seen her.

One of the council members, a man named Sadler, stepped forward, a scowl growing across his sagging, aged features.

"If you have an important question, then please ask it. Otherwise I think you ought to leave the widow Searus to her grief."

"Very well." Lothain clasped his hands behind his back. "What I would like to know, is if you are aware of any clandestine meetings that First Wizard Baraccus might have had?"

Magda frowned at the prosecutor. "Clandestine meetings? What do you mean? What clandestine meetings? With whom?"

"That's what I'm asking you. Are you aware of any secret meetings he had with the enemy?"

Magda could feel her face go red with rage. "Get out."

Her own voice surprised her with its calm power. He studied her eyes a moment, then turned to leave.

"I do hope that First Wizard Baraccus was the hero so many think he was," he said back over his shoulder, "and not involved in a conspiracy."

Taking long strides, Magda closed the distance to the man. "Are you accusing my husband of conspiring with the enemy?"

He turned back at the door and smiled. "Of course not. I merely think it strange that the men Baraccus sent to the Temple of the Winds failed, and that he would then go himself on such a mission when the war burns hot and he is desperately needed here. After all, approaching enemy troops threaten our very existence. It seems a strange priority for him to take, don't you think?

"And even more curious, when he returned, he rushed to kill himself before anyone could so much as ask him if he made it into the Temple to repair the damage."

He held up a finger. "Oh, but wait. It just occurs to me that with the moon still red, he must not have gotten in or it would have returned to normal while he was still there." His frown returned. "Or at least, if he did get in, he must not have repaired the damage. After all, had he done so, the red moons would have ceased. Now, as the red moon slowly wanes, apparently even the Temple has given up hope."

He was still fishing. Magda said nothing.

His antagonistic smile returned. "You do see my point, I trust. Treason is an offense that can taint even the dead. And, of course, knowingly aiding a person committing treason is treason as well, and would cost such a person their lovely head."

He started away again, but then again turned back.

"One last thing, Widow Searus. You will make yourself available to answer questions should I deem a formal investigation to be necessary."

Magda trembled with rage as she glared at the man's smile. She didn't give him the satisfaction of an answer before he finally turned and left.

CHAPTER
4

After watching the door close, Councilman Sadler turned back to Magda. "I must apologize, Lady Searus."

"No need for you to apologize." Magda arched an eyebrow. "Unless you support Lothain's accusations against my husband?"

Sadness softened his expression. "Baraccus was a good man. We all miss him. I fear that bitter sorrow over recent events may have clouded Lothain's better judgment."

She glanced at the other five. Hambrook and Clay nodded their agreement. Elder Cadell made no show of his feelings. The gazes of the last two men, Weston and Guymer, dropped away.

"He did not seem to me to be a man possessed by sorrow," she said.

The hunched elder, Cadell, gently touched the back of her shoulder. "There is grave concern in the air, Magda." His hand left her shoulder to gesture past her and the other councilmen toward the shuttered window overlooking the city of Aydindril. "All of us stand at the brink of annihilation. People are understandably afraid."

Councilman Sadler let out a troubled sigh. "Added to that, there is great confusion as to what happened with

First Wizard Baraccus. It doesn't make sense to us, so imagine the rumors and gossip spreading through the Keep, much less down in the city. Everyone expected First Wizard Baraccus to always stand with his people, to defend them, to protect them. Many feel that he instead deserted them. They don't understand why. Prosecutor Lothain is merely giving voice to suspicion and unease, merely speaking aloud what whispers are saying."

Magda lifted her chin. "So you believe that it is proper for Prosecutor Lothain to give voice to gossip? Do you also believe that such talk from anonymous people who know nothing of the true reasons behind events calls for fabricated accusations from the head prosecutor himself and quick beheadings in order to quell gossip and discontent? Is that your position?"

Councilman Sadler smiled somewhat self-consciously at the way she had framed it. "Not at all, Lady Searus. I am merely suggesting that these are stressful times and perhaps Prosecutor Lothain is feeling those stresses."

Magda didn't relent or shy from his gaze. "Since when do we allow fears and misgivings to guide us? I thought we stood for more. I would think that a head prosecutor, of all people, would only be interested in his duty of seeing the truth brought out."

"And maybe that is exactly his purpose," Elder Cadell said, speaking softly in an attempt to make what was a sharp point sound less harsh and at the same time bring the disagreement and criticism to an end. "It is the rightful duty of the head prosecutor to question. That is how we discover where the truth lies. Beyond that, the man is not here to speak to his reasons for asking the questions he asked, so it is only right that in his absence we in turn not speculate or fabricate accusations of our own."

Magda had dealt with Elder Cadell for several years. He was open-minded and fair, but she knew that when he made it clear that he was finished hearing a point of view, he expected it to end there. She turned away to rest a hand on the smooth, rounded edge of the worktable and changed the subject.

"So what would be the purpose of this visit from the council? Have you all come to discuss some of the matters I have pending before you?"

There was a long silence. She knew, of course, that that wasn't the reason they were there. She turned back around to face all the men watching her.

"Those are matters for another time," Sadler said.

"And will I be heard when I return to the council chambers at another time? Will the concerns of those I speak for be heard by the council, then, when I am no longer the wife of our First Wizard?"

Sadler's tongue darted out to wet his lips. "It's complicated."

She leveled a cutting look at the man. "Maybe to you, but not to me."

"We have a great many matters before us," Councilman Weston put in, trying to turn the issue aside.

"Our immediate concern is the need for a man to replace First Wizard Baraccus," Elder Cadell said. "The war rages on. Aydindril and the Keep itself could soon be under threat of siege. Those matters require our full attention."

"Alric Rahl has also just arrived from the D'Haran Lands," Sadler said. "That man has turned the Keep upside down with his own urgent demands. He had been hoping to meet with First Wizard Baraccus. Something to do with some rather startling claims and even more startling remedies. With your husband dead, there are an endless variety of urgent problems that must be attended to."

"As you can no doubt appreciate," Councilman

Guymer, down at the end of the line, added, "we have any number of pressing issues of rule which require our full attention for now."

"Ah." Magda smiled without humor as she looked at each man in turn. "Pressing issues. Matters of state. Great questions of warfare and rule. You must all be terribly busy with such work. I understand.

"So you are here, then, about one of these momentous issues? That is what brings you out of council chambers to see me? Vital business of state? Matters of war and peace?"

To a man, their faces turned red.

Magda strolled past the line of six. "So how may I help with such important issues that require the council's full attention? Please tell me what urgent matter of state brings you to me this particular day, the same day we all stood by and prayed that the good spirits would take my departed husband, our leader, our First Wizard, into their gentle arms? Speak up, then. What urgent matter takes you away from your vital work and brings you all up here today?"

Their expressions turned dark. They didn't like being mocked. At that moment, Magda didn't much care.

"You know why we're here," Cadell said in an even tone. "It is a small duty, but an important one that demonstrates our respect for our heritage. It shows people that even in such times, tradition still has meaning to every one of our people, even those in high places. Sometimes, ceremony is essential for the continued cohesion of society."

Councilman Sadler's bony fingers fidgeted with the sky blue band of rank sewn on the sleeves of his black robes. "It demonstrates to people that there is continuity of the ways that have been handed down to us, that the customs of our people, that the practices that govern civilization itself, still matter and will not be abandoned."

Magda glared at the man a moment before turning her back on them and sitting on the chair before the table.

"Do it, then," she said in a voice finally gone lifeless and empty. "Carry out your critical custom. And then leave me be."

What did it matter anymore?

Without another word one of the men pulled out a bloodred ribbon and handed it to her over her shoulder. Magda held it a moment, feeling the silken material in her fingers.

"This is not something we take pleasure in doing," Cadell said quietly from behind her. "I hope you can understand that."

"You are a good woman, and have always been a proper wife to the First Wizard," Sadler said, his words rambling on, apparently in an attempt to cover his obvious discomfort. "This is merely an upholding of custom that gives people a sense of order. Because of your high standing as the wife of the First Wizard, they expect us in this case, as the Central Council, to see this done. It's more for them, really, that they might see that our ways endure, and thus, despite the perils of the times, we will endure as well. Think of it as a formality in which you play an important role."

Magda hardly heard him. It didn't really matter. None of it did. An inner voice whispered promises of the loving embrace of the good spirits awaiting her beyond the veil of life. Her husband, too, would be there waiting for her. Those whispers were reassuring, seductive.

She was only distantly aware of her hands gathering her long hair together in the back and tying it tightly with the ribbon near the base of her skull.

"Not that short," Cadell said as his fingers gently took hers away and slipped the ribbon down until it was just below the tops of her shoulders. "Though you may not have been born noble, you have proven yourself in your own right to be a woman of some standing, and besides, you are, after all, still the widow of the First Wizard."

Magda sat stiff and still with her hands nested in her lap as another man used a razor-sharp knife to slice through the thick rope of her hair just above the ribbon.

When it was done, Cadell placed the long hank of hair, tied just beneath the fresh cut with the red ribbon, in her lap.

"I'm sorry, Magda," he said, "I truly am. Please believe that this does not change the way we feel about you."

Magda lifted the length of brown hair and stared at it. The hair didn't really matter to her. What mattered was being judged by it, or by the lack of it, rather than by what she had made of herself. She knew that without the long hair she would likely no longer have standing to be heard before the council.

That was just the way it was.

What mattered most to her was that those whose causes she brought before the council would no longer have her voice to speak for them. That meant that there were creatures without an advocate who very well might die out and cease to exist.

That was what having her hair cut short meant to her, that she no longer had the standing needed to help those she had come not merely to respect, but to love.

Magda handed the severed hair back over her shoulder to Elder Cadell. "Have it placed where people will see it so they might know that order has been restored, that tradition and customs endure."

"As you wish, Lady Searus."

With her place in the world now corrected, the six councilmen finally left her alone to the gloomy room and her bleak thoughts.

CHAPTER
5

Warm summer air rising up the towering outer Keep wall and spilling over onto the rampart ruffled Magda's shortened hair, pulling strands around in front of her face. As she made her way along the deserted rampart, she reached up and drew her hair back. It felt strange, foreign, to her touch now that it only just brushed her shoulders rather than going down to the small of her back.

A lot of people, women mostly, paid very close attention to the length of a woman's hair because, while not always absolute, length was a fairly accurate indication of their relative social standing and thus their importance. Ingratiating oneself to the right person could bring benefits. Crossing the wrong person could bring trouble. Hair length was a valuable marker.

Being the wife of the First Wizard meant wearing her hair longer than most women. It also meant that many women with shorter hair often fawned over her. Magda never took such flattery seriously, but she tried to always be gracious about it. She knew it was not her, but her position, that drew the interest of most of them.

To Magda, having not been born noble, her long hair had merely been a way to open doors, to get an audience and be heard on matters important to her. She had cared about Baraccus, not how long she was allowed to grow her hair simply because she was married to him. While she had come to like the look of it on her, she didn't attach worth to that which she had not earned.

Since her long hair had begun to be a part of her life for the year Baraccus had courted her and the two years since she had been married to him, she had thought that she might miss it.

She didn't, really. She only missed him.

Her grand wedding to Baraccus seemed forever ago. She had been so young. She still was, she supposed.

With the long hair gone, in a way it felt as if a weight had been lifted from her shoulders in more ways than one. She no longer had a responsibility to live up to what others expected of her. She was herself again, her real self, not a person defined by an artificial mark of worth.

To an extent, she also felt a sense of liberation from her standing, from the need to act in a manner befitting her place as others saw it. Now, she had no place, no standing. She was in a way free of the prison of standing. But none of that mattered now, for far more important reasons than the length of her hair.

Baraccus had given her a new life because of what they meant to each other. Without him she had no life. Her standing didn't really matter in that equation.

Reaching the right spot, the spot forever burned into her memory, Magda stepped up into the opening in the massive, crenellated outer Keep wall. She inched out toward the edge. Beyond the toes of her boots peeking out from under her skirts, the dark stone of the wall dropped away for thousands of feet. Below the foundation of the Keep, the cliff dropped even farther to the ledges and boulders below. Feathery tufts of clouds drifted along the cliff walls beneath her. It was a frightening, dizzying place to stand.

Magda felt small and insignificant up on the top edge of the towering wall. The wind at times was strong enough to threaten to lift her from her perch. She imagined that it might even carry her away like a leaf in the wind.

The beautiful city of Aydindril lay spread out below, flowing across rolling hills that spilled from the foot of the mountain. Green fields surrounded the city, and out beyond them lay dense forests. From its place high on the mountain, the monolithic Wizard's Keep stood watch over the mother city sparkling like a jewel set in that verdant carpet.

Magda could see men leading horses and wagons as they returned from their work in the fields. Smoke rose from chimneys all across the valley as women prepared the evening meal for their families. Slow-moving crowds, visiting markets, shops, or going about their work, made their way through the tangled net of streets.

While she could see the activity, she heard none of the hooves of the horses, the rumble of wagons, the cry of street vendors. From this distance the lofty world up at the Keep was silent but for the calls of birds wheeling overhead and the sound of the wind over ramparts and around the towers.

Magda had always thought of the Keep, more than anything, as mute. Though hundreds of people lived and worked in the enormous stone fortress, went about their lives, raised families, were born, lived, and died there, the Keep itself witnessed it all in brooding silence. The dark presence of the place stoically watched centuries and lives come and go.

These massive battlements where she stood had

watched her husband's life end. This was the very spot where he had stood in the last precious moments of his life.

She thought, fleetingly, that she didn't want to follow him, but the whispers from the back of her mind overwhelmed those doubts. What else was there for her?

Magda looked out at the world spread out far below, knowing that this was what he would have seen as he stood in this very place. She tried to imagine the thoughts he must have wrestled with in his last moments of life.

She wondered if he thought of her in those last moments, or if some terrible, weighty matter had taken even that from him.

She was sure that he must have been sad, heartbroken even, that he was about to leave her, that his life was about to be finished. It must have been agony.

Baraccus had loved life. She could not imagine him taking his life without a powerful reason.

Still, he had. That was all that mattered now. Everything had changed and there was no calling it back.

Her world had changed.

Her world had ended.

At the same time she felt shame for focusing so narrowly on her own world, her own life, her own loss. With the war raging, the world had ended for a great many people. The wives of the men Baraccus had sent to the Temple of the Winds still waited in silent misery, hoping their loved ones might return. Magda knew that they never would. Baraccus had told her so. Yet they still clung to the hope that those men could yet come home. Other women, the wives of men gone off to war, wailed in anguish when they received the terrible news that their men would not be returning. The corridors of the Keep often echoed with the forlorn cries of the women and children left behind.

Like Baraccus, Magda hated the war and the terrible toll it took on everyone. So many had already lost their lives. So many yet would. And still there was no end in sight. Why couldn't they be left in peace? Why must there always be those seeking conquest or domination?

There were so many other women who had lost their husbands, fathers, brothers, sons. She was not alone in such suffering. She felt the heavy weight of shame for feeling so sorry for herself when others, too, were going through the same agony.

Yet she could not help being smothered beneath the whispers of her own grief.

She also felt a deep sense of guilt over those she was abandoning. She had given voice before the council to those who had no voice. Over the last couple of years she had gradually become the conscience of the council, reminding them of their duty to protect those who could not protect themselves. The night wisps, for example, that she had seen only days before, depended on others to speak for them and their need to be left in peace lest their fragile lives be silenced for good.

Because of her standing, she had often been able to go before the council and remind them of their duty to all those who lived in the Midlands. Sometimes, when she explained the situation to them, they did the right thing. Sometimes she shamed them into doing the right thing. Sometimes they looked forward to her recommendations.

But without standing she could no longer be that voice before the council. It was wrong that being married to a man of standing in turn gave her standing, but that's the way the world worked.

She was proud that she had made friends of those rare and secretive beings that few had ever seen, or ever would see. She was grateful for all the friends she had made of far-flung peoples of the Midlands. She had made the effort to learn many of their languages, and because of that they had come to trust her when they would trust no other. She was proud of what she had been able to do to protect their peaceful, isolated lives.

She thought that maybe she had also been able to bring some understanding between different peoples, different tribes and communities, and in so doing helped in some small way to make them all feel a part of the larger Midlands.

But when her husband had ended his life, he had also inadvertently taken away her voice before the council.

Her life no longer had a noble purpose, except to herself.

And at that moment, her own life meant nothing to her but insufferable anguish with no end in sight. She felt as if she was caught up in a raging torrent of sorrow.

She just wanted the hopeless agony to end.

Inner whispers urged her to end the suffering.

L ooking down at the frightening drop over the edge of the wall, a drop of thousands of feet, Magda saw that the towering wall in this section of the Keep wasn't perfectly vertical but actually flared out as it descended toward the foundation within the rock face of the mountain. She realized that when she jumped she would need to get herself some distance out away from the wall to ensure that she cleared the steeply angled stone skirt of the Keep or it would be a long, gruesome fall.

Her muscles tensed at the thought of a drawn-out, tumbling descent, repeatedly smacking the steeply angled wall and breaking bones all along the way down. She didn't like the thought of that. She wanted a quick end.

She placed her hands on the stone battlements flanking the notched opening as she leaned out farther for a better view. She also checked back and to each side to make sure that no one was around. Like her husband, she didn't need to worry much about anyone trying to stop her. Because it led to the First Wizard's enclave, this particular rampart was restricted, leaving it a lonely, out-of-the-way area of the Keep. The guards back at the access stairs that spiraled up from below knew Magda and had offered their sincere condolences. Since they knew her so well, they hadn't tried to prevent her from going up top.

Peering down the mountain, Magda tried to judge how far out she would need to jump in order not to hit the wall on the way down. She wanted it to be over before she had time to feel the pain of it. The whispers promised her that if she got out far enough, she would fall free until she finally reached the rocks at the bottom, where it would all be over in a single instant.

She hoped that Baraccus had been able to do the same and that he had not suffered.

But he must have felt a different sort of suffering all the way down: the suffering of knowing that he was leaving life and leaving her. She knew that she, too, would have to endure that final terror of leaving life behind.

But it would end quickly enough and then she hoped to be in the protective arms of the good spirits. Maybe then she would again see Baraccus smile at her. She hoped he wouldn't be angry.

She wasn't angry at him giving up his life because she knew him well enough to know that he had to have had a compelling reason for what he had done. She knew that a great many people had sacrificed their lives in the war so that others might live. Those sacrifices were made out of love for others. She knew that Baraccus would only have given his own life for just such a powerful reason. How could she be angry at him for making that sacrifice? No, she couldn't feel anger toward him.

She felt only crushing sadness.

Magda gripped the top corners of the rough stone to each side. Even though the sun was setting, the stone was still warm. While the battlements were spaced quite a ways apart for her size, they would still be useful to help push herself off.

Not far away, out in front of her in midair, a raven rode an updraft, its glistening black feathers ruffling in the wind as its black eyes watched her prepare to leap.

Magda bent at the knees, readying herself for a maximum effort to jump clear of the wall. In a daze, she felt as if she were only watching herself. The whispers urged her on.

Her heart hammering, Magda took a deep breath, crouched down even more, and started rocking back and forth, swinging farther out each time, standing, crouching, standing, crouching, back and forth, farther out over the edge of the wall, farther out toward the drop that would take her pain away, building up speed for the final, big push.

In a swelling moment of doubt, she heard a voice within whisper for her not to think, but to simply do it.

As she swung herself out past the wall on the last rocking arc before the great leap, she realized in a single, crystal-clear instant the true enormity of what she was doing.

She was ending her life, ending it forever, ending it for all time. Everything that she was would be no more.

The voice became more insistent, telling her not to think, telling her to end her misery once and for all.

She was struck by how odd that seemed. How could she not think? Thinking was critical to any important decision.

In that icy flash of comprehension, in spite of the whispers, she realized just how terrible a mistake she was making.

It was as if, since learning of her husband's death, she had been carried along in a raging river of emotions, urged onward by an inner voice pressing her toward the only thing that seemed like it could make the agony stop. She realized only now that she hadn't thought it through, she had simply allowed herself to be swept along toward the spot where she now stood.

She was making no loving sacrifice. She was not trading her life for something she believed in, offering it for something of value as she knew Baraccus had. She was instead throwing it away for nothing. She was giving in to weakness, nothing more.

She was thoughtlessly rejecting all she believed in, all she had fought for. How many times had she gone before the council to speak for the lives of those who couldn't speak for themselves? How many times had she argued for the importance of their lives, for the value of all life?

Was hers not just as important? Was her own life to be so carelessly, so foolishly, thrown away? Was she not going to fight for the right to her own life as she had fought for others?

She remembered telling Tilly that every life was precious. This was her only life and, despite her crushing agony, her life was precious to her. In her grief, she had allowed herself to be blind to that.

As if coming out of a fog, she realized, too, that there were things going on that didn't make sense. There had to be more to everything that had happened than she was seeing. Why had Baraccus killed himself? What had been his purpose? Who was he protecting? For what had he traded his life?

She suddenly regretted thinking that she wanted to die, regretted being up on that wall. In fact, it now seemed to her as if she had somehow arrived at that spot in a dream.

As much as she hurt, she wanted to live.

But she was already moving too fast to stop, already flying out toward empty space.

CHAPTER
7

Magda's fingers clawed frantically at the stone to each side, but it wasn't enough to halt her momentum. She swept out through the opening in the battlement toward the terrifying drop, with a scream caught in her throat.

Just as she lost her footing going over the brink of the stone wall, a powerful gust of wind rising up the side of the mountain caught her body, lifting some of her weight as she snatched at the wall to each side and helping her get herself back to solid footing. The push from the wind coming up the mountain had been just the help she needed to stop herself from going over the edge.

As she started to fall back toward the Keep, her left hand came up off the wall and she wheeled that arm in the air, trying to maintain her balance. As she toppled back, she grabbed at the wall to the right side and caught a joint of stone blocks. With the help of her grip on that joint, she was able to hold on tight enough to get her balance and keep herself from falling back off the wall. Finally solidly back on her feet, she let out a deep, frightened sigh. She knew that it would be a while before her galloping heart would slow.

Her head was suddenly more clear than it had been all day.

She was alive. She wanted to stay alive. She suddenly had a thousand questions and wanted the answers. She clutched at the stone block for support so that she wouldn't accidentally fall, now that she knew she didn't want to go over the side.

That was when her fingers felt something odd in the joint between the blocks.

It wasn't rough like the stone. Rather, it had a smooth edge.

In the fading light, Magda frowned as she looked over at the joint in the massive granite blocks. There, wedged between the dark, mottled stones, was a folded piece of paper.

She couldn't imagine what a folded piece of paper was doing, stuck there. It made no sense. Who would put a piece of paper there in the joint at the edge of the wall? And why?

She leaned close, narrowing her eyes, trying to see better. The paper looked to be wedged tightly in place. She could only get ahold of the very edge of it with a finger and thumb. Being careful not to tear it, she gently wiggled the folded paper from side to side to loosen it from its hiding place.

At last she was able to work it free.

Careful not to let a gust of wind catch it and pull it from her fingers, she stepped down off the wall onto the deserted rampart as she unfolded the paper.

There was something written on the paper. She immediately recognized her husband's handwriting. With trembling fingers, she held the paper close in order to read it in the last light of the dying day.

My time has passed, Magda. Yours has not. Your des-

tiny is not here. Your destiny is to find truth. It will be difficult, but have the courage to take up that calling.

Look out to the rise on the valley floor below, just outside the city to the left. There, on that rise, a palace will one day be built. There is your destiny, not here.

Know that I believe in you. Know, too, that I will always love you. You are a rare, fierce flower, Magda. Be strong now, guard your mind, and live the life that only you can live.

Magda blinked the tears away and again silently read it to herself. In her mind, she could hear her husband's voice speaking the words to her.

Magda brought the paper to her lips and kissed the words written there.

She looked up from the paper, out through the opening in the stone wall, and below saw a beautiful green rise that overlooked the city of Aydindril. For the life of her, she could not fathom what Baraccus meant about a palace, or about her destiny there.

Baraccus was a wizard. Part of his talent was prophecy. She swallowed past the lump in her throat, wondering for a moment if what he meant was that he wanted her to go on with her life and marry another.

She didn't want another man. She didn't want to marry anyone else. She had married the man she had loved.

And now he was gone.

She read the words yet again. There was something more to them, she knew there was. There was something more important than a simple prophecy, or even the simple message asking her to embrace life.

Wizards existed in a complex world all their own. They rarely if ever made anything simple to understand. Baraccus was no different.

There was a purpose to these carefully chosen words, a hidden message, she knew there was. He meant for her to know something more.

Your destiny is to find truth. It will be difficult, but have the courage to take up that calling.

What could he possibly mean by that? What truth? What truth was he expecting her to find? What calling did he expect her to take up?

Her head spun with thoughts scattering in every direction. She began to imagine all sorts of things he could have meant. Maybe he meant the truth of what he had done at the Temple of the Winds. Maybe the truth of why the moon had stayed red even though he had told her that he had gotten inside.

Maybe the truth of why he had returned from the world of the dead only to end his life.

It seemed to her, though, that there was more to the message than any of that. There was meaning hidden with the words. There was a reason he had not made the message clear.

Baraccus had told her in the past that foreknowledge could taint prophecy and cause dire, unintended consequences. Knowing a prophecy could alter how one behaved, so it was sometimes necessary to withhold information in order for free will to be able to let life play itself out.

Even without understanding the meaning of the note, she knew that Baraccus was telling her as much as he could without tainting it with what more he knew.

Magda knew that Baraccus had given her a message that involved life and death. She grasped just how important the message had been to him. From that, she knew that it was perhaps even more important to her.

Magda gazed out again over a landscape growing more dark by the moment.

She had to know what Baraccus had been trying to tell her with his last words. She couldn't let his effort, his sacrifice, be in vain. She had to find out what he had really wanted her to know.

Her life suddenly had a purpose.

Your destiny is to find truth.

She had to find out what he had meant by that.

Baraccus had reached out from the world of the dead and given her a reason to live.

He believed in her.

She kissed his words again as she slumped to the ground and wept at all that was lost to her, at all that she had just gained. She wept with grief for her loss, and with the relief of being alive.

CHAPTER
8

N ear her rooms, in a quiet corridor softly lit by reflector lamps hung at regular intervals on the dark wood panels to each side, men-at-arms blocked her way. A lot of men. They weren't regular soldiers, nor were they the elite Home Guard. At first, from a distance, Magda had found herself worrying that they might be troops from the prosecutor's office.

As head prosecutor, Lothain had his own private army, men who took orders from and were loyal to him and him alone. It was a privilege of his high office that no other in the Keep enjoyed. It was argued that to be independent and remain above outside influence, the prosecutor's office had to have its own guard to protect the office from coercion and threats, and to enforce decrees against those who would otherwise resist.

These men, though, were not dressed in the dark green tunics of the prosecutor's office. These were hulking men, towering men, with bull necks, powerful shoulders, beefy arms, and massive chests. Under their leather armor they wore chain mail that was well used, scuffed, and discolored by tarnish. She could smell the oil they used to help keep rust from their mail and weapons. The whiff of slightly rancid oil mixed disagreeably with the smell of stale sweat.

There was no mistaking that the armor these men wore was not meant for show. The weapons they carried—swords, knives, maces, and scarred battle-axes—likewise had the single-minded purpose of life and death.

These grim-faced men were not the kind who marched on a field of review or a polished patrol.

These were men who had looked death in the eye and grinned.

Magda stood frozen, unable to reach the door to her rooms, not knowing quite what to do. They in turn stood silently watching her like a curiosity come into their midst, but made no attempt to advance on her.

Before she could ask the men what they were doing there or tell them to move out of the way, another man, long locks of blond hair to his shoulders and dressed in layers of dark traveling clothes and leather, stepped out from behind the wall of men. He was just as big as the men all around him and likewise heavily armed, but he was a bit older, perhaps just entering his forties. Character creases had begun to take a permanent set.

As he moved forward through the armored soldiers he pulled off long gauntlets and tucked them behind a broad leather weapons belt. Two men, larger even than him or the soldiers, stayed close behind him but a little off to each side. Like all the others, they, too, had blond hair. Magda saw that above their elbows the two men wore metal bands with wicked blades jutting out, weapons for brutal, close-quarters combat. Instead of mail, the two wore elaborately fitted leather armor sculpted to the contours of their prodigious muscles. On the center of their powerful chests a stylized letter "R" was engraved into the leather breastplates.

The man with the long hair and the cutting, raptor gaze dipped his head in a quick bow.

"Lady Searus?"

Magda glanced to the blue eyes of the guards behind his shoulders, then back to the man who had spoken.

"That's right."

"I am Alric Rahl," he said before she had a chance to ask.

"From D'Hara?"

He confirmed it with a quick nod.

"My husband has spoken highly of you."

His cutting gaze remained fixed on her eyes. "Baraccus was more than merely a good man. He is the one man here at the Keep that I trusted. I am deeply grieved to hear that we've lost him."

"Not as grieved as I am."

His lips pressed tightly together with what looked to be heartfelt sorrow as he nodded again and then gestured to her door, off behind him.

"Would it be possible to speak with you privately?"

Magda glanced toward her door as the wall of men parted to provide a corridor lined with muscle and chain mail.

Magda dipped her head. "Of course, Lord Rahl."

While she had never met the man before, Baraccus had spoken of him from time to time. From what she had gathered from the things Baraccus had told others, this was not a man to be trifled with. He looked the part of the stories she'd heard of him. She knew from comments made by members of the council that many didn't think much of Alric Rahl, but Baraccus had. He had told her that, despite his audacity, he was a man to be trusted.

As Magda made her way toward the doors to her room, the grim soldiers spread out to take up stations up and down the hall.

She glanced back over her shoulder. "Are you expecting trouble, here, in the Keep, Lord Rahl?"

"From what I've seen," he said cryptically, "the Keep is no safer than anywhere else these days."

Magda frowned. "And what have you seen, if I may ask?"

"Three of my men have died since we recently arrived."

Magda halted and turned back to take in his grim expression. "Died? Here in the Keep? How?"

He hooked a thumb behind his weapons belt. "One was found in a corridor, dead from over a hundred stab wounds. Another died in his sleep for no reason we could find. The third suffered a mysterious fall from a high wall."

Magda had almost had such a fall. She still felt strangely disoriented, as if she were only now escaping the grip of a terrifying, otherworldly nightmare, rather than simply a grief-stricken moment of weakness.

"Perhaps the man who was stabbed had gotten into a fight with the wrong people over something?" she suggested.

"All three can be explained away if you try hard enough," he said, making it obvious that he didn't buy the easy explanations.

Magda worked to gather her composure as she started out once more, making her way past the looming, silent soldiers watching her. She didn't like to think of the Keep as a place where danger lurked. Yet Baraccus, too, had been troubled by what he had thought to be suspicious deaths at the Keep.

Besides that, the Keep was, after all, the place where her husband had died as well. The silent Keep had almost watched her follow him to a grisly death on the rocks below.

She was beginning to grasp that there was more to her husband's death than it had at first appeared. It no longer seemed a simple suicide. The note in her pocket, his last message to her, certainly made it clear enough that there was something more going on beneath the surface.

With all the people living and working at the Keep, and with the war going on, to say nothing of the gifted working with profoundly dangerous magic in an effort to create weapons they could use to turn back the horde from the Old World, it wasn't exactly surprising that people at the Keep would die. Lord Rahl's three men were not the only unexplained deaths she'd heard about. But still, even healthy infants died unexpectedly from time to time.

Such deaths didn't prove that something evil was going on within the walls of the Keep, though she knew that there were those who believed as much. Death, though, was a part of life. There could not be life without death always shadowing it.

Magda unlocked the heavy doors and spread them wide in invitation as she entered. The two big guards followed Lord Rahl into the room, then closed the doors and took up stations to either side, feet spread, hands clasped behind their backs.

Magda gestured toward the two men. "I thought you said that you wanted to speak privately."

Alric Rahl glanced back at the men and caught her meaning. "We are speaking privately. These are my personal bodyguards."

"A wizard who needs muscle?"

"Magic does not ensure safety, Lady Searus. Surely your husband must have told you as much."

"What do you mean?"

"In a land of blind men, sight is an advantage. But when everyone can see, your eyesight offers no special benefit. Among the gifted, the ability to bend magic to your will is not a weapon that makes you exceptional, much less invincible. Magic can be countered by the magic others possess, so having the gift does not in itself make one all-powerful, or necessarily safe."

Alric Rahl turned and cast a hand out, bringing flame to the wicks of several lamps on nearby tables and half a dozen candles in an iron stand. "Not to say that it doesn't have its uses."

With the added light to aid him, he strolled deeper into the quiet room, scanning the collection of books in carved walnut bookcases standing against the wall to the right. He rested his palm on the silver handle of a knife at his belt as he moved down the line of shelves, pausing to gaze in at volumes behind glass doors. He squinted a bit as he read the titles.

"What's more," he added as he finally straightened his broad shoulders, "we are all flesh and blood, and a simple knife will cut my throat the same as it would cut yours, and it takes no magic at all to do that."

"I see your point. Baraccus never put it in exactly those terms, but I have heard him say similar things. He once told me that the gift was coveted by those who didn't have it because they wrongly believed that it would protect them, or that with it they could win in battle, but what they didn't realize was that it offered only a fluid, ever-escalating form of checkmate. I guess I never realized his full meaning until I heard you explain it."

Alric Rahl nodded, still looking at the books. "That is the whole issue in a nutshell: the balance of power. Even as we speak, wizards of great skill here and in the Old World work to come up with new forms of magic that will offer an advantage in the war. Both sides seek ever more deadly weapons crafted by the gift, hoping to find one that will have no counter from the other side.

"If we succeed, we will turn the tide of war and survive. If they succeed, we will be enslaved if not annihilated."

A vague sense of apprehension settling into her, Magda gazed off at her empty quarters. "Being the wife of the First Wizard, I have often heard such worries."

Finished perusing the books, Lord Rahl returned to stand before her.

"That's why I'm here. That balance of power has shifted. We now stand at the brink of annihilation."

That is frightening news." Disheartened, Magda slowly shook her head. "But I'm afraid that there's not much I can do to help you. I'm not gifted."

Alric Rahl paced off a few strides, seeming to consider how to proceed. "Baraccus and I were working on something together," he finally said. "I've been dealing with my part of it while he was working on a separate issue. I need to know if he was able to accomplish his objective, but I didn't get here in time to speak with him." He turned back. "Absent Baraccus, I'm hoping you can help me with what needs to be done, now."

Magda reflexively reached to pull her hair back over her shoulder, but her hair barely brushed her shoulders, now, so there was nothing to pull back. She let the hand drop.

"I'm sorry, Lord Rahl, but with Baraccus lost to us I don't know what help I can be."

"You know people in the inner circles of power here at the Keep. You know who would listen. You can talk to the council. You could help convince them to take seriously my warnings. That would be a good start."

"Talk to the council? The council won't listen to me."

"Of course they will. You're the closest thing they have to the word of Baraccus himself."

"The word of Baraccus?" Magda shook her head. "I am no longer the wife of the First Wizard, so I no longer have standing with the council, or anywhere else for that matter." She held out a short strand of hair for him to see. "The men of the council are the ones who cut my hair to make that clearly evident to everyone."

"Who cares about your hair? Baraccus may be dead, but you're still the wife to the First Wizard. His passing does not change the fact that you knew him better than anyone, or that you were the one he trusted. He confided in you, I know he did—he told me so himself. He said that because you weren't gifted you were often the best sounding board he had."

"Baraccus is dead." Magda looked away from the man's blue eyes. "The council will soon replace him. Without Baraccus alive, I no longer have any status. That's why they cut my hair.

"It's an age-old custom among the people of the Midlands. The length of a woman's hair shows the world her standing. It matters for everything here in the Midlands and especially in the Keep. This is the seat of power for the Midlands, so such issues of rank, influence, and power always matter."

He gestured impatiently. "I know about the custom. It's absurd. I can understand petty people paying attention to such trivialities when deciding the seating arrangement at a banquet, but beyond that it ceases to be useful. This is a serious issue. What does the length of your hair have to do with matters of life and death?"

"It has everything to do with it, here in the Midlands. I'm no longer worthy of recognition because I was not born noble and my husband, who when he was alive gave me standing, is dead. That means that I'm back to where I was before I was married to him. This isn't by my choice, it's just the way it is."

Lord Rahl closed the distance back to her. "How do you think you came to be the wife of First Wizard Baraccus? Do you think that Baraccus sought out a weak, unimportant wife?"

"Well, I—"

"You became wife to First Wizard Baraccus because you were the only woman who was worthy of being his wife. Are you suggesting that Baraccus, the First Wizard, a war wizard, would want to marry a woman who was weak? He married you because you were a woman of strength."

"That's very flattering, Lord Rahl, but I'm afraid that it's simply not true. I was a nobody when he met me, and with him gone I am once again a nobody."

He looked genuinely disappointed by her words. The fire seemed to go out of his eyes. His expression sagged.

"You were his wife, so I guess you would know him better than anyone." He shook his head with great sadness. "I admit to finding myself disillusioned to learn that Baraccus was not the man I had thought him to be, that he was instead nothing more than a rather common fool, like so many other ordinary men."

"A common fool? What are you talking about?"

He lifted an arm and then let it drop to his side. "He had the wool pulled over my eyes all along. You've made me see the unpleasant truth. I always thought him intelligent and strong, but it turns out that Baraccus was simply an ordinary, weak-minded man who like so many would marry even a lowly woman of no standing and no worth simply because she batted her eyes at him.

"You apparently came along in one of his weak moments, stroked his male pride with a bit of feminine flattery, and just that easy, you had yourself a man of

standing. It's clear now that he must have been too inse-
cure to think that a woman of standing would be interested in him, so he was willing to trade the standing you
lacked in return for your affections. I guess he wasn't the
man of character I thought he was.

"I can see now that by marrying you he was hiding his
lack of confidence with women. It's clear now that he
was ready to settle on the first shapely woman, no matter her standing, who swayed her becoming ass before
his weak-minded gaze."

In a blink, Magda had the point of her knife poised
motionless a hairsbreadth from his throat.

"I will not stand here and listen to you insult a righteous
man who is not here to defend himself," she growled.

"Apparently, my old friend Baraccus taught his nobody wife a thing or two about using a weapon."

"A thing or two," she confirmed. "Tell those two that
if they take another step you will be breathing through
something other than that foul mouth of yours."

She in fact knew far more than a thing or two about
using weapons. Baraccus had actually used his gift to aid
in teaching her a great deal about weapons. He said that
as wife to the First Wizard, she would always be a target. He wanted her to be able to protect herself when he
wasn't around.

"I can't believe that he ever considered you a friend. I
think it's high time that you were on your way back to
your D'Haran Lands. I want you and your little army
gone first thing in the morning. Do you understand me?"

A sly smile overcame the man at the point of her knife
as he signaled the two men near the doors to stand down.
Magda was surprised by his smile, but her anger kept
her focused, and kept her knife where it was.

"What's this? A nobody, a woman not born noble
woman with short hair, a woman of no standing, w

has the nerve to tell me, the Lord Rahl, what I will and will not do? What gives you the right to speak this way to the leader of D'Hara, a man who commands the army outside your room, and guards inside it? How dare you think that you can speak to me in such a manner? Where do you, a woman of no status, a nobody, get the gall to think you have such a right?"

"Such a right?" Magda raged in fury.

But then she saw the twinkle in his eye and realized what he was doing. Her fury faltered. She suddenly felt foolish. She couldn't keep a shamed smile from overcoming her.

Magda bowed her head in a gesture of exaggerated respect.

"It would seem that the Lord Rahl is not so stupid as some on the council say."

His grin widened. "Magda, I knew Baraccus long before you met him. I've fought beside the man. I knew his character. He would never be attracted to a weak woman. He never cared about the length of your hair or standing when he met you, did he?"

Magda shook her head, remembering the first time she met him. He didn't even look at her hair. He looked into her eyes and asked her name.

"He cared about your character. He cared who you were. Baraccus was a man of power. He was only attracted to strength and temperament that could complement his. He could have had any woman he wanted—I know because many sought him out and he always turned them away. Yet he chose you. He chose you not because you were weak and common, but because you were rare, and his equal in every way that mattered."

She smiled again, but this time in appreciation. "Thank you for the kindest words about my husband—and —that I have ever heard."

"They are true words, Magda. He chose you because you were worthy of him. He was lucky to have you. I'll not have you selling my friend's wife short."

Her smile turned downhearted. "I don't think I could begin to tell you how much I miss him, how lost I am without him."

"I understand. Now, let's put this nonsense aside; we have urgent matters that must be addressed. With Baraccus gone, you are the only one I can turn to for answers. This is a time for courage and honesty if we are to have a chance."

Magda finally lifted her chin. "What can I do to help you, Lord Rahl?"

CHAPTER

10

"Y ou must speak to the council and let them know of the threat, make them understand how serious it is," Alric Rahl told her. "With Baraccus dead, it's up to us, and we're running out of time."

"What threat?"

A bit surprised, he cast her a suspicious look from under a lowered brow. "Surely, Baraccus must have told you about the dream walkers."

Magda stilled. She wanted to help the man, but she didn't like the idea of talking about anything Baraccus had told her in confidence. The two of them had always had an understanding that, because of his position, the things he discussed with her were meant to remain strictly confidential. She never spoke about such matters without her husband explicitly telling her that it was all right.

She remembered, then, the note in her pocket, the note Baraccus had left for her up on the battlement. Those were his last words to her.

Your destiny is to find truth. It will be difficult, but have the courage to take up that calling.

It seemed clear that Baraccus meant for her to act. His note didn't ask her to keep silent, or to stay out of things. said that she must have the courage to act.

Magda realized that with Baraccus gone she needed to trust someone. While she knew a number of the people her husband had worked with and trusted, she never heard him speak about his trust in anyone the way he spoke of his trust of Alric Rahl.

"He did," she said at last.

"Good. Tell me what you know about them, anything Baraccus said."

Magda took a deep breath to gather her thoughts. "Well, when enemy gifted in the Old World not long ago created dream walkers, Baraccus told me that such weapons, made out of people, could mean the end of us all. He said that there was only a small window of opportunity to act. In secret, he worked tirelessly on the problem. In the course of that work he discovered that the dream walkers were created through the use of a constructed spell."

Lord Rahl nodded. "He told me that much of it when he traveled through the sliph to warn me about the dream walkers."

Magda bristled at the mention of the sliph. She hated that creature made from a woman. The sliph took Baraccus away from her to travel great distances in a short time. Yet one more of the abominations created by wizards out of human beings.

Magda reminded herself not to be so harsh. Had not wizards created some of the things they did, all of them would be dead by now, or worse. There were wizards who created weapons, such as the dream walkers, to cause harm, but there were many wizards who used their ability to create things that saved a great many lives. The sliph, as much as Magda didn't like her, was one of those things.

"Baraccus and I discussed the situation and ma plans as to how we could deal with the dream walke

Lord Rahl said, "but I've not heard what happened since. I don't know what Baraccus was able to accomplish, if anything. That's one of the reasons why I'm here."

"Well, because Baraccus understood what the spell did, he was able to work in reverse from there to create a close replica, even though it was not entirely functional, of what he believed the constructed spell would have had to be like. From that approximation, he was able to ignite an artificial verification web. Once he had a functioning verification web, he back-traced the spell's unique nodes and core elements to the men who would have created the real one."

His brow had lifted in surprise as he listened. "That's quite remarkable. I didn't know that such a thing was possible."

She confirmed that it was with a nod. "I saw it one night. It was a frightening thing made of glowing lines tracing their way through midair. Baraccus ignited the web around himself in order to trace the nodes. I was terrified for him while he floated motionless inside it."

He eyed her as if seeing her in a new light. "For one not born with the gift, you certainly have a remarkable grasp of it. I doubt that one gifted person in a hundred would even understand what you have just told me." Lord Rahl rolled his hand impatiently. "So what did Baraccus do then?"

"He had contacts with a shadowy group. I never saw them and I don't know who they were, but I suspected that they might have been resistance fighters from the Old World. He met with them in secret and sent them on a covert mission to the Old World."

Lord Rahl arched an eyebrow. "Did the council know bout this?"

"No one knew. The replica spell, the artificial verifica- n web, its ignition and node traces, the meetings in the dead of the night with those men, no one knew any of it. Baraccus said that with dream walkers now a reality, it would jeopardize everything if anyone knew about any aspect of it.

"Not long ago, he came home a few hours before dawn and told me that the men he'd sent had gotten in and killed the team of gifted in the Old World who had constructed the dream-walker spell. He could share his excitement with no one but me. He was nearly in tears with relief and said that it meant that in all likelihood such a constructed magic could never again be brought to reality."

Lord Rahl let out a great sigh of relief. "That was the confirmation I've been hoping to hear. I can't imagine how he managed to pull off such a feat, but all of mankind owes Baraccus an enormous debt of gratitude." His frown returned. "What about the constructed spell itself?"

Magda leaned in close and lowered her voice. "When he came home that night, Baraccus told me that the men had not only succeeded in killing the team that had created the dream walkers, but they had also stolen the constructed spell and brought it back with them. They gave it to Baraccus."

Lord Rahl looked truly shocked. "No."

"Yes," she said with a firm nod. "Baraccus showed me the small box made of bone, its sides and lid stitched together with cords made from strips of dried human flesh. Inside was something wrapped in buckskin. He held it out and laid back the folds of buckskin to show me that it held a round thing about the size of a hen's egg. It was as black as a moonless night, like something forged in the darkest depths of the underworld, with shadowy shapes moving across its surface. It looked liked death itself brought into the world of life." Mag pressed the flats of her hands to the tense knot in her stomach. "It seemed as if that evil thing might suck the very light from the room."

Pulling herself away from the memory, she looked back up. "When Baraccus opened the spell with his gift, it ignited into a framework, taller than he was. It was a structure of thousands of glowing, colored lines of light all linked together in an intricate, circular gridwork, very similar to the verification web he had crafted before. It was both beautiful and terrible all at the same time. Baraccus said that when it was used for its intended purpose, it would have been opened around the person who was to become a dream walker."

Magda took a few steps away to stare off into the dark end of the room. "I can't imagine being one of the people who stepped inside that thing to become something other than they were born. I can't imagine allowing yourself to become a weapon created by magic."

Alric Rahl watched her in silence for a moment more before quietly urging her on to the rest of the story. "So then he was able to deactivate it?"

"Deactivate it?" She looked back over her shoulder at his grim gaze. "Unfortunately, no. He said that it was far too complex to safely dismantle such a thing. He said that he didn't even know if it was possible to deactivate it."

Lord Rahl rubbed his chin as he considered. "So it's here, then?"

She shook her head. "He took the spell with him to the Temple of the Winds so that it could be safely locked away."

"The Temple of the Winds!" Lord Rahl let out a deep sigh of relief. "That's the best news I could have heard. And even better, with the team who created it dead, those in the Old World will not likely be making another."

"It would appear so. Baraccus eliminated the threat, so maybe we don't stand on the brink of annihilation after all."

He rested his palm on the hilt of his sword. "Did he say if he was able to terminate the power that had already been unleashed here, in the world of life? Was he able to eliminate those dream walkers that had already been brought into being?"

Magda tapped a finger on a small side table inlaid with silver leaves as she recalled her husband's exact words.

"Baraccus said, 'We will have to deal with the ones they've already created, but at least they will be minting no new dream walkers and no more will be born into the world. That magic is now safely locked away.' Then he stared off and under his breath added, 'For now.'"

CHAPTER

11

F or now'? What did he mean by that?"

Magda shook her head. "I don't know. That was all he said. He was quiet and distracted after he returned from the Temple of the Winds. I wasn't even sure that he had intended for me to hear that last part of it."

What she remembered the most was the way he had held her for a long time, as if she were the most important thing in the world to him. She longed for the feel of his sheltering arms around her again. So why then, if he cared that much for her, and there were so many pivotal issues facing them, had he killed himself? Magda swallowed and tried to put the memory from her mind lest she be overwhelmed by tears.

"As I had hoped, Baraccus once again managed to accomplish the seemingly impossible and eliminated their ability to create more dream walkers." Lord Rahl regarded her with a determined look. "Unfortunately, that doesn't do anything about the ones that already exist. They are easily trouble enough to annihilate us. That element of the threat must be countered as well."

Magda knew the truth of that. Baraccus had told her that after a person had been enclosed by that constructed spell, the power from it was fused into their being, into their very souls. They were in part the same person, but now they were more. They became beings with powers and abilities that others didn't possess and couldn't defend against.

From their name, Magda had at first thought that they were able to steal into a person's dreams while they slept, but Baraccus had explained that it was more sinister than that. They actually slipped into the infinitesimal empty spaces between thoughts, like water seeping into the voids of a sponge. It wasn't that they used dreams to enter a person's mind, it was more like they became the victim's real-life nightmare.

Magda paced a few steps away, thinking, worrying. She hadn't wanted to press her husband for details when he had returned. She had been so thankful that he had come back safely to her that she had just wanted to hold him.

She turned back. "Can a dream walker invade anyone's mind?"

"Technically, yes, however entering a person's mind is profoundly difficult, so, to help them, dream walkers use the victim's gift. In essence, they seize control of a person's own magic and turn it against them. Where dream walkers are concerned, having the gift is a dangerous liability."

"What about the ungifted, like me?"

"It's much more difficult for dream walkers to get into the mind of an ungifted person and even more difficult yet to control them. Not that it can't be done, but it requires great effort. The real question is why would they want to? After all, dream walkers were created as weapons, so they would be expected to seek out high-value targets. That implies the gifted."

"That makes sense," Magda said as she tried to put

the pieces of what she knew together with what she was learning. "But the person would be aware of it, wouldn't they? They would know the dream walker had invaded their thoughts."

"No, not necessarily. A dream walker can be in your mind, watching, listening, and unless they want you to know, you would be completely unaware of their presence. Once there, without you ever realizing it, the dream walker not only has access to all your thoughts, he can also overhear anything you hear—plans, defenses, names, anything that might be useful to the enemy.

"But if he wishes to, a dream walker can make his presence known and force you to do anything, or use you for any purpose he chooses. He can, for instance, use you to help him identify other important targets. You would be helpless to stop yourself.

"A dream walker often uses a seemingly harmless individual as an extension of himself, as a tool—in other words, as a surrogate assassin. People who are gentle or even timid offer a perfect cover. If he wants, a dream walker can force even such a person to assassinate their closest friend or a loved one.

"A dream walker's control is absolute. He can remain hidden and you won't even know he's there, or be an insidious presence, whispering suggestions that you interpret as your own thoughts. If he wishes it he can make his presence all too clear by exerting complete control over your actions, or, as I've seen with my own eyes, give pain beyond imagining."

Magda folded her arms as she paced, her alarm growing by the moment. As she walked past them, she cast a suspicious look at the two towering, silent guards standing with their broad backs to the doors. Their eyes rarely left her. For all she knew, a dream walker could be in their minds.

"Then they could be here in the Keep already. They could already know all our defenses, all our plans." She tapped her temple. "For all we know, they could be in our minds right now, listening, watching, waiting to pounce."

Lord Rahl's brow twisted with doubt. "I don't think so. Dream walkers are newly created weapons. They haven't had those abilities for very long. Imagine how difficult it would be for someone newly turned into a dream walker to learn to accomplish anything useful."

"What do you mean?"

"Well, if you right now had the power to enter the mind of the enemy down in the Old World, how would you pick a useful person? Even if you knew the name of a target, if you weren't looking right at them how would you find that one person out of all the millions of minds down there? How would you know who to look for, or where they might be? How would you search for the one mind you wanted? If you were trying to target enemy officials, how would you even know who they were? How would you identify them and then find them? Where would you look?"

He shook his head. "It can't be easy to establish the right links. I have no doubt that they will soon enough be able to spread like a wildfire through our ranks—and through the Keep—but if we're lucky we still have a bit of time."

"Time? Time for what? Dear spirits," Magda said as she lifted her arms in frustration, "we're helpless against them. What good is a bit of time going to do us? We really do stand at the brink of annihilation."

"Not entirely," Lord Rahl said. "Baraccus's task was to eliminate the source of the dream walkers. My part in this was to create a counter for the ones who already exist."

"But without a dream walker how will you know how

their power functions, or be sure what they're capable of? For that matter, how can you know for certain that any counter you create really works?"

At that moment, at seeing the look that came into his eyes, Magda for the first time fully understood why this man was so feared. There was terrible resolve there, and terrible conviction.

"Because," he said, "we captured one."

Magda was stunned into silence for a moment. "You actually captured a dream walker?" she finally asked. "Are you sure?"

"Absolutely sure."

"How do you know he's really a dream walker?"

"There is no mistaking them. Looking into their eyes is like looking into a nightmare. Their eyes are entirely black, black like that evil thing you described that Baraccus showed you and then took with him to lock away in the underworld. When a dream walker looks at you, clouded shapes shift across the inky black surface of their eyes, eyes so black that they seem as if they might suck the sunlight out of the day and turn the world into everlasting night."

"I remember well the black thing Baraccus showed me." Magda rubbed her arms, unable to turn away from the look of bottled fury in Lord Rahl's eyes. "Were you able to gain his cooperation, or learn anything useful from him?"

The knuckles of his fists were white. "He killed a lot of my people, people I loved, and he forced me to kill some of those innocent people he possessed lest he kill me by their hand. He caused us a great deal of trouble, but in the end I was able to use him to unlock the secrets of their power."

Magda didn't ask how he had gained the dream walker's cooperation. It was wartime. They were in a struggle for their very existence. Every day lives were being lost in that struggle. Countless more innocent lives were at stake. From what she had heard, if there was one thing the D'Harans were good at, it was knowing how to make people tell what they knew.

"I had to devote a great many resources to the task," he said, "but it was necessary and the results were worth it. I finally created a counter to block their ability."

Magda wasn't sure that she had heard him correctly. She took a step closer. "You mean you can actually stop them?"

Lord Rahl nodded. "I was able to construct a very complex spell that I actually propagated within myself. That magic is now part of who I am, a part of every fiber of my being. In a way, I, too, have become more than I was before, much like the weapons we create out of people. That new ability now completely shields my mind from the dream walkers."

She gripped his forearm. "You're certain?"

"Yes. I tested it on our dream walker."

"But how can you be certain that he wasn't pretending that he couldn't enter your mind?"

He arched an eyebrow. "With what was being done to him at the time, and for as long as it was being done, I promise you, if he could have gotten into my mind to stop me, he would have."

"So the magic you created is our salvation, then."

"Yes and no."

She felt her hopes yet again slipping away. "What do you mean?"

"I was able to create a counter to the dream walkers, and it works perfectly. The problem was that it only worked for me. I tried but I can't re-create a similar ability in others. It's a power specific to me, to my inherent nature."

Magda's heart sank. "So the rest of us are to remain at the mercy of the dream walkers."

"Not exactly. I finally succeeded in creating a way to protect other people as well. Part of the ever-escalating balance of power I spoke of before. Those in the Old World may have gotten a temporary advantage with the dream walkers, but I created a counter for them—and I now have a way for that counter to protect others as well. I can check the enemy's plans."

Magda eyed him suspiciously. "What's the problem, then?"

"The Central Council. Most of the D'Haran Lands have accepted the solution I've created and are now safe from the dream walkers. We need the council to help us implement the same protection here. That's why I need you to speak with them. I've already tried to convince them of the danger we're in and the necessity of my solution, but without Baraccus to lend his support they won't listen to me."

Magda pressed her fingers to her forehead, frustrated that he still thought she could somehow tell the council what to do. "If they won't listen to the Lord Rahl, the leader of the D'Haran Lands, they certainly aren't going to listen to me."

"They've listened to your arguments for several years and know that your appeals are always important and well reasoned. They're used to having you speak before them. They've often gone along with your proposals. On the other hand, they've always been suspicious of me and aren't inclined to listen with a open mind to anything I say."

"Lord Rahl, I wish it was otherwise, but I don't think—"

"If they won't listen to you now about something this important, and they don't do what is needed, then the people of the Midlands will have no way to guard their minds."

Magda paused, struck by those words.

They were close to the same words in the note.

Be strong now, guard your mind . . .

She wondered if that could possibly be what Baraccus had meant. She wondered if he had been trying to tell her about the dream walkers. But how could that have been what he meant?

She felt an icy sense of unease as she remembered, then, the whispers in her mind urging her to jump off the wall.

Was it possible?

Dread welled up inside her. "What do people have to do to be protected? What solution have you created?"

"With the spell I forged, the spell that is now part of my being, I'm immune to dream walkers entering my mind. But like I said, I can't create that same counter within other people. I tried, but it isn't possible. So I instead created a way to link others to my protective magic. That link shields them from dream walkers entering their mind the same as I am protected."

"Are you sure? How is such a thing even possible?"

"Everyone, even those like you who are ungifted, has a spark of the gift within them. That living spark enables everyone to interact with magic, even if they can't create it themselves. Through that flicker of the gift, anyone who accepts me as their ruler becomes my subject and they are thus linked to me. We become bonded. Them to me, and me to them. I become their magic against magic"—he gestured toward the two men watching from their position at the door—"and they in turn protect me."

Magda blinked. "Do you mean to say that to be protected from dream walkers, people must swear loyalty to you?"

"Yes and no. Sincere belief in my sovereignty over

them is actually the link that powers the bond. In reality that's all that's needed. Swearing loyalty, though, helps a lot of hesitant minds fully commit."

"How can simply swearing loyalty possibly accomplish such a thing as powering this link to your ability?"

"It's not the swearing of loyalty that's the real secret of it. It's the realization—the conviction—that they are my subjects and I their sovereign ruler that actually powers the spark of their gift to link to my magic. It has to be sincere in order to connect them with the spell I carry within me. They don't have to like it, but they have to accept the fact that I am their ruler."

"I just don't understand—"

"That's always the problem, and we don't have time to try to make people understand the nuanced intricacies of conjured links to constructed spells." He gestured irritably. "It's complicated and hard to explain to people, even the gifted, even wizards. Fortunately, I've found that an oath serves to bring about acceptance, ignites the link, and forges the bond."

"An oath?"

"Yes. All that is really necessary for the bond to work is the person's solemn acceptance of my authority over them. But, like I say, the oath is a great deal simpler and works in most cases. It's nearly infallible if fear is a component—fear of dream walkers, or even fear of me. Fear triggers need, need powers sincerity. Sincerity is the required element.

"Once established, the bond becomes a kind of conduit, through the spark of the gift, that draws upon the constructed protection I have within me to protect them as well. I worked long and hard to create an oath that fires the forge of that living link within the supplicant."

Magda stared up at the man. "And what is this oath?"

"To be protected, people must swear as follows. *Master*

Rahl guide us. Master Rahl teach us. Master Rahl pro-tect us. In your light we thrive. In your mercy we are sheltered. In your wisdom we are humbled. We live only to serve. Our lives are yours."

Magda was stunned. "And you expect people to swear this oath to you?"

"I'm trying to save their lives, Magda." He gestured dismissively. "But calling it an oath does motivate some people to refuse, so I instead call it a devotion. Softens it a bit. I find that it works with near certitude if it is delivered from a kneeling position, bent forward at the waist, forehead to the floor. Something about kneeling and swearing loyalty helps build fear and makes it real to the supplicant."

No wonder the council had rejected Lord Rahl's plan.

He was asking them to help him rule the entire New World.

From the things her husband had told her in the past and from what she had learned from Alric Rahl, Magda was coming to fully grasp the mortal danger they were in. It was only a matter of time until the dream walkers learned to use their abilities to find their way into the minds of those in the Wizard's Keep. If something wasn't done to protect people, such an event would be the beginning of the end.

Not only was the Keep the seat of power in the Midlands, it was in many ways also its heart and soul. The council lived and worked there, but so did representatives from various lands along with military officers, administrators, and officials of every sort. Perhaps even more important, while vast armies along with gifted support clashed in the field, some of their most brilliant wizards lived at the Keep, working on everything from counters to the weapons being created in the Old World to new weapons of their own.

Those gifted down in the lower reaches of the Keep worked day and night, many in secret, on things that Baraccus rarely talked about. Magda remembered Tilly's chilling gossip about some of the projects. While Magda didn't necessarily believe everything Tilly said, she knew that it likely wasn't far off the mark.

If the council didn't go along with Alric Rahl's plan, and the gifted didn't come up with a counter of their own, the New World would be lost.

But on the other hand, it meant making Alric Rahl more than a mere king. It meant making him the ruler of the entire New World. It meant allowing him to create an empire and make himself its ruler.

Even if Magda could influence the council, would she want to be a part of such a thing? Would Baraccus have wanted her to?

She remembered, then, being up on the wall earlier that same day, seemingly in a fog, preparing to throw herself to her death. Even though it had only been hours ago, it was beginning to feel more like a dream in the dim past.

Had she really been serious? Had she really, in her heart, wanted to die? To kill herself? Of course she was still heartbroken and the future still seemed bleak, but not in quite the same way.

She remembered the whispers urging her to jump.

Was it possible?

If it was true . . .

Her mouth felt as dry as dust.

"I see what you mean, Lord Rahl." Magda laced her fingers together as she paced off a few steps, trying to come to grips with the enormity of everything that had happened. In the last few days her life had been turned upside down. Everything had changed. Despite the uncertainty of the war, her husband had been her security. Now, there was no more security. Now, she had only herself to rely on.

"Then you must act," Alric Rahl said. "You must do your best to convince the council to help me protect the Midlands from the dream walkers."

Magda, staring off into the dark end of the room where the glow of the candlelight hardly penetrated, finally turned back. She looked up at his grim concern.

"You're right. I don't know if I can convince them to listen to me, but I have to try. I must find a way to get the council to go along. We have truth on our side. Maybe I can make them see that and make them see that they must act for the good of us all."

He let out a deep sigh as he nodded. "Thank you, Magda. Let us hope that you can convince the council. It may be our only chance."

But then pain slammed into her so abruptly, so unexpectedly, so violently that it took her breath.

Magda's muscles locked stiff as the searing pain ignited in her head. It felt as if half a dozen hot needles were all at the same time being thrust into her ears, through her temples, and up into the base of her skull.

A razor-sharp spike of pain lanced into the nerves just below her ears as if yet more of the searing-hot needles were being thrust in right behind her jaw on either side. Her eyes watered and her mouth opened wide, but she couldn't make a scream. She couldn't draw a breath. The weight of the terrible agony locked her muscles rigid.

Lord Rahl frowned. "Magda?"

She could see the puzzled concern on his face, but she couldn't speak to tell him what was happening. She wanted to scream, but she couldn't do that, either. Mostly, she wanted to somehow make the unexpected, savage pain stop.

She couldn't endure it for another moment. As much as she wanted to live, she welcomed death if only it would bring her release.

In that helpless, desolate instant, she knew.

The initial violence of the pain unexpectedly eased up

just a bit. She didn't know if it was a depraved game, or if the crushing hurt was going to ram back in at her again with even more force. In that brief break, Magda gasped a breath.

Before she could cry out, the pain slammed into her again, but with immensely more force than the first time. She hadn't thought it possible for it to hurt more, but it did. The startling power of it left her senseless.

Staggered, she began to lose her awareness of where she was. Her skull felt as if it were being slowly crushed.

A powerful blow came out of nowhere like a bolt of lightning, striking her in the middle, doubling her over. Her muscles strained against a force squeezing her chest. She heard snapping and felt her ribs break, sending yet another kind of pain ripping through her.

In insufferable torment, her eyes wide, she saw Lord Rahl rushing toward her, yet his movements seemed impossibly slow. He almost looked to be a statue, unable to make any headway. At the slow, dreamlike rate at which he appeared to be moving, she didn't think he would reach her before she was dead.

She felt something warm and wet running from her ears and down along her jaw. She saw bright blood splattering on the stone floor under her.

Magda dropped heavily to her knees.

Her vision narrowed to a dark tunnel. Everything seemed far away. She thought she heard voices but she couldn't make them out over the piercing, painful, high-pitched noise she was hearing.

Just at the dark edge of her restricted vision, she saw Lord Rahl's two big guards draw their swords as they, too, started toward her. She knew that they now saw her as a threat.

The blood running from her ears and dripping from her chin merged into a wet, red pool on the floor beneath her. She could feel the wet warmth soaking her knees and dress.

Through the stunning torment, through the paralyzing pain spiking down through her head and ripping up through her abdomen, Magda, like the guards, realized what was happening. As disoriented as she was, she was all too aware of the alien presence roaring out from the dark corners of her mind.

If the thing within didn't kill her, the guards surely would. Magda recognized that she had only precious moments to live.

With that awareness, she realized how desperately she didn't want to die. Despite how much she wanted the pain to stop, she didn't want to die. She had never felt so strongly about wanting to live. But she could feel herself slipping ever closer to the dark rim of the underworld.

Magda remembered then her husband's last words on the note in her pocket.

Be strong now, guard your mind, and live the life that only you can live.

Lord Rahl was right there, right before her, his boots in her blood. He was leaning down, his hands on her shoulders as he yelled something.

She couldn't hear him. She could hear only the ripping howl of pain in her ears.

Magda clutched Lord Rahl's pant legs in her fists as the pain darkened her vision, threatening to blind her. She knew that in brief moments she would not only lose her vision, she would lose consciousness. She knew that she had only those brief seconds before everything was lost to her.

She could hear Alric Rahl above her yelling urgently, but she couldn't make out the distant words. She could feel his powerful fingers grasping her shoulders as he leaned over her.

She knew that this was her only chance.

But she didn't know if she could summon the strength. "Master Rahl . . ." she managed in a hoarse voice. Blood dripped from her lips. She could taste it in her mouth.

Terror tightened her throat. Her heartbeats came weaker and weaker. She knew that she was about to die. She could feel the glimmer of life itself slipping away. It seemed too much effort to hold on to it.

It was even too much effort to draw another breath.

Some part of her, though, desperately didn't want to surrender to the lure of release.

Magda summoned all her remaining strength and gasped in a last breath.

With her lungs filled by that last gasp at life, she forced herself on in a desperate rush, giving herself over to the words, giving herself over to their meaning.

"Master Rahl guide us. Master Rahl teach us. Master Rahl protect us. In your light we thrive. In your mercy we are sheltered. In your wisdom we are humbled." She put her heart and soul into the words. "We live only to serve. Our lives are yours."

Darkness passed through her, shadowing her soul. She thought that it must be too late.

But then the pain abruptly lost its hold on her.

Magda, panting in relief as the full force of crushing torment released her, crumpled to the ground, weeping in lingering agony and sweet gratitude for Baraccus's words of *guard your mind*.

They had just saved her life.

Baraccus had just saved her life.

Lord Rahl had just saved her life.

CHAPTER

13

Free of the alien presence, but still in agony, Magda lay in a warm, velvety pool of her own blood. The pain in her head, still radiating into her ears and down through her jaw, was horrific. As much as she hurt, though, she was profoundly thankful that it was at least not the same kind of agony as the crushing pain the dream walker had been inflicting from within.

As much as she didn't want to suffer the pain of being touched, she didn't have the power to offer much resistance as Lord Rahl and his two bodyguards gently rolled her over. She cried out at the torture of being moved. She could feel broken ribs grate together with each shallow breath.

"Easy, now," Lord Rahl said in a surprisingly gentle voice as big hands caught her weakly flailing arms. "It's going to be all right. You have to be still, though. Don't try to get up."

In a daze, Magda was only dimly aware of where she was and what was happening. It seemed like it all was happening to someone else and she was only watching it. Her whole body throbbed in terrible pain. But even that, too, in an odd way seemed strangely distant.

"At least that bastard is gone from her now," one of the big guards said.

Lord Rahl grunted his agreement before looking down at her. "It's going to be all right, Magda. I'm going to help you."

Magda nodded. She didn't really know why. She had to swallow back the blood in her mouth.

Lord Rahl leaned in closer over her. He had the strangest look in his eyes. Magda realized, then, that it was fear.

At seeing that look, at comprehending that it was fear for her, she started to panic. With a firm grip on her shoulders, he forced her back down.

"Listen to me, Magda. You need to be still. Don't fight it. Let me do that."

She tried to ask what he meant, but the words came out in a jumble that even she couldn't understand.

He smiled just a bit. "No need to talk anymore. You got the right words out when you needed them." He patted her shoulder. "You're safe from the dream walker, now."

Magda sagged in relief. At least that monster was gone from her mind. She had felt that evil presence for only a brief time, but it was something she knew she would never be able to forget. Tears of gratitude at being free of the dream walker ran across her cheeks. Even if she had to endure the lingering effects of his attack, even if she was to die, she was at least free of his vile presence.

"I need to get into your mind, Magda—"

She had just escaped that very thing. She didn't want anyone in her mind ever again. She didn't want to have anyone controlling her in that way. In a panic at the thought of it, she thrashed, trying to escape his grip.

"Listen to me," he said as he held both of her wrists firmly in one of his big hands. "It will only be to heal the damage. You're still losing a lot of blood. I have to hurry. You have to let me help you. Just lie still and don't fight me, all right? Can you do that? Can you trust me? It will be easier if you do."

This was a chance at life. This was a chance to be pulled back from that terrifying dark void. She had fought for her life. She couldn't let herself slip beyond the veil. At last, she let the tension go from her muscles and nodded.

"Thank you, Master Rahl," she managed with the greatest of effort.

He offered a brief smile before putting his hands to either side of her head. His hands muffled the distant sounds of the world, muffled what she only then realized were the sounds of her own sobs.

She looked up at him, and his blue eyes reminded her of looking up into a blue sky. As she stared, unable to blink, she was drawn into that calming color. His eyes became the sky. She felt herself falling into that azure forever that became sapphire that became cobalt that became midnight blue that became simply midnight.

She felt the weight of his power press in on her mind as the cold flood of his magic cascaded down through her whole being.

She had been healed by Baraccus before, but that had been for relatively minor things—a deep cut, a twisted ankle, a crippling headache—so she recognized the unique feel of Additive Magic. What in those instances had been a trickle was now a massive icy torrent overwhelming her with its power.

Even more, though, she felt the red-hot touch of what she knew had to be Subtractive Magic. She imagined that he was removing residual traces of the damage done by the dream walker's presence.

She gasped at the sudden, sharp, searing heat deep

inside her ears. She recoiled at the smell of burning flesh, realizing that he must be cauterizing the wounds to stop the bleeding.

Even though she felt lost in a strange, empty place, she knew that she was not alone. He was there with her, working, trying to help her. It was something like when the dream walker had made himself known in her mind, but at the same time it was the opposite side of that alien presence. The dream walker, she knew, she could feel, had been malicious and had fully intended harm.

This, by contrast, was a benevolent presence. Despite the pain pulling her ever downward inside herself, she could feel that his purpose was only to help her, only to eventually be able to lift her pain away.

She could feel every thread of Additive Magic stitching through her torn muscles and broken ribs. It didn't exactly hurt, but the odd sensation made her queasy. She wanted to squirm away, yet she knew that this was her only chance and so she surrendered to it. The warm power seeping deep into her ears was equally uncomfortable.

At the same time, she was aware of him trying to force her to let him lift the agony away. Magda resisted, holding on tight. She didn't want anyone else, especially Master Rahl, to have to feel the agony she felt. She clutched it tight, trying to shield him from the full force of the suffering.

It did no good. He was stronger than she was. With a fearful sense of concern for his safety, she felt the pain's grasp slipping from her. With that impediment lifted away, his gift was able to twist down through her inner being, going deeper into her core in order to heal her.

As she felt the last of that icy agony stripped away, she reveled in the mercy of being free of it and at last began to feel the warmth of his healing magic warming her.

She hung suspended in that glowing warmth, only distantly aware that anything else existed but that comforting support.

Magda lost all sense of time. She didn't know how long she floated in that place of serenity. It could have been mere moments, or it could have been days. In that silent void, time lost all meaning. In that strange inner place, time ceased to exist.

Gently, she became aware that it had ended.

Her eyes at last opened and the room around her came into focus. She realized that she was lying on a couch. Lord Rahl stood over her, his brow beaded with sweat. He looked exhausted.

The candles on the iron stand nearby were burned down to nubs. She knew, then, that it had lasted most of the night.

Magda reached up and touched her ear, letting her fingers trail down along her jaw. It didn't hurt anymore.

Her chest didn't ache inside, either. She placed her hand on her ribs, testing. They were sound and no longer hurt.

But there was more. While she still missed Baraccus, still hurt that he was gone, it was different, now. The pain of losing him wasn't so crushing as it had been. She still grieved, still felt the suffering of the loss, but she recognized that the sharpest edges of that misery were now softened just a bit.

She would always miss her husband, always love him, but she knew, now, that she was going to be able to go on. She had to go on.

"Thank you," she whispered up at Lord Rahl.

He showed her a weary smile. "I would suggest that you rest, but I fear that we can't afford the time right now."

Magda sat up, wiping at her eyes, getting her bearings. "Is it still night?"

His smile widened. "It's a new day, Magda. Has been for a while now."

"Then we need to get to the council chambers. They will be in session. I need to convince them of the imminent danger. They must act."

Lord Rahl glanced down at her clothes. "Maybe you had best get cleaned up, first."

Magda stood, feeling remarkably steady. She had expected to at least still feel wobbly, but she didn't. She felt alive. Really alive.

She looked down at her dress. Large areas of it were soaked with blood. He was right, she needed to change. She touched her hair and found that it, too, was matted with dried blood. She glanced over at her reflection in a small mirror on the wall. Blood stained the sides of her face and neck.

"I guess I do look a shocking mess. I had better clean up, first, before we go to see the council."

Alric Rahl nodded as he gestured at his two big bodyguards. "We'll wait outside while you change and wash up."

Magda caught his arm as he started to turn toward the door.

"No."

He frowned. "No?"

"No. I want the council to see me like this. They need to see the reality of the blood that will be shed by our people at the hands of the dream walkers if they refuse to listen."

Lord Rahl smiled. "I don't think that the council has yet ever really encountered the true resolve of Magda Searus."

She returned a haunted smile. "They are about to."

Magda kept her eyes straight ahead as she marched past towering, polished black marble columns to each side of the gallery leading toward the council chambers. Rounded moldings covered in gold atop the columns supported a thick architrave carved with robed figures meant to represent the members of the council.

A gridwork of golden squares overspread the long, vaulted ceiling. Each square held a bronze medallion with a scene of a different place in the Midlands. Supposedly, as council members passed through the gallery they were walking beneath a grand display of the diversity of the Midlands so that they would be reminded to be mindful of all the far-flung people they represented as they went about their official deliberations. In Magda's experience, it took more than bronze medallions to remind the council to be mindful of all the far-flung places of the Midlands.

Magda passed beneath a line of long red silk banners hanging from the vaulted ceiling. They were meant to represent the blood that had been shed in defense of the people of the Midlands. The carpet she walked along, with the names of battles woven along the edges, was also red and meant to be a reminder of the struggles fought and the lives laid down so that others might live.

Magda usually found passing through the gallery to be a somber experience. On this day, it was more somber than usual.

The red banners and crimson carpet only served to help draw attention to the blood covering Magda. More than ever before, she felt a connection to those who had bled in defense of their motherland. If the council refused to listen to her, then a great deal more blood would be shed.

As she marched down the long carpet, men to the sides paused in midconversation to stare openly. Women moved back. The drone of talking withered to whispers and then people fell silent as she passed, leaving a hush in her wake.

As she entered the great rotunda not far from the council chambers, Magda saw small clusters of people all through the enormous room standing around talking, no doubt discussing matters waiting to be brought before the council. The conversation echoing around the room tapered off as people watched her advance through their midst, trailed by the Lord Rahl of the D'Haran Lands and his two huge bodyguards.

Overhead, the high windows around the lower border of the golden dome let in early-morning sunlight to bathe the towering reddish marble pillars around the edge of the room in harsh light. Between the columns, against the stone wall, stood imposing statues of past leaders.

Magda knew that one day a statue of Baraccus would take up a place of honor in this room leading to the Central Council.

It was a strange thought that touched her with pride, yet at the same time served to highlight how Baraccus was slipping inexorably into her past.

It wouldn't be long before Baraccus became a figure left to history. People would no longer come to know him, they would only know bits and pieces about him. She wondered if the stories people in the future learned would bear any resemblance to the reality she had known with Baraccus. History, like memories themselves, tended to become distorted with the passing of time, or worse, corrupted with the agendas of those writing it.

As much as she wished it were otherwise, Magda could do nothing to alter the past or to bring Baraccus back. He was now in the hands of the good spirits. Meanwhile, life went on. He had wanted her to go on.

The great mahogany doors to the council chambers stood open, as they usually did. The doors were three times her height and as thick as her thigh, both sides carved in intricate designs meant to represent spells, although they were not actually spells. As Baraccus had often told her, drawing out real spells was dangerous. The intention was to remind all that it was the gift that guided them in everything.

The open doors were meant to convey a sense of the council's openness, but Magda knew that it was an illusion of receptivity. Where the council was concerned, nothing was as simple as it seemed.

At the great doors, the guards posted to either side, their pikes standing perfectly upright, saw that she didn't intend to stop. Their pikes tilted as they hesitantly stepped away from their positions onto the great seal set into the stone before the doors.

One of the guards lifted a hand out, thinking she needed assistance. "Lady Searus, you're hurt. Let me get someone to help you."

"Thank you, but the members of the council are the only ones who can help any of us."

"I'm afraid that they're in session," he warned.

"Good," she said as she pushed his pike up out of her way.

"Lady Searus," the other guard said, "I'm afraid that the agenda is full for today and they are not taking up any new business."

"They are now," she said on her way past.

The guards weren't sure what they should do. They knew her quite well as the wife of the First Wizard who often spoke to the council. But even though they knew her, they were not accustomed to women with short hair walking in to speak to the council. More importantly, though, she was covered in blood and they didn't know why. If the Keep was under attack, they clearly needed to know about it, but then, so did the council.

Other guards inside the council chambers started to close in to slow her until they could find out what was going on. They took in Lord Rahl and his two men behind her. Confused by the sight of the First Wizard's wife covered with blood, to say nothing of the leader of the D'Haran Lands accompanying her, they finally parted, apparently thinking that stopping her could potentially be more trouble than letting her through. Not only was Lord Rahl a dignitary, but it was the council, after all, that decided who would speak.

Magda was glad that she had told Lord Rahl to leave his small army waiting in the corridors farther back and out of sight. Having a force of armed men try to enter the council chambers would only have complicated matters.

Once inside the big doors and past the knot of guards, she turned back to Alric Rahl. She put her hand on his chest to urge him to a halt.

"Why don't you wait back here? Your presence beside me will only make them think that I ask this on your behalf."

His brow creased with displeasure as he stared off at the council on the dais in the distance at the far end of the room. He shifted his weight and hooked his thumbs on his belt.

His blue eyes finally turned down to her. "As you wish."

Magda offered him a brief smile before she turned her attention to the room she had visited many times. A runner of blue and gold carpet leading off toward the council split the grand room. Fluted mahogany columns supported soaring arches to the sides. Leaded windows high up in the arches let in muted streamers of sunlight. Below the windows, balcony galleries held seating for observers. The seats were packed, which told her that the council was not dealing in restricted military matters.

The open floor beneath the balconies had no windows, making it a rather dark and gloomy place. The windows up high were meant to represent the light of the Creator, while the darker regions down below were a reminder of the eternal darkness of the afterlife in the underworld. It was a subtle reminder of the forces of nature, life and death being the most notable, that always had to be held in balance.

Groups of people who had come for an audience with the council crowded the floor farther off to each side, beneath the shadows of the balconies. As was often the case, there were military men in dress uniforms with clusters of staff around them, officials in dignified robes with color-coded bands to denote rank and position, wizards and sorceresses in simple robes, and aides accompanying well-dressed, important women. As in most places in the Keep, there were even children here and there with their parents.

The sunlight slanting in through the windows high to the right revealed a slight haze from men smoking pipes as well as the dust that the constant traffic carried into the vast room. As she marched down the blue and gold carpet and through isolated patches of sunlight from windows that had been designed to let the light penetrate down to the center runner, no one could miss Magda's blood-soaked dress. She knew from seeing herself in mirrors that her face and hair were quite a sight as well.

Despite the relatively hushed quiet of the room, out in the world a war raged. Baraccus had confided that the fighting was horrific. Men died by the thousands in desperate battles, their bodies torn apart in the mad rush to attack or defend. The fury, the panic, the blood, the noise, the desperation were said to be beyond imagining.

In contrast, the vast room where the council went about its stately work was an ordered and dignified place where business was conducted at a measured pace. Panic, blood, and naked desperation seemed very far away.

Magda knew that it was an illusion. While everyone worked very hard to preserve the appearance that this place was the balance to the madness of the war, that war was on every mind.

As in the outer halls, people quietly discussing business fell silent as they spotted Magda marching resolutely along the long ribbon of carpeting through the center of the chamber. Most of these people knew her. Most of them had seen her standing before the flames that had consumed her husband and their beloved leader. Many had come to her to offer their condolences.

Atop the dais, the council sat at a long, ornate desk that curved around in a half circle. Staff and assistants sat at the desk beside them. Even more sat behind. People stood in the center of the dais, with that desk curving halfway around them and the audience at their back, to be heard by the council.

Magda recognized the woman standing in that spot, speaking passionately to the council. Her words trailed off as she looked over her shoulder to see Magda step up behind her.

The woman first quickly took in the length of Magda's hair and then scowled down at her bloody clothes. "I don't appreciate being interrupted when I am addressing the council."

"I'm talking to them now, Vivian," Magda said as she showed the woman a very brief smile. "You can speak to them later."

Vivian pulled a long lock of hair forward over her shoulder. "What makes you think that you can—"

"Leave," Magda said in a voice so calm, so quiet, so deadly that Vivian flinched.

When the woman made no move to leave, Magda leaned even closer and spoke in a confidential tone that no one else could hear.

"Either you walk out now, Vivian, or you will have to be carried out. I think you know that I'm not bluffing."

At seeing the look in Magda's eyes, Vivian turned and dipped a quick bow to the council before hurrying away.

A hush fell over the room.

"What is the meaning of this interruption?" a red-faced Councilman Weston asked. "What matter could be important enough for you to dare to think you can intrude in this fashion?"

Magda clasped her hands. "A matter of life and death."

Behind her, whispers rippled through the room.

"Life and death? What are you talking about?" Weston demanded.

Magda met the gaze of each councilman, now that one of them had made the mistake of inviting her to speak on the subject.

"The dream walkers are in the Keep."

15

The room erupted with noise and confusion as everyone behind Magda started talking at once. Some people yelled questions. Others called out their disbelief. Yet others shouted denunciations. Many, gripped by fear, remained silent.

Elder Cadell, ever the arbiter of decorum in the council chambers, held up a gnarled, arthritic hand, calling for silence.

When the crowd quieted, Councilman Weston went on. "Dream walkers? Here in the Keep?" His eyes narrowed. "That's absurd."

Elder Cadell ignored Weston's charge. "Lady Searus," he said with practiced patience, "first of all, the council is in session and—"

"Good," Magda said, not at all patient. "That means I don't have to hunt you all down. Better that you are all gathered to hear this. Time is short."

Councilman Guymer shot to his feet. "You have no standing to speak before this body much less to interrupt us! How dare you dismiss someone who was speaking on important matters and—"

"Whatever matter Vivian was wound up about this time can wait. I told you, this is a matter of life and death. I was just invited by Councilman Weston to speak. I intend to do so." She arched an eyebrow. "Unless you want to have me dragged away before I can make known the mortal danger to our people as well as how the council can help to protect them?"

Assistants shared looks. Some of the councilmen shifted uncomfortably in their chairs. Not all of them wanted to so publicly silence her before she could reveal what the council could do to help to protect people. That reluctance gave her a window of opportunity.

Councilman Hambrook leaned back and clasped his hands together over his ample middle. "Dream walkers, you say?"

Guymer shot to his feet and turned his wrath on his fellow councilman. "Hambrook, we're not going to be diverted from our agenda to allow this outrageous interruption to continue!"

Magda closed the distance to the desk in three long strides, placed her hands on the polished wood, and with a glare, leaned toward Councilman Guymer.

"Sit down."

Taken aback by the calm fury in her voice, and somewhat stunned to be spoken to in such a way, he dropped into his chair.

Magda straightened. "Dream walkers have made their way into the Keep. We must—"

This time it was Weston, to her right, who interrupted her. "Disregarding your bursting in here in such an insolent fashion, what makes you think we would believe such a claim?"

Magda slammed the flat of her hand on the desk before the man. The shock of the loud smack made all of them jump. She could feel her face going red with rage.

"Look at me! This is what a dream walker did to me! What you see—the blood all over me—is what your countrymen and loved ones are going to look like before they die in unimaginable agony! This is what is coming for all of us!"

"I am not going to sit here and—"

"Let her speak," Elder Cadell said with quiet authority.

Magda bowed her head to the elder in appreciation before collecting herself and going on. "A dream walker entered my mind without my being aware of it. I don't know how long he was hidden there. I fear to think what he overheard while he was lurking in my mind without my knowledge."

"What could he have overheard?" Councilman Sadler asked in a suspicious tone.

"For one thing, the reason I was coming here today: the solution to prevent the dream walkers from having free run of the Keep and destroying us all. Once he heard that solution, and knew that I was going to come here for the council's help in implementing it, he acted. His intent was to kill me so that I couldn't speak to you. His intent was to keep you in the dark so that we would all be vulnerable."

As Magda looked at each councilman in turn, out of the corner of her eye she could see the crowd moving in closer so that they wouldn't miss what she had to say. She straightened and stepped back to the center of the semicircle of councilmen so that she could make sure that everyone could hear her.

"While I don't have any idea how long the dream walker was hidden there in my mind, watching, listening, his presence became all too obvious once he decided to rip me apart from the inside." She slowly shook her head as she turned her back on the council to look out into the frightened eyes of all the silent people watching her. "You cannot imagine the pain of it."

The spectators stared in silent anxiety.

Weston broke the silence. "Do you expect us to trust—"

"No," she said without looking back at him. "I expect you to look with your own eyes at the result of what was being done to me by the dream walker who had slipped into my mind, here, in the Keep, where we thought we were safe. We are not safe." She held out the skirt of her dress. "As I fell to my knees, dying, blood running from my ears, blood choking me, I could feel the dream walker break each rib, one at a time." Some in the crowd gasped. "The pain was beyond endurance, yet there is no way to avoid enduring it."

She walked slowly across the dais to be sure that everyone out in the crowd, as well as all those behind the desk, could get a good look at the blood all over her. The sound of her shoes on the wooden floor of the rostrum echoed through the room.

"The blood you see all over me," she said, "is the evidence of the torture he was inflicting. If it is shocking to see, I promise you, you would not have wanted to hear my screams as I lay in a pool of my own blood and on the brink of death."

"And so I guess that the good spirits swept in and saved you at the last moment?" Councilman Guymer asked, bringing a smattering of laughter.

"No," she calmly answered as she gazed out at the crowd. "Though I prayed they would, the good spirits did not come to my rescue. I saved myself."

"And how, may I ask, did you do that," Sadler asked, fingers skyward, "if the dream walkers are in fact such fearsome beings?"

"You're right. They are fearsome. They are also powerful. But I invoked magic even more powerful and as a result I was protected from the dream walkers."

"You are not gifted," Guymer scoffed.

"You don't have to be gifted to be protected," she said out to the crowd watching, addressing them rather than the council. "You must choose, though, to accept the solution. At the last moment before I was about to die, I came to understand that, and I chose to do what was needed to save myself.

"That's why I'm here. I want all of our people to know that there is protection for them, for all of them. Believe me, the dream walkers can steal into the minds of anyone and they will show no mercy. But none of you need fear them. None of you needs to suffer and die."

"And how do you know that you really are protected?" Guymer asked.

"If I wasn't protected, the dream walkers would have torn me apart where I stood so they could prevent me from coming here to tell you how to protect yourselves and our people from their abilities."

Concerned chatter rippled through the room. People among the onlookers shouted out over the noise, wanting to know what was needed to be protected from the dream walkers.

Magda let the worry build for a time before she finally lifted her arm, pointing to the back of the room near the great doors. Everyone turned to look where she pointed.

"There stands Lord Rahl, the key to your survival," she said in a voice loud enough that all could hear her. "He alone created a protection that shields him from the dream walkers. That protection constructed of magic is powerful enough to protect anyone bonded to him."

"Lord Rahl!" Guymer shouted. "Not that nonsense again! Lord Rahl has already come before us with his plans to rule the world."

Magda turned a glare on the man. "And since when is toiling to protect your life and the lives of all the other innocent people of the Midlands as well as the D'Haran Lands interpreted as wanting to rule the world?"

"This is about the oath he insists we must swear to him, isn't it?" Elder Cadell asked.

Magda spread her hands. "We are all on the same side in this. We of the Midlands and those of the D'Haran Lands share a common interest as well as a common threat. Those in the Old World want to subjugate all of the New World. They don't care about our internal boundaries. They want to rule us all. If they win, there will be no Midlands, no D'Haran Lands. We will all be either dead or their slaves. This is about our survival, not petty matters of rule."

"Petty?" Sadler asked. "I don't see bowing to the rule of Lord Rahl as petty."

"You will think it petty enough," Magda said, "if a dream walker silently slips into your mind and becomes your master, if he makes you do his vile bidding. They can make you betray those you care about, even kill people you love. If you're lucky, that master will choose instead to rip you apart from the inside."

Sadler licked his lips but didn't speak up to argue.

The whispers in the crowd fell silent as a man who had been watching from the shadows at the back of the room behind the councilmen stepped out into the light.

It was Prosecutor Lothain. His menacing gaze was fixed on Magda.

Lothain's smile looked every bit as deadly as a skeleton's grin. "And how do you know, Lady Searus, that it was not really Alric Rahl's own magic that was in fact tearing you apart from the inside, as you put it?"

"Lord Rahl's magic?" Magda gaped at the man. "Why would he do such a thing?"

Lothain arched an eyebrow. The grace of his smile, as mocking as it had been, vanished. "Perhaps for the exact reason that brings you to stand before us—to have you put on a show to frighten people into going along with his scheme to seize power and become the leader of all of the New World."

He stood as motionless as a rock, challenging her to deny it.

"That is not what is happening." Magda wished her own voice didn't sound so inadequate and defensive.

"Because your husband had convinced you that Alric Rahl was to be trusted?"

Magda blinked. She didn't want to agree with the man, but she had to say something. She pulled herself up straighter.

"My husband told me of the very real danger from the

dream walkers. As a war wizard he knew all too well exactly what they are capable of. Like everyone else, I have for years admired Baraccus's knowledge and wisdom. He was, after all, named First Wizard because of the respect in which he was held. As First Wizard, he had a great deal of trust in Alric Rahl. They were both fighting on the same side in this war. They both have fought from the beginning to keep all our people from being slaughtered."

Lothain smiled just a bit, as if he had caught her in a slip of the tongue. "It would appear by your own admission that your husband carefully shaped your thinking in a great many areas." He stroked a finger across the stubble on his chin as he took a few slow strides toward her. "Are you saying, then, that your husband was all along a secret party to Alric Rahl's plot to rule the New World? Perhaps that was the reason for your husband's secret dealings and covert midnight meetings with strangers?"

Magda's hands fisted at her sides. This time she had no trouble bringing power to her voice.

"My husband has from the beginning fought this long war for no reason other than to protect us all."

"This long war that we are losing."

"Your accusations are as insulting as they are groundless."

Lothain bowed his head. "Your loyalty to your husband is admirable, Lady Searus. But it is to be expected."

"This is all quite beside the point," Elder Cadell said. "Motives aside, we have been through all of this before quite exhaustively and in the end we made our decision to decline Lord Rahl's offer."

Magda closed the distance to the elder sitting at the imposing center of the council's desk. "But things have changed. There is no time to waste. The dream walkers are here, now, in the Keep."

"No one is doubting that you may in fact believe

that," Prosecutor Lothain said from behind her. "However, even though there may be those who are inclined to trust your sincerity in what you believe, it is the truth of that belief that is in question. Dream walkers will no doubt pose a threat at some point in the future but when they do I would expect that they will come after important targets."

Magda rounded on the prosecutor and held out her bloodstained arms. "They came after me!"

Lothain smiled dismissively. "At such a great distance from down in the Old World, how would a dream walker know of you, or find you, and more to the point, why would they bother with you? But Alric Rahl was in the Keep, right there in the room with you, and he had motive enough to want to make you believe it was a dream walker who was attacking you."

"That's absurd," she said. "The dream walkers are real and a threat."

"Of course they are," Elder Cadell said. "But in any event, we have decided on our own solution to protect our people."

"Your own solution?" Magda's brow twitched into a frown as she rounded on the elder. "Surely you don't mean the towers?"

Councilman Weston, to the side of the elder, leaned forward, his hand clenching into a fist on the desk. "We don't need to hear your skepticism of a matter that is the council's concern and not a topic meant for public discussion."

Magda knew that, for obvious reasons, they would of course want to keep the true nature of the project a secret. Baraccus had never agreed to the proposal, or to keeping the plan a secret. He thought that if the situation was grave enough, the idea was something that would reluctantly have to be considered, but he thought it had to be considered publicly. Apparently others thought so as well. As a result, the tower proposal was one of the worst-kept secrets in all of Aydindril.

"We have a solution and we are working on it," Elder Cadell said in his typically calm tone of authority. "That is all that matters here."

Shocked, Magda paused only briefly. "Do you mean to say that you've actually gone ahead with the plan? You began implementing it without Baraccus's knowledge?"

"The First Wizard had his own responsibilities; this was under our jurisdiction." Elder Cadell gestured, glossing over the question. "Once completed, the towers will not only protect us from the dream walkers, they will seal away the Old World and protect us from anything that the enemy gifted might create and send to destroy us. The towers are not a partial solution such as Lord Rahl proposes. They are a complete solution that will not only protect us from all manner of onslaughts, they will seal us off from the Old World and end the war."

She knew that he was making a statement for public consumption. In so doing, he was only revealing the virtuous aspects of a monstrous idea.

"If it's even possible to complete them," she said.

"They will be completed," a glowering Councilman Guymer said, dismissing the concern.

Magda was horrified. She looked back at Elder Cadell. "But the towers would mean the death of untold numbers of our wizards."

"It is a price that must be paid," he said. "It will end the war."

Magda was incredulous. "At what cost? How many thousands of our best and brightest will you condemn to death to create your towers?"

Looking down at the desktop, Cadell scratched an eyebrow. "They will be volunteers."

"Volunteers?"

"Yes." The elder frowned as he looked into her eyes. "Your husband in his capacity as First Wizard did much the same thing, did he not? Didn't he choose volunteers from among the most talented of the gifted to go to the Temple of the Winds in the underworld? When each failed to return, he sent another, and then another. Baraccus knew that he was likely sending those men to their death. The men knew it as well. It was a risk that was judged to be necessary, and a price that was paid willingly. This is no different, here. It is a sacrifice that our people, including those you often advocate for, might survive."

Magda took a step back. "And even if the price is willingly paid by those thousands, it will take time before the towers can be completed. The dream walkers are coming. We can't afford to wait."

Elder Cadell's frown began to show anger. "Do you suppose that the towers are the only solution we pursue? Do you think we are foolish old men, leaving the matter to languish while our people are in jeopardy? We have gifted who as we speak work feverishly to find a way to shield us from the dream walkers."

"I'm not saying that you are foolish, Elder Cadell," Magda said with a bow of her head. "But the dream walkers are here now. What if the gifted can't create a shield? What if the dream walkers cut through the ranks of those gifted who are working on the problem in order to prevent them from coming up with a solution? We have a solution through Lord Rahl that works, and it will work immediately."

"You claim," Lothain said. "The question for us here remains, do you say this because you have been duped into believing it, or because you are a willing participant, a traitor plotting against the Midlands?"

The prosecutor cocked his head, as if inviting a confession.

"Plotting against . . . ?" Magda's surprise darkened into a murderous glare. "I say it because it is the truth."

"So you say. It remains to be determined what Baraccus may have been up to. For all we know, you, too, could be part of a conspiracy. After all, you were the wife to the First Wizard, yet you advocate surrendering our sovereignty to Alric Rahl. And no wonder, since you now tell us that Baraccus himself, a man who was supposedly our noble leader, confided in you his trust in the Lord Rahl of the D'Haran Lands over the council of the Midlands. That does not strike me as the kind of thing that would be said by a woman who has always claimed to be an advocate for those of the Midlands. It sounds to me like a woman who advocates for D'Haran interests over ours."

The crowd broke into a drone of whispering. Magda thrust a finger toward the prosecutor.

"Your twisted accusations could very well cost uncounted thousands their lives!"

As the echo of her voice still rang around the room, the whispering behind her died out.

"You are avoiding the true issue before us," Lothain said.

"The true issue? The true issue is that you see conspiracies lurking in every shadow, spies hiding around every corner, traitors behind every door. You care only about chasing inventions of your imagination in order to advance your own personal fame and power!"

The crowd gasped.

Magda spread her arms before him. "In your fixation on coming up with conspiracies designed to elevate your own status, you deliberately ignore the bloody truth standing before you."

Apparently so surprised that anyone would dare to speak to him in such a tone, much less publicly accuse him of inventing conspiracy theories for personal gain, Lothain was for the moment struck speechless.

Before he could recover and say anything, Magda wheeled around to the crowd watching in rapt attention.

"The dream walkers are among us," she said loud enough for all to hear. "These men on the council choose to be blind to the bloody truth before their eyes while the clever head prosecutor chases phantoms only he sees. If you follow the lead of the council or Lothain's self-serving gossip about conspiracies, then you risk what I suffered. Know that without protection you very well could die in unspeakable agony.

"As well-intentioned as the council's choice may be, you are the ones who will pay the bloody price for their mistake."

The crowd again buzzed with anxious chatter. Some people shouted out over the racket, wanting to know what they could do. Magda held up her hands, calling for order so she could answer.

"Let the council do as they will," she told them. "But if you wish to live, then to save your own life go to your knees, bow forward, place your forehead to the ground, and speak the following devotion to the Lord Rahl:

"*Master Rahl guide us. Master Rahl teach us. Master Rahl protect us. In your light we thrive. In your mercy we are sheltered. In your wisdom we are humbled. We live only to serve. Our lives are yours.*

"Repeat the devotion three times to ensure that you invoke the link to Lord Rahl's magic so that your mind will be shielded from the dream walkers.

"Do it in secret if you don't want to have to explain to these men your reasons or if you fear reprisal. Realize that it does not make you a traitor to the Midlands to swear your allegiance to the Lord Rahl; rather it makes you loyal to your own life.

"Lord Rahl is not an enemy of the Midlands, he is a fighter for all of those in the New World. We are all one. We are all fighting for the right to live, the right to be free from bloody tyranny.

"You cannot help the Midlands if you are dead." Magda thrust an angry fist high. "Choose to live! Swear your loyalty to Lord Rahl and you will be protected from the dream walkers!"

Magda saw the council frantically signaling for the guards to lead her from the council chambers.

Before they could come to escort her out, she lifted her chin and marched toward the doors. The crowd parted, falling back out of her way as if she were someone of power and authority.

Some whispered their thanks as she passed.

Magda kept her eyes straight ahead and her expression blank, not showing her emotions as she made her way toward the great doors.

Magda spotted the stony Lord Rahl standing just outside the great doors watching her long march out of the council chambers. His two grim bodyguards waited not far behind him. Glancing back over her shoulder as she passed the massive, mahogany doors, Magda saw the council guard who had been following after her slow to a halt when they were sure that she was indeed leaving and looked to have no intention of returning.

Far off across the rotunda Magda saw Lord Rahl's small army standing ready to draw weapons and defend him if there was trouble. She realized that they would not be in a good mood after word of all the angry charges and accusations that had been leveled against Lord Rahl reached them. As far as the soldiers were concerned, they must believe that they were in a potentially hostile place. What's more, three of them had already died mysterious deaths since arriving at the Keep. At a signal from Lord Rahl, though, their hands eased off their weapons.

Back inside the council chambers, despite the calls for order, things were not returning to normal. The crowd didn't want to go on with the agenda. They wanted an swers to pointed questions about the threat from dream walkers.

Magda hoped that the council would think it over and see the wisdom in using Lord Rahl's solution to shielding people from the threat. In her experience, it was often the case that upon further reflection the council saw that her suggestions made sense. She hoped that was the case this time.

"I must apologize, Lady Searus," Alric Rahl said with a deep bow. "I was terribly wrong."

"Wrong about what?" Magda asked, her own temper still burning hot as she started out once again.

As he fell in beside her, he gestured back through the door to the council chambers, where a near riot was taking place. People were shouting at the council, demanding to be heard, demanding to know if it was true that danger was really that close at hand.

"I must beg your forgiveness. I was wrong and you were right." He leaned down toward her a little and arched an eyebrow. "I can see now that having shorter hair has indeed lowered your status to that of a nobody and that you are now completely defanged."

Magda's fury faded in the face of his satire. She couldn't help but to smile. "Well, the truth is the truth, no matter your status."

He glanced back briefly toward the council chambers. "Unfortunately, I think that speaking the truth has made you some enemies."

Magda's smile faded. "I almost died twice this day. The second time you brought me back as I was passing through the veil into the world of the dead. I was nearly in the embrace of the good spirits. I was dead but for you pulling me back to the world of life.

"Every moment I live now is a gift. All anyone can do

is return me to that place where I should rightfully be. If I am to live, then I will live free of pretense."

"You're wrong that you should rightfully be dead, Magda. You chose life and you lived. That is the fact of the matter. We can't live our lives according to what might have been. We have to live by what is. You're alive and that is what's important."

To Magda, though, life without Baraccus seemed dismal and empty. Despite the pain she had been in, she had thought that she was about to be with him again. Despite wanting to live, she was in a way sorry to have been snatched back.

"You lived and you have given other people the gift of also being able to choose to protect themselves so they can also live," one of Lord Rahl's big bodyguards said.

Alric Rahl glanced back at the man and nodded. "The choice is now their own, not the council's."

He turned his attention back to Magda. "But by helping people make their own choice, you have put yourself in jeopardy. Perhaps you should come with me back to the People's Palace. You will be safer there."

With the world at war, Magda wondered if there was such a thing as a safe place. If one place fell, then the next would come under siege until it, too, fell. Eventually, there would be no safe place left to run to. Either the New World survived together, or all of it would fall under the swords of the invaders.

Though he didn't return the stares, people watched Alric Rahl as he passed. Their eyes betrayed their fear of the imposing figure of Lord Rahl, a man that few in the Keep had ever seen. But they would have heard the stories of him.

As they passed through the great rotunda, she noticed others, back in the shadows, a collection of worried people who glanced her way as they talked quietly among themselves. She saw the silent dread in the eyes tracking her.

In that moment, she realized that while some feared Lord Rahl, most of the others were not watching him, they were watching her as she passed by. They were looking to her for something, for answers, or salvation, or maybe simply a reason to hold out hope. They weren't seeing her short hair. They were seeing Magda Searus, a woman covered in blood who had declared that it didn't have to be.

Magda finally shook her head. "I grew up in Aydindril. Since I married Baraccus I've lived in the Keep. This is my home. We are at war and my home is under threat. I have to stay and fight for it. These are my people. I have to stay and fight for them.

"People are accustomed to doing as the council says. I don't know if any will choose to become bonded to you and your protection, but at least I'm shielded from the dream walkers. That means I will be better able to fight for these people. Maybe I can convince others to join in accepting the same protection.

"Besides, the dream walkers are not the only threat. There are things going on that don't make sense to me. I know that Baraccus, too, always thought that there was something wrong here at the Keep."

"Lothain's conspiracies?"

Magda pursed her lips as she considered. "Knowing my husband I don't think it's that simple. There is something terribly wrong here, something much deeper."

"What do you mean?"

"Well, for one thing, the Temple team was supposed to take the most dangerous things of magic away into the Temple for safekeeping. They betrayed us, supposedly to help protect mankind from the tyranny of magic."

"But they've all been caught and put to death."

Magda was beginning to think that whole story was too simple, too neat and tidy. She was beginning to wonder if they all really were traitors.

"But how could such men turn against us? How is mankind suffering under a tyranny of magic? Dear spirits, they were wizards, creatures of magic. They weren't tyrants.

"For the Temple team itself—a hundred men—to have been working for the enemy was horrifying. No one, not even Baraccus, had suspected such a thing. So if no one suspected, do you really think that Lothain managed to catch and execute every last one of the traitors?"

"It is hard to imagine such a widespread conspiracy here at the Keep, and especially among such trusted men. But I'm sure that Lothain tortured confessions out of those men before they were executed and would have rounded up any others if there were any."

"You told me that three of your men died mysteriously since arriving here," she reminded him.

"There is that," he said.

"Baraccus left me a note. It was his last words to me. He told me that my destiny is here. He asked me to have the courage to find the truth."

"The truth? The truth about what?"

Magda let out a deep sigh. "I don't know."

"How do you know that the note really meant anything specific? Maybe Baraccus, knowing your nature, simply wanted to let you know that you were in his heart."

"In that note, he told me to guard my mind."

Lord Rahl missed a step. "Guard your mind? You mean from the dream walkers?"

She cast him a sidelong glance. "You tell me."

Some of his long blond hair fell forward over a shoulder as he looked over at her. "So you think he also wanted you to stay here?"

"Yes. He said that my destiny is here. Baraccus was a war wizard. He had the gift for prophecy. I think that he knows that something dark is going on here and he wanted me to find it."

Lord Rahl thought it over as they walked past soaring marble columns supporting an arched ceiling with scenes of great events painted between the ribs of the vaulting.

"But Baraccus was a war wizard. You're, well, you're not. What can you possibly do that he couldn't?"

"Try and guess how many times I've tried to make sense of that very thing."

Lord Rahl grunted his understanding of her point. "You have no idea what it is you are supposed to look for?" he asked.

"I guess that I'm supposed to look for the truth."

"But what truth?"

"Maybe the truth of why Baraccus killed himself."

Lord Rahl considered that for a moment. He finally gestured in frustration. "Perhaps after venturing into the world of the dead, he was simply overwhelmed by the experience and lost all hope."

Magda again glanced over at the man. "None of the Temple team killed themselves after they returned. None of them seemed overwhelmed. Baraccus was stronger than those men."

Lord Rahl clasped his hands behind his back as he walked silently beside her, thinking it over.

"Baraccus never did anything without good reason," he finally said.

"Exactly. I think that he had a purpose in killing himself. I think it must have been the only way he could accomplish something profoundly important. I think that

Baraccus sacrificed his life for a calculated, powerful reason. I need to know what that reason was. I think he wanted me to look for the answer to that question.

"I have to stay and find the truth behind all of the things that have happened. I'm the only one who seems to care why he killed himself. I may be the only one who can find the answer. In any event, Baraccus seemed to have faith that I could. In fact, he charged me with that mission as his last request. He said for me to live the life that only I can live."

As they entered the long gallery Lord Rahl glanced up at the red banners hanging above them. "Where will you start?"

"I'm not sure, yet."

For a time he walked in silence along the crimson carpet with the names of battles woven into it before finally glancing over and smiling. It was not a happy smile, but rather a sad, grim smile.

"I understand. These people are fortunate to have you fighting for them. But know this. You are not the only one here who is safe from the dream walkers."

Magda frowned up at the man as they passed immense black pillars. "What do you mean? The council rejected your help."

He clasped his hands behind his back and waited until they had gone by a knot of onlookers and were out of earshot before answering.

"I expected that they might, so when I first arrived I went to those who do the work of protecting us—the officers and the gifted working here—and laid out the situation. Military men understand threat all too well and grasp the value of an effective defense."

"You are a devious man, Lord Rahl."

He grinned, looking happy with himself. "I knew better than to put all our necks in the hands of the council.

That's why I went to a number of important people here at the Keep, first."

"And they've sworn loyalty to you?"

"Not all. But some comprehended the true dimension of the threat and spoke the devotion as you have." He chuckled softly. "Though none of them had to bleed first."

She smiled with embarrassment. "Baraccus mentioned a few times that he found me stubborn."

"Officers Rendall and Morgan are with us," he said. "They command troops in and around Aydindril. Grundwall too. He leads the Home Guard."

Magda nodded. "I know them. They're good men. What of the gifted?"

"Since it involves magic, they tended to understand the true dimensions of the threat and therefore the wisdom of the solution. Some didn't take to my offer, but many did. That means we have a fair number of allies who can go about their work without worry of dream walkers subverting what they do."

Magda sighed. "Still, not all have accepted the protection of the bond to you. Maybe I can help convince them."

When they reached his big, brawny soldiers at the far end of the great gallery, Alric Rahl turned to face her.

"I have to be on my way. Now that I've done what I can here, there are pressing matters that I must attend to."

Magda looked up into his blue eyes. "Before you go, tell me something."

"If I can."

"Are the council and prosecutor right? Are you after rule? Is power what you really care about, what drives you? Is that why you created the bond to work in the way it does, so that people must swear loyalty to you? The truth, now."

He hooked his thumbs in his weapons belt as he gazed

down into her eyes for a time. His intent resolve didn't waver.

"Know this, Lady Searus. I have agents in the Old World as we speak. They seek out the dream walkers. They are there to hunt down and kill every last one of those bastards. I couldn't tell you before, before you were sworn to me, because I couldn't risk the dream walkers learning of it. If my purpose was to rule, I would let the dream walkers live so that people would have to swear loyalty to me. If the men I sent succeed in the mission I've given them, no one will have any need of swearing loyalty to me."

Magda smiled. "Thank you, Lord Rahl. In your wisdom I am humbled."

CHAPTER
18

Holding up her small tin lantern, Magda tried to see ahead into the blackness. She thought that she knew where she was, but she wasn't entirely sure. The dank maze of stone passageways beneath the more heavily used portions of the Keep was as black as death, making it all the harder to get her bearings. While up above many of the areas were expansive, elaborately decorated, and comfortable, the little-used passageways Tilly led her through resembled cramped caves. Magda could see the vapor from her every breath lifting into the cool, damp air.

Water seeping from joints in the rough stone blocks of the walls had in places over many years built up spongy, slimy mats across the floor. At times Magda had to hold her breath against the stench of rat carcasses rotting in puddles of stagnant water. The inky pools reflected flickering yellow lantern light in twisting patterns across the low ceiling.

"Tilly, are you sure that you're not lost?"

Walking in front because the passageway was too narrow for them to walk side by side, Tilly looked back over her shoulder and spoke without slowing.

"I often go this way, Mistress. Other routes are sometimes crowded and noisy. I find that this way is faster, and besides, I would rather be alone with my own thoughts."

Magda understood that well enough. As much as she didn't like the confining, dark passageways, they did have the advantage of being virtually unused. In the more direct routes by way of busy corridors she would have encountered a lot of people.

"Is it much farther?"

"A ways yet, Mistress."

The two of them worked their way around an awkward jog in the passageway that skirted a protrusion of wet, gray, speckled granite on the right. It was the bedrock of the mountain itself, left in place to serve as a wall, evidence that they were at the margin of the Wizard's Keep, deep in the mountain into which the vast structure was built. Much of the lower Keep was pinned directly into the stone heart of the mountain.

At an intersection, they followed the passage that cut off to the left, heading in the direction of the Keep's interior. The walls were even closer together, the ceiling lower.

Not long after they had taken the turn, a deep thump shook the stone floor. Magda could feel the concussion in her breastbone. Grit rained down from joints in the stone. They both paused. She then heard a distant scream echo through the cramped corridor.

"What was that?" Magda asked, her words echoing back to her from the darkness.

Tilly glanced back and saw that Magda had stopped. "Not far ahead be where some of the gifted work on creating weapons. Sometimes, people get hurt. It might be nothing more than that."

"Are you saying that you think it might be something else?"

The old woman leaned closer and lowered her voice. "I know that I be the one who planted the seed of this idea in your head, Mistress, but that was before people started turning up dead down here. Like I told you when you asked to show you the way, I didn't know if this still be such a good idea. As much as I would like to believe your suspicions, I don't know if I share the explanation."

Not long after Baraccus's death, people had begun to find mutilated bodies down in the lower Keep. Tilly's fears were understandable, especially since she had found one of the bodies herself. People didn't know who was to blame, and that only heightened everyone's fears.

At least Lord Rahl was long gone so they couldn't blame him, though a few still tried. For some people, it was better to blame anyone than to fear the unknown.

Magda's suspicion was that the killings were most likely the work of the dream walkers, just as she had warned the council. Since giving the devotion to Lord Rahl, Magda was protected from the dream walkers by that bond, so she wasn't too worried about the danger to herself in the lower Keep. Tilly wasn't so sure that it was the dream walkers. She was worried for Magda's safety down in the areas where the victims had been found. Despite suspecting dream walkers, Magda couldn't help sharing that nagging worry in the back of her own mind.

Magda ruffled her short hair, ridding it of the bits of stone and dust that had rained down from the joints in the ceiling. "If you don't think it's the dream walkers, have you heard any suggestion of who else might be responsible?"

Tilly checked the darkness ahead and behind. "Not who, Mistress, what."

Magda's frown deepened. "What does that mean?"

"From what I hear, no one knows much about the killings and no evidence has been discovered. I have heard it said, though, that such as was done to the poor souls they found dead does not appear to have been done by people. At least, not people who could be in their right mind. Considering what I saw, I am inclined to agree."

"Dream walkers can rip a person apart, or make them attack someone else as savagely as any animal."

Tilly straightened. "Maybe so. Please promise me that you will be careful when you are down here? You are ungifted. Promise me that you will be on guard at all times?"

Magda nodded. "You've no need to worry about that. As soon as I'm done with what I came to do, I'll be headed back up. I have no desire to stay down here any longer than necessary."

She followed after as Tilly started out again, moving quickly enough to reveal the slight hitch in her gait. Magda heard the screams several more times before they finally died down to a brief murmur of weeping and then even that mercifully ended. She hoped it was wizard's work that had injured someone and not something else. If wizards were involved, then help would at least be at hand for the person in pain.

If dream walkers were involved, there would be no help at hand.

Magda was well aware that Tilly could go just about anywhere in the Keep and few people ever paid much attention. Most people didn't even seem to notice her, almost as if she were invisible. She was just a lowly worker, one of many, going about her work. People rarely gave her a second look.

Magda had been worried that dream walkers might see the significance of that as well, see an opportunity in such anonymity, and take Tilly in order to use her fo their ends. To protect her, Magda had convinced Tilly to take on the protection of the bond to Lord Rahl by giving the devotion. Though Tilly was now protected from dream walkers, she still feared what else might be on the loose in the Keep. Magda didn't entirely dismiss those fears.

The old woman stopped and moved to the side, pressing her back to the stone-block wall to make room for three men who suddenly appeared, approaching from the darkness ahead. The three, dressed in simple robes, were in a hurry. Magda pulled the cowl of her cloak forward to hide her face as she backed up against the wall beside Tilly.

"Tilly," the first of the men said in greeting as he dipped his head. While most people didn't even know Tilly's name, there were apparently at least a few people, like Magda, who did notice her and know her name.

"Do you know who screamed?" Tilly asked.

The man had to turn sideways a little in order to shuffle past. "Yes," he said, anger charging his tone. "Merritt just got another two men killed. A third was injured. That's who you heard screaming."

Magda thought that she recognized the name. Baraccus must have mentioned it before. She spoke before she thought.

"How did this Merritt get the men killed?"

The first man looked up at her, indignation clearly evident in his eyes. Magda held her lantern off to the side, making it look as if she were trying to stay out of the way, but in doing so it put her face in shadow and lit his.

"Merritt refused to help us any longer in crafting a critical weapon. Five brave wizards went to their death as a result." The muscles in his jaw flexed when he clenched his teeth. "Now two more have just died trying to accomplish the task Merritt abandoned instead of leading. The third man, at least, will recover, though he may be blinded. I don't know how many more we will lose until, the Creator be willing, we are successful."

"I'm sorry," Magda said in a sympathetic tone.

"Merritt should have been there," the second man in line said.

The first man grunted his agreement as he moved on past Magda. She noticed that he smelled of smoke and burned flesh. As he passed close, she saw specks of blood splattered across his robes.

Magda lowered her head so that the second two men, holding glowing spheres that cast cold, greenish light up across their heated expressions, wouldn't recognize her. All three swiftly disappeared back into the darkness.

Once the men were out of earshot, Tilly leaned closer. "Wizards," she confided before starting out once again.

Magda had suspected that they were wizards by their simple robes. She had known they were when she had looked into their eyes.

While she had no gift for magic, she did have the rare knack of being able to see the gift in the eyes of those who possessed it. She'd always thought of it as merely a form of intuition. Baraccus had said that it was more. He had told her that, while she was ungifted in the overt sense, she had latent abilities that set her apart in at least some small ways from others who were ungifted.

He'd said that the spark of life was stronger in her than in most people. That, he said, was what he saw in her eyes, that she was not merely beautiful but intelligent, unusual, rare. He had sometimes looked into her eyes and whispered to himself how bewitching she was, as if she weren't there hearing him, as if he were all alone looking upon some exceptional specimen rather than his wife.

Magda never thought of herself as exceptional, but she did feel lucky that he thought so.

She recalled quite clearly the first time she had looked into Baraccus's eyes. She remembered feeling momentarily lost for words as she gazed in those gentle, knowing eyes. Looking into his eyes had made her feel safe. She had known that he was gifted, of course, but she'd also seen a handsome older man behind those abilities that she was inexplicably drawn to. Who knew the ways of love?

Besides being aware of the presence of the gift in the eyes of all three men, Magda was pretty sure that she recognized the first two. She didn't know their names, but she thought that she had seen both of them before. Magda had occasionally gone with Baraccus on some of his frequent visits down into the lower Keep to see his wizards. She thought that she must have seen the men one of those times because she didn't recall them ever coming to see Baraccus in their apartments.

She also thought that she recalled the name Merritt. Baraccus met with a lot of gifted people and he didn't always introduce her. She knew when he preferred that she remain in the background or even out of sight, such as when people came to discuss confidential matters or to report trouble. There had been times, after such visitors left, that he would stand at a window, stoically staring out at the city of Aydindril below.

Sometimes, though, when visitors left he would tell her their names and what it had been about. On occasion he talked to her about people he'd met with down in the lower Keep. The name Merritt sounded familiar, though she couldn't place a face with the name. It could be that she'd never seen him, merely heard Baraccus mention him.

Magda would rather not be returning to the lower reaches of the Keep. It was an unnerving place in the best of times, to say nothing of some of the things she had heard from Baraccus, but it was even more so, now, in light of Tilly's warnings, yet Magda didn't know what else to do. She had run out of ideas and needed to find answers.

After Lord Rahl had left, she'd spent weeks making discreet inquiries, all to no avail. She had spoken to every wizard and sorceress she knew, at least the ones she felt comfortable enough to approach. Most were sympathetic, but no one knew anything that was in the least bit useful to her.

Magda knew that Baraccus confided little in others, even the gifted, except for specific things they needed to know. Her questions had only confirmed it. Others knew only small bits of the picture. Magda had been a bit surprised to come to the realization that she knew a great deal more about Baraccus and his activities than did anyone else, even the people he regularly worked with.

Through Baraccus, Magda had seen more of the larger picture of the war, complex alliances, and covert activities than any of them, even if she didn't know some of the finer details. Other people saw the details of small segments, while she in many cases glimpsed the overview of all the things with which Baraccus dealt. She had a deeper insight into how all the parts that various people knew about were connected.

Even Lord Rahl, one of the men Baraccus trusted most, was not a great deal different. Baraccus might have trusted him with more vital missions than he entrusted to others, but he hadn't trusted him with everything. Even with as many details as Alric Rahl knew about the dream walkers, he didn't know as much as Magda about the larger picture.

Her husband had been a man who closely guarded not only his secrets, but his activities and the reasons behind most of the things he did. He'd often said that keeping things to himself was a matter of survival.

Yet even with as much as she knew, Magda still didn't know nearly enough about the various matters he had been involved in. She still didn't know why he had killed himself.

A number of those she had spoken with had been more interested in talking to her, than about Baraccus. They wanted to know about the dream walkers, and if what they had heard from people who had been at the council meeting the day she had gone before them, covered in blood, was true. When Magda had confirmed that it was, they asked about the devotion that was said to be able to protect people's minds. She had given her counsel to anyone who had wanted it. Some of those people had listened with open minds and had been grateful. Some weren't interested in being allied with Alric Rahl.

A few of the gifted, she learned, had already met with Lord Rahl and had already taken up the bond to him.

At first, after Lord Rahl had left the Keep, Magda had been worried about the bond working once he was gone. To her surprise, she had discovered that she could sense him through that bond. It was the strangest feeling, but through that link she could feel her connection to him, tell the direction he was in, and sense the distance. It was a reassuring connection that let her know she was safe from the dream walkers.

Now, with the summer wearing on and the secrets behind Baraccus's death haunting her at every turn, the only thing left was to try Tilly's original suggestion. She still didn't like the idea, especially in light of the new dangers down in the Keep, but Magda had reached a dead end in her search for answers. In the back of her mind, she also feared to lose the chance should the dream walker get to the woman first.

Despite her misgivings, Tilly seemed to understand

Magda's need to find answers as to why Baraccus had killed himself. Tilly thought that if she went to see the woman, it would at least help bring peace to Magda's heart. Magda was looking for more than peace. She wanted answers.

The passageway finally emptied them out into a vast, narrow chamber that rose up like an enormous split inside the mountain. Fine-grained granite blocks lined the soaring walls. The chamber was perhaps half a dozen stories high, yet only as wide as the public corridors up in the Keep where merchants sometimes sold their wares from small carts or stands.

The narrow hall was so long that Magda couldn't make out faces of people at the far end. In some cases she couldn't even make out their gender. She was able to make out the dots of various colors of robes, denoting rank and duties.

Magda found herself somewhat relieved to see people again, relieved not to be alone in the dark passageways. The screams she had heard, and learning that men had just died, made her own loss fresh again.

Up near the lofty top of one of the long walls, slits were open to the night sky. Bats up high darted about, chasing bugs.

One of the Keep's young cats sat on its haunches, peeking around the corner, its big green eyes watching the bats. It was obviously hungry. Feeling sorry for the scrawny black cat, Magda pulled a small bundle of chicken strips from her waist pouch. She unwrapped the meal she had brought along and tossed a small piece down to the hungry cat. As long as she had it out, Magda handed Tilly a strip and took one for herself before replacing the bundle in her waist pouch. The cat pounced and devoured the unexpected prize as Magda and Tilly went on their way, each nibbling at her own snack.

Magda had been to the enormous room several times, though by a more agreeable route, so she knew that it was a central hub leading to a number of important areas of the lower Keep. The first time she had been to the place, Baraccus had told her that the slits along the top of one of the walls helped the chamber serve as a ventilation chimney, drawing air through the lower Keep in order to provide a bit of fresh air.

The open slits were also one of the ways that birds sometimes found their way into the Keep. It wasn't uncommon to find a small bird lost in the halls. Sometimes grackles found their way into dining halls, where they hopped around on the ground looking for crumbs, or even boldly stole food right off people's plates.

Magda could see several sparrows that had obviously found their way in via the high slits, roosting on supports near the tops of the wall. She even spotted a raven perched on a beam, its feathers fluffed up, its black eyes watching the people down below.

With it being hotter outside than in, the ventilation openings seemed to be working in reverse this night, letting muggy air sink into the room and leaving the place feeling clammy. A haze of smoke coming from work areas had stratified throughout the room.

Stone stairs built tight against the wall to the right led to long, narrow balconies with widely spaced openings. Some had doors, while most were passageways to different areas.

Many of the people in the room seemed in a hurry, but Magda was used to seeing people in the Keep in a hurry. As large as the place was, it wasn't uncommon for a journey between areas to take hours. Delaying for any reason, such as to chat, could in certain cases cause an errand to end up taking the better part of the day. That was probably why Tilly preferred the mostly deserted secondary passageways.

When Tilly saw Magda staring at carts piled high with bloody bandages parked haphazardly along one wall, she leaned closer and whispered, "Down here, in the matters these people deal in, errors are costly. Even worse, they are frequently punished by death."

Magda didn't have to ask what Tilly was talking about. She had escorted Baraccus to the place several times when he needed to speak with some of his wizards working on weapons for the war effort.

They were entering the area of the Keep where some of those weapons were created out of people.

While she understood the need, she was still appalled by the very idea of using magic to alter a person's nature, to change who they were—in some cases to something no longer even human. She found the practice of changing people in such ways to be beyond abhorrent.

O ver there." Tilly gestured to an entryway, set back into the shadows, some distance down on the far side of the vast chamber. "We must go down that way."

Magda nodded. She knew of the place, of course, though she had never had reason to go down there before. She pressed a hand against the pang of anxiety tightening in her stomach.

As they made their way along and diagonally across the chamber, she tried as best she could to keep her face concealed by the cowl of her cloak. She wasn't going to go out of her way to prevent people from recognizing her, but she wasn't going to deliberately let people know she was there if she didn't have to. The echo of her every footstep, though, whispered through the cavernous room, as if to betray her.

Glancing out from the edge of the hood of her cloak, Magda saw gifted people she recognized. Even though she was doing nothing wrong, she didn't want to stop to talk with them or have to explain her purpose. It was nobody's business. She kept the hood pulled forward.

Baraccus had often told her that if she was doing something important, she shouldn't tell people anything they didn't need to know. He lived his life by that rule. In fact, he often wouldn't even tell Magda about things he thought she didn't need to know.

Like why he had killed himself.

She was certain that what Baraccus had done was not the simple suicide it had appeared to be to those who didn't know him as well as she did. Magda knew that it was more complicated than that. Suicide was simply not consistent with his character, so she knew that there must be more to it, that there must be a larger purpose to it. She also knew that for Baraccus to sacrifice his life, that purpose had to have been vitally important.

She also suspected that this time it was different in that he really did want her to find the reason behind it. His last words, in the note he had left for her, seemed to say as much. His voice still rang in her head with his words from the note.

Your destiny is to find truth.

One way or another, Magda intended to discover the truth behind his death.

As they made their way through the immense room, she saw that the series of arched recessed areas in the wall to the left served as workstations. People stood over the workbenches filing, hammering, cutting, and shaping metal, but in some cases wood. Back beyond some of those arched work areas were large rooms, most with big rolling doors pushed open to each side, probably to provide fresh air.

Reddish light from the fires of a forge deep in one of the dimly lit rooms revealed feverish activity that drew Magda and Tilly's attention. Men yelled instructions as they urgently worked to contain the damage from what appeared to be a serious accident.

Through the broad opening Magda could see that the room was a shambles. The forge had been partially torn open. Broken brick and burning embers lay scattered across the floor. The metal hood that belonged over the forge, along with its chimney, was nowhere in sight. Acrid-smelling smoke and glowing ash still rising from the remnants of the fire rolled across the ceiling and out the open doors. Iron bars set into the brick around the forge were twisted and bent outward, as if there had been a violent explosion.

Ominous flashes of lightning still flickered around the damaged forge, sparked through the dimly lit room, and arced off through the smoke hugging the ceiling. The twisting strands of lightning crackling through the room all seemed anchored at the forge, evidence of the magic that had been involved in the labor, and probably the source of the catastrophe.

The shuddering lightning lit the lines of men in spasms of bluish light as they rushed in carrying buckets, heaving water on the fire. Hot coals hissed and steamed. Other men rushed in with glowing spheres to provide more light.

Magda spotted the body of a man slumped on the floor against a far wall and another sprawled nearby. Both men were torn and bloody. It was obvious they were dead. One of the men's blackened robes still smoldered.

A long, gleaming section from a shattered sword was embedded in his chest. Magda could see that he was missing an arm at his shoulder. She could see by how still the piece of blade jutting from his chest was that he wasn't breathing. Coals still glowing red lay strewn among the abandoned bodies, along with polished fragments of the broken blade. One piece stuck in a far wall shined out from the shadows.

A small clutch of people surrounded an injured man on the floor. The circle of kneeling men, all seeming to be working together, were clustered together, bent over the moaning man, tending to his injuries. One of the man's legs bent at the knee, then straightened, then the other, back and forth as if he were in great agony. Some of the men held him down while others appeared to be using their gift to try to help him.

Magda knew that this had to be the source of the screams she had heard. She felt an urge to go help the man, but the gifted were already doing that.

From what the three men they had met in the corridors had said, none of it would have happened if the wizard Merritt hadn't abandoned these men. She couldn't imagine why he would leave people who needed his help. Now men were dead because of it.

She also couldn't imagine how a sword could have exploded to do so much damage.

Magda and Tilly kept moving through the busy room. There was nothing they could do to help.

Other rooms, dark but for the intense glow from forges and furnaces, were beehives of activity. Despite the accident that had happened close by, work continued unabated. Furnaces and molten metal could not be left untended. Teams of men lifted heavy containers and pushed them into furnaces with the aid of long poles. In other areas, men lugged blazing crucibles from the furnaces to pour luminescent, liquid metal into molds.

In other rooms, men rushed with glowing steel from the forges to massive anvils where other men with hammers waited. As the hot metal was held in place, the hammers worked in unison. The steady beat of cold steel against hot metal at various stations rang through the large chamber as the men shaped the malleable metal. The ringing of hammers mixed with the roar of fires being fed by bellows, shouting, conversation, and the dull background rasp of files.

Magda could smell molten metal, smoke from fires, and steam from salt water and oil used to quench the glowing steel. The haze of smoke and steam that hung motionless the length of the enormous room was in places tinted yellowish orange by the blush of light from forges and furnaces off under archways and rooms to the side.

Despite the accident, work looked to have hardly paused. The war raged on. Every day the enemy drew closer. These people knew that they could not slow their efforts.

The threat overhanging them all was almost palpable.

CHAPTER
21

When they reached the far side of the long chamber, Magda glanced around, checking to make sure that the people were going about their own business and not paying any attention to her. Satisfied, she and Tilly slipped into a sheltering entryway.

Though its style mimicked many of the grand places in the Keep, the recessed entry was, in contrast to most other areas, rather small and intimate. Fluted limestone columns lined either side of the gloomy alcove. The small pillars, not much taller than Magda, were topped with long entablatures that provided support for arches elaborately decorated with complex, carved stone moldings framing tiles laid out in dark, geometric patterns. Benches to each side had been intricately embellished to match the forbidding architectural details of the rest of the entry.

The benches seemed to suggest that visitors sit and reconsider before going any farther. Or maybe that they pause in their weary grief and rest to steady themselves before continuing on.

Surrounding the pitch black opening at the rear, larger-than-life stone figures in grim, contorted, distraught poses clearly conveyed a sense of desolation and tragedy for what lay beyond.

For good reason. The brooding figures surrounding the doorway were meant to tell all that this was not a region to be entered lightly.

This was the threshold to the place of the dead.

Without pausing to reconsider or to rest, Tilly vanished into the dark maw. Magda followed swiftly behind. Their lanterns, along with more hung at intervals, revealed stone steps descending down into blackness. The stairs were wide enough that the two of them could walk side by side.

"Do you come down here often?" Magda asked.

"No, Mistress. Only when a wizard or sorceress asks that I come down to clean a specific area for them. Some like their rooms kept tidy. Most don't like anyone coming into the places where they do their work. Other members of the staff are assigned to the common areas down here, the same as up above."

Magda glanced at the meticulously maintained and polished stone balustrade. She supposed that it was a sign of respect for the dead that the place be kept presentable for visitors.

In contrast to the marble staircase that gave the descent a sense of grandeur, the walls and ceiling were nothing more than a broad shaft hollowed out of rock. Flight after flight of stairs, each ending at a landing from which the next run turned, were all part of a massive staircase that spiraled ever downward. There were no rooms or side corridors along the way, nor areas set aside to sit and rest.

It surprised Magda how far down they had to go before they finally reached a spacious cavern at the bottom. The chamber had been carved out of the rock, much as the tunneling descent had, with tool marks and drill holes from the excavation still in evidence on the rough stone walls. Only the floor was finished off, in a circular pattern of light and dark stone tiles. A table veneered in burl walnut sitting alone in the center of the room held a simple white vase filled with white lilies.

At intervals around the room, openings cut into the stone led off into darkness. Each looked like a cave. None of the nine passageways were trimmed or decorated, except for a symbol that had been carved into the stone above each opening.

Without delay, Tilly entered the ninth opening, a number that she knew from Baraccus had great meaning in things having to do with magic.

The walls of the passageway were the same roughly hewn stone as the chamber had been. Almost immediately, they started down yet more steps, except that these, rather than being built, were carved directly from the stone itself. The treads were rugged and uneven, so Magda had to be careful lest she fall.

It was another long descent down the twisting tunnel before the stone abruptly changed. As the tunnel leveled out, they found themselves within a vein of softer sandstone. Unlit corridors branched off in every direction but Tilly led them on through the largest, main hallway. Before long, rooms carved out of the sandstone began to appear on both sides.

Almost immediately, Magda began seeing the dead.

As they passed by room after room, their lantern light revealed niches carved right into the stone walls of the rooms. Each cavity looked to hold at least one body; most held more. Some of the hollowed-out chambers seemed to have entire families laid out beside one another.

Magda slowed to take a better look into a larger area off to the right. She saw that in places the resting chambers were half a dozen high, the uppermost niches reachable only with a ladder. Most of the bodies laid to rest in the honeycombs of cavities were wrapped in shrouds that were so old and dirty that they looked to have been carved out of the same tan sandstone as the rooms themselves. A number of the recesses held coffins, all of them stone, most with carved decorations, all of them layered in dust and partially encased within masses of cobwebs.

As they went on, they encountered rooms of niches that held massive numbers of bones. Each recess was filled to the top with neatly stacked bones, sorted by type, covered in dust. Several of the chambers held only skulls. Many of the resting places looked untouched for decades, if not centuries. Very few looked tended.

"These are the oldest tombs," Tilly said. "As more space was needed, the oldest bones were brought together and stacked here to make room. As time went on, catacombs had to be extended deeper and deeper in order to make new places to bury the recently deceased. The excavation goes on to this day. Many of those living up above will one day end up down here."

Above many of the hollowed-out resting places could still be seen a family name in faded paint, or a name and a title of the deceased. Some were decorated around the edges with crudely carved decorations, probably done by family members.

Many people preferred to inter their family members so that they could come to visit them. Other people, especially the relatives of more famous people, preferred to let fire consume their loved one, rather than allow their bodies to become an attraction, or provide rivals a corpse to spit upon.

Magda had chosen to have the shell that had contained Baraccus's spirit to be consumed by fire as that was also said by some to purify the spirit of its worldly trappings for its journey to the underworld. Some couldn't stand the thought of a loved one being reduced to ashes. Magda didn't see that empty vessel as her loved one. Her loved one was gone to be among the good spirits. The choice being forced upon her, she chose to have his vessel reduced to ash rather than to rot.

The passageway they hurried down widened out, so that the two of them could again walk comfortably side by side. As they descended level after level, past the dead numbering in the thousands, they eventually came to newer sections of the catacombs. The bodies Magda saw wrapped in white shrouds were not yet layered in centuries of dust.

Torches in rusty iron brackets were lit in these newer sections, providing enough light to see without the need of lanterns. Tilly blew out the flame in hers.

"Besides the dead," Tilly said, "here, too, be places where some of the gifted choose to work."

Although her guide didn't mention it, Magda recalled Tilly telling her that some of the gifted down here worked with the dead. Magda didn't like to contemplate such a concept, and tried hard not to imagine what such work could entail.

Before long, Magda began to hear the whisper of conversation. They soon encountered people coming out of passageways to the sides. Some hurried past in the opposite direction. Most of them were alone, but she also saw groups of four or five people talking in low voices among themselves, absorbed in debate on formulas or the order of prophecy.

Magda finally saw rooms that were something other than burial chambers. They looked like crude work areas cut out of the sandstone. Some were lit by torches, but a number of the rooms were brightly illuminated by glass spheres.

Inside a few darker rooms Magda saw glowing verification webs surrounded by people studying them, pointing out certain elements to others, or casting in additional branches. Some of the webs hummed. The colors of the webs reflected off faces focused on the work.

There were several large libraries, lined with shelves from floor to ceiling, all filled with books. Magda knew from Baraccus that these would be valuable and profoundly dangerous books that needed to be kept away from more public areas. Some such books had been taken away to the Temple of the Winds.

People sat at tables, quietly studying volumes opened before them, while others stood in the aisles, searching the shelves, apparently looking for particular information. Other rooms had heavy doors. At one door, flashes of light crackled and flickered through the gap at the bottom of the door, as if there were a thunderstorm inside.

Tilly gestured down a passageway to the right. "This way."

The long corridor was noticeably different from any that had come before. It was wider than the others, with carefully carved straight walls and a flat ceiling. It was also completely deserted and silent in a way that was oppressive.

As they left the occupied areas far behind and made their way down the passageway, something about the place made the fine little hairs on the back of Magda's neck stiffen.

At the far end they reached a single arched opening, its significance highlighted by the broad corridor that had led up to this lonely archway. A textile with long-faded colors in vertical geometric designs hung over the entryway.

Tilly paused to the side of the covered opening. "Here be where you need to go, Mistress. I can take you no farther."

"Why not?"

Tilly glanced at the hanging. "The gifted who I sometimes work for, and who have told me about the woman, also say that I am not to go beyond these symbols hung here. They say that it is only for the gifted to go beyond."

Magda frowned. "I'm not gifted."

"But you are Magda Searus. As the wife of the First Wizard you had to live up to responsibilities others don't have, but with those responsibilities came liberties not always enjoyed by those who are not gifted."

Despite Tilly's confidence, Magda wasn't so sure that she would be welcomed. The fact that Tilly wasn't allowed beyond was a troubling sign that Magda hadn't anticipated.

Tilly pulled a small piece of paper from her pocket and handed it over. "This map was given to me by a friend I trust. It will show you which passageways you must take. Pay close attention so that you don't become lost in the maze. When you reach an archway covered over with red cloth, that be the place.

"Inside there is said to be a blind woman named Isidore who tends the spiritist. I have never met her, but as I hear it told, if the spiritist is willing to see you, Isidore will take you to her.

"You must understand that the spiritist may not wish to see you. Her purpose is to help the gifted to see into the world of the dead, not to grant audiences to petitioners. She may choose to turn you away."

"But you're the one who suggested in the first place that I come to see the spiritist. You mean you don't even know that she will see me?"

"You are the wife of the First Wizard now in the world of the dead. Though I can't say for certain, I have believed from the first that you are one she would agree to see."

Despite looking somewhat apologetic, Tilly tried to allay the concern by going on with her advice. "If you are allowed to speak with the spiritist, she will need to reach into the spirit world to find what you seek. My advice would be to think carefully about what you most need to know."

"I understand." Magda glanced down at the paper covered with lines and intersections, unsure if it was all worthwhile. "Thank you, Tilly. I appreciate you showing me the way."

"If she agrees to help you, I have heard that it takes some time. With your permission, I would leave you to your search for answers. I should be back to my work before I am missed."

Magda could tell by the way the woman stole glances back up the strange entrance tunnel that she was afraid of the place. Magda didn't feel all that comfortable there, either.

"Of course, Tilly. You've done enough bringing me down here. Please, go on back. I'll be fine."

Tilly offered a brief smile. "Can you find your way back from here alone?"

Magda nodded. "Yes. I know how to return."

Tilly touched Magda's arm. "I wish you well, then, Mistress. I hope that you can find the answers you seek and that your heart can at last be at peace."

Magda didn't know if her heart would ever be at peace, but she nodded anyway. She was at least determined to find answers.

Tilly leaned close and lowered her voice. "Be careful, Mistress."

"What do you mean?"

"The spiritist is said to be a dangerous woman."

Magda frowned down at the old woman. "Dangerous in what way?"

Tilly arched one brow. "She deals with the dead."

Magda let out a sigh as she again took in the cloth hanging in the dead-still air of the arched opening.

"I will be careful."

She watched as Tilly hurried back through the cavernous passageway and vanished around a bend.

Standing in the silence before the hanging textile covered with a simple geometric pattern, Magda looked at the map again to get her bearings.

For a long time she stood alone, debating the wisdom of going to see such a woman. At last, she let out a deep sigh. She had no other ideas.

She had tried everything else she could think of. It would be foolish to turn back when she was this close.

CHAPTER

22

Magda lifted the rough cloth aside and cautiously entered what the map showed to be a complex maze. She held the lantern out, trying to see into the darkness, but she could see little of what was ahead. As she moved deeper into the carefully carved tunnel, she encountered layers of coarsely woven, raw linen hanging motionless across the passageway. It was unnerving to abruptly encounter the walls of cloth suspended in the darkness. She couldn't imagine their purpose. She speculated that perhaps they were there to make the maze more confusing to trespassers. They were certainly confusing her.

The hanging cloth also hid many of the side passageways, making it difficult to know for certain where she was on the map and if it was merely a cloth hanging in the middle of the hall, or a cloth covering the opening to another passageway. Sometimes there were four cloth walls forming a square, several with passages behind them, some with none. Over and over, she had to check behind the hangings and then consult the paper Tilly had given her. Several times she had to retrace her steps and start over again, trying to be sure of the proper turns to take.

Even though she carefully studied the map as she slowly made progress deeper and deeper into the warren of tunnels, it seemed that the complex network didn't match the drawing. It was frighteningly confusing. She was having trouble reconciling the map to the tunnels she found herself in and feared becoming lost in the maze.

After a time, though, Magda realized that the short marks along the line of the route she was to follow were not side corridors, as she had thought at first. The short lines were actually intended to designate the locations of the layers of cloth that hung across her way. She confirmed her theory by counting the hangings between side tunnels. Once she was properly oriented to Tilly's drawing, she was more confident in selecting the proper turns when she reached intersections.

The place was dead quiet. The only sound was the soft swish of her boots on the sandstone floor. She noticed that the floor was relatively rough, while the others they had been in had been worn smooth by foot traffic. Apparently, not many people ever ventured this way.

Magda turned when she thought she heard a soft sound from behind. She stood motionless for a time, breathing as slowly as she could while she listened. When she didn't hear it again, she finally moved on, quickening her pace.

To the sides, a few of the inky black tunnels didn't have the hangings covering the openings. There were no doors anywhere in the maze, as there had been in the areas where people worked. It was as if doors were not needed because the oppressive darkness itself barred the way into the side passages. That, or the ominous, dread-still curtains.

The place smelled dusty and dry with little hint of th burning pitch from the torches back in the occupie areas. Magda cautiously checked each room as best s could as she passed by, but she saw no one. Each room was completely bare, without any furniture or indication of purpose. None of them looked to have ever been inhabited. She heard no voices. It was as if she had entered an empty world entirely devoid of life.

She paused and turned back when she thought she heard a sound from behind. She stood stone-still for a time, holding her breath, listening, but she didn't hear it again. Finally, she let her breath out and continued on, but from time to time she checked back over her shoulder.

She couldn't ever recall being anywhere in the Keep that felt so lonely. She had never been down into the catacombs so she hadn't really known for sure what they were like. Even the resting places of all the dead had seemed less desolate than the passageways leading to the spiritist. She hadn't been aware that such strange deserted areas existed down below the Keep.

Every tunnel of every corridor looked the same. It would be all too easy to become lost in the complex network of tunnels. As she checked her map at every intersection, she was thankful that Tilly had obtained it for her.

Magda abruptly found herself at the end of the corridor. An archway covered over with a coarse red cloth loomed up before her. This was where the map ended. It was the place Tilly had told her about.

She stood stock-still for a time, not knowing for certain what to do. There was no door for her to knock on.

"Is anyone there?" she finally called out. Her voice echoed back to her from the cold corridor behind.

"We are here," came a woman's voice from deep within. "Why are you here?"

"I have come to speak with the dead."

The only sound was the hiss of Magda's lantern as she ꜱod motionless, watching the vapor of her breath slowly rise into the still air. She glanced back into the darkness as she waited, listening for the sound she'd heard before.

"Enter, if you have need enough," the woman finally said.

Something about the voice made Magda wonder if she should turn back now, while she had the chance.

CHAPTER
23

efore she lost her courage, Magda pushed the
dead-still, faded red cloth aside and ducked under
it into a narrow hallway. Under a low, arched
ceiling the hall led back through darkness toward an
area of mellow light. At the end of the entryway she
found a roughly round chamber lit by dozens and dozens of fat candles. The room was hollowed out of the
same pale sandstone as the rest of the catacombs. Ledges
carved into the walls all the way around held all the candles. The candles gave the whole room a soft, warm amber glow.

To the right Magda saw a dark doorway, presumably
leading farther back into the quarters. She suspected that
the spiritist would be in that back area.

In the middle of the room a thin young woman sat
cross-legged on the floor. She had very short, fine brown
hair and wore a dark, loose-fitting wrap of a dress that
covered her legs entirely but left her shoulders and slender arms bare. Her hands remained nested in the lap of
her dress.

A strange, thick leather blindfold fastened around her
head covered her eyes. It was a uniform width except for
notch cut in the middle to fit around her delicate nose.

The blindfold went temple to temple, held in place with a leather thong tied at the back of her head. Magic symbols and spell-forms had been carefully tooled into the leather with some of the lines colored in with paint. By the way the leather edges were worn and smooth it looked to have been in use for quite some time.

It was beautifully made, but covering the young woman's eyes as it did struck Magda as rather foreboding.

The woman cocked her head as if to use an ear to better locate her visitor. "Welcome."

"Thank you," Magda said. She glanced into the dark opening to the side, but saw no one. "Are you Isidore?"

The young woman smiled, making her bony cheekbones stand out all the more. The smile, while pleasant enough, did not put Magda entirely at ease. The woman's expression and the lines around her mouth had an uncompromising toughness to them that seemed at odds with her young age. It reminded Magda a bit of the look she had seen in the eyes of orphan girls who lived by their wits in the alleyways of Aydindril. Those girls were tough beyond their years.

"I am Isidore. Strangers are most uncommon down here. Who would you be, then?"

"Magda Searus."

"Ah. Wife to Baraccus. I have heard of you."

Magda didn't know if that was a good thing or not. She glanced again to the dark doorway, wondering if the spiritist could hear the conversation.

While most people had heard of Magda, and a number of people knew her and genuinely liked her, she knew that there were also those who didn't like her. Some women had been jealous of her, resentful that she had somehow attracted and married the First Wizard. Some men thought marriage in general, and to an attractiv younger wife in particular, was a distraction that the Fir

Wizard didn't need. A number of people simply resented her for marrying such a great man when she herself was ungifted. They thought it improper.

She also knew that a few people, besides some on the council, had come to loathe her after that bloody day in the council chambers. They didn't like to have trouble come into their lives at the Keep. It was as if by warning them of the danger she had personally brought the threat into their midst. As frustrating as such an attitude was, the truth was the truth.

"I'm sorry for your loss," Isidore said. "The First Wizard was a great man."

"Thank you. I am here about that great man. I would like to speak with the spiritist, if I may."

"I'm afraid not. You see, the sole purpose of the spiritist is to serve the wizards in their work here. I don't know what you've been told, but she does not give spirit consultations for either the solace or the pleasure of others. She has instructed me to tell people that her work is vital and consumes all her effort and strength, so she can see no one else. I am sorry."

Magda knew what was being implied. "I was told only that it might be possible for an ungifted person to see her."

Isidore considered Magda's words. "Is it important?"

"It is to me," Magda said. "And I can assure you, it would not be for either my solace or my pleasure. I would just as soon leave the dead to their eternal peace."

The young woman smiled vacantly for a time. "I meant, is it important to us?"

Magda was a bit surprised by the question. "It very well may be essential to all our survival."

"Come back another day."

Magda stood frozen, surprised by the abruptness of the rejection. She hadn't even been given a chance to plead her case. She decided that she had not come this far to give up so easily.

"This has to do with the continued existence of our people and our way of life. We are at war and we are all in danger. I need the help of the spiritist. I'm afraid that I must insist."

"Insist?" The woman leaned back a little as if to look up from behind the blindfold. "And you think that because you were married to an important man you should be granted special favors? Do you believe that because you were married to the First Wizard himself you can insist and we must obey?"

Magda thought that the woman's words actually sounded more innocently curious than bitter, so she decided not to let the questions unnerve her and instead answered calmly.

"Not at all, Isidore. I admit, my status often gained me access, but I sought that access to plead on behalf of others who have no voice, not to obtain special favors for myself. It is much the same now. I am not asking for special favors because I was married to an important man. I am asking to see the spiritist because I have need of answers so that I might help keep others safe. I admit that my safety is at stake along with theirs. I am trying to find a way to help us all survive.

"That important man, my husband, the First Wizard, in his last words to me told me to seek truth. He believed that I had a purpose in life. That is why I'm here, and why I must insist, not because of who I am, but because I have been charged with finding the truth."

"What truth?"

"For starters, the truth behind my husband's death. Baraccus was not the kind of man who would kill himself out of despondency. He would have had a crucial reason for what he did. Something happened when h went to the Temple of the Winds. I know that there was a purpose behind him leaping to his death, a purpose meant to help us all. It was not a suicide; it was a compassionate sacrifice of his life to give ours a chance to go on in safety. I need to find out what was behind that act so that his sacrifice will not be in vain."

Isidore smiled to herself. It was a curious smile that softened her angular face.

"I am sorry." The woman lifted her hand toward the entryway where Magda had come in, inviting her to leave. "As I said, the spiritist has her job to do and cannot see others. That job is also to help us all. Admirable as your effort may be, it is not our problem."

Magda took a deep breath and let it out as she reminded herself to be patient. "It very well might become your problem sooner than you think, and then it will be too late."

Isidore's hand lowered and then nested back in her lap. For the first time, the woman's brow wrinkled with a hint of worry.

"What do you mean?"

"All is not right in the Wizard's Keep. We are at war and the enemy is already here, among us."

The woman showed no emotion, but she lost a bit of color. "The enemy is inside the walls of the Keep?"

"Yes."

"What are you talking about?"

"Have you heard of the dream walkers?"

Isidore sat silently for a moment. It was clear by her expression that she had.

"I have heard of them. But they are distant, down in the Old World."

"The council thinks so as well. But the council is wrong. The dream walkers are slipping into the minds of people right here, in the Keep. I fear that they may have help from spies or traitors inside the Keep. A number of strange murders point to the enemy."

"I am all too aware of murders taking place down here in the catacombs. For that reason, surely you must realize that it could be dangerous for you to be down here. But dream walkers? Here, in the Keep? Are you really so sure?"

"Yes. They attacked me."

Isidore seemed surprised and fell silent. She finally gathered her thoughts.

"If that were true, you would be dead, yet you seem unharmed."

"I was very nearly killed. I thought for certain that I was about to die. I was in fact at the veil, very near to passing forever into the spirit world, but I was able to obtain a defense against the dream walker in time to save my life. That same defense can also protect your mind being taken by a dream walker."

The smile returned. "Ah. So, you wish to bargain. You wish to offer me this protection if I can get the spiritist to agree to see you."

It was not a question. It was an accusation.

"Not at all," Magda said. "I would offer you the protection without any precondition, before we go on with anything of substance, and before you agree to anything. In fact, I intend to insist, even if you refuse to help me."

The frown returned. "You think that if you are kind by offering this help freely, then we will relent and be inclined to indulge you?"

"No," Magda said. "Make no mistake. It is not a kindness at all, but an act of self-interest on my part. Dream walkers can invade an unprotected mind and that person can be completely unaware of it. The spiritist is at great risk of being taken because she is valuable. I believe that there are traitors in the Keep. If I'm right, then they would likely direct the dream walkers to the spiritist. Once so identified, the dream walkers would obviously want to control her so as to spy on important matters, or they might simply choose to eliminate her so that she could no longer help our cause.

"For all I know, a dream walker could already be in your mind, watching, listening, hoping to hear what I would ask, and especially what answer I would be given. I can't take that chance. Too much is at stake."

The frown deepened. "Do you mean to say that you offer this protection so that you will know that you are safe in my presence?"

"That's right. I know all too well what the dream walkers are capable of. I nearly died because of them. I don't want to risk that I could be given answers from a spiritist who is unknowingly being controlled by a dream walker intent on hiding the truth. They could send me off in the wrong direction so that I would fail and we all die.

"I suspect that there are traitors in the Keep. Among other things, I think they are guiding the dream walkers. I have to believe that such traitors could be plotting something even worse. Perhaps this is what Baraccus intended me to find. I know that assassins of some sort are among us. We are running out of time. I need to trust that the spiritist helping me is guided by the truth, and not by a dream walker."

Isidore turned her head to the side, as if looking off into her own personal darkness.

"More than that," Magda said, "I fear that if a dream walker is secretly lurking in your mind, he might tear you apart from the inside to prevent me from having the chance to get the answers I need. So you see, while I would not want to see you harmed, I am more concerned for myself and everyone else than I am just for you."

Isidore had lost even more of her color. She looked ashen. Magda could see goose bumps prickle up on her bare arms. Her head turned up toward Magda.

"I value my mind," Isidore said. She reached a hand out. "Please, sit with me, Magda Searus. I would very much like to be protected—for the reasons you give, and for my own reasons."

Isidore had just confirmed Magda's suspicion.

Once Isidore had completed the three devotions, she pushed herself up from the floor and folded her legs under her as she sat back down.

"Thank you, Magda Searus, for teaching me how to be bonded to the Lord Rahl in order to be protected from the dream walkers."

Magda noted what Isidore did not say. She bowed her head, but then remembered that the woman couldn't see. "You are very welcome. And Magda is name enough for a friend."

Isidore smiled. "You have a shadow, Magda."

Magda leaned in. "Excuse me?"

Isidore's smile widened as the pointed back toward the entrance. "Your shadow walks on nearly silent feet."

Magda turned and saw a pair of big green eyes looking at her. The skinny black cat arched its back and rubbed bashfully against the side of the hallway opening. It looked like the cat Magda had seen before, the one she had fed a scrap of food. It must have followed her, hoping for more. It was a relief to realize that the sound she had heard before hadn't been something more sinister.

Magda couldn't help smiling. "It's a cat," she told idore.

"What color?"

"She's black."

Isidore nodded knowingly. "That's why she is not afraid to come in here."

Magda frowned. "What do you mean?"

"People fear black cats, thinking that they are evil. They are not evil. It's just that they have some small ability to see between worlds. Black cats catch glimpses of the spirit world. That's why people fear them, and why she wasn't afraid to follow you into this place. This place is not entirely alien to her, as it is to those who only see the world of life."

The catacombs filled with the dead certainly did seem to be nearer the spirit world than anywhere else Magda had ever visited. The whole subterranean region of the Keep seemed to be very far removed from the life up above.

When the cat again voiced a small cry, Magda asked, "Are you hungry, little one?"

The cat meowed, almost as if she were answering, and rubbed the side of her face against the doorway, fearing to come close, but at the same time aching to approach.

Magda pulled the small bundle from her waist pouch and unwrapped the chicken strips. She knew that the temptation of a meal would overcome the cat's caution. She asked Isidore if she was hungry. When Isidore nodded, Magda held the woman's hand out and placed a piece of chicken in it. The cat sidled up to Magda and rubbed against her leg. Magda pulled off a small strip and held it out for the cat.

"Here you go, little one, have something to eat."

As Magda ate the rest of the strip, the cat hunched forward and devoured the welcome tidbit.

"She seems to shadow you," Isidore said. "You shou" name her Shadow."

"I don't need a cat," Magda said as she gave the hungry cat another small piece of chicken.

"For those who understand their talents, a black cat is good to have around."

"Talents?" Magda couldn't imagine what good the cat could do her. "You mean being able to see into the spirit world?"

"I mean seeing things from that world that are here in this world."

Magda realized that this was no longer idle chitchat. Isidore meant for her to be mindful of her words.

"You mean you think they can see ghosts?"

"Some think that cats, black cats in particular, can see the presence of spirits, or perhaps the essence of spirits. We don't always know when such an essence has drifted into this realm and is near, but such a cat would be aware of it. For this reason, black cats have long been linked to death. Ignorant people wrongly fear them for this association. But just because they can see into the spirit realm, that does not mean that black cats are agents of death, or that they are evil.

"Sometimes, we need to heed subtle signs, for such signs may be more than they seem. Especially down here. I never let any sign down here go unnoticed, or unheeded."

"But what use could having such a creature be?"

"While it is rare for spirits to drift through our world, it could possibly be useful to know when they are near."

Magda didn't know what good that could be to her, but she didn't want to dismiss Isidore's words out of hand. "So you think that this cat coming to me is a sign that I should keep her around to know when spirits are near?"

"She is shadowing you. Perhaps you should heed such sign." Isidore shrugged. "It could even be that a spirit guided the cat your way to be a comfort to you in your loneliness."

"So you really think that she may be a sign from the spirit world?"

Isidore smiled. "I couldn't say. She might have simply been hungry and smelled the food you had with you." Isidore's enigmatic smile ghosted away. "But I wouldn't dismiss such a creature coming into the circle of your life energy."

Magda had come to a spiritist seeking answers. It occurred to her that it might not be a bad idea to listen to her advice.

"Shadow it is then." She stroked a hand along the sleek fur of the cat's back. "Do you like that name? Shadow?"

The cat meowed as if to answer. Before long, Shadow was in Magda's lap, hoping for more chicken. Magda pulled off pieces, giving her a much-needed meal. When the cat had had her fill, she curled up and started cleaning herself.

"How long have you been a spiritist?" Magda asked as she stroked the warm little cat. Shadow purred in appreciation.

Isidore feigned shock. "Me? A spiritist? No, I am only—"

"You are the spiritist, Isidore."

Isidore had wanted to be protected herself, but had not asked for protection for the spiritist. In her alarm at hearing about the threat, and then with the distraction of the cat showing up, she had forgotten to keep up the pretense. That told Magda what she had suspected all along, that there was no one else. Isidore was the spiritist.

Isidore stiffened a little, falling back into her role. "I am flattered that you would think I am such a woman, Magda, but I am merely her humble servant."

"You play the role of aide to the spiritist so that you will not have to entertain appeals directly. That insulates you and gives you an easy way to turn people away, saving time and trouble. You work with the gifted, so you need to be able to keep others at arm's length without having to turn down the appeals directly. More than that, you are empathetic and don't like to disappoint people, but you have more important work and this small deception enables you to remain focused on that work without the streams of suppliants who would be eager to contact deceased loved ones if word got out that you were a spiritist and you would be willing to help them."

Isidore sat quietly, hands nested in her lap, not offering any comment.

"I will not betray your secret, Isidore. But there is no one else. You are the spiritist. Your eyes are covered to help hide this world from your vision so that you may look into another world. That is what you do. You look into the spirit world.

"I have helped you to be safe from the dream walkers as you go about your important work. Please, Isidore, my work is important as well. Let's not play games."

As Isidore finally released a deep sigh, her posture sagged a bit. She was apparently relieved to no longer have to lie.

"You have it mostly right."

"What do you mean?"

"It is more than a blindfold keeping me from seeing this world."

Magda reached out and laid a hand over Isidore's. "Show me."

As the cat curled up for a warm nap in Magda's lap, Isidore nodded, then reached up behind her head to the leather thongs holding on the blindfold. When at last it was untied, she slipped it away and sat a bit stiffer, nesting her hands again, letting Magda look at her face.

Isidore's eyelids were closed over sunken sockets where her eyes should have been. They were not sewn shut. There were no eyelashes. It looked as if she had never had eyes, or as if they had been injured and healed over.

Magda knew better. She knew that Isidore had not been born this way, nor had she been injured.

"How did you lose your eyes?" Magda asked, fearing that she already knew the answer, fearing that this was wizards' work.

"Is that the question you have come to ask the spiritist?"

"No. It is a question I would ask from one woman to another, because the reason for it greatly concerns me."

Isidore thought a moment, her head turning blindly as if trying to see Magda.

"My eyes were taken from me so that I could see."

"You were altered by wizards."

"Yes."

"I am sorry for your loss," Magda said in soft sincerity.

The woman's brow bunched with the ache of tears that could not flow.

She cleared her throat. "No one has ever been sorry for my loss."

"That makes it even worse, then, doesn't it?"

The young woman nodded. "In a way. But the loss is far greater than you could suspect."

"Tell me why you would allow this to be done to you."

"I did not allow it, the way you may think. I sought to have it done, asked to have it done, so that I could see into the spirit world."

Magda was incredulous. "Why would you do such thing?"

"I had need enough."

"Need enough? Why would you request wizards to alter you in such a way? Why would you have him take away your eyes?"

"It's not a pretty story. Either to tell, or to hear."

"I imagine not." Magda steeled herself. "But I would hear it, if you are willing."

CHAPTER
25

I sidore nodded, then started to reach up as if to wipe away tears. Her hand paused when she realized that she could no longer make tears any more than she could see. The hand sank to her lap.

"I lived in Grandengart. The name means 'guardian at the gates.' It's an old name that signifies Grandengart's place at the southern fringe of the New World and long standing as an outpost in the trackless lands of the wilds. The Old World lies beyond to the south.

"Because of its location it has long been a crossroads of trade routes in the New World. Rare trade goods also came up from a few distant places down in the Old World. Grandengart had for ages been an outpost as well, the place where people first come over from the Old World. Trade relations with peoples of the wilds and distant places to the south had always been good.

"The several thousand people who lived there mostly made their living in one way or another because of the trade. For many of the peoples who inhabit vast stretches of inhospitable land of the wilds, and the merchants who dealt with them, we were a trusted place to do business. As a result, with all the different kinds of people an goods passing through, it was an exciting, vibrant pla to live, with different cultures and beliefs, as well as plenty of fascinating stories of far-off places from all the travelers.

"A while back we began to see the first signs of trouble. Rare spices, foodstuffs, and other commodities from the South began to slow and then halted altogether. Everyone considered that a worrisome sign in and of itself. For a time there was no word. Then trickles of people fleeing the new rule down in the Old World began to come through, headed north.

"When trade stopped, timber coming down from the North, a scarce commodity down in that part of the world, began piling up, awaiting transport to arrive from buyers in the South. That transport never arrived. Foods waiting to be moved rotted.

"With all that trade halting, people began to worry about how they would make a living. They worried, too, about what the distant signs of trouble could mean, not just for themselves, but for people they know to the south.

"I was the sorceress assigned to serve the people of Grandengart. People from the South, down in the Old World, didn't hold much with magic. They always stayed well away from me as they passed through. But the people of Grandengart relied on me for my abilities, my skills, but mostly for protection from shapeless worries.

"To most people I possessed inscrutable abilities, so in a way I was not exactly one of them. As a result I sometimes felt that I was little more than their talisman meant to somehow keep shapeless evil from their door. People seemed to think that merely having a sorceress's powers nearby was a vaguely beneficial thing, that it would somehow ensure good fortune, much like their prayers to the good spirits for a safe journey.

"Their worries about the increasing signs of trouble to

the south, though, were not so shapeless. They looked to me for help with this troubling development.

"I didn't know exactly what I could do about it. Magic didn't offer any solution that I could see, although it seemed as if it must to those who knew little about it. In the end I traveled here, to the Keep, to see the council, hoping they could help. They told me that they would take the concerns of the people of Grandengart, as well as the details I had offered, under consideration, along with other reports they were receiving. They suggested that the unrest would likely soon calm down and trade would resume. One of them even suggested that perhaps a bridge had washed out and it was nothing more than that. I told them that from what I had heard from people fleeing from the South, there was a new ruler and his forces were the source of the unrest. They seemed disinclined to see such a change in rule as necessarily a bad thing, because the old rule was so fragmented and inefficient.

"While I could get no immediate help from the council, they did promise that as soon as troops were available they would send a detachment to investigate the situation. I decided that until the troops could be sent, it would be best if I returned home at once. I knew how nervous people were, and I wanted to be there for them.

"I arrived home the day after General Kuno and his forces from the Old World flooded across the border and swept through Grandengart. Even if some of us saw the storm building, until the day Kuno arrived, the world had been at peace."

Magda stiffened in alarm. "General Kuno? Right hand to the emperor?"

Isidore nodded. "Emperor Sulachan himself sent Kuno north and through my home place."

Magda took a deep breath and let it out with a s

She knew from Baraccus that General Kuno was ruthless. He struck fear into the hearts of anyone in his path.

Emperor Sulachan wanted the world under one rule, the rule of the Old World. He wanted everyone to bow to him as emperor of it all. She knew, too, that the start of the war had been both swift and violent. Apparently, it had started in Isidore's hometown.

"General Kuno had everyone brought to the town square," Isidore said, "where he told them that this was a new day, that the world order was about to change, and they had been selected to be given the opportunity to join the cause of the Old World, and bow to Emperor Sulachan. He told the men that the choice was theirs to choose for their families to either stay a part of the New World, or join the empire of Sulachan. He asked for a show of hands of those who would side with the emperor, or those who would decline the offer.

"Remember, we were not yet at war, so people mostly didn't yet realize the danger of choosing to side against Emperor Sulachan. This was to be the day that the world would learn of that danger.

"The men with General Kuno kept track of how each person voted, then they divided up the people of the town. Those choosing to bow to Emperor Sulachan were put on one side of the town square, those against on the other. It was then that people began to panic. Soldiers grabbed anyone who tried to run and kept the two crowds packed together, surrounded by a ring of steel. A number of those trying to flee were brutally cut to pieces before everyone's eyes to discourage anyone else from attempting to escape.

"Soldiers took the people who had voted against bowing to the emperor out to dig holes along the side of the road into Grandengart. They then made the people erect poles with the timber that the townspeople used for trade.

"To the full, screaming panic of the people, most of the men who had voted against, along with their family members, were hoisted by their wrists up onto the poles. A small number of old men were made to watch as General Kuno's soldiers walked up both sides of the road, slashing the terrified people hanging by their wrists. The soldiers pulled down strips of their flesh, leaving muscles and ribs exposed. Other people were stabbed in the legs or stomach, but left alive in their panic to hang there in helpless agony.

"The townspeople who were left, those who had chosen to side with Emperor Sulachan, after watching what was done to their friends and neighbors, were taken as slaves and sent south.

"The small group of old men who had been made to watch were released. They fled to later recount the terror far and wide so that other places would panic before the advancing forces of General Kuno and dare not resist Emperor Sulachan's will.

"When I arrived the next day after Kuno's forces had left, the road into Grandengart was lined on each side with poles, each holding a victim. Men, women, children—all were treated the same. There were over fifteen hundred poles, each holding a person, each person alone in their agony, but close enough to their neighbors, friends, and family to see them suffering and dying.

"Mothers, watching their children screaming in terror and pain, blamed husbands for voting against joining the side of the Old World. Husbands had to endure the dying hatred of their wives and unimaginable suffering of their children for the decision they had made.

"Beyond the poles, at the end of the road, smoke from the smoldering ruins of the town rose in the still air high into the blue sky. Not one building was left standing. Everything had been burned to the ground by Kuno's men.

"Dogs and coyotes hounded the condemned, pulling and tearing at the strips of skin still attached to them. They set upon the already dead. I threw sparking flashes of fire to chase them away. Flocks of birds had come to feast as well. I used booming bolts of air and scattered most of those as well.

"In the bright sun, exposed rib bones of the victims stood out white against the red meat still left on them. Many of the bones had been picked clean. Most of the people were clearly dead, their middles torn open so that scavengers could get at their organs. Between the blood, the fluids, and all those who had lost control of their bodily functions, the stench was staggering.

"While a number had died over the course of the night, many of the victims, perhaps one in every four people, were still alive. Most of those had long since lost their voice from screaming. But they moaned, they cried, and they whispered prayers that went unanswered.

"I walked up that road, between those poles as those still alive watched me, hoping that I, their trusted sorceress, could do something for them. Some cried out with their last breath for help.

"Inky black ravens perched on the poles, warily watching me as I came up the road, waited for me to pass before they resumed the feast. Some cawed loudly, hoping to drive me away from what they had claimed as theirs."

Isidore's head turned to the side a bit, as if she was staring off into another place in her mind's eye. Her breathing was ragged and labored.

"What did you do about the people on the poles who were still alive?" Magda finally asked. "Could anything be done to help them? Could you use your gift to save some of them, at least?"

Isidore sat motionless for a time, staring at nothing in

her lonely blindness, as if reliving the vision of what she had seen that terrible day.

"They were beyond healing," she whispered at last. "Those still alive used all their strength to beg me to deliver them from the unendurable pain. They begged for death."

"Could you heal none of them?"

"All but one were well beyond healing of any kind, even from wizards far more talented than me. There was nothing I could do to save their lives. Nothing."

Magda leaned in. "So what did you do, then?"

Isidore turned blindly toward Magda. "All I could do was spare them their remaining suffering so as to ease their souls' final journey into the spirit world. As I hurried up the road, I first used a slash of my power to sever the ropes holding each of them up on the poles. Hanging there like that had made it difficult to breathe. Many of the dead had suffocated. Each person in turn collapsed to the ground as I parted the ropes.

"Then, I went from one of those still alive to the next and held their hand for a moment as I offered each a few quiet words of comfort, sympathy, and a promise of a gentle end to their agony.

"It felt as if I were outside my own body, watching myself moving from one person to the next, holding their hand, offering words of comfort, and then stopping their heart. I couldn't believe I was doing such things. I had never envisioned my abilities being put to such a use as to have to end the lives of those I was supposed to be protecting.

"But I knew that I had to do it. I was there to serve these people, people who had rarely thanked me for my efforts, and this was the only service I could now offer them. To think, after living among them, each perso thanked me more than ever before for what I was abo to do to each of them. They wept with joy and whispered their deepest appreciation that I was about to end their life."

Isidore's breathing came with difficulty as she labored to continue the story. "Then I used my gift to stop their hearts, each one in turn, one at a time, over and over. I had to do it more than four hundred times in all.

"It took until long after nightfall before I had delivered all but one of the people of Grandengart from their agony. I was not quite through with my work. I had silenced the moans, and stopped all but one heart."

26

I t was long after the moon should have been high in the sky when I finally reached the last man," Isidore said. "But there was no moon because a thick overcast had gradually covered the sky, like a shroud of gray darkness pulled over the dead. I knew that it would soon begin to rain.

"The last man alive was trembling and having difficulty breathing. His name was Joel. He was a baker. Every day he had used to bring me a small loaf of bread. He would never accept payment. Joel said that it was his small part to make sure that Grandengart's sorceress did not want for a meal.

"Truth be told, Joel had feelings for me, though he never spoke of those feelings or acted on them, except to bring me that loaf of bread. I think it was an excuse for him to see me.

"Joel's wife had died in childbirth before I came to Grandengart. He was lonely and terribly sad. There was something about him, something beneath the sadness, that I liked, but knowing about the death of his wife and unborn child I felt uncomfortable saying much to him, other than to ask as the town's sorceress how he was and if there was anything I could do for him. He always said that he was fine and turned down any offer of help.

"Over time, my feelings for him grew, but in light of his loss I felt that it was not my place to speak of such things. I knew that he would be a long time in getting over such a loss and felt that I had to respect the pace of grieving and felt that I shouldn't interfere. So, as much as I longed to tell him of my feelings, I kept my distance. Yet every day he would bring me a loaf of bread, as if that was the only way he could reach out to me.

"I was exhausted by the time I reached Joel lying there on the ground in the dark beside the road. By then I could barely walk. I was in shock and covered in the blood of the people I had just helped to die.

"I fell to my knees beside Joel and took up his hand, knowing that I had to be strong enough to bring death to one last person. I held his hand to my own heart and put all my strength into sending as much comfort as I could into him.

"But in so doing I sensed that, unlike all the others, he was not entirely beyond healing. I knew that there was a small chance to save his life.

"I remember seeing his cracked lips move. He wanted to say something. I gave him a sip of water from a waterskin, as I had for so many others, and then bent close.

"He told me that he was sorry for my ordeal. I told him that I was shamed that I had not been there for them, that had I been there I might have done something. He said that he had been there, and he knew for certain that I could have done nothing against such brutal men.

"He said that they'd had gifted among them, men with fearsome powers. He said that had I been there, I would be hanging on a pole along with the rest of them, and then I would not be there to help end the suffering.

"Joel said that he thought it was meant to be this way so that I could help the people.

"I told Joel that I thought I could save his life, that he could be healed. I told him to hold on, to be strong. I spent several hours hunched over him in the dark, healing what I could. I knew, though, that he needed more than I could provide.

"I knew that Whitney, a town to the north, would have the healers needed. I helped him onto my horse and we started riding north to Whitney. I rode as hard as I dared push the horse. We rode the rest of the night and the next day. I often had to use my gift not only to give the poor animal endurance to continue, but to give Joel the strength to hold on to life.

"We almost made it to Whitney. Joel cried out in pain. I tried to hold him up, to keep going, but he couldn't ride any farther and begged me to help him to the ground.

"As I knelt beside Joel, I realized then that the one person I thought I might be able to save was now beyond help. I knew through my gift that despite how desperately I had worked to help him, his internal injuries were too severe. I could sense his life slipping away. It was a cruel blow after such hope I could save him. In that moment there wasn't anything I could do to prevent Joel from dying.

"As I bent close, clutching his hands in mine, tears running down my face, he said that he was sorry for what he had done. I asked him what he meant. Joel said he had clung to the memory of his dead wife to the exclusion of everything else. He said that he had loved her but she had passed. He should have gone on and embraced the life he had left to live. He said that he knew I was remaining silent out of respect.

"He said that if he had told me of his feelings, maybe I would have been open to him and then we both could have had happiness for that time. Instead, he had clung to the dead rather than turning to the living. He said he should have lived his life, but now it was over and it was too late.

"He wept as he told me that he was sorry that he had never given himself, or me, the chance to seek that happiness, and now it was too late and he was so sorry. His life was over without having lived what was right there all the time.

"I sobbed uncontrollably as I confessed that I, too, had lived for the dead, fearing to reach out to him. I told him that I should have known better, that I should have sought to comfort him while encouraging him to use the time he had to live his own life.

"He said that he wished he had known that I would not have pushed him away. He said he should have tried to get closer to me than to just bringing me a loaf of bread every day. I laughed through the tears at that. He said that by respecting his feelings for his dead wife, I had shown true compassion, and that he wished he had returned it.

"Joel knew that the others of the town would be with the good spirits. He told me that he would soon see his wife again in the spirit world, and regretted only that he had not lived the last couple years of his own life. He told me that one day when my time too was done in this life, I would be back with them, with the people of Grandengart, where I belonged and would be welcomed. He promised to be waiting for me where we would all be safe in the light of the Creator among the good spirits.

"Joel's last words were for me to pray on the behalf of all those who had died that terrible night. He asked me to pray that the good spirits welcome them all and give them peace at last.

"I promised that I would use my abilities to help guide

them all into the spirit world. He smiled, and as he thanked me and squeezed my hand . . . his last breath of life left him and he was gone.

"On my knees, as the gentle rain began, I hunched over him and rained my own tears down on this poor man for all that he and the others had suffered, wept for what might have been had we each had the courage to let the past go and embraced what life still had to offer."

Magda understood all too well that desolate agony of loss.

"So, there I was beside the road to Whitney with the dead body of my friend, while back in Grandengart lay the corpses of my charges, my town. The corpses of the people I had failed."

Magda laid a hand on Isidore's arm. "You did not fail them, Isidore. Emperor Sulachan's minions are as powerful as they are ruthless. Joel was right, you could have done nothing to stop it. Don't take on the guilt that rightly belongs to the killers.

"Not many would have shown the courage you did in such a difficult situation. You did your people the greatest kindness possible. You were there for them to end their suffering when there was nothing else that could have been done."

"I thought so too. But as it turns out, after reaching Whitney and burying Joel, that was only the beginning of the nightmare."

CHAPTER

27

Magda stroked a hand along the silky back of the sleeping cat curled up in her lap. The cat's contented purring served to emphasize the stretch of empty silence.

"The beginning of the nightmare?" Magda finally asked. "What do you mean?"

Isidore took a deep breath. Her shoulders slumped as she let out a weary sigh. "After Joel died, I managed to lift him up and over the back of the horse." She flicked a hand in an aside. "I used to be stronger than I am as you see me now. I've lost weight and muscle since then. I find that I rarely have much of an appetite.

"Anyway, I rode most of that night, stopping only for a brief nap when neither I nor the horse could go on. It was the first sleep I'd had since arriving home to Grandengart. It was also the first of the terrible dreams that haunt me to this day. The short rest was at least enough for me to be able to resume the journey. By late the next afternoon I finally reached the wheat fields and scattered farms at the outskirts of Whitney.

"A man and his wife working a field saw me and must have realized that I was having trouble. They both rushed out to the road to help. When they saw the body slung over the back of the horse, they said that he needed to be buried at once. They were kind enough to lead me to a small graveyard beside a clutch of oaks, the only trees in sight out on the plains of the southern reaches of the New World. There, they helped me lift Joel down and then bury him.

"I was in a numb daze from the whole ordeal, from traveling so long and hard with the dead body of my friend, with tormented thoughts of what might have been between us, and worse, what I might have done to stop the madness had I returned home from seeing the council just a little sooner. I hadn't eaten in days and I was near delirious with exhaustion. Even so, I knelt beside Joel's fresh grave and prayed earnestly to the good spirits to welcome him and all the others into their arms.

"Hunched over his grave I again promised Joel that I would keep my word, given just before he died, that I would use my abilities to help make sure that they all made it safely into the embracing shelter of the good spirits.

"After that, the man and his wife, feeling sympathy for me, gave me some food and water and then escorted me the rest of the way into Whitney. I think they thought that I might not make it on my own.

"In Whitney I learned that a few of the terrified old men from Grandengart, the ones who had been released by General Kuno to carry word of what had happened so as to spread panic, had done just that, coming through and telling everyone of the horrifying fate of Grandengart's people. The whole town of Whitney was buzzing with the news, so the town officials were not surprised when I briefly recounted my story.

"There were gifted there and they listened with even greater interest than the officials, though they said nothing, when I told them what they had not heard yet, that

I had gone from one dying person to the next, ending their suffering.

"A number of the town's people were already packing their belongings and more yet had already left, all headed north. No one knew where General Kuno and his army would strike next, but they wanted to flee to a more distant place where they thought it would be safer. I couldn't really fault them.

"A detachment of troops, sent by the council to look into the reports of trouble brewing to the south, happened to have just arrived in Whitney. I talked with the commander and reported what had happened. I told him that I couldn't bury well over a thousand bodies by myself and I needed help. I didn't want my people to lie there and rot in the open or be scavenged by animals. All I could think of was that it was my duty to at least see them buried.

"Fortunately, the commander was an understanding man. He and his troops took me with them. We rode hard all the way back to Grandengart to attend to the dead as swiftly as possible.

"When we got there, the dead were missing."

Magda blinked, not sure she had heard correctly. "Missing? What do you mean, they were missing?"

Isidore lifted a hand in frustration and then let it drop back into her lap.

"They were gone. Not a single corpse was there by the road where I'd left them. The town had been burned down. The rain had since doused the smoldering rubble. There were no bodies in the town, nor were there any beside the road where the poles had been erected, where I had delivered them from their suffering."

"Did the troops believe you? Believe your story?"

Isidore grunted bitter confirmation. "The ground was soaked with clotted blood. They believed me. The poles, each with the ropes still attached, were covered with blood as well. There were some remains still scattered about—the viscera of those that animals had ripped open. After inspecting the remains the commander confirmed that they were human."

Isidore again weakly lifted a hand. "But there were no bodies. None."

Magda hooked a lock of her short hair behind her ear, at first having expected it to be long. She still wasn't used to it being short.

"I don't understand. How could there be no bodies? What could have become of them?"

"Well, I saw tracks that hadn't been there before, so my first thought was that maybe General Kuno's army had decided to turn back to the safety of the Old World and they had come back through Grandengart. I thought that maybe on the way back through they had decided to bury the dead rather than let them decay out in the open."

"No," Magda said. "That doesn't sound at all like what I know about Kuno. Baraccus told me that Sulachan personally selected Kuno to lead their forces because he was so ruthless. Kuno wouldn't care about any such decency as burying his enemy's dead. Like Sulachan himself, he's the kind who would have deliberately left the bodies there in the open as a ghastly warning to anyone who had thoughts of resisting. He uses tactics of terror to sap the will of those who will eventually have to face him."

Isidore was nodding as she listened. "Though it was the beginning of the war, before we had learned how truly brutal Emperor Sulachan and his forces were, the commander I was with harbored no delusions. He said that any army that would come in and torture and murder innocent people like that would not care about burying them. And then his men, as they searched, found evidence that the bodies had been taken."

"Taken? What do you mean, taken?" Magda asked. The whole thing was not making any sense to her.

"The soldiers said that there were a lot of tracks showing that an army had come back through and crossed over the road, headed south. There were drag marks on the ground where it looked like the bodies had been collected into piles. The ground there was covered with even more of the gore. The drag marks ended at wagon tracks. Lots of wagon tracks."

Magda frowned. "You're saying that Kuno's army came back through and . . . took them?"

"They came back and harvested the dead," Isidore confirmed in an icy tone.

Magda's hand paused on the cat's back. "Harvested the dead?" She tilted her head toward the woman. "For what purpose?"

Isidore shrugged one shoulder. "The officer was only able to say that it appeared that they had taken the dead with them, south, back to the Old World."

Magda pressed her fingertips to her forehead as she tried to make sense of it. "But why would they do such a thing? What would they want with the bodies?"

Isidore's hands opened a little in a vague, noncommittal gesture.

Magda could only imagine the grisly state the bodies would have been in. Collecting hundreds and hundreds of days-dead corpses and taking them away in wagons would have been a sickening task. No one would have done such a thing without a powerful reason.

Isidore offered no immediate insight into the mystery of what that reason might be. Magda thought that maybe it was simply such an outrage that the woman didn't want to think about it, much less discuss it. By

Isidore's guarded response, though, Magda suspected that she knew more than she was revealing.

Rather than press, Magda thought it best to try to soothe the woman's terrible memories and let her tell the story at her own pace.

"That certainly is gruesome. I can see what you mean about the nightmare just beginning."

Isidore's head was hanging. She didn't lift it.

"No. That is not what I meant when I spoke before of the nightmare only beginning."

Surprised, Magda stared at the woman for a moment. "Then what exactly did you mean?"

Isidore finally lifted her head. "Well, after that, the troops went south after Kuno's army to make sure that they weren't going to turn back and head north again into the New World by a different route. But also, the commander thought that, burdened as Kuno's forces were with so many wagons, there was a good chance that if they rode hard he could catch them. He was confident that he had a large enough force to fully extract vengeance when he did.

"I didn't know what to do at that point. With the commander and his troops gone, I was again alone. Most of my people from Grandengart were dead with the remainder captives, and my friend Joel dead and buried. I had no one.

"I decided to go back to Whitney."

Magda thought that made some sense—there was nothing left of Grandengart and Whitney was the closest town. Yet, there seemed better options, such as going to Aydindril, where she could have given what information she had to the council at the Keep, and to the army. After all, this was an enormously significant event. It was the first attack in a war that many had long feared would eventually erupt and had now begun.

Magda suspected that there was more to Isidore's decision. "Other than Joel being buried there, did you have some reason for choosing to go back to Whitney?"

Isidore rubbed a thumb back and forth on the side of her knee for a time before answering. "Yes. I went back because I knew that there was a spiritist there."

"A spiritist?" Magda's brow tightened. "Why did you want to see a spiritist?"

"I was so distraught by everything that had happened, and by the final injustice of the bodies being taken, that I wanted to consult the woman. I guess I wanted what most anyone else who goes to a spiritist wants. I wanted to know that Joel was safely in the fold of the good spirits. I wanted to keep my promise to him."

Magda at last resumed stroking the cat. "I guess I can understand how you felt. So, did this spiritist help put your mind at ease?"

Magda watched as Isidore's thumb continued to rub back and forth on her knee. She spoke without lifting her head.

"Sophia was much older, and quite experienced, although she told me that in recent years she had not practiced her craft. She said that while she was proud of the work she had done, she had spent a lifetime at it and was finished with the whole business of dealing with the spirit world. She said that she wanted only to live the remainder of her life in peace. She refused to help me.

"I persisted. I told her that it was important, that I had made promises. Promises not only as a friend, but as a sorceress. She angrily waved away the request and said that my promises were not hers. I asked if she couldn't see her way to helping out of compassion for all those innocent people, so that I would know they were now at peace. She said that even if she wanted to, which she didn't, she couldn't help because my loss was too fresh for me and that I was too distraught.

"I asked if I could return later, after I had gained a bit of perspective. She told me that delving into the spirit world wasn't what most people thought it was, that her craft wasn't intended as a means to commune with the dead to find comfort for the living. She said that there were dangers involved that I couldn't begin to understand. Sophia again, and very emphatically, refused to help me."

Isidore smiled. "I guess I learned from Sophia much of my reluctance to see people who want to consult with the spirits. She advised me, as one sorceress to another, to forget the whole thing." The smile ghosted away. "As it turned out, it was very wise advice. Perhaps I should have listened."

Magda didn't say anything, instead waiting for Isidore to go on at her own pace. The frail young woman brushed the back of a slender hand against the opposite cheek, as if wiping away an invisible tear, before she finally did.

"Much like you, though, I had no intentions of taking no for an answer." Isidore's head turned up. "As it turns out, that persistence is a requirement."

Magda's brow lifted in surprise. "A requirement to having a spiritist help you?"

Isidore nodded. "I waited a few days, got some rest and spent some time thinking, then I went back. Sophia still refused to consult the spirits on my behalf. I couldn't understand why not. I decided to stay in Whitney and try again later.

"Since I'm a sorceress, I made myself useful by helping some of the people in Whitney with ailments and such. I made a pest of myself with Sophia, asking to help around her home, until she started giving me little things to do to help her. I asked roundabout questions as I cooked her meals, brought her firewood, banked her hearth, fetched her water, always trying to sound innocently curious—you know, conversational. I listened carefully to anything she would tell me. I was doing my best to get lessons out of her in any way I could.

"I figured that if she wouldn't give me the help I needed, then maybe I could learn enough to do it on my own. I'm a sorceress, after all, so I'm not without abilities. Although the methods involved were a mystery to me, I thought that maybe it wouldn't be so complicated to learn just enough to check on the souls lost to me and find out if they were at peace. I guess I felt guilty for failing to be there for the people of Grandengart when Kuno had shown up and wanted to make up for it.

"The old woman, of course, knew what I was up to. She finally asked what it was I hoped to accomplish by contacting the spirit world so directly. I explained my promise to Joel to help make sure that he and all of the people of Grandengart had made it safely into the embracing shelter of the good spirits.

"She chuckled and asked what I thought one of the living could do to influence events in the spirit world. How did I think I could help souls gone to the underworld? Did I think I could take them by the hand and lead them into the glory of the light of the Creator? Did I really think that the souls in the underworld would never be able to find peace until I found it for them? Of course I had no answers.

"So I told her, then, of how the bodies of those killed in Grandengart had been harvested and taken away. I told her that I was greatly worried about what the gifted down in the Old World were doing with the dead people of Grandengart. I told her that I had a terrible feeling that the souls of those people were not at all safe.

"That gave her pause.

"Sophia became darkly moody and said again that such things were not the responsibility of the living, and besides, no matter what we might wish we could do to help, we had no say in the spirit world. But the worry about why the corpses had been taken nagged at her. I could see her demeanor change with the mystery surrounding the harvesting of the dead.

"One evening, she finally said that she would help me see that the people of Grandengart were at peace, but on a condition.

"Because I was a sorceress, and not the typical person who came to her for consultation, she wanted me, in exchange for her help, to first learn from her to be a spiritist. She explained that it was an old and honorable craft, but with an unfortunate stigma attached to it. She said that she was nearing the end of her life and wanted to pass her lifetime of knowledge on to someone of a new generation. She wanted the skills to live on.

"I told her that I had no desire to become a spiritist. Sophia smiled and said it didn't matter to her if I wanted to or not, only that I did. She said that it was a dying art and she had never found anyone willing to learn the old craft. She said that young sorceresses nowadays don't really want to have anything to do with the world of the dead. They figured that they would have an eternity of being dead and so they would rather spend their time living.

"Sophia said that it was understandable for people to feel that way, but she believed in the value of what she did and didn't want to see the old ways die out. I certainly believed in the value of what she did. In fact, it seemed the only thing of real importance to me at the time.

"Still, as much as I wanted her help, I admit that I was repulsed by the idea of taking up such a profession myself. She reminded me of how much I'd wanted the help of a spiritist, and said that there would be others in the future who would also need such help. Sophia said that without younger people like me learning the old ways, they would vanish forever and that help would be lost to them.

"She told me that it might be my chance to make a difference for the future of the living. I told her that I would have to think on it.

"Then we got the reports that the soldiers who had gone back with me to Grandengart and then gone south after General Kuno's forces had been slaughtered."

Magda gasped at the news. "Slaughtered? All of them?"

Isidore nodded. "It had been a trap. Sophia thought that the bodies the enemy took had been the bait for the trap. Two men had escaped to tell what they saw."

"More likely Kuno let them escape to spread fear."

"I think you're probably right. The men said that they were charging south and thought they were getting close when they were ambushed. All of our men, other than the two who had escaped, were killed or gravely injured.

"After the battle, Kuno's men tied all of our fallen soldiers together into bundles of a dozen or so, tied them by their wrists, and then fastened groups of them to the wagons of the dead from Grandengart. One of the two men said that it reminded him of stringers of dead fish. Kuno's army dragged all the dead and dying soldiers away with them, some of them still alive and screaming in pain, or moaning in mortal agony."

Magda was incredulous. "I've never heard of an army hauling away the soldiers they'd killed."

"They harvested the dead," Isidore confirmed, "as I have since heard they have done in other places as well. At the time, I thought that maybe it was yet more bait to entice others to chase after them. In a way, I was right.

"After hearing about them taking the dead soldiers, I knew that I had to get Sophia to help. Something was going on that no one understood but we all feared. I thought that the spiritist might be the way to discover the truth.

"Sophia told me then that if I agreed to learn the craft, then I would be able to draw more from the experience than simply having her report on what she saw. She said I would be able to see the truth I needed to know for myself, the truth that only I could grasp, the truth that only I could understand.

"Though the idea frightened me, I could no longer shy away from what I needed to do, so I agreed.

"Sophia then told me that the spirits had surely sent me to her for a reason, that there was a purpose, that I was meant for something.

"She began teaching me that very night."

ow long did these lessons take?" Magda asked.
"Less time than I had thought they would. Being the daughter of a sorceress and a wizard, I had a good start on what I needed to know. My father, in particular, had a lifelong fascination with the underworld. He had learned a lot in his 'adventuring,' as he called it, adventures dealing in where we all eventually had to end up, he would say.

"My mother would say that adventure was just another name for trouble. Some people whispered that my father had a death wish. I knew that wasn't true, but I was fascinated by the fearless way he liked to challenge death. At the same time, I shared my mother's worry about it being trouble.

"His adventures were mostly experiments with spell-forms, learning how the interplay with Additive and Subtractive Magic worked. That was how he had learned so much. It was how he learned to balance on the cusp between worlds. That, and racing horses on overland courses through dangerous countryside."

"I see what you mean about him liking to challenge death," Magda said.

Isidore confirmed it with a nod and a sigh.

"He even taught other wizards about the things he had discovered. From a young age, much to the discomfort of my mother, he told me stories of his exploits with experimental magic and the enthralling things he'd uncovered in how the interaction between worlds worked. I would sit wide-eyed as he spun tales of riding the rim, as he called it. He said that he believed that life and death were connected in much the same way as Additive and Subtractive Magic depended upon each other to define their nature.

"He saw that connection in everything, even in something as elemental as light and dark. Consequently, he also saw such interdependence in simple things as well."

"Simple things?" Magda asked. "Like what?"

Isidore lifted one shoulder in a matter-of-fact shrug. "Where I saw a shadow cast across the ground, he saw the shadow, but also what he called the negative shape created by the shadow. He said they were inextricably linked, locked together, the positive shape and the negative shape, each depending on the other to exist. He said that to truly appreciate one, you had to at least recognize the contribution of the other.

"Thus, he would tell me, you need the dark to show light, so you shouldn't curse the darkness. You needed death to define life.

"Hence, the delight he found in his 'adventuring' into areas others found terrifying. I guess you could say that his quest for understanding of the world of the dead contributed to a greater appreciation for life. My mother would roll her eyes when he would tell me about such things, but sometimes, out of the corner of my eye, I would see her flash him a private smile.

"So, perhaps more than most, I already had a pretty good working knowledge of the Grace, how it is drawn and how it functions, how magic itself is connected to

Creation and death through Additive and Subtractive Magic, and how spell-forms can draw on these elements for power. My father did not view different aspects of the world, such as life and the underworld beyond the veil of life, as independent things, but rather as interdependent elements that were all part of a great, unified whole. In that way, he said, we were all part of all things.

"Sophia said that such an upbringing, learning, and understanding put me years ahead of most in becoming as a spiritist. She said that I had come to it as if it were my destiny, although she said that she didn't believe in fate.

"The hardest part of Sophia's lessons was that from my father's teachings I was accustomed to thinking in terms of the whole, so learning not to see this world, but rather to exclude it from that whole, was difficult for me."

Magda frowned. "What do you mean, learning to exclude this world?"

"To see into the spirit world, Sophia told me that I had to be able to look beyond what was around us in order to see into that other realm. She said that, while she didn't herself know if it was true or not, some people believed that the underworld was all around us in the same place we existed, but at the same time it was separate and so we couldn't see it. I can understand that now that I am blind; I can hear things I never before knew were there, but always were.

"She blindfolded me for all our lessons. She said that it would help me to learn more quickly. It was a few weeks after starting that she told me that it was time to venture on my first journey to look into that other place.

"By then, of course, after all I had learned—the warnings, the cautions about the smallest mistakes, the grim stories of small things gone horrifically wrong—I was properly terrified.

"Sophia believed in safety through preparation. We drank teas in the morning to cleanse our auras lest they snag on the veil and trap us. We took powerful herbs in the afternoon to dull our senses to the world around us so we would not fail to see the dangers lurking in the dark world. In the evening we began the soft chanting to condition our minds to open. The whole day, of course, in addition to the tea and herbs, we had been laying out spells and conjuring various forms of wards and protections. As the sun went down, we banked the fire. She said that flame was an anchor to this world and that if anything went wrong it could light our way back through the eternal night."

Isidore lifted an arm, gesturing around the room. "This is the reason, even though I am blind, that there are candles lit in here." She smiled just a bit. "That, and of course so that others don't stumble and fall on me."

Magda wasn't able to appreciate the humor. "So once you were ready, then what?"

"Sophia had me cut my finger and use blood to draw a Grace around where we were to sit on the floor before the hearth."

Though Magda was not gifted, she had certainly spent a lot of time around the gifted. She had also been married to the First Wizard. She knew full well the significance of drawing a Grace in blood. A Grace connected Creation, the world of life, and the world of the dead via pathways of magic.

"I remember that it was an overcast, windy night, and dark as pitch," Isidore said in a tone half to herself, as if drifting back to that night. "The black world outside the two tiny windows of Sophia's home seemed foreboding and oppressive."

Isidore looked to be trying to return from her haunting memory. She paused to wave a dismissive hand.

"None of the details would matter to you. Not being gifted, you likely wouldn't understand most of it anyway. The important thing is that we had to invoke the darkest forms of magic to summon up the darkness of the underworld. Then we drew spells with Subtractive threads that brought about the parting."

"The parting?"

"In the veil to the underworld," she managed with difficulty.

Magda thought that Isidore looked at the edge of composure. She covered her mouth with a hand, as if in her mind's eye seeing again the horror of what she had seen that night. Her brow wrinkled into tight furrows. Her chest heaved with each ragged breath. Magda realized that Isidore was sobbing in the only way she could even though she had no tears.

Feeling a sudden pang of sorrow for the woman, for her terrible loss and crushing loneliness, Magda lifted the cat and scooted around to sit close beside Isidore. Magda set the cat down to the side, where she stretched from her long nap. Magda put a comforting arm around the frail young woman. Isidore melted into the embrace, burying her face against Magda's shoulder.

Magda held Isidore's head against her shoulder. "I'm sorry for asking you to recount such terrible memories."

Isidore pushed away, swallowing back her emotion. "No, I wanted to tell you. I've never had anyone to tell, except, of course, for the one who took my eyes from me. I wanted you to know, much like I had to know, what it means to be a spiritist, to practice such a sorrowful skill that puts you there in the midst of death."

"I understand," Magda said.

"I'm afraid that you really don't." It wasn't said in a cruel or condescending way, merely as Isidore's expression of the simple reality. "I didn't understand myself until we actually pulled the veil of life aside and faced the un-imaginable."

Magda listened to the silence for a while, then finally had to ask, "What did you see beyond that veil?"

Isidore stared off blindly into the memory.

"I saw a place of darkness beyond dark," she finally said in a haunted voice. "An endless place of souls that would take forever to see, and yet I glimpsed it all in an instant.

"In that instant I saw what I had come to see, learned the truth I had come to learn . . . and I was horrified."

"Horrified by seeing the world of the dead?"

"No," Isidore said. "Horrified by the truth."

CHAPTER
30

"I don't understand," Magda said. "What truth did you see?"

For a time, the only sound was the sputtering of a few of the candles glowing around the room. The cat sat silently on her haunches, as if waiting to hear what Isidore would say.

"I saw Joel there," Isidore finally said. "His spirit, anyway. That much of it was a comfort—seeing the light of his soul there at peace."

Magda, her arm around the woman, squeezed Isidore's opposite shoulder. She didn't want to sound suspicious, or disbelieving, but she found it hard to imagine.

"How is it possible, Isidore, considering how many millions upon millions upon millions of souls there are in the underworld—the souls of everyone who has ever lived and are all now there in the world of the dead—for you to be able to immediately see the one you were looking for out of the multitude?"

"Well, it's rather hard to explain." Isidore considered the question briefly. She frowned as she tilted her head up in thought. "You know the way you could walk into a vast gathering in the Keep, and despite how many hundreds and hundreds of people are there, you could always spot Baraccus immediately, pick him right out of all those people?"

Magda smiled sadly at the memory. "Yes, as a matter of fact I do recall such events."

"It's something like that," Isidore said. "It's not the same, but that's the only example that I can think of that you might be able to grasp. Things don't work the same way in the underworld as they do here. Time, distance, numbers, things like that are all different there. It's like the same rules you are used to don't work that way there."

"Baraccus traveled the underworld," Magda said, her mind wandering, "just before he killed himself."

She wondered what it had been like for him, what he had seen, and how it must have affected him.

"It's not the same for a spiritist." Isidore squeezed Magda's hand in sympathy. "Baraccus was a profoundly powerful wizard who journeyed through the world of the dead. We don't have that kind of power and are not venturing into the underworld. A spiritist is only parting the veil just enough to look beyond for an instant.

"Rather than going into that place, as Baraccus did, a spiritist is a sorceress invoking her gift in a unique way. We are calling together a number of forces through spell-forms, along with both Additive and Subtractive Magic conjured to a very specific task.

"He was in that place. We are only looking in through a window."

"I see," Magda said. "So when you looked through that window, what did you see?"

"In that cauldron of magic, at the center of a storm of power, it all happens in an instant, yet that instant seems to last an eternity.

"In that terrible spark of time, I saw the truth."

"And what was the truth that so horrified you?"

Isidore bit her bottom lip as she gathered her courage. "The truth that the others, the people of Grandengart who had died, were not there."

Magda frowned and leaned in close to the woman. She was unsure exactly what Isidore had meant.

"You mean you couldn't find them? You couldn't tell in the vastness of the underworld that they were safe and at peace like you could with Joel?"

Isidore shook her head emphatically. "No. I mean they were not there."

"I still don't understand. They're dead. Of course they're there. Maybe you were only able to find Joel there, that way I could spot my husband across a room of people, because you cared deeply about him, but you couldn't do the same with the others."

"No," Isidore said with forceful certainty. "That is the truth that I saw in that instant. I saw that their souls were not in the eternal world of the dead. Their souls, their spirits, whatever you want to call them, were not in the underworld."

"Then where are they?"

"I don't know," Isidore said. "I've been looking for them ever since that day and I have not yet found them. All I know is that the spirits of the people of Grandengart, the people whose bodies were harvested, are not in the world of the dead. And neither are the souls of the other bodies that have been harvested."

The silence felt suffocating. Magda had to remind herself to take a breath.

"How can the dead," she finally asked, "not be in the world of the dead? How is that possible?"

That was the very thing I wanted to know," Isidore said. "I knew, as soon as I grasped the truth of it, that I had to find the answer."

"But how?" Magda swiped her hair back off her face. "You said that you only hold the veil open for an instant."

"Yes, but in that moment where all that magic, all that power, comes together, that spark of time seems to last an eternity. In a way, it isn't an instant at all. In a way, it is an infinitely large piece of forever."

Magda felt as if she were getting lost. "How can that be?"

"The reason, as I had learned from my father, is that there is no time in the eternity of death. Because there is no beginning, no end, there is no way to measure how long you're there."

"But there has to be a way to measure how long an event lasts. Time still exists. A day is still a day."

"Here, but not in the underworld. Here time is finite. Days start and end. There it's eternal night."

"I still don't understand," Magda said.

"Imagine encountering a rope stretched across your path. There is no beginning to your left, and no end to your right. The rope is infinitely long. It started forever ago and runs on forever. How could you take a measured portion of it? A portion of infinity is a contradiction. How could you, for example, measure out a fourth of forever? If you tried to cut a section out of such an eternal rope, it too would be eternal because the rope has no ends, so you cannot create them in something that does not have them as part of its nature. Just because you want a beginning and an end for your convenience, that does not mean that they exist. While they certainly exist here, in the underworld, those beginnings and ends do not exist.

"In the center of that vortex of power, time itself does not exist. A minute, a day, a year, they are all the same.

"So, in that eternity of time, that instant I was there in eternity, I had all the time I needed to search. In a way, I had forever. I searched forever.

"I tried to ask Joel's spirit where they were, but before I even began to form the question, he told me that they were not there.

"I saw people I knew from Grandengart, people who had died in the past, before that terrible day Kuno's army arrived, people who had been old, or sick, even a boy I had tried to help but who had died of fever. None of them knew where the rest of the people were, the people of Grandengart who had died out on the road that day.

"Everyone I knew could only tell me that the others were not there. They were not in the underworld."

"How is that possible?" Magda asked. "How can they be dead, but not dead?"

Isidore showed the slightest hint of a smile. "That is the question that has led me to be down here, among the husks of the dead."

The smile melted away, as if she were again lost in the vision of the memory.

"I saw tormented spirits, evil itself, lost in the black

sorrow of eternal darkness. I dared not let my attention linger too long on such entities, lest they pull me into everlasting night with them and tear my soul apart.

"I saw the glory of the good spirits. I saw them at peace in gentle light. I didn't want to disturb them, but I had to find the people who were missing. I had to ask them to help me, to tell me what they knew.

"One turned toward me, then, and I saw that it was Sophia's spirit looking back at me through the soft golden glow. She said that I had already learned the truth. She said that there was nothing more to learn there."

Magda's brow drew together. "Sophia's spirit? How could Sophia's spirit turn and speak to you in the world of the dead?"

Isidore licked her lips. "Because she was dead."

"What?"

Isidore cleared her throat. "It was her final journey to the spirit world. I knew then that she would not be returning back through the veil with me. She had given me the answer, and it was as simple as could be."

Magda was shaken to realize that Sophia, a woman she didn't know except through Isidore's story, had died on the quest.

"What do you mean, the answer was as simple as could be?"

Isidore gently laid her hand on Magda's arm. "It wasn't complicated at all. I had learned it the very first thing. They weren't there. The spirits of those people weren't in the underworld. That was the simple truth."

"If the simple truth is that they aren't there, in the underworld, then that would have to mean that their spirits are still here, in this world, that they haven't yet crossed over."

Isidore's only answer was a hint of a smile.

CHAPTER
32

Magda couldn't believe what she was hearing. "Is that what you're saying? That the spirits of all those people are still here in this world? I mean, if they really aren't there in the world of the dead, then they could only be here, still in this world, still with us." She caught herself glancing around the room, half expecting to see spirits hovering around her. "Is that what you're saying?"

Isidore pressed her lips together for a moment, but then finally answered. "I'm afraid so. The truth is, though those people died, their spirits, their souls, have not yet been able to cross over to where they belong."

Magda didn't know how that was even possible, or if it really was possible. It occurred to her that maybe they had crossed over to where they belonged, but then they had somehow been pulled back.

But why?

She wiped a weary hand across her face. She feared to imagine the reasons for such a thing. She couldn't begin to imagine the implications, the consequences. Her mind spun with a confusing tangle of thoughts. Isidore went on without Magda needing to prompt her.

"Sophia's spirit swept in closer, then. Her arms spread open like a falcon swooping in to stop right before me. Even though I knew Sophia, I was terrified and felt as if I were frozen in place, unable to move. The spirit's eyes—Sophia's eyes—blazed with the same light that enveloped her.

"She stared out at me from the underworld and said, 'You have the truth you came to find.' I didn't know what to do. As if to answer, her spirit came closer yet, right up to my face, and said, 'Find them!'

"In that terrible instant, I had the answer I had come to find, the answer to everything I needed to know. I knew, then, what I had to do.

"I returned, having learned the truth I had journeyed to find. I returned a spiritist, but I returned without the spirit of the woman who had taught me. I returned in her place, taking her place.

"Sophia lay dead beside me in the center of the Grace, her hand clutching the blindfold she had used when she had taught me to be a spiritist."

Magda could tell how much Isidore had come to like Sophia. She could see the grief etched in Isidore's sightless face. Magda felt terrible for Isidore that the search for answers had cost Sophia's life.

"I'm sorry about your friend."

Isidore smiled distantly. "Yes, she ended up being a good friend in many ways. She helped me learn what it was that I needed to do to help my people."

Magda cocked her head. "Are you saying that in making this discovery, that you thought it had become your duty to, to, what? Somehow escort missing ghosts to the world beyond?"

"I am saying that I knew then that the battle wasn't over just because I had gone to the underworld and found part of the truth. The war that had started with the murder of the people of my town had only just be-gun. I realized then that I am a warrior in this struggle."

"But you—"

"The same as you are here because you, too, have be-come a warrior."

"Me?"

Isidore turned to Magda, almost as if she were able to look right into her eyes, the way Magda imagined that the spirit of Sophia had looked into Isidore's eyes.

"You were wife to Baraccus, but since he died, you, too, have been searching for answers to troubling ques-tions. You, too, came here, to a spiritist, because you need to learn the truth. You, too, want answers from beyond the grave, not unlike your husband had done. You do these things because you have the spirit of a warrior.

"Though you are not gifted, you have knowledge, abili-ties, and heart that make you a uniquely capable individ-ual. You may think that anyone would do the things you do, such as confronting the council, but in fact they wouldn't, they couldn't. Only you could do the things that you have done, and you may be the only one now able to uncover the terrible truth. Make no mistake, Magda Searus, the enemy fears you, and with good reason, even if you don't know it."

"Fears me?"

"Yes. That is the mantle you have taken up. By com-ing here seeking a way to find the truth, you too have shown yourself to be a warrior. You have also shown yourself to be dangerous to them."

Magda remembered all too well, then, how the dream walker had been there, lurking in her mind, and then had tried to kill her.

"I guess I have. I hadn't thought of it in that way, but I guess I have. I'm not even gifted, but they for some rea-son don't want me looking for the truth."

"The journey to reveal the truth sometimes takes us to places we never expected to go," Isidore said. "But it is vital that the right person walks that path because we are fighting against those who can enter our minds and steal our souls. Perhaps they see, somehow, that you are the right person, and so they fear you. Because they fear you, they will come after you."

Magda couldn't argue. From the day up on the outer Keep wall, when she decided that she wanted to live, she knew that she was seeking something essential.

CHAPTER

33

S o where did your journey to discover the truth take
you after you returned and found Sophia dead?"
Magda asked.

Isidore gently ran a hand along the silky back of the
cat curled up between them. "After I buried Sophia, I
stayed at her house for a time, making several more jour-
neys to the spirit world. In doing so I came to realize
that my battle was not there in the world of spirits, but
here, in the world of the living. I knew that I had to find
help where our fight is centered."

"You came to see the council," Magda guessed.

Isidore confirmed it with a nod. "I came to report
what I had learned. I requested to speak before a session
closed to the general public. I felt that my information,
if spread among people who didn't understand such
things, might cause a panic. I wanted to speak only to
other gifted, only to those who had some understanding
of the work of a spiritist.

"I finally found myself in the council chambers, standing in line in a closed session waiting my turn to speak.
I had thought that such a closed session would be more
private than it actually turned out to be. Even a closed
session had a sizable crowd of important people. All of

them, it seemed, were there with news, reports, or concerns about the war.

"A number of army officers started out with confidential reports on battles along with the details of intelligence that had been gathered. I could hear only bits and pieces, but I grasped the general nature of their reports. A number of wizards then brought forth information on what was being discovered about new weapons of magic we are up against. I could only hear bits of that as well, but what I could hear was frightening enough. Other gifted had proposals that needed approval, mostly for weapons of our own.

"Some of the officers and wizards, as they reported on enemy activity, leaned in and spoke in low voices as council members gathered in close, listening in stony silence to what I couldn't hear at all. I didn't have to hear what they were saying, though. I could read the worry on the faces of the council, worry that the war was not going well.

"After the war reports, an old wizard not far ahead of me in line limped up when it was his turn and spoke at length on the need to create another sliph so that we could quickly get information from place to place out ahead of the enemy."

Magda recoiled at the very idea of them creating another. She was not at all fond of the sliph. As far as she was concerned the one they had was one too many. She forced her mind back to listening to Isidore's story.

"The council elder was respectful, but told the man that it had been a great deal of effort to create the sliph, and it had ended up causing trouble that no one had anticipated. The wizard started to argue his case but the council elder cut him off, saying that when the war started, the enemy had found their way into the Keep through the sliph."

Magda clearly recalled the ensuing carnage. Baraccus had ordered that one of the gifted guard the sliph at all times to prevent anyone from again slipping in to attack them.

She knew one of the wizards, Quinn, who was assigned the lonely task of standing watch over the sliph. He had grown up with Magda in Aydindril. It was a grim duty guarding the sliph, but Quinn didn't seem to mind. He said it gave him time to write in his journals. He was fond of recording details about events at the Keep, information about people he knew, and his thoughts on the state of political intrigue. Magda had asked if she could one day read his journals. He promised that she could, but said she would likely be bored.

"The old wizard hadn't known about this breach and fell to stunned silence," Isidore said. "They thanked him but denied the request. They told him to instead create some additional journey books to help with his communications problems.

"As the old wizard bowed and departed, the next man in line right ahead of me impatiently stepped up. He was a tall, broad-shouldered wizard not much older than me. He wore a beautiful sword—a rare thing for a wizard to do. That's why I noticed it. Nor did he wear the more common robes that most wizards wear.

"Since I was next in line behind him, I was able to hear the entire conversation. The faces of the council turned sour at the sight of the young man. One of the councilmen asked, 'What is it this time, Merritt?'"

Magda remembered the name. The wizards that Tilly and she had encountered in the dark passageways earlier that day had told them that Merritt had just gotten some more men killed. They had been quite angry about Merritt's refusal to help.

"Merritt told the council that he was now confident

that his method to create a person who could elicit truth was achievable." Isidore tilted her head toward Magda. "That caught my attention."

It did Magda's as well, but for a different reason. Magda had never liked the idea of altering people with magic.

"The council only listened briefly before interrupting him to say that they'd heard his proposal before and in their judgment his idea was beyond the ability of any wizard. Merritt insisted that since he had last talked with them he had studied every aspect of the process and then worked through an extensive series of verification webs to satisfy himself that he was right. He said that not only was it achievable, he believed he could do it. He told them that the purpose was critical enough that it needed to be pursued.

"They agreed about the theoretical value of the objective, but asked, if he thought it was possible, why hadn't he done it? Why hadn't he already succeeded in accomplishing such a thing?

"Merritt said that he would first need some arcane celestial calculations to complete the process, and then a willing subject. They asked what celestial calculations he needed. I couldn't hear his answer, but several members of the council laughed. Another smacked a hand on the table in anger and told Merritt that he was out of his mind.

"Merritt was not cowed when they told him that the existence of such templates were only speculation. In a clear, quiet voice he told them that he knew what he was doing. He said that he had been able to learn through his research that such occulted calculations would have to exist. He said that he was sure that the formulas from before the star shift had survived. He said that at the least there had to be charts for a seventh-level breach from which he could plot his own templates.

"Merritt assured them that if he could get the rest of what he needed, he could create a weapon, a person, who could infallibly pull truth from any lie.

"All the councilmen started talking at once. The elder interrupted them and told Merritt that, based on what he had heard and what he knew, the attempt to create such a weapon would likely result in the death of the subject. He said that the enemy took such risks with lives, but we did not.

"Merritt didn't answer. He stood with his back straight and let the other councilmen similarly denounce his ideas. By the things they were saying, I'm not sure that the council even understood Merritt's concepts. The things he was talking about were well over my head, yet I was able to grasp sparks of his brilliance in the things he said. But I don't know enough to judge the accuracy of Merritt's claims. The council certainly didn't seem to think highly of them.

"The elder asked if he was correct about the danger to the subject. Merritt was silent for a time and then quietly said that while he was confident that he could do it, he had always been honest about the lethal risks involved. But, he asked them, how many would die without his weapon. They sat back in their chairs, unable, or unwilling, to say.

"The elder finally leaned forward again and said that there was nothing they could do to help him because they didn't know if such seventh-level rift calculations even existed, but if they did, the council didn't possess them. Merritt then said that since the council wasn't able to provide him with the zenith formulas he needed, he would have go to the First Wizard himself. Several councilmen laughed and said that he could try."

Magda now knew why she had recalled the name Merritt when she had heard it back in the passages on the way to see the spiritist. She remembered Baraccus coming home after a private meeting that had unsettled him. Magda had asked what troubled him. He had stood at the window looking out at the moon for a long time before he finally said that a brilliant wizard had come to him seeking some valuable and rare rift calculations for creating a seventh-level breach. Magda hadn't known what that meant, but there was no doubt in her mind as to the seriousness of the issue. She asked if Baraccus had given the man what he needed.

Baraccus had said, "I couldn't give Merritt the formulas he needs. I wish I could, but all the breach calculations are locked away in the Temple of the Winds, out of reach in the underworld."

Magda knew, in Isidore's story, that Merritt was not destined to get what he needed by visiting the First Wizard.

"Finally," Isidore went on, "the elder suggested to Merritt that he go back to work on lesser tasks until he could come up with something worthwhile, something not outside the realm of possibility.

"When Merritt passed me on his way out, I could see that his jaw was set and his teeth were clenched. His fist was tightly gripped around the wire-wound hilt of his sword. I felt sorry for him because I heard something in his voice that I liked."

Magda came out of her thoughts and glanced over at the woman. "What do you mean?"

Isidore shrugged. "I don't know. Sincerity. Competence. I could tell that he knew what he was talking about even though the council wasn't taking him seriously.

"And his eyes . . ."

"What about his eyes?"

Isidore shrugged self-consciously. "I don't know. They were an unusual color for one thing—on the green side of hazel. But it was what I could see in his eyes that caught me up.

"When he looked at me, I was stopped dead by his gaze. It was like he could look right into my soul. Even though he was quietly angry at the council's rejection of his request, there was still something gentle about his eyes. Through the anger in them, I could also see his compassion."

Even in the soft candlelight, Magda could see that Isidore was blushing. "He made you feel safe," she guessed.

Isidore nodded. "And I felt bad for him. I thought they were failing to recognize his true ability, his potential. I guess that because I'm a young sorceress I know what it feels like to have people not take you seriously when you really do know what you're talking about. Sophia had taken me seriously, but few others ever did."

"What about your meeting with the council?" Magda asked. "Did they agree to help you?"

Isidore let out a deep sigh. "When my turn came, the council sympathized with my story, but said that there was nothing they could do about the tragedy.

"I suspected that they didn't entirely believe me. I can't say that I blamed them. Most people, even most wizards, don't really know much about the underworld, so the council couldn't grasp the significance, the danger, of the things I was telling them any more than they could grasp the insights Merritt had brought them. My father would have, but these men hadn't spent a lifetime studying the underworld the way he had.

"The council's view was that as tragic as it was, the people from Grandengart were dead and therefore beyond help. The elder said that they needed to worry about the living.

"No one on the council could see that my discovery

had a direct bearing on the living, and especially on keeping the living alive.

"The elder looked me in the eye and said that they had a great many important things to worry about. Though he didn't say it, I got the distinct impression that he meant to scold me for wasting their time.

"I said that with the war growing day by day I completely understood, but, as a sorceress and a spiritist, I believed that this had something important to do with that war and that it was somehow tied into it all. I said that I feared there was more going on than anyone was aware of and that we were all at far greater peril than anyone realized."

Magda had been before the council a number of times and knew full well their capacity for detachment.

"What did they say?"

"Well, after a moment's thought, the elder leaned back in his chair and suggested that perhaps I could find a wizard willing to help me. He said that if I could find such a wizard, I was welcome to his help.

"One of the other councilmen chuckled and suggested that I seek the help of young Wizard Merritt, that maybe I could take his mind off his daydreaming."

Magda was afraid that she knew all too well what had happened next.

CHAPTER
34

S o," Isidore said, "considering the possibilities of what the enemy could be doing with the bodies they had harvested and what they might be doing to prevent the spirits of those poor people from finding their rightful way into the spirit world, and why they would do such ghastly things, I decided that my best chance was to look for Wizard Merritt."

Magda was not liking where the story was going, especially since she already knew that a wizard had taken Isidore's eyes, and it seemed that Merritt was a man already engaged in the secretive business of altering people with magic into something other than the way they were born. She knew that some such alterations were relatively minor, but some, like the sliph, were monstrous transformations.

"Inquiring where I could find Merritt, I began to learn that people didn't laugh at him, the way the council had. People were afraid of Merritt."

Magda was surprised by this news, especially in light of the way the council had dismissed him. "Afraid of him? You mean because he alters people into weapons?"

"Well, yes, to an extent, but it's actually more than that. They are afraid of him because he's a maker."

"A maker?" Magda leaned in. "Are you sure?"

She knew that the things made by such wizards often frightened people, and with good reason. She also knew that true makers were exceedingly rare and opinions of them tended to be contentious. She was beginning to better understand why the council hadn't wanted to deal with Merritt.

Isidore nodded. "That's one of his gifted talents. He makes all sorts of things, everything from exquisite leather bindings heavily invested with wards for books of magic, to piles of edged weapons that cut in ways that steel alone can't, to complex metal creations I couldn't even begin to describe and can only wonder at. He even carves beautiful statues from marble.

"His place was littered with an array of metal objects left all over the floor, sitting around the statues, and piled in corners. There were knives stacked on some tables and swords neatly arranged on others. I'd never seen the likes of it in my life. It reminded me a bit of the blacksmith places I've seen, except cleaner and, I don't know, more refined, I guess."

Magda smiled. "I'm familiar with strange objects left in corners. My husband was a maker, though I rarely heard that name applied to him."

"Really?" Isidore asked. "Baraccus was a maker as well as a war wizard?"

Magda nodded. "When I met him he was already First Wizard, so that's the way people referred to him, the way they thought of him."

In fact, people were hesitant about calling him a maker, so they were eager to refer to him as "First Wizard."

"Despite his duties and responsibilities," Magda said, "Baraccus was always making things. He would often sit at a worktable late at night and craft the most intricate things I've ever seen, yet I always knew that some of those things, despite how beautiful they may have been, were actually quite deadly.

"Not long after we were married I asked him why, with so many responsibilities and other things to do, he took the time to sit at that table and make things. He smiled and said that he was a maker, and driven to make things."

"That's a maker," Isidore said. "That's the way they are. Creativity in large and small ways defines their nature in everything they do."

When he had first mentioned that he was a maker, Magda had confessed to Baraccus that, although she'd heard whispers about "makers," she didn't really know much about them. At that time, a lot of things having to do with his abilities were a mystery to her. He had patiently explained how the gift manifested itself in various ways in different people. He said that as a war wizard his gift contained a number of these discrete elements.

Magda had been surprised. She'd always thought that being a war wizard was a unique talent in and of itself. She remembered him smiling and saying that a war wizard's power was not a singular ability, but its strength actually came from a combination of components.

He explained that prophecy sometimes guided a war wizard. If combat was called for, such a man could envision a battle plan, or wield a blade, or sometimes focus the force of his rage into destructive power, or do the opposite and call forth his ability to heal the gravely injured. He said that in his case, if a stronghold and defenses were needed to protect people he also knew how to build them because he was a maker. All of those things and more, added together, he said, made up his unique ability as a war wizard.

She recalled how his eyes lit up when he explained that makers were more, though. They were actually artists, he said, and true artistic ability was as rare among wizards as it was among those without the gift. And, like true artistic ability, a lot of people thought they had it, but few actually did.

According to Baraccus, this genuine artistic ability enabled exceptional makers to use magic in creative ways that others had never imagined. He said that all new spells, all new forms of magic, all new uses for spells, were first envisioned by these kinds of makers.

Baraccus had told her that while a number of wizards could make things, the same as the ungifted could make things, it was this component of artistic ability in creating new things that took it to another level and made true makers more rare than true prophets.

That was also part of the reason that people feared them. They could conceive of and conjure what had never before been done. New things were frequently treated with suspicion, while new things having to do with magic were usually treated with great suspicion.

Baraccus held that without makers magic would stagnate, its scope left to accidental discoveries and to those who learned what to do through rules, formulas, and methods. Without that element of imaginative artistic ability, the gifted couldn't expand on magic or build it into new forms. Without makers to show them new ways, show them new forms of magic, the gifted were left with doing only that which been done before.

Magda had always heard that there were rules and procedures that had to be followed in order to make magic work properly. She thought it must be rather like baking bread, that it had to be done correctly. She asked Baraccus how a maker could get magic to work properly if they weren't following rules, formulas, and methods.

He laughed and asked how she thought all those things arose in the first place. Where did the rules originate? Where did the formulas come from? How were the methods first discovered?

Who created the first shield? Who first used the gift to mend a broken bone? Who first cast wizard's fire?

Makers, Baraccus told her, first conceived of all those things and more. They created forms of magic that others then went on to mimic and copy and use. What was at first remarkable in this way became common, eventually acquiring rules and formulas and methods. But it was the creativity of makers that first showed the way. Makers created new recipes, as it were. Those who couldn't wield magic creatively had to follow the recipe someone gave them.

Magda remembered the passion in his voice as he told her about such things. Making things was in his soul. Creating new things seemed to be his spark of life.

"Baraccus told me that without makers there would be no new conjuring and magic would be forever confined to simple things that were endlessly copied. He said that it takes makers to think up and create what never before existed."

Isidore smiled as she nodded. "That's the secret about magic that most people, even most of the gifted, don't really understand. The things created by a maker are endlessly imitated and copied to the point where people cease to think about where such things originated. People who have lived with a particular form of magic their entire life tend to assume that it always existed."

"I guess that's because true makers, such as my husband, are so exceedingly rare."

"You are a rare person as well, Magda Searus. You seem to know more on the subject than even most of the gifted I've ever encountered."

"I would never have understood about makers, either, had it not been for Baraccus teaching me about them. It was a subject close to his heart." Magda shook her head as she remembered some of the things Baraccus had done. "He made such beautiful things. I still have all his tools. Since he died, I sometimes go to his worktable and pick them up, trying to feel a bit of him."

Isidore was smiling as she listened. "I wish I could have known him."

Magda's own smile ghosted away. "Some of the things he made, I feared."

Isidore frowned. "Really? Like what?"

Magda stared off into her memories. "At the start of the war, Baraccus created an achingly handsome amulet of precious metals surrounding a bloodred ruby. Despite its mastery, its beauty, its intricacy, that amulet was at the same time invested with meaning I couldn't begin to understand. Yet I knew how important its meaning had to be to Baraccus because he always wore it.

"One night, after a particularly disturbing report from some of his wizards, I found him again at the window, staring out at the moon. I knew that he was thinking, as he often did, about the Temple of the Winds off in the underworld. He was clutching that amulet in his fist. I asked him what the amulet meant to him, what its meaning was.

"At first, I thought he wasn't going to answer. But then, in a haunting voice, he said that it represented the dance with death. I was rather horrified by that. He said the dance with death was the way of a war wizard.

"I sat on the floor beside him that night, him standing, staring out the window, me with my back leaning against the wall beneath it while I held his hand, as he held his private thoughts close, and that amulet in his other hand.

"He was a remarkable man, a man that in many ways I don't think I really knew.

"And now he's gone."

Isidore gently touched her arm.

Magda came out of her thoughts to look over at the spiritist. "I'm hoping that you will soon know his spirit . . . at least enough to bring me the answers I need, or at least answers that can guide me in the right direction."

Isidore gave Magda's arm a sympathetic squeeze. "We will find your answers, Magda. You've found your way to the right person, a person with the right kind of vision."

Magda put thoughts of Baraccus out of her mind as she returned to the matter at hand.

She couldn't bring herself to ask Isidore if Merritt had been the one to take her eyes. She skirted the subject and asked something else instead to steer the conversation back to the subject at hand.

"So what about you? What happened with Merritt? Was he able to help you with your efforts to find the lost souls of Grandengart?"

"Well, when I finally found his place"—she pointed a finger toward the ceiling—"up under the southern rampart, of all places, Merritt seemed to be distracted by his own problems, but he was kind enough to allow me in and at least listen to my story. He listened as you have, and far more seriously than the council had. I guess people closer to your own age are more inclined to take you seriously.

"He didn't say much as I told him what had happened. He stared down at that beautiful sword of his, lying on a table, as he listened. He asked a few questions, though, and I got the sense from those questions that, perhaps even more than me, he considered the implications of bodies being taken, and worse, their spirits missing from the underworld, to be quite ominous. In a way, his concern made me worry even more and served to reinforce my conviction in what I knew I had to do.

"When I finished with my story he asked what it was I thought he could do to help. I told him that I believed that there was a threat that everyone was ignoring. He didn't argue the point. I told him that because of my abilities as a sorceress and a spiritist I thought I had a unique understanding of the problem, an understanding that the council was not taking seriously. He seemed in harmony with that as well.

"I told him that while I believed the enemy was somehow meddling with the world of the dead, I at first had not been able to come up with any solution to finding the truth until I finally began to consider how I could use my ability to do what had never needed doing before. I told him how I had eventually come to understand that I needed to search the world of life for the dead, and for that I needed a new way to use my abilities, a way that had never been conceived of before.

"Up until that moment, he had listened with great interest to the things I was telling him, but now he was even more intently focused."

Magda had no doubt of that.

Isidore smiled self-consciously. "I guess that I was trying to appeal to his nature as a maker, trying to talk to him in a language he would understand and appreciate. It seemed to be working, as he was acutely interested in what I was telling him.

"Finally, I told him that I had come at last to understand what was needed. I told him that I needed to have a new way to see, a way to see what no other could, and to do that I needed to have my vision of this world removed. To see, I had to first be blinded. I said that I wanted him to do it.

"Merritt was shocked and angered by my unexpected request. He refused to listen to anything else I had to say. He ushered me to the door and sent me away."

Magda for the first time thought better of Merritt.

"Over the course of time, I had gradually become used to the idea of trading one kind of sight for another and had accepted its necessity. I was used to the idea. But I realized that it was a shocking request to make of Merritt, so for a while I left him alone to think about the things I had told him. I knew that he needed time to absorb it all.

"After a while, I went back to see him. I would have liked to have given him more time to consider the situation, but I knew that time was working against me—against all of us.

"Before he could say anything or send me away, I asked him to first tell me one thing. He folded his arms and looked down at me, waiting for me to pose the question. He's a tall man—you are more his size than me. For a moment I had trouble summoning my voice under the scrutiny of his hazel eyes. I finally did, of course, and asked him to tell me why General Kuno's forces would take the corpses of our people. He stared down at me for a long time.

"Finally he told me, in a quiet voice, that he feared to imagine. I told him that I did as well and asked him to allow me to explain.

"He at last stepped aside from his doorway and allowed me in. I again told him that I needed to be blind. Anticipating what he might say and before he had a chance, I told him that I needed to be really blind, not blindfolded, in order to see what I needed to discover. I explained that I was searching for the answers to real problems, and I couldn't use pretend methods.

"Merritt told me that if I wanted to be blind so bad, all

I had to do was stab out my own eyes. I remember him pacing around his room, gesturing with his arms as he told me that he would be cursed with a lifetime of nightmares if he were to do such a dreadful thing. He said that it was a cruel request for me to make of someone.

"He grew more and more angry as he paced. He finally told me again to leave and said that if I decided to stab my eyes out for such a crazy cause I would be doing him a great favor if I made sure that he never learned of it.

"As he held my arm and led me to his door, I told him that if he cared about all the people who had been slaughtered, and all those I feared would be slaughtered, he needed to listen to me. I insisted that he wasn't understanding what I was saying or what I was asking for.

"He finally calmed down and let go of my arm. He leaned back against a table covered in swords all neatly laid out on a red velvet cloth. He picked out one particularly stunning sword from a raised place at the center and held the wire-wound hilt tightly in both fists as he rested the sword's point firmly on the floor. He then looked up at me and said he was listening. It was a warning that it was my last chance.

"I told him that it was not actually blindness that I sought. I was actually seeking vision.

"When he frowned, I went on and told him that of course I could blind myself, but I could not give myself the sight I needed, so it would be pointless to do so. Even more curious, he leaned toward me a bit and asked what I meant.

"I told him that being blind to this world was only half of it—the easy half. I said that what I really needed was a wizard with enough of an imagination and ability to be able to create a new kind of vision.

"I told him that I needed to be invested with a singular ability, the ability to see what no one else could."

Magda arched an eyebrow. "I would imagine that by then, with him being a maker, you had his full attention."

"I did indeed," Isidore confirmed. "He began to realize that I was not asking him to blind me so much as I was asking him to take my vision so that he could replace it with a new kind of sight, a better kind of sight. The kind of sight that no one had ever conceived of before.

"I told him that in my mind, my vision had already been taken by the enemy. They had blinded me to spirits so that I could not fight against them.

"This was about getting the vision I needed so that I could fight back.

"I told Merritt that I needed him to create in me the ability to be able to hunt spirits in this world."

Magda watched Isidore silently rubbing a thumb on the side of her knee for a moment, gathering her thoughts before she went on. Magda could not imagine what it must have been like for this woman, all alone, haunted by her calling of working with the spirit world and by the spirits that were missing from it. Despite how thin and frail she looked, this was a woman of enormous determination.

"I remember the last day I had normal sight," Isidore finally said.

Seeing the woman's courage flag as her jaw trembled for just a moment, Magda placed a reassuring hand on Isidore's back, but said nothing.

Isidore spoke softly as she picked up the story. "After giving him the details he would need, all the things I knew as a spiritist that he would likely be unaware of, I'd let Merritt work on the problem. I had told him that it was in his hands and asked him to come to me when he was ready.

"He worked for weeks. Not once did I go to see him. I let him create what he would in his own way.

"Merritt hated the thought of taking my eyes, he truly did, but he understood that I wasn't really asking to be blind. I was actually asking for something far greater than the sight we are all born with.

"I was asking for wizard-created sight."

Magda stared at the candle flames wavering slowing as they burned, trying to imagine such a thing, trying to imagine what she would feel like, knowing that she was about to be changed forever by a wizard's power. She knew from Baraccus that when a wizard changed a person in such a way, there could be no going back. Such changes could not be reversed.

"One day a messenger delivered a note. It was from Merritt, saying that he was ready and would arrive shortly. It asked that I be ready." Isidore took a deep breath, letting it out with a sigh. "I remember how my heart started hammering when he knocked on my door that day. My heart was pounding against my ribs and I could hear each beat whooshing in my ears. I had to stop for a moment, hold on to the back of a chair, and make myself slow my breathing before I went to the door.

"I had made preparations for the day when he would finally arrive. I had gone over everything countless times as I waited. The waiting had been agony, but I knew that the last thing I wanted was to rush him. I needed him to get it right.

"I remember frantically looking at everything on my way to the door, trying to take it all in, trying to remember what everything looked like. I tried to remember the shape of the pottery bowl on the table, the simple design of the chair, the grain of the wooden table.

"It was a small place, but I had arranged the few pieces of furniture in it so that once I could no longer see I would be able to get around and find things fairly easily. I had tried to anticipate every aspect of being blind, tried to set things out that I would need to find, move things that might trip me, ready everything I could think of.

"Still, despite my preparations, I was terrified.

"I had several scarves laid out in a line on my small sleeping mat. I'd selected them because they were each a different color. For some reason, color seemed more important to me, more dear to me, than anything else.

"I desperately wanted to remember color.

"I had tied knots in the ends of each scarf, a different number of knots for each different color. One knot meant that it was a red scarf, two knots was brown, three green, and so on. I don't really know why I thought that was so important, considering that it could make no difference if I couldn't actually see the color, but I remember being panicked that I might forget what color looked like, what flowers looked like, what sunlight looked like, what a child's smile looked like.

"I guess that those scarves with the knots in the ends were my connection to all those things. They were my talisman to recall what color looked like . . . and so much more."

Magda felt tears running down her cheeks and dripping off her jaw. She tried to imagine eyes in the sunken hollows Isidore was left with. She must have been a beautiful woman, with big beautiful eyes looking out from a beautiful soul.

"I plucked up those scarves on the way to the door. I held them in a death grip, as if I could somehow hold on to color itself."

Isidore cocked her head, as if recalling the scene. "When I opened the door, I was surprised to see that Merritt's eyes were red. To this day, that, and not the scarf with one knot, is my memory of red.

"He told me in a quiet voice that he had figured out how to do what it was I wanted. He asked if I was sure, if I still wanted to go through with it. In answer, I took up his hand, kissed it, and held it to my cheek for a moment as I thanked him for what he was about to do. He nodded without saying anything.

"I was joyous for the lost souls that I hoped to be able to find. Merritt was miserable.

"He had a roll of papers he'd brought along with him. He unfurled them on the table and I saw then that each one had some kind of drawings all over it. He arranged them just so, putting various pieces where they belonged so that together they became parts of a larger drawing. When it was all arranged, I could see that he had drawn what looked to be a complex maze with odd symbols at various places."

"A maze?" Magda managed to ask without the tears surfacing in her voice.

Isidore nodded. "I asked him what he thought he was doing. I told him that drawings for a maze had nothing to do with the new kind of sight that I needed.

"He straightened then—he is an imposing man—and asked what I thought I was going to do. Walk all over the New World looking for ghosts? Look in dark corners and under beds? He said that it wasn't enough to be able to see such spirits as I was hunting. He said that I needed something more to help me find them.

"He said that he had not merely thought of a way to create a new kind of sight so that I could see them, but a way that might attract them, draw them to me.

"I was stunned. It was brilliant. I hadn't thought it through, thought about how I would actually search, but Merritt had. He had considered the entirety of the problem and he'd come up with a way for me not only to see spirits, but to draw the dead to me."

Magda glanced around the circular room, imagining what was out beyond, remembering the way she had come in through the maze to find Isidore's place.

"You mean to say that Merritt designed this maze

down here? That maze out there, that confusing place with all the dead ends, all the twists and turns, all the confusing passageways, all the hanging cloth, and the empty rooms?"

"That's right."

"I don't understand. How can it help you? Why the passageways to nowhere that dead-end? The hanging panels of cloth? The empty rooms? What's the purpose?"

"To make them feel safe," Isidore said.

Magda blinked in surprise. "To make the . . . spirits feel safe?"

"That's right. The dead ends make them feel a sense of safety, feel that others can't sneak up on them. The cloth gives them the comforting sense of being shrouded. Did you notice that the cloth panels have protection spells either painted on them or woven into the fabric? Most of it is very faint, but spirits can see them, or maybe they are aware of the spells in their own way."

"I guess I hadn't noticed," Magda said.

"Some of those spells on the hanging fabric are my own creation, born of my work as a spiritist. They're powerful and significant." Isidore leaned toward Magda a bit. "The dead must heed them."

"And the empty rooms?"

"The rooms are refuges that give the dead a sense of place. It has to be hard for them, not knowing where they belong. The rooms are empty so that the spirits don't feel like they are intruding into someone else's place. You see, the whole maze is a sanctuary for the spirits who find themselves trapped in this world.

"That day in my room, standing over the papers, Merritt said that he knew the right place to build such a sanctuary. He said that it would be down in the lower reaches of the Keep, below the crypts, where there were countless dead laid to rest. The crypts, he said, were a place of such specific energy that spirits trapped in this world would already tend to haunt that area. He said that the refuge he would build below would then draw them in to me.

"He said, then, that he would personally oversee the construction." Isidore swallowed. "I knew what he meant. He meant that it was time for him to first take my sight."

"I don't see how you could allow a wizard to alter you in such a way," Magda said, unable to contain her emotion any longer.

"Sometimes, it is necessary to step beyond what you have known and to reach for something more."

Magda had intended not to bring her own views into the conversation—after all, what was done was done—but she couldn't help herself. "I'm sorry, Isidore, but I can't see how you could allow it. How could you stand to give up so much? How could you allow a wizard to alter you from the way you were born?"

Isidore smiled then. "It's not that way at all, Magda. You were born unable to speak a language. Without people changing you from that natural, unaltered state, you would to this day not understand the spoken word, or be able to communicate."

"That's different," Magda said. "A person is born with that potential."

"A person is born with the potential to change, to learn, to grow. It's not always an easy step to take. You were changed by being taught to read and write. Reading and writing aren't natural abilities. They were instilled in you. Aren't you happy that people cared enough to change you so that you would be better than you were born and thus have a better life? Aren't you better for it? Didn't the struggle make you stronger?"

Magda swiped back her short hair. "But Isidore, he took your sight. How could you stand to lose—"

"No," Isidore said, holding up a finger to cut Magda off. "It's not that way at all. Yes, I lost something, but I gained something truly remarkable. I gained far more than I lost. Do you know that I've never again bothered to hold those scarves with the knots?"

"Why not?"

"Because I don't need them. That memory is the past. I can see so much more now."

Magda frowned. "What do you mean? See what?"

Isidore lifted an arm, slowly sweeping it around the room. "Well, I can see . . ."

The cat hissed as she suddenly jumped to her feet and rose up onto her toes.

Isidore's arm halted in place.

The cat arched her back high. Her black hair stood on end as her mouth opened wide. Her muzzle drew back, exposing her teeth as she hissed.

Magda blinked at the cat. "Shadow . . . what's the matter with you?"

"You should run," Isidore whispered.

Magda looked up. "What?"

"Run."

Magda sprang to her feet, following Isidore up. Shadow's black fur stood out straight, making her look bigger than she really was. Her tail puffed out to twice as fat as normal. Hissing with her fangs bared, she looked ferocious.

Isidore swept her arm out, pushing Magda behind her. "It's too late to run. It's in the hallway."

Magda thought that her own hair might stand on end along with the cat's.

"What's in the hall?"

A gust of wind swept in low along the floor and then up through the room, swirling around the wall, extinguishing all the candles. The air turned icy, as if someone had opened the door into the dead of winter.

The cat growled in a way that Magda had never before heard a cat growl. It was a ferocious, feral sound.

The frigid, whirling breeze died away, leaving the room to settle into murky stillness. Fortunately, the shield door on Magda's lantern had been closed. The flame hadn't been blown out by the strange gust of wind, so it was still providing some light. But sitting off to the side as it was, and with the shield door closed, it wasn't much help at lighting the uncomfortably dark room.

Magda squinted, trying her best to see in the dim light, looking for any sign of movement, something out of place, something that didn't belong. She didn't see anything that would have Isidore and the cat in such a state of alarm, but it was so difficult to see in the near darkness that she couldn't be sure there wasn't something she might be missing.

Using an outstretched arm, Isidore began backing Magda through the room, following the curve of the circular wall. The blind woman was obviously able to tell quite well where she was in the darkness. Now it was Magda who was at the disadvantage.

Magda pulled her knife. With her other hand she clutched Isidore's arm so if she had to she could pull the spiritist back out of harm's way. Even though Magda knew how to use the weapon to defend herself, with the unseen nature of the threat the knife offered less comfort than she would have hoped.

Not seeing anything, Magda leaned close and whispered, "Maybe we should go into the back room."

Isidore had both arms out, crouched a bit, as if she, too, was readying herself to fight the invisible opponent.

"No," Isidore said. "If we go back there we'll be even farther from the way out. We would be trapped."

"Trapped by what?" Magda asked, holding her knife out as she scanned the room to both sides. "I don't see anything."

Isidore came to a slow, fluid stop as she crossed her lips with a finger, urging silence.

Slowly, quietly, each step taken with care, Isidore began ushering Magda closer to the side of the room, all the while facing the entrance.

For the first time, Magda heard something coming from the entry hall. The strange sound sent goose bumps tingling up her arms. It sounded like fingernails dragging along stone.

The cat, facing the black maw of the entrance hall, hissed and growled even louder. Magda didn't know if Shadow intended on making an escape or attacking whatever it was that she and Isidore had first sensed in the entry.

With a sudden roar that made Magda gasp, a dark shape burst out of the blackness of the hall and into the room. In the dim light, Magda could see that it was a man. As Magda brought her knife up, Isidore ignited a bolt of power between her palms that lit the room in a blinding flash of light.

In that flash, Magda saw that the man didn't look the way she had expected. The folds of skin on his face seemed dry and stretched. It was difficult to see clearly in the crackling flashes of light, so she couldn't be sure exactly what she had seen. His scraps of clothes were dark and clung tightly, as if stuck to him.

Isidore flicked her hands, casting the sizzling point of light toward the intruder. The cat screeched and sprang for his face.

A dark arm caught the cat in midair and flung it aside. At the same time the bolt of power that Isidore sent flying at the man seemed to glance uselessly off the dark figure as he advanced through the room. Stone shattered where the flickering light of Isidore's power hit the wall, sending shards flying and dust boiling up.

Isidore didn't waste any time. Another bolt of powerful light ignited. This time, Magda had to turn her face away from the searing heat that slammed into the advancing figure. The shimmering heat turned to white vapor as he pushed through it without slowing.

"Try to get around him and run," Isidore said.

"I'm not leaving without you," Magda told her as she

tried to think of a way they could get past the hulking man.

"Forget about me—I am already lost!" Isidore yelled as she pushed Magda back.

"You're not lost!" Magda regained her footing and seized Isidore's arm. "We both have to get out of here!"

"We can't both get away."

"Yes we can. Hold my arm. When I cut him that will give us an opening. Stay with me."

"You will only have one chance," Isidore said, ignoring Magda's command and shaking her arm free. "When that chance comes, take it! Don't lose your life in here, Magda. You have to get away! You are more important than I am."

Magda had no intention of leaving a blind woman to her fate with whoever, or whatever, was in the room with them. She grabbed Isidore's arm again and yanked her back just in time from what the woman couldn't see. A powerful arm swept past them both.

Magda used the opening to duck under Isidore's outstretched arm and to slam her knife up into the ribs just under the man's extended arm as it swung past them. It was a solid strike. She pulled back in time to miss the elbow that cocked back, trying to get her. The arm swept around again, inches from her face. She tried to slash the arm but missed. Magda saw that the fingers were like shriveled, blackened claws.

Isidore pushed both hands out, using all her strength to send a concentrated, focused fist of air at the center of the figure. It bent him only a little. He staggered back a half step but then kept coming forward again as Magda and Isidore kept circling away from him.

The cat leaped out of nowhere up onto the man's back. He twisted and threw it off. The cat hit the wall hard.

With an angry roar and sudden, ferocious speed, the man lunged toward them. Magda snatched for the blind woman's arm to yank her back out of the way, but she caught only air as Isidore leaned in and again tried to force a focused wall of air at the attacker.

Magda felt as if she were moving in a dream. Even with all her strength put into the effort, her legs wouldn't move fast enough to get her within range to stab the man, to stop what she knew he was about to do.

Lashing out with lightning speed, his clawed hand raked through Isidore's middle. Isidore's scream turned to a grunt with the impact of the blow.

An arc of warm blood and flesh splattered across Magda and then in a diagonal line up across the wall.

Isidore's legs began to buckle.

"Run! Now!" she cried out at Magda as she was going down.

Magda instead rammed her knife into the side of the man's neck. She had to stop him before he did any more damage. All she could think was that she had to stop him and then get help for Isidore.

Driving the knife in deep didn't feel like stabbing into muscle and sinew. It felt hard and leathery and dead. She tried to yank the knife back so that she could stab him again, but it was stuck fast.

She gripped the handle with both hands, trying to pull the blade back out of his neck. It was then, when she was close enough, that she saw in the dim light that the man, though he moved with impossible speed and power, didn't look like a man.

He looked like a corpse.

His face was sunken and partially decayed. His jaw hung crooked to one side; his dark teeth were exposed behind shrunken, shriveled lips. He looked like a rotting cadaver.

But even as dead as the rest of him appeared, his eyes were something altogether different. The look in his eyes sent an icy chill through her.

It wasn't just that they glowed with a kind of inner light. It was that the glow was fired by the gift, yet unlike any light of the gift she had ever seen before. It was at once dead and empty, but alive with menace.

Magda was so shocked by what she saw that it stopped her cold for an instant.

Then, that frozen instant shattered with a crack that made her ears ring. The room suddenly spun in her vision. Her back smacked the wall, driving the air from her lungs. Her head hit the stone so hard that it knocked her senseless. Through the pall of pain she only dimly heard the terrible roar of the thing, only dimly saw blurry movement in the swirling room.

Magda could taste dry stone dust and blood. She realized then that the man had struck her with a blow so powerful it had lifted her from her feet and thrown her back across the room.

She was distantly surprised to realize that she still had her knife gripped tightly in her fist. Isidore's warm blood ran down Magda's arm and over her hand, making for a slippery hold on her knife.

Magda blinked, trying to clear her vision as she struggled to get her breath back. Looking up from the floor, she saw the man in a wild fury ripping into Isidore. He tore off the side of Isidore's face and the top of her skull with one powerful blow, the rest of her head with the next.

The dark figure roared as he flailed and ripped at Isidore's body. Blood and gore from the poor woman splattered across the floor and up against the walls as he swung both arms in mad fury.

In a strange pall of quiet shock, Magda told herself

that it was too late to do anything but escape. If she didn't get away, she would be next.

As the man bellowed in a wild frenzy of savagery, she told herself that there was nothing she could do for Isidore. This was her only chance to get away. She knew that she had only a few fleeting seconds if she was to live.

She told herself to move.

Magda scrambled to her feet and staggered toward the black entrance to the hallway out. She snatched up her lantern on the way past.

Once into the hall, she looked back over her shoulder as she ran. She was still stunned from the blow, and her wobbly legs wouldn't move fast enough. She could see the man back through the entrance, finished ripping Isidore apart, turn toward her.

A cry of anguish for Isidore caught in Magda's throat as she struggled to run. The cat appeared out of the dark doorway and raced after her.

CHAPTER
38

I n a daze, Magda stumbled as she ran. Tears streamed down her face. Blood dripped from her fist holding the knife. Glancing down at her arms, she thought it looked as if she had just butchered someone.

As she ran, she struggled to comprehend what she had just seen. She knew that something only remotely human, or maybe only once human, had just slaughtered Isidore. It made no sense.

It was such a horrific sight, such a shock, that she was already questioning if she had really seen what she knew she had seen when she had looked into the man's face. She began to wonder if it could have been a trick of the shadows.

But she knew it wasn't.

She cried out in fright when she suddenly ran into one of the walls of hanging cloth. It caught her, flapping around her like arms grabbing for her. She slashed wildly with her knife, frantically trying to get away from what she thought for a second was the man who had killed Isidore trying to seize her.

She shoved the cloth aside and started running. She could only see a short distance ahead into the empty maze of halls.

She looked down as she ran, fumbling with the lantern door, trying to get it open so that she could see better. It finally sprang open, casting a bit of useful light into the passageway.

She realized that, lost in the maze as she was, she would soon be the next victim of the thing that had killed Isidore. It was coming for her. If she was wandering around aimlessly it would likely be able to catch her in short order.

Magda thrust a hand into her pocket, frantically searching for the map that Tilly had given her. She dug around with trembling fingers but couldn't find the map. She didn't know if she'd dropped it as she was running, or if she'd lost it in the fight. All she knew for sure was that the map wasn't in her pocket.

She turned back the way she had come, holding the lantern up, trying to see if she had dropped the map when she had fought her way out of the embrace of the hanging cloth. She didn't see it on the ground anywhere.

She heard a sound. She thought she saw a dark shape move back in the direction she'd come from.

Then she saw the glow of his eyes off in the darkness, like some goblin from her childhood nightmares come to life.

Magda abandoned the search for the map and started running. She knew that it was foolish to run in a maze without knowing where she was going, but she was too panicked to stop herself.

Besides, what choice did she have?

She ran with wild abandon, taking random passageways at intersections. From time to time she could hear the dead man in the distance behind her. He let out a growl of rage as he came, his feet sometimes dragging on the floor. Magda ran all the faster, imagining the goblin from her nightmares hot on her heels. She knew that she didn't stand a chance fighting against him. She had to get away.

She was suddenly brought up short in a dead end. She spun around and saw the man step into the passageway from a side hall, blocking her way back. Magda stood panting, knife clenched tightly in her fist, trying to decide what to do.

His glowing eyes watched her, and then he started toward her. As he got closer, the cat sprang out of the darkness onto the man's head, clawing at his gleaming eyes with wild fury. He twisted to the side, his arms thrashing, trying to swipe the cat off his head.

Magda knew that it was her only chance. She didn't hesitate. She ran toward the man and the only way out. As she reached him, she bent low and slammed her shoulder into his ribs, knocking him to the side. He lost his balance and fell against the wall.

Pain shot through her shoulder from the solid impact with his rocklike torso. Magda was already past him and running at full speed as the cat sprang off the man and raced after her.

Magda took intersection after intersection, ducking around heavy panels of hanging cloth whenever they appeared unexpectedly out of the darkness. She didn't know where she was or how to escape the maze. She was simply trying to lose the man close on her heels. The man who had killed Isidore.

Charging down a long hallway, she suddenly came upon another hanging cloth that loomed up out of the darkness. Magda pushed it to the side with an arm as she went around it. When she did so, she realized that it was different from the others she had encountered. Unlike the others, this one was light and airy.

Almost immediately, before she could wonder at the silken nature of the cloth, she saw in the weak lantern light that it was a dead end. She couldn't go any farther.

Magda spun around. The man had already reached the other side of the cloth wall blocking the passageway. It was too late to go back the way she had come.

The man slowed. He had her trapped in a dead end.

Magda stood frozen in panic, gulping air. She could see the reddish glow of his eyes through the gauzy cloth.

She had nowhere to run.

CHAPTER
39

Magda could see his boots just on the other side of the hanging cloth. Her back was to the wall at the dead end of the corridor. The delicate cloth hung perfectly still, not three paces away from her.

She tried to think what to do, how she could get away. She thought that maybe, if he came around one side, she could dash out the other side at the same time and run.

But where? She didn't have the map. She realized, then, that even if she had the map it likely wouldn't do her much good. There was really no way to run and read the map at the same time. It had been hard enough to decipher when she had been able to stand still, study it, and count intersections.

The truth was she was lost in the maze. A maze designed to attract the spirits of the dead. Magda didn't think that this man, or creature, or whatever it was, had been what Isidore had been trying to attract, but in dealing with dark forces perhaps she had inadvertently gotten the attention of things she hadn't intended to attract.

An arm thrust around the cloth, clawing at the air, as if trying to feel around to find her, hoping to snag flesh.

Magda pressed her back against the wall behind, trying to stay as far away from the sweep of the clawed hand as possible. The cloth was sheer enough that had there been light beyond in the tunnel she would probably have been able to see the man through it. With her lantern, she thought that he could probably see her. She turned the lantern window aside, hoping not to illuminate herself for him.

She leaned to the side away from the arm reaching blindly for her and carefully peered through the small gap between the wall and the other end of the cloth. The hall wasn't as wide as some. She could see that if she went for the gap opposite the man he would likely be able to reach over and grab her.

Again he swung the arm, groping into the dead end, trying to catch her up. She was far enough away from where he was standing, though, that he couldn't reach her.

But as soon as he came around the flimsy, hanging cloth, he would be able to snatch her unless she could somehow get past him as he came for her. She was fast, but from what she had seen back in Isidore's place, he was faster. Making it worse, the hall wasn't very wide. There was no maneuvering room.

Magda wondered how long it would be until he came around and had her. She kept imagining being ripped open the way he had ripped open Isidore. She knew that the end was going to come at any moment.

But instead, he moved to the other side of the cloth, reaching around with his other hand, clawing the air on that side. He didn't even lean over and look around, probably because his glowing eyes could see her on the other side of the cloth. She could see those eyes clearly enough, and they only added to her terror.

Even as she gasped for air, trying to get her breath as she struggled to figure out what to do, Magda frowned. Why didn't he simply come around the cloth to get her? It was obvious that he knew she was back there.

He roared in frustration, slashing wildly, blindly, around the side of the cloth. He raced over to the other side, trying again to reach back and snag her. But he wasn't leaning in far enough to get to her. She couldn't imagine why not.

It seemed like the silky cloth was somehow keeping him back.

Magda wondered . . . could it be?

She remembered Isidore saying that some of the spells on the hanging fabric were her own creation. Isidore knew more about the underworld and the dead than most people.

Magda held the lantern up. She could see then, through the diaphanous cloth, besides his glowing eyes, that there were symbols all over the other side. They were drawn rather crudely with what looked to be a thin wash of paint that wrinkled the fabric. Magda could see that they were definitely spell-forms. She tried to picture in her mind what they would look like if she were on the other side and wasn't looking at them backward.

She had frequently seen Baraccus draw spells. She tried to think if she recognized these drawn spells. They were unusual; they didn't look like anything she had ever seen Baraccus draw.

The man lunged, reaching around the side, grasping empty air with his clawed fingers. Magda ducked in and jabbed at the filmy cloth, pushing it toward him. He stepped back with a surprised, angry growl, then raced to the other side to try again to reach around and get her while she was close.

Magda remembered Isidore saying that the spells she had drawn were born of her work as a spiritist, and that they were both powerful and significant.

Magda remembered Isidore saying *The dead must heed them.*

The man on the other side hadn't yet tried to come past the cloth but he showed no signs of giving up. She knew that he would not leave until he had her. If anything, he was getting ever more frantic to reach her.

There was no telling when or if someone, someone like a wizard, would be coming down to the maze to see Isidore. But even if someone did come to visit the spiritist, it was possible that they wouldn't come this way. The maze was a sprawling complex. For all Magda knew, she could be far off the regular route in. Even if someone did come to see Isidore, they might never come this way and happen across Magda.

Worse, even if someone did come this way they very likely would be killed just as swiftly as Isidore had been murdered. Isidore had used powerful magic and it hadn't saved her.

Magda could be stuck down in the deserted tunnels forever, with the crazed killer ready to strike at any moment. For all she knew it was possible that his fear of the symbols on the cloth might only be a stopgap measure that wouldn't hold him back for long. Once he got past that thin piece of cloth, it would be a horrific, painful death.

Magda realized that if she was going to escape certain death, she was going to have to get away on her own.

She had an idea. An idea she didn't like one bit.

With her heart pounding nearly out of control, she clutched the knife tighter in her fist.

She didn't see that she had a choice.

CHAPTER
40

As the man beyond the hanging cloth moved from one side to the other, when he was about in the middle, Magda shoved the cloth toward him as hard as she could. Through the cloth, she could feel his body on the other side. His middle didn't feel at all soft like a living person's. It felt more like a tree trunk.

He roared at the contact with the thin cloth and stepped back. Recovering quickly, he lunged to one side, his arm coming around, trying to grab her as she was still pushing at the cloth. His clawed hand caught a few strands of her short hair. Magda jerked her head away before he could get a better grasp.

As he reached, sweeping the air, trying for more of her hair, Magda used all her strength to stab the blade deep into his hand. The blade pierced through his palm, coming out the back of his hand. He didn't cry out in pain, but instead yanked the hand back, pulling it off the blade to free it. He shoved the hand back toward her, sure that she was close and he would get her when she stabbed at him again.

Magda used the opening as he was occupied in reaching for her, thinking he had her, to race to the other side of the fabric panel. Without pause, she shot around the cloth. His dark shape turned abruptly when he saw her dash past him.

Magda sprinted at full speed down the corridor, too frightened to look back. But she didn't need to look back. She could hear him coming. As hard has she ran, she could hear him getting ever closer. He was as tireless as he was powerful.

Magda ducked around another hanging and took a turn to the right, then at the next intersection another right, then a left, in her mind marking the turns she took. The heavy hangings she encountered along the way didn't seem to trouble him the way the wispy one at the dead end had. He kept coming.

Even holding the lantern out as she ran, she still couldn't see very far ahead. She feared that she would run into another dead end, but one without the protective cloth, and then he would have her trapped.

As intersections appeared she took them at random and without hesitation, but still took note of each turn in case she came to a dead end and had to retrace her steps. As fast as she was running, and the way he was getting closer all the time, she knew that if she came upon another dead end, it would likely be the end of her. Even so, she knew that she couldn't afford to slow for anything.

Despite her fear, despite how hard she ran to escape, she couldn't keep the horrific memories of Isidore being slaughtered out of her mind. She knew that she had to think, but the thought of such a fate also happening to her was filling her mind. She could only imagine the pain and the terror of such a death. The only mercy was that it had been swift.

Magda looked up when she heard the cat yowl. The cat, a bit out ahead, turned back toward her. When Magda met the cat's gaze, the cat took a side passageway and started running.

The thought occurred to Magda that the cat had found the way in to Isidore's room on its own.

Magda wondered if maybe Shadow could find her way out as well.

She didn't know what else to do and she had no better idea, so she started chasing after Shadow, taking every turn the cat took. With her tail high in the air, the tip hooked forward, Shadow raced through the halls.

Magda glanced back over her shoulder and saw the glowing eyes. He had gained on her and was only two or three strides behind. She would have screamed, but she knew that if she did it would slow her just enough for him to grab her. Instead of screaming, she focused all her effort on running as hard as she could, trying to keep up with the dark streak of the cat.

The cat cut to the right at an intersection, but then abruptly stopped and looked off into the dark. It reversed direction and took to the left instead. Magda hesitated for just an instant, not knowing if she should keep up her momentum to stay out of the reach of the man, or follow Shadow. She chose to follow the cat rather than risk losing her only guide out and again being trapped in a dead end.

That instant was all the man needed. His arms circled around her middle.

Magda spun around before he completely closed his arms around her. She struck hard, slashing the knife across his throat. She saw bits of dried flesh fly off from the deep gash, but no blood. The wound didn't slow the man.

She slammed the knife into his chest, fist deep, over and over, then dipped her head under his arm when he tried to hook it around her neck.

As Magda slipped through his grasp, she spun around to the side of him. Hard as she could, she kicked the back of his knee. His leg buckled and he started to fall but staggered back and caught his balance before he fell.

Even though he stayed on his feet, it was just long enough for Magda to bolt away, out of his reach. Bellowing a deep growl that echoed through the halls, he charged after her.

As she ran after the cat, trying to keep it within the limited range of the lantern light, Magda couldn't see well enough and took a turn in the corridor too wide. The man took the inside, shorter line around the corner.

In that instant, he darted ahead of her, blocking her route. The cat stopped and looked back at her. The dark silhouette between them waited to see what she would do, where she would run.

Back beyond the man standing in the center of the corridor blocking her way, back beyond the cat, Magda saw light. She realized that they were at the entrance of the maze.

Despite the welcome light beyond the man that offered the way out, Magda couldn't get to it. The man started stalking toward her. Magda didn't want to run back into the dark passageways. She was close to being out of the maze, but with his feet spread and his arms out to the sides, she knew that there would be no getting by him this time.

As she started backing up to keep some space between her and the man, Magda thought she heard people in the distance yelling. She yelled back to them.

Hearing her yell for help, the man started to run toward her. Just then, something dark swooped in, hitting the back of his head. Magda could see the cat in the distance, waiting for her, so she knew it wasn't the cat.

When she heard the loud cry, she realized that it was

a bird. She saw broad, inky wings fluttering and realized that it was a raven.

It must have been one of the birds she had seen earlier that had come in one of the high windows in the large chamber and gotten itself trapped down inside the Keep's vast network of halls. She knew that it was a relatively common occurrence and that when they became desperate they sometimes panicked.

The raven let out a piercing cry as it attacked the man's head. He swiped at it, trying to fight it off. The raven withdrew every time he swung, avoiding his arms, only to dive in again and renew the attack.

The man stumbled to the side, careening into the wall as he tried to get the bird away from him.

When Magda saw her opening she didn't hesitate. She raced past him, toward the light. She no longer needed the cat to show her the way. She simply followed the distant glow of light.

Coming around a corner Magda abruptly encountered a small cluster of men. Some had torches while others had spheres that cast a greenish light. She recognized the gift in their eyes.

"What is it?" one of the men asked. "What's happened?"

Magda pointed back. "A man—a dead man. He murdered Isidore. He came in and killed her."

The wizard leaned in and frowned. "A dead man?"

Magda swiped sweaty stray strands of hair back out of her eyes. "I don't know. I don't know what he was or who he was. But he looked dead and he wasn't stopped by her magic." She lifted the bloody knife. "And he wasn't stopped by this. I stabbed him a dozen times at least. It didn't even slow him down."

The men shared looks before peering off down the

dark passageways. She thought they would question her, or argue with her. They didn't.

The raven suddenly burst out of the darkness and flew past them, back toward the lighted corridors.

"Those birds are always getting lost down here," one of the men grumbled.

"Come on," the first man said to the others.

As afraid as she was, Magda followed after the men, expecting that at any moment they would encounter the dead man. Despite the men being wizards, she wasn't entirely confident that they grasped the true danger of the threat. She wasn't entirely sure, despite their numbers, that they could handle the man who had killed Isidore.

Some of men broke away from the main group to take different routes through the maze to search for the intruder. She followed not far behind the man she took to be the one in charge, the one who had spoken to her at first, until they made it all the way back to the sight of Isidore's slaughter. In the light of torches and the light spheres it was, if anything, an even more horrific sight than she remembered.

The men didn't waste any time once they saw that the spiritist was well beyond any help. In grim silence, they quickly searched her quarters before they began retracing their steps through the maze. Along the way they looked in every room and behind every cloth hanging over the entrances to side halls. It was not hard to see how angry the men were as they searched for the one responsible for such a crime.

Eventually they found themselves almost back at the entrance without coming across any sign of the man who had killed Isidore. Guards at the entrance told them that no one had tried to come through. The man in charge told the others that they would keep searching until they found the killer.

As they again made their way off into the dark maze to continue the search, Magda paused. She stood alone after the men had gone, listening to the hiss of her lantern as she considered what she should do. Considering what she dared to do.

She remembered the route at the end when she was being chased. She had counted the turns. She knew the way back. At least back far enough.

She knew what she had to do.

Magda scooped up the cat and started back into the darkness.

Magda stood when the six men filed into the quiet room. A row of small, high windows let in glowing streamers of early sunlight that cut diagonally across the gloomy space.

Elder Cadell gestured without looking up at her before pulling out his own tall-backed chair. "Please, have a seat."

Magda did as he asked, sitting in the single, simple, and rather uncomfortable wooden chair set before a highly polished mahogany table in the council's private chambers. Though her chair was simple, the six chairs on the other side with Elder Cadell and Councilmen Sadler, Clay, Hambrook, Weston, and Guymer were quite elaborate, as were the three walls of floor-to-ceiling bookcases packed tightly with faded leather-bound volumes.

The furniture was intended to emphasize to people the difference in status between any of the council and those coming before them. Magda suspected that they had sent word that they would like to see her privately, before they began the day's session, so as to avoid a repeat of anything like the last time.

A steady stream of people had sought Magda out

since that day in the council session, asking her to help them with swearing the oath to Lord Rahl in order to protect themselves against the dream walkers. She had met with hundreds of people who had heard about what she said before the council that day and who were afraid of the dream walkers. With good reason.

While the council had not forbidden such an oath—after all, D'Hara was part of the New World and on the same side in the war—they privately chafed at people giving a devotion to Lord Rahl. Their official position was that while dream walkers were indeed real and presented a danger, the enemy was not yet advanced enough to put such a weapon into use, so while the threat was genuine, it was distant in the future.

Other than the attack against herself, Magda could provide no proof otherwise. But many people didn't want to take the chance and learn too late that the council was wrong.

"I had been expecting to see you sooner," Magda said when they were all seated.

"The war grows more desperate by the day," Elder Cadell said without looking up as he lifted one paper after another from the table before him, glancing over each briefly before setting it aside and going on to the next. "We have been trying to keep from losing the effort."

Councilman Sadler only briefly glanced her way between selecting specific papers from his own stack and handing them to the elder. Some of the other men were not interested in the papers. They were glaring at her.

"Of course," Magda said, dipping her head respectfully. With the elder continuing to look through papers, and several of the others staring at her, she felt compelled to say something. "Have you found the . . . person responsible for Isidore's murder?"

Elder Cadell looked up from under bushy brows. "Some people seem to think that you are responsible."

"Me?" Magda felt her face flush. "And have these people managed to explain how I could rip a person apart like that with my bare hands?"

The elder grunted before returning his attention to a paper that Sadler handed to him.

"That's true," Councilman Clay said. "She isn't gifted, after all."

"She had a knife," Councilman Guymer reminded him. "A bloody knife."

"Isidore's skull was torn in half," Magda said. "An axe could do such damage, but not a mere knife, especially not one wielded by me."

"I didn't say that we believed you are responsible," Elder Cadell intoned. He looked up and lifted an eyebrow. "I said some people think you are."

Magda didn't know what he was getting at.

"People often believe a lot of things that aren't true," she said. "I wish I had a way to reveal the truth for you, but I don't."

"The spiritist was doing valuable work for the war effort," Guymer said. "And now, while you were alone with her, we lost her rare talents."

Magda came up out of her chair. "If you are suggesting—"

"What were you doing down there?" Councilman Sadler asked in a quiet voice meant to override Guymer's accusation. "What business did you have with a spiritist?"

Magda sank back down into her chair. "What do you think I was doing seeing a spiritist?"

Sadler shrugged. "You tell me."

"I had what business anyone going to see a spiritist would have. I wanted to contact the spirits."

Councilman Weston lifted an eyebrow. "Contact spirits? For what purpose?"

"I miss my husband," Magda said. "What other purpose would there be to see a spiritist? I wanted to know that he is safe in the arms of the good spirits, to know that he is at peace. Perhaps none of you miss Baraccus, or worry and pray for his soul, but I do."

Looking rather uncomfortable for the first time, some of the men leaned back.

"You are not the only one who misses him," Sadler said.

Magda thought that he sounded sincere.

"And was the spiritist able to help you?" Weston asked. "Did you find out what you needed in order to put your mind at ease about Baraccus?"

"No. She was killed before . . ." Magda turned away and swallowed at the terrible memory. She cleared her throat and looked back to the men watching her.

"So, has the murderer been found?" she asked.

Elder Cadell swished a hand back and forth just above the table, as if he wished he could brush the problem away. "The lower reaches of the Keep have been searched extensively. Nothing has been found. There is no trace of the killer."

Magda looked from one face to the next. "But how is that possible? How could he have gotten away?"

"This dead man?" Guymer asked in a mocking tone. "The one you say killed our spiritist?"

"I reported what I saw," Magda said. "Are you suggesting that I lied?"

"No," Guymer said with a smirk, "only that in the heat of panic you may have imagined him to be more fearsome than he actually was, imagined that a killer would have had to be a monster. Your description was hardly useful. How would anyone searching know what he really looked like so as to know who to look for?"

Magda returned the glare in kind. "I told you what I saw."

Councilman Clay leaned forward. "And what you say you saw was not of any help in identifying the person responsible so that we could find him, now was it? There have been several such murders in the lower Keep. You are the only one who has actually seen the killer. Or, should I say, you are the only one who has survived the encounter."

"It was an invaluable opportunity to help us catch the killer," Guymer said. "We need to stop him before he kills again. But because you didn't keep your head and imagined a monster, we have lost the chance to identify the attacker and capture him. Because of your emotional reaction, we still have a killer loose in the Keep and we don't know his identity, much less what he looks like. He is undoubtedly a traitor or an infiltrator sent to kill important people. We might have had him if you could have kept your wits about you so that you could tell us what he looked like. Because you couldn't do that simple thing, we missed our chance and as a result we don't have a clue who it could be."

"We are left to wonder why," Clay added.

"She can't be faulted for being afraid," Sadler said.

Magda sat quietly, refusing to allow herself to rise to the bait. There were more important things at stake than proving herself to these men. It was not only the lives of the people in the Keep that were at stake, but all the people of the New World. She didn't know why the council had summoned her, but it wasn't to get at the truth. There was no point in defending herself when they had already decided that it was more convenient to blame her than listen to her. They didn't want the truth; she did.

Elder Cadell waved his hand again. "That's not why we called you here, Magda. We called you in because Councilman Weston had a valuable suggestion."

"And what would that be?" she asked without looking over at Weston's smug expression.

"That we appoint you as a representative of the council for the people in outlying lands. It's an important post. We value your experience with such distant lands. You would be our contact with these remote peoples of the Midlands, as you often were on an informal basis in the past. As Councilman Weston pointed out, there is simply no one better suited to the post."

Magda frowned as she looked from one grim face to the next. "You want to appoint me to a post to advise you on the peoples of the smaller lands?"

"No, not advise us." Weston leaned an elbow on the polished table. "You would travel to these far-flung lands and represent the views and decrees of the council to the peoples who inhabit those distant places. They are, after all, part of the Midlands. They need to know what is happening here at the Keep, what is being decided. They need to know about the war and such."

"After all," Sadler added, "should we lose this war, they, too, would fall under the merciless rule of Emperor Sulachan. You know as well as we do that if they win this struggle they will slaughter any who possess magic. The forces of the Old World are ruthless in their objective to wipe magic from the world.

"You would be the council's roving ambassador, filling people in on what we're doing in our effort to protect them from such a threat. Imparting such information, you would be helping to keep them safe. At the same time, you could also solicit their help with anything they might be able to contribute."

Despite Sadler's enthusiasm for the idea, Magda saw through the proposal. They wanted to get rid of her, or some of them did, anyway. The widow of the First Wizard was becoming an ever larger, ever sharper thorn in their side. They were trying to make the cause sound noble so that she would happily accept, or at least wouldn't be able to refuse.

"I am honored that you think highly enough of my abilities to suggest such a post," Magda said without committing to it. "You flatter me with your confidence, Councilman Weston."

Though the smile spread on his lips, it didn't make it to his eyes.

"There is also the matter of appointing a new First Wizard," Elder Cadell said. "We need a First Wizard to lead us in our fight. Our very survival is at stake. Things are not going well. We dare not delay any longer in finding someone to replace Baraccus as First Wizard. We have large numbers of the gifted coming to the Keep to help. They need a First Wizard to direct them in how best to work to defend the New World. These new arrivals need quarters, as will the new First Wizard.

"I don't mean to sound callous, but if you were to become our representative you would be traveling, and wouldn't need the space. So, a side benefit of you taking up such a mission would be that the quarters belonging to the First Wizard would once again be free. We don't want to push you from your home, but the new First Wizard will need a place to work and meet with his wizards, as Baraccus did."

Magda bowed her head. "I understand, Elder. No need to feel you are pushing me from my home. My home, the home I have come to love, is the Keep and the city of Aydindril. It is the people here I have come to love, not the walls. I will of course vacate the First Wizard's quarters.

You are right that the new man will need the apartments."

The elder brightened with a brief, relieved smile. For some reason it appeared that he thought it would have been more difficult. The council seemed to have formed an opinion of her that was based to some extent on accusations about her.

"Thank you for understanding, Magda. So you will take the appointment, then?"

Magda had no intention of taking such an appointment and leaving the Keep. There was something going on, something that threatened the Keep, threatened their very existence. She seemed to be the only one who understood that the threat was real. She was not going to abandon her search for answers just to make life convenient for the council.

That search for answers was a mission that Baraccus himself had given her, both as her husband and as First Wizard.

At the same time, she didn't want to get into a battle with these men. That would only back them into a corner and make her search for answers all the more difficult.

"I appreciate the generous offer, Elder Cadell. I will certainly give it my most earnest consideration. But in the meantime, I would like to give over the First Wizard's apartments. I have modest needs and will have no trouble finding a place. I know that there is space under the southern ramparts."

The elder blinked. He was left momentarily speechless. The quarters under the southern ramparts were the least desirable in the Keep, so there was always room there. As much trouble as she was to them, even the council would think that such quarters were beneath the widow of the First Wizard. It reflected poorly on them that they would force her out of her apartments to live beneath the southern ramparts.

Magda didn't really care where she slept. She was only concerned with finding answers before they were all killed the way she was nearly killed by a dream walker, or as Isidore had been killed by that walking nightmare.

Before Elder Cadell could say anything, she asked, "Have you selected the man to become First Wizard, then?"

Sadler leaned back in his chair. Hambrook and Clay shared a look. Weston and Guymer showed no reaction to the question.

Elder Cadell cleared his throat. "We have had discussions and have someone in mind." He smoothed his bushy brow. "We will reveal our choice at the proper time and in the proper manner."

In other words, he wasn't about to tell Magda what they had decided. She hoped it was one of the men Baraccus had worked closely with. There were good men among them.

"Of course, Elder Cadell. I am sure that the council will choose wisely. They certainly did the last time."

With the war going badly, they needed someone strong. Someone like Baraccus. Once the man was selected, she had important information to convey to him.

He would need to know what she knew, what she had dared tell no one.

It seemed to her like Baraccus was already just a figure in their history, lost to the advance of time.

The world was moving on. It was up to her to convey knowledge from that past history.

But only to the right person.

Magda dipped a quick bow and departed before they could insist that she accept the post they wanted her to take.

As she was pushing closed one of the heavy double oak doors to the council's private chambers, she heard footsteps. Turning, she saw Prosecutor Lothain and a dozen men of his personal guard. Magda stepped to the side to make way for them.

"Lady Searus," Lothain said with a smile. "I hear that you have been at the center of yet more trouble."

"Shouldn't you be down in the lower portions of the Keep searching for a killer to prosecute?"

The menacing smile remained in place. "I don't believe that the threat to our security is confined to the lower portions of the Keep. I think dangers to our cause are closer than most people think."

She knew what he was getting at, but she didn't want to be distracted by Lothain any more than she had wished to be drawn into arguing with certain members of the council. She had to get back to her search.

"I'm afraid that you would know about such threats better than I would. If you will excuse me, I have things to do."

His smile returned. "Such as finding new quarters?"

"As a matter of fact, yes."

"Rather sad that with a new First Wizard soon to be named you have to give up such luxurious apartments."

Magda wondered how he seemed to already know all about it.

"It's not sad at all. It is just a place to sleep. I am joyous that a new First Wizard will soon be named. The people I care about are what really matter to me, not an apartment."

"And which people are they, Lady Searus, that you really care about?"

"The innocent people of the New World who are being slaughtered in the name of a cause."

Before he could say anything else, Magda started

away. He caught her arm, stopping her. His grip was hurting her arm but she didn't give him the satisfaction of showing it.

"No need to be in a hurry to move your things, Lady Searus. I may be able to help you out with an accommodation so that you can remain where you are comfortable."

Magda's only answer was a brief, noncommittal smile before she pulled her arm away and marched off. She kept her eyes straight ahead and didn't slow for the wall of men in green tunics blocking her way. The prosecutor's big personal guards stepped back at the last moment and just enough to let her pass.

She couldn't imagine what Lothain was talking about and she wasn't particularly interested in coaxing it out of the man. She was sure that was what he had wanted her to do. When she glanced back she saw him vanishing into the council chambers.

Magda wondered what business Lothain had with the council that he would be seeing them in a private session.

It was apparent to Magda that the city of Aydindril, though as busy and active as ever, was on edge. Concern weighed on every face. People in small groups eyed passing strangers as they talked in low, worried tones.

Every day brought new stories of enemy advances, of bloody battles, of the numbers of men lost, of cities that had fallen, of innocent civilians being slaughtered by the approaching forces of Emperor Sulachan. She knew that some of the stories were nothing more than rumors and gossip. She also knew that the truth was far more gruesome than most people knew.

Glancing up between spaces in the tightly packed, two-story buildings as she made her way down the crowded cobblestone street, Magda could see glimpses of the lush forests covering the foothills and lower sweep of the nearest mountain. Higher up, the pines and spruce thinned as they reached granite ledges at the base of sheer cliffs. Beyond a few passing wisps of clouds and flocks of birds that lived in the stone face of the mountain, the massive cliffs supported dark, soaring stone walls of the Keep. Above the walls, even at this distance, she could see ramparts, bastions, lofty spires, and towers joined by high bridges.

For as long back as Magda could remember, the dark shape of the Keep had loomed over the city, at once protector and threat, the magic it embodied both guardian and target.

Magda had always had mixed feelings about living in the Keep. She loved the vibrancy of Aydindril, so with a soon-to-be-appointed new First Wizard needing the apartments, she had given thought to moving back down to the city. But she couldn't do that until she found out what was behind Baraccus's death and the other things that were happening at the Keep.

While no one seemed to believe her, Magda was sure that everyone at the Keep was in danger. She couldn't leave the Keep until she knew that the people living there were safe. While people were focused on the distant war, no one but her seemed aware that the enemy was already closer than anyone thought.

Magda knew the enemy was already slipping in among them.

Even as Aydindril sweltered in the summer heat, there was talk that by winter the enemy troops might be within striking distance of the city. Magda feared to consider how devastating such a strike would be to the place where she'd grown up. If the city was overrun, that would also mean a siege of the Keep. The Keep could withstand a siege for a long time, but not forever.

Besides, it was impossible to win a war defensively. The forces from the Old World had made it clear that there would be no mercy. While some of Sulachan's forces held the Keep under siege, others would lay waste to the New World. When the Keep finally fell, they would make examples of every last person.

That was what they did to every village, town, and city in their path. Either people surrendered, or they were made to suffer for refusing.

Simply hiding behind walls and iron doors would not eliminate the threat. Sooner or later even the Keep's walls would fall. Evil had to be defeated or it would only grow stronger.

How they were going to destroy this evil, Magda didn't know. All she knew for sure was that it was not only getting closer every day, it was already among them. She had felt the painful presence of the dream walker. She had seen the monster that had come out of the dark and killed Isidore. Those were not random events; they were connected. Magda had to find the truth behind those connections.

Making her way past crowds on the streets was at times like trying to move upriver. The peddlers shouting out the many benefits of their goods stood like rocks in that river as streams of people continually flowed around them.

Some of the street merchants tended carts with salted meats and fish, fresh vegetables, or a variety of ready-made goods. Other vendors carried trays stacked high with long loaves of bread. There were also hawkers draped with jangling strings of amulets prowling the crowds as they shouted out singsong warnings of curses and plagues. They attracted flocks of bouncing children wanting to hear about curses of magic as parents rushed in and pulled them away.

Magda sometimes crossed the street to avoid particularly aggressive hawkers she saw grabbing the arms of passing women, insisting that they listen to why they needed the protection of a magic charm. Potential customers were warned that when the enemy got closer, the supply of charms and talismans would all be gone and then it would be too late to get what was needed. Some people gave in to the warning or bought the least expensive of the amulets simply to free themselves from the hawker.

Warm as it was, as she passed throngs of people Magda, like many women, kept the hood of her light cloak pulled up. People down in the city weren't as likely to recognize her as were people up in the Keep, but she had been the wife of the First Wizard and as such it often surprised her how many people she'd never met recognized her.

With time working against her, she couldn't afford delays. As much as she would like to, she couldn't stop to give guidance to people on the oath to avoid the dream walkers, or convey news from up in the Keep. There were also those who hated Baraccus and might want to give her a piece of their mind, or worse.

Most people understood that surrender was suicide at best, slavery at worst. But not everyone could recognize the face of evil when it presented itself in the guise of salvation. She could hardly defend herself if a mob wanted to stone her because her husband had decided that they would go to war rather than surrender.

Panicked people didn't listen to reason and didn't want to hear the truth. Sympathizers frequently stirred up resentment against the authority of military officers, the council, and even the First Wizard for being unwilling to accept the peace that the emperor had offered. Peace, these people said, was as simple as letting Emperor Sulachan rule instead of the council. They wanted to believe, and so they did, that the rule of either was the same difference in their lives.

If other people wouldn't accept the wisdom of their notion of "peace," the advocates were all too willing to use violence to make their point. It struck Magda as ironic that those who professed to want peace the most were quickest to use bloodshed to try to get their way.

Magda pulled her cowl farther forward as a knot of people moved past her. Unshaven men leered at her shape, even though they could see little of it under the cloak. They knew only that she was a woman, and therefore must be worthy of ogling. When a passing group of women happened to get a glimpse inside her cowl, Magda's short hair told them that she was a nobody. They didn't give her a second look as they went on about their own business.

At a cross street, Magda peered around the corner of a two-story brick building that housed a tailor. On the other side of the street was an inn with a blue pig painted on the sign hanging over the door. The narrow street around the corner followed rolling, uneven ground. Despite how confining and confusing this part of the city of Aydindril was, she knew that this was the turn she needed to take.

Magda had searched under the southern rampart but had learned that he was no longer living there. As much as she needed to find him, she hadn't wanted to bring undue attention to herself by asking too many questions. Those kind of questions would sooner or later get noticed.

Isidore's murder had made Magda more than a little cautious. She had nearly been a victim, too. A dream walker was no longer in Magda's mind, but she had no way of knowing if one might be in the mind of any person she talked to. A dream walker could no longer follow her through her own eyes, but she didn't want them following her through the eyes of others.

So, she had gone to Tilly. Tilly had been horror-stricken over the death of Isidore. At first she blamed herself, believing that if she hadn't shown Magda the way, then maybe none of it would have happened.

Magda had convinced the woman that she was wrong. They were fighting evil, and the evil was not Tilly's doing. Magda had told her that Isidore herself said that they were warriors in this war. Evil would not rest. It had to be fought.

Tilly had been silent for a moment and then asked if she, too, was a warrior in this war. Magda told her that indeed she was, and in fact she had been more help than any of the council had been. Magda said that since no one else would help her find Isidore's killer, she intended to do it herself, and to that end she again needed Tilly's help.

It had taken a few days, but Tilly had discovered that the man whose help Magda sought was nowhere in the Keep. After several more days of discreet inquiry she had finally been able to learn where he lived. Magda was surprised that he would have moved out of the Keep and down into Aydindril, and frustrated that it had taken so long to find where he now lived. She knew that time to act was slipping away.

After glancing around to make sure that she wasn't being followed, Magda turned up the quiet street. There were no shops, only houses, mostly multi-family structures. She could see that trees beyond the buildings shaded an alley. The houses and two-story dwellings were tightly packed together and in some places connected with common walls. Out back people planted gardens and laundry hung on lines. She could hear chickens and a hog or two. A crudely painted sign on one gate said eggs for sale.

After following the street over several rises, she came to the place that was set back beside a two story stone building. There was a forked plum tree in the front of the little porch. At the side of the small place she could see down the narrow passageway between the buildings that the back was heavily shaded by oaks. She also saw the corner of a shed along with wood scraps and odd bits of metal neatly laid out beside it.

On the porch, in under a low overhang, Magda tucked her small bundle under an arm and knocked firmly on the simple plank door. After a moment, she heard someone coming through the house from the back. He stopped on the other side of the door.

"What is it?" he asked without opening the door.

"Are you Wizard Merritt?"

"I'm sorry but I can't see anyone right now," he said from the other side.

"This is important."

"I told you, I can't see anyone now. I'm busy working. Please be on your way."

She could hear the footsteps heading away from the door toward the back of the house.

"P lease, I need to see you," Magda called to the door. "I come with news of Isidore."

She heard his distant footsteps pause.

As she waited in silence, Magda wasn't sure if he would come back and open the door or not. She wiped away a bead of sweat trickling down her temple as she idly watched a lacewing hunting for aphids on the lush green leaves and stems of a vine climbing one of the posts holding up the overhanging roof of the porch. At last she heard his footsteps returning.

The door opened enough that Magda could see that he was as imposing a figure as Isidore had said. After all Magda had heard about him—from Baraccus, from the men down in the Keep, from wizards she knew, and from Isidore—she found it was a somewhat strange feeling to finally see him in the flesh. After all the things said about him, he wasn't exactly what she had pictured.

He was somehow more.

He was tall, and without a shirt it was plain to see that he was handsomely built. He was a good deal younger than Baraccus. In fact, he didn't look much older than her—maybe a couple of years at most.

Magda had seen hundreds of wizards. The Keep was

full of them. Merritt, especially without a shirt, didn't look at all like her idea of what a wizard looked like.

His skin glistened with sweat and grimy smudges. There were a few streaks of soot on his face behind stray, wavy locks of light brown hair that was struck through with a lighter, sun-bleached, blondish brown. Disheveled as it was, it added to his rugged looks.

Somehow, impossibly, the sweat and the soot made him look all the better.

But it was his hazel eyes cast with a shade of green that caught her breath. It felt as if he was looking right into her soul, weighing it for worth. At the same time, she felt that she could see in his eyes that he was open about who he was, without pretense or deception.

Though they contained the same basic trait, the eyes of the gifted tended to appear quite different to her. In some people, such as warriors, the glimmer of the gift that she saw had a menacing aspect to it. In healers it had a softer, more gentle appearance. The aspect of the gift in Baraccus's eyes had been passionately wise, resolute, formidable.

Just as Isidore had said, Magda, too, could see both sincerity and competence in Merritt's eyes.

Yet unlike Isidore, Magda could also see the gift.

In Merritt's eyes, the gift was different from anything she had seen in her life. It was a look that was at once breathtaking and dangerous, but at the same time softened with an undertone of warmth. Under his intent gaze, she had to remind herself to let her breath out.

On second consideration, she decided he did indeed look to her very much like a wizard.

"What news have you of Isidore?"

His voice matched the look of him perfectly. It almost felt as if her whole being vibrated in harmony with the deep, clear tone of it. Magda swallowed and forced herself to speak.

"Before I can say anything else, I must ask you to swear an oath."

His brow drew down. "An oath?"

"That's right. I need you to first swear an oath of loyalty to Lord Rahl, which will protect your mind from dream walkers. Only in that way can I know that we are talking in confidence."

He did the oddest thing, then.

He smiled.

It was an easy, warm smile that betrayed a shade of private amusement.

"A bold, if not highly strange request from such a lovely stranger at my door. We haven't even been properly introduced."

Magda pushed the cowl back off her head. "I am Magda Searus."

The smile vanished in a heartbeat. "Magda Searus?" His face turned red. "Wife of First Wizard Baraccus? That Magda Searus?"

"Yes."

The frown revisited his expression. "I was there, among all the people at the ceremony the day your husband's remains were purified in the funeral pyre. I saw you there that day, in the distance. You had long hair."

"Well, with Baraccus dead, the council wanted it cut off. They were quite insistent about letting the world know that without Baraccus I am a nobody. Elder Cadell, personally, saw to cutting it."

He dipped his head respectfully. "I'm sorry about the loss of your husband, Lady Searus. Baraccus was a truly great man."

"Thank you."

He stared into her eyes a long moment, head still

bowed, then remembered himself and straightened. "Please," he said as his face reddened again, "wait there a moment, will you?"

He abruptly shut the door.

Magda realized, then, what else was different about him from most men. The entire time he had been in the doorway, he had looked into her eyes, his gaze wandering no farther than to her hair. The gazes of most men invariably wandered elsewhere. Merritt hadn't done that, even though the black dress she was wearing under her light cloak did tend to reveal her shape to advantage.

Magda heard him stumble over something inside that then rolled across the floorboards. There was a thud as something heavy hit the floor. Then, it sounded like a chair fell over. A few more things clattered when they fell. It went silent inside the house for a time.

Magda glanced up and down the street to see if anyone else was hearing all the noise or paying attention to the visitor at his door. She saw a woman across the narrow street and up a ways come out and shake a rug. She folded it over an arm and went back in without noticing Magda in the shadows of the porch. Through small gaps in a screening lilac bush, Magda could see a few people in the distance talking, but they were too far away to be able to see her standing behind the greenery.

The door finally opened wide. Merritt was still tucking in a dark shirt. The long, wavy locks of his light brown hair had been hastily brushed back, revealing that his face had been hurriedly wiped clean.

"Sorry to make you stand out there, Lady Searus." His face flushed again. "I'm afraid that I was out back working on a few things and—" He paused, apparently afraid that he was beginning to ramble. He made himself start over as he lifted a hand out in invitation. "Please, won't you come in?"

As Magda stepped through the doorway, she could see an overturned chair and a small statue lying on its side. The place was small, with the strangest things stacked everywhere. Strange metal objects, not unlike the things she had seen Baraccus make, sat all around the room, making it difficult to tell what she had heard fall to the floor and what had already been there.

As odd as everything was, there was a strange kind of order to it all. Books stood in tall columns in places at the side of the room. A wicker couch also held books, but they were lying open and piled one atop another, as if to keep a place marked. A variety of small tables held mounds of scrolls between candles, bottles, boxes, and bones.

A small, tightly rolled scroll sticking out of a shelf had a variety of small clay figures collected all around the end of it. As far as she could tell, they were all floating around the end of the scroll with nothing holding them up. It was an inexplicable and disorienting sight.

There were also profoundly beautiful statues standing in random places around the room, not as if they had been placed to be admired, but simply, it appeared, put wherever there had been an empty spot at the time. There was a soldier about to unsheathe a sword carved from a gray stone, there were several smaller statues of men in robes carved from pale butternut wood, and, carved from pure white marble, there were several statues of the most graceful women Magda had ever seen.

Draped over the table beyond the overturned chair was a large square of red velvet. The tabletop was the only place in the entire room that wasn't cluttered. A single gleaming sword sat in the middle on a raised portion of the red velvet.

Magda noticed an ornate gold and silver scabbard attached to a baldric lying on the floor. The scabbard was so striking that it could only belong with the sword.

Merritt righted the chair, then hung the baldric and its scabbard over the back before he hurriedly removed books from the wicker couch. "Sorry for the mess. I don't ordinarily live in such clutter. It's just that this place isn't as roomy as my place at the Keep. Please, Lady Searus, won't you have a seat?" He looked around. "Tea. I should make tea."

"No, none for me, thank you," she said as she made her way to the wicker couch.

He looked relieved. Magda wondered why he no longer lived at the Keep, but didn't ask; she had more important matters to get to first. She waited until he turned around to her again.

"I need to talk with you, Wizard Merritt."

"So talk." He gestured to the couch. "What about Isidore?"

Magda wasn't ready to sit. "What about the oath?"

He put both hands in his back pocket as his posture relaxed a little. He grinned boyishly. "You mean the devotion to the Lord Rahl? Master Rahl guide us. Master Rahl teach us. Master Rahl protect us. That oath?"

"Yes. You're familiar with its purpose, then?"

He was smiling as if it was a private joke. Magda didn't think it was funny. She could feel her own face heating to red.

"Actually, you see, Alric is an acquaintance of mine."

"You know, then, that he's a good man, and that he means the devotion to protect us from dream walkers?"

He still had a hint of a crooked smile as he kept her locked in his gaze. "Yes. Their side creates a weapon, we have to work to counter it. That's why I helped him in creating the power contained within its bond."

Magda blinked in surprise. "Are you saying that you helped him create the magic that protects people from the dream walkers? That power? You helped him with that?"

Merritt nodded. "To a certain small extent. I don't know exactly how he crafted magic that could do such a thing, but I do know that he's as smart as he is determined. He was stuck at a point that was keeping the bond from taking hold and igniting in others, at their end. It worked for him, but he wanted it to work to protect other people as well, and it wouldn't go to root in them, I guess you could say. He knew that I happen to be familiar with unusual calculations for spell couplings, so he asked for my help."

Magda tilted her head toward him. "You helped Alric Rahl create the magic of the bond."

He nodded again, looking quite earnest. "I provided the authentication routines for the verification web, from inside of it, in order to complete the validation process. That was what initiated the unification of the spell components he was trying to combine so that the bond would activate in the proper sequence.

"Once it ignited, locking down the series reductions, I was the first one to speak the devotion. When I did, I did it from inside the completed web. I wanted to test it first to ensure that it wouldn't inadvertently harm people when they gave the devotion to invoke the bond."

Magda couldn't help staring openly at him. She touched her fingers to her forehead, trying to take it all in. "You mean that you were the one who made it work?"

He shrugged one shoulder. "No, not really. Alric did most of the work. He came to me because he knew that I would be able to understand what he was trying to do. There aren't many people who understand such complex combination routines well enough to discuss it with him. He thought I might be able to see why the verification web wasn't functioning exactly the way he intended and hoped that I would know what was needed."

"So it wouldn't have worked without what you did," she said.

"Alric Rahl created something masterful. I guess you could say that I just added a little seasoning to his stew."

"Then you are bonded to him?" Magda asked. "You are protected from the dream walkers?"

His smiled vanished. "Oh yes, I am protected. He tested me with the dream walker he held captive. That's how Alric knew that the bond he created finally worked in others. I was the first one protected by the bond. So, you see, there is no chance that a dream walker is hiding in the shadows of my mind, listening and watching, if that's what you're worried about.

"Now, what is it you wanted to tell me about my friend Isidore?"

Magda's heart sank.

"I'm afraid that I got Isidore killed."

CHAPTER
45

Merritt's face took on the look of chiseled stone, much like his statues. The aspect of the gift she saw in his eyes had a decidedly dangerous cast to it.

"What do you mean, you got Isidore killed?"

In that calm yet emotionally charged question, she could see that this was a man with more than a simple temper. It was a refined sort of bottled fury that had the potential to be devastatingly violent, and yet at the same time he was also a man able to control it.

That meant that he could focus it.

"It takes a bit of explanation."

While at first a bit shy, once the subject became somber he turned all business.

"So explain."

Magda rearranged the bundle under her arm as she finally sat on the wicker couch. It gave her the excuse to look away from his intense expression.

"I was at first in shock over my husband's death," she began. "I couldn't understand why he would take his own life, couldn't understand why he would leave me like that, leave all of us. People said that his journey to the Temple of the Winds in the world of the dead must have crushed his spirit and sapped his will to live.

"Everyone accepted that story. They believed it was a straightforward suicide. And while it may have made grim sense to them, it didn't make sense to me. As I thought about it, I kept coming back to the core truth that Baraccus was not the kind of man to be so despondent that he would kill himself.

"Besides, I was there when he came back from the Temple of the Winds, and while there was no doubt that he was troubled and distracted, I wouldn't characterize him as depressed.

"He had too much to live for, too many things that mattered to him, too many people he cared about, too much important work yet unfinished. He wouldn't kill himself to end any kind of personal despair. He cared about us all too much to do such a thing. With all of the New World in danger he had every reason to want to fight for us."

"Then why would he do it?" Merritt asked as he went to the table to gaze down at the sword.

"That's what I'm trying to find out. Baraccus knew that I wouldn't believe that he had simply wanted to end his life. He was counting on me to realize that something about it didn't make sense.

"He knew that I would recognize that he would only have done such a thing if it was to somehow protect all of us. That's the way he was. That was his mission in life. That was why he was First Wizard. He was a war wizard, after all. He took that mission very seriously.

"War wizards don't give up. They find a way around any obstacle, even if that way results in their own death. He called the way of a war wizard the dance with death.

"Shortly after his death, I found a note he'd left for me, telling me to seek truth. Somehow, for some reason, he couldn't do that himself. Baraccus, not merely as my husband, but as First Wizard, charged me with finding truth.

"This is about something bigger than Baraccus. It involves all our lives. Even before I found the note, I knew that I had to find answers, not only for Baraccus, not only for myself, but because all our lives are at stake. For reasons I can't yet fathom, he left the task to me.

"His note said, 'Your destiny is to find truth.'"

Merritt, standing over the table, looking down at the sword as he listened, turned with a frown. "You mean the note said, 'Your destiny is to find *the* truth.'"

Magda's brow furrowed as she tried to recollect the exact words. She didn't have the note with her. She had hidden it back at the Keep in a secret compartment in his workbench.

She didn't know why the exact wording mattered to Merritt. It seemed an insignificant point. She knew, though, that wizards saw the world differently. Things that might seem insignificant to anyone else were often centrally important to them.

"Now that you mention it, I guess I can't recall, exactly. I suppose that what you say makes more sense. Find the truth."

Merritt nodded as he turned his broad back to her once more. "What happened then?"

"Not long after I found that note, the same day in fact, Lord Rahl was waiting to see me. As I talked to him, a dream walker that had apparently been hiding in my mind all along nearly killed me before I could start looking for answers. In a way, that was the beginning of an answer.

"I was able to give the devotion to Lord Rahl in time to protect myself. But why would a dream walker be hiding in my mind in the first place? I'm not even gifted."

"You just said that you believe Baraccus left an important mission to you," Merritt said, "a mission that is somehow critical to all our survival."

"That's true," Magda said, "but the thing is, how would a dream walker have known that in the first place? Why would he have been hiding in my mind to begin with?"

"I see your point," he said as he clasped his hands behind his back while pacing off a few steps as he thought about it. "Maybe with Baraccus dead, the dream walker was simply trying to find out what you may have known about the First Wizard's business, his plans for fighting the war, weapons we're developing, things of that sort."

"I guess it makes sense," Magda said. "I don't know how it could be possible for me to be important to the future of our people, but Baraccus believed it. The dream walkers obviously had to have thought I was important enough to be worth watching in the first place, and then certainly after I found that note. Once I saw what it said, they would have seen it, too.

"But before that, why would they care about the thoughts of a nobody?"

"You aren't a nobody," Merritt said in a surprisingly compassionate voice as he looked over at her. "They may have cut your hair after Baraccus's death, but that doesn't change you into a nobody. You are still Magda Searus, the same as before, with the same abilities, the same potential, the same mind, the same capacity to think for yourself."

"I wasn't born noble or gifted. That makes me a nobody in the minds of most people in the Midlands."

Merritt stopped before the table and again stood gazing down at the gleaming sword lying on red velvet. "As long as their cutting your hair doesn't make you a nobody in your own mind then it doesn't make any difference what others think, now does it?"

Magda had to smile. "That's always been my attitude. It frequently gets me into trouble, though. Before I met Baraccus, people often told me that I didn't know my place. I've never much cared what most people thought about me, or what they thought my place should be. I always believed that I should think for myself and act accordingly. My status sometimes hinders me, but I don't ever let it guide me."

"Good." He turned away from the sword and folded his arms as he leaned back against the table to face her. "So what did you do next?"

"I talked to a number of the people who had been closest to Baraccus, trying to find clues. That got me nowhere.

"So I went to the spiritist hoping that her unique abilities could help. Isidore told me that she was only the spiritist's assistant and that the spiritist couldn't see me.

"I was desperate, so I told her that I believed Baraccus had sacrificed his life in order to protect all of us and I was hoping that the spiritist could reach out to him for answers. I told her that I thought something important had happened when Baraccus had gone to the Temple of the Winds in the world of the dead. I needed her to contact him there, in the underworld, since this time he wasn't coming back.

"I told her that all is not right in the Wizard's Keep, and that I believe the enemy is already here, among us. After all, how would a dream walker know about me from all the way down in the Old World? I told her that the council wouldn't believe me. I told her that if I was right, then the enemy would likely direct the dream walkers to the spiritist to prevent her from assisting the wizards in developing defenses.

"I finally got Isidore to admit that she was the spiritist. I convinced her that because of her importance, she was in great danger that the dream walkers would take her mind. That persuaded her to give the devotion to protect herself.

"After she did, she told me the story of the slaughter of the people of Grandengart and how she had learned that their spirits were not safely in the world of the dead, where they belonged. She told me, too, the story of how you had taken her eyes."

Magda gestured uncomfortably. "I couldn't understand how she could do such a terrible thing. I couldn't understand how she could . . . well, how she could let a wizard so fundamentally alter her, change her into something other than she had been born."

"If you think it's upsetting, imagine how I felt," Merritt said.

Magda looked up into his eyes. She had to look away from the shadow of pain she saw there.

"Through Isidore's story, I did come to realize how reluctant you were to do such a thing, and how determined she was to go through with it. While I of course felt sorry for what she was giving up, I also felt sorry for you, for the awful burden she placed on you.

"She was just starting to tell me that it wasn't so terrible, like I thought, and what a wonderful new vision you had given her. But before she could finish explaining and then contact the spirit world for me, we were attacked by some kind of monster and—"

Merritt lifted a hand to stop her story. "What do you mean, a monster?"

Magda shrugged. "It appeared to be a man, close to as big as you. He was impossibly strong. At first I thought that he had to be gifted and that he was using magic.

"When I stabbed him, though, he didn't bleed. When I got a good look at him, he looked like a dead man. He smelled like something dead, too."

Merritt's frown deepened the creases on his brow. "A dead man? What do you mean he looked like a dead man?"

"He was blackened, his flesh shriveled, and it even looked decayed and pulled apart in places. He looked like a corpse."

He folded his arms across his chest. "That does indeed sound like a dead man. But was it dark? Are you sure you saw him clearly enough?"

"It was pretty dark," Magda admitted. "But I still had a lantern. I got a good enough look.

"I stabbed him a number of times, hard and deep. The blade, deep as it went, didn't seem to harm him at all. Isidore used her powers as well, but that didn't stop him either. We tried. . . . We tried."

Magda swallowed and had to look down at the floor away from Wizard Merritt's gaze before she could go on. "He . . . he ripped Isidore apart. It all happened so fast. He killed her before we could stop him, before we had a chance to run.

"I realized later that a dream walker had to have been secretly lurking in her mind all along, listening. When I told her that I needed information from the spirit world, I never thought that a dream walker might already be there, in her mind. I had thought that I needed her to give the devotion in case a dream walker ever tried to take her. I should have realized that he might already be there.

"The dream walker had invaded my mind and spied on my thoughts without me being aware of him, but then he had failed to kill me because I was able to give the devotion and banish him from my mind in time.

"He must have then been spying on me and Isidore from the shadows of her mind, but he didn't want to spoil his second chance by trying what had failed before.

He wanted us both. So he didn't reveal himself, didn't try to kill her before she could give the devotion, as had happened with me.

"He instead let us believe we were safe. He probably slipped away, then, as she started to give the devotion. He probably wanted to lull us into feeling secure in order to make it easier for him to send the man who attacked us.

"I should have realized that he might already be there watching Isidore because she was important. I was just a lucky additional catch who happened along. I foolishly revealed too much before having her give the devotion.

"If I'd made Isidore give the devotion first, he would not have heard how important I thought she was to un-covering the answers Baraccus wanted me to find. He would not have realized that he needed to kill her before she could help me."

Against her will, the vivid memory of that awful slaughter returned to fill her mind's eye.

"That's why you asked me to give the oath before you would talk to me," he said, half to himself.

Magda nodded as she watched tears dripping onto the floor at her feet. "If I had thought it through, first, and had her give the devotion from the beginning, she would still be alive. She would have freed her mind from the dream walker before he overheard what I needed, and how much she mattered in my search for the truth."

"But a dream walker didn't kill her," Merritt said.

Magda swiped the tears from her cheeks. She knew how much Merritt meant to Isidore. She knew how re-luctant he had been to help the woman. Magda knew, too, that even though Merritt had taken Isidore's sight and altered her with magic, he had come to consider her a friend.

Magda sucked back a sob. She couldn't bring herself to look up at him.

"No, the dream walker didn't kill her. He must have gone to his contact in the Keep, and they sent that monster to slaughter her before she could have the chance to help me.

"It's my fault. If I hadn't gone to her she would still be alive. Or if I'd had the presence of mind to realize how deeply the Keep has been penetrated by dream walkers and traitors, and had her take the protection of the bond right at first, she would be alive.

"It's my fault she was murdered."

Merritt crossed the room and sat beside her. "I see now why you think you're to blame, but it wasn't your fault, Lady Searus. You didn't know that a dream walker was listening to the things you told Isidore."

Still, Magda couldn't look him in the eye. "No, but I should have realized that it was a strong likelihood. I should have thought it through. Had I taken the precaution of having her swear loyalty to Lord Rahl first—"

"It wouldn't have changed anything."

Magda finally looked up at him through her watery vision. "How can you know that?"

"The dream walkers know that you're looking for answers, right?"

Magda swallowed past the lump in her throat. "That's right."

"Then if they know that much, they would know that you would sooner or later go to see the spiritist to try to find those answers. After all, with Baraccus dead, the spiritist would be the next logical place for you to go looking for answers—answers, after all, that they want as well. In fact, they were already there in her mind, secretly listening in on our other activities of the Keep's business as they waited for you."

"So if I had first had her swear loyalty—"

"It would have made no difference. Don't you see? We have to assume that they already learned everything they could by covertly searching through her mind, so they were probably hiding in the hopes of hearing any new bit of information that you or anyone else might happen to divulge to Isidore. They were there to spy, to collect information. Information is the coin of war. When she agreed to swear the oath, they knew that was the end of them being able to learn any more from her, so they killed her before she could help you discover anything."

"But had I thought to—"

"Had you thought to have her give the oath right at first, they would have killed her just the same. Talking to her first only delayed her murder for a brief time while they eavesdropped.

"They would have wanted Isidore dead for reasons beyond you. She was seeking vital answers in her work, answers about what the emperor's wizards are up to. She was trying to discover why the enemy is harvesting the dead and what they're doing with both the bodies and the souls of those dead. The dream walkers wouldn't want her to help us understand what they're doing, or why the souls of those dead aren't with the spirits in the underworld, where they belong."

"Then they know everything Isidore knew," Magda said. Her gaze flicked around as if driven by her racing thoughts. "Everything Isidore knew has been compromised. They know it all."

Merritt nodded. "It would appear so, and because of that we have even bigger trouble than we realized. Because of what Isidore knew, and what she was working on, she was already marked. By talking to her, you likely actually delayed her death. The important thing now is to find out what she knew, and therefore what the dream walkers learned by spying on her mind."

Magda wiped a hand back across her face to dry her tears as she considered the implications. Her search for answers, for the truth, had just become even more critical.

"It sounds like you may be right that my failure to have her give the oath at first made no real difference in the outcome."

"You aren't to blame," he agreed. "You could just as easily say that it's my fault she's dead. After all, I'm the one who gave her abilities that made her a threat to the enemy. Had I refused, she very likely would still be alive, doing nothing more dangerous than helping to advise those in mourning about the souls of their dead relatives.

"But in the end, we can't live our lives by 'what if' and 'if only.' We can only do the best we can to the best of our ability based on what we know. That's why the truth is so important.

"Sometimes, as in Isidore's case, it's our skills that bring the attention of evil. Evil abhors those with ability. Emperor Sulachan wants to destroy just about everyone with the gift in order to make everyone helpless before him. He has already made significant strides in purging the Old World of magic. He can't afford to let it flourish here.

"In the process, he is willing to lay waste to the gift itself, strip it from mankind, all to be able to consolidate power for himself and rule through brute force. The gift—our abilities—stand in his way and mark us as targets."

"That's true," Magda said. "Baraccus told me once

that Sulachan would rather annihilate us than allow us to live in peace, because that would mean the risk that his people would want the same freedom to live their lives that we have."

Merritt nodded his agreement. "People like Isidore, like you, are not going to stand aside and do nothing as he slaughters people. Isidore was fighting for us all. She was well aware that she might lose her life in this struggle. In fact, I told her as much. That didn't stop her.

"She was a warrior in our cause. So are you, or you wouldn't be seeking the truth at the risk to your own life. If you were any less, you would give up your search and move away to somewhere safe. Yet you stay in the Keep, right in the midst of the danger."

"There is no safe place, or at least there soon won't be," Magda said. "Safety is only an illusion when evil is on the hunt. I can't stand by and watch. I have to act."

"We all can be only who we are, no more, no less," Merritt said.

"That's a beautiful sentiment." Magda smoothed a wrinkle in the skirt of her dress lying across her knee. "Is that why you gave in to her wishes when you could have said no?"

He stared off across the room for a long moment. "It was the path she chose. People have to live their own destiny."

That sounded very much like what Baraccus had said in his note to Magda about her following her own destiny.

Magda wasn't sure that Merritt was right, but it was an inviting notion to believe that she wasn't responsible for Isidore being murdered.

"Thank you, Wizard Merritt, for helping me see it another way. I can see now that there is more to finding safety than me simply having Isidore give an oath. I must admit, though, that I do feel a bit ashamed for allowing myself to feel better. It isn't easy to absolve one's self of guilt."

"Lady Searus, you were not the cause of her death. Evil likes to shift guilt to the victims. Don't you let them."

Magda nodded as she hooked some of her hair back behind an ear. "Please, I would feel better if you would call me Magda."

His smile added a warmth that made his face all the more agreeable. "And I am just Merritt."

Magda returned the smile, but it quickly faded.

"I'm afraid that I must ask some questions, Merritt, that you will not like me asking, but I need answers if I'm to get at the truth."

He leaned back a little. "Really? And what do you need to know about?"

Why have you moved away from the Keep?"

He stood and strolled to the table with the sword. "I wanted to be alone to work in peace," he said with his back to her. "I find the Keep to be . . . a distracting place."

"Really? From the quantity and quality of what I can see in this room alone, to say nothing of what Isidore told me, I'd say you are a man of great focus and intensity. I think that you must have had more reason than that."

He glanced back over his shoulder. "Well, besides that, it isn't safe there."

"I see. And why not?"

"You said yourself that the dead walk the dark passages of the Keep."

"And you knew that before I told you about Isidore, did you?"

Magda wondered why he'd really left the Keep. It didn't make sense to her that a wizard that Baraccus thought so highly of would leave what must have been important work at the Keep, where he would have been surrounded by a wealth of resources, everything from books, to tools, to an abundance of reference items invested with magic, as well as being able to draw on older, more experienced wizards for guidance.

Besides that, if it was a matter of safety, there were places at the Keep protected by guards as well as shields. She had seen no indications that his little home had any such shields to protect him as he worked.

But even so, that was really only a side issue. She was trying to find a way to ease into her relevant questions. He seemed to sense as much. He turned around, fixed her with a serious look, and again folded his muscular arms.

"Why don't you tell me what it is that you really want to know, Magda?"

She lifted her chin. "All right, then." She hated repeating hurtful words, but she didn't know how else to get at the underlying truth without airing the charges so that he could at least have the chance to give his side.

"I hear it told that you are responsible for getting a number of wizards killed—good men who were important to our war effort. I've also heard it said that besides those deaths being on your hands, you have abandoned the men you led and refuse to help with important work for our defense. Some even say that you're a traitor. Is any of that true?"

He stared down at her a moment. She had thought that the gift in his eyes might take on a dangerous appearance. Oddly enough, it didn't. His expression was a strangely unreadable mask. In a way, that was worse because it hid his inner feelings. She felt like a traitor herself for asking him to answer such inflammatory charges, but too much was at stake and the charges were too serious for her to ignore.

"As long as we're airing what 'people say,' " he finally said in a chillingly calm voice, "I hear it told that you and Lord Rahl put on quite the show before the council to make it appear that dream walkers are in the Keep and invading people's minds, all so that the two of you could frighten people into swearing loyalty to Lord Rahl."

"But you know Alric Rahl." Magda could feel her face going red. "You know why he created the oath."

"Maybe I don't know him as well as I thought I did. What with everything else I'm beginning to hear, what am I to believe? People say that according to no less an authority than Head Prosecutor Lothain, Baraccus had secret meetings with people who might very well be enemy agents. The prosecutor has said publicly that he suspects that Baraccus might have been part of a plot, and that he may have convinced you to go along with the scheme."

Merritt clasped his hands behind his back as he paced before her, going on without pause.

"Worse, many people both up in the Keep and down here in the city of Aydindril wonder openly if Baraccus is responsible for the war going so badly. They wonder if he wrongly took us into war in the first place and lied about the reasons. They say that if he really had our best interest at heart, we wouldn't be losing the war. They say that Baraccus must have finally committed suicide because of his sense of guilt over dooming his own people."

Magda shot to her feet. "But Baraccus didn't take us into war. We were invaded!"

Merritt shrugged. "People say otherwise. They say we weren't invaded at all, that our side started it. They say that you, Lord Rahl, and Baraccus plotted all along to start a war and use it as an excuse so that Lord Rahl could seize rule of the Midlands and take it over as part of D'Hara."

"But you know that the dream walkers—"

"Yes, yes, I know that dream walkers are real, but am

I to believe the preposterous story that they are already here, on the loose in the Keep, just because you say they are, when there is no proof except your own self-serving stories of how they attacked you and sent monsters to kill Isidore when you were alone with her? Am I to discount the credible charges against you and Baraccus brought by no less an authority than our eminent prosecutor and some members of the council, all saying that your wild stories of plots against our people and traitors in our midst are really meant to distract people from your own guilt? How can I be expected to disregard such serious accusations?"

He opened his arms before her. "So you tell me. Are you a traitor to the Midlands, as so many people say?"

Magda swallowed. She was sure that her face was bright red.

"For not living up at the Keep any longer, you certainly seem to have heard some of the ugliest gossip."

He arched an eyebrow in a way that would have made her back up a step if the couch hadn't been at her heels.

"Gossip? Not merely gossip, but the suspicions of even high officials. People say that since the charges are so serious there must be something to them. So, you tell me, Magda. Are they true? I need to know if I'm talking to a traitor. I think I have a right to know before I answer any of your questions."

Her hands fisted as she glared at him. "None of it is true. It's all lies. Hateful, despicable lies." Her gaze fell away. "But I admit that I have no way of revealing the truth to you. I wish I did, but I don't."

He did the oddest thing, then. He smiled. "And I would wish for a way to reveal the truth to you as well. But the truth can seem awfully small and insignificant when compared to a mountain of lies."

Magda was angry. She hated to hear such terrible

things said about Baraccus. She knew that some people believed those very lies while the truth was that he had given his life to protect the people of the Midlands. She didn't know why, yet, but she knew that was why Baraccus had died.

Merritt spread his hands. "Do the accusations make Baraccus guilty? Make you guilty?"

"No."

"Ah, but you worry that similar accusations make me guilty. You worry that, because the accusations are so serious, they must be true."

"I see your point." She looked away from his eyes as she wiped a tear from her cheek. "I'm sorry, Merritt, for being so unfair. I'm sorry to come to you out of the blue, without invitation, and dare to question you about things I've heard.

"But this is about our very survival. If I make a mistake, and trust the wrong person, we could all pay with our lives."

"At least you had the courtesy to come and ask me for the truth instead of simply accepting the lies." Sadness haunted his smile. "It's ironic that so much of my life's work has been devoted to being able to find a way to ensure that we know the truth when it's important enough, when lives are at stake, and now lies are used against me and that work."

"I see what you mean," Magda said, "I really do. I feel like I need to prove my innocence to you, and at the same time I feel helpless because I can't."

His smile was reassuring. "Baraccus was quite a remarkable man and no fool. I've always thought that there had to be a good reason why he considered you worthy to stand beside him. Baraccus believed in you. That says a great deal to me."

Magda felt conflicted. She didn't want to ask him

about the things she'd heard, didn't want to give the accusations credibility, but at the same time she needed to put the issues to rest and so far they hadn't been.

"I can tell by the look on your face how troubled you are. You don't know me, so it's understandable that you don't know what to believe. Why don't you go ahead and ask the things you need to know about."

Magda nodded as she took a seat once more, hoping that by sitting it might take some of the hostility out of her question.

"I've heard accusations from wizards who were there that men died because you had abandoned your duty to them. I need to know why they think you are responsible for the deaths. I need to know if you are the kind of man who would walk away and let other men die. I realize that it isn't fair of me to repeat such charges from others, or to expect you to answer them. You certainly don't owe me the truth."

She looked up into his eyes. "But please, Merritt, I'm trying to find answers to what is really going on. I believe that the Keep, all of our lives, are in grave danger. I need to find out what is really going on before it's too late. Would you please not take offense at my asking these questions and simply tell me the truth?"

"And how will I prove to you that I'm telling you the truth?"

She smiled a bit. "As it so happens, the truth has always mattered a great deal to me. Baraccus often said that I was the bane of liars. I'd like to think that I'm a person who can recognize the truth when it's told to me, or detect a lie, and often I can, but I guess that in the end I have no real way of knowing truth from lies.

"I'd still like to hear your side of it."

CHAPTER
48

Merritt nodded as he pulled a footstool closer and sat facing her on the wicker couch.

"There are people who want things," he said, "but they aren't willing to listen to the truth about the things they want."

"That's true enough in a general sense, but what does it have to do with people saying that men died because of you?"

"If you want to know the truth, then it takes some explaining so that you can understand. Bear with me?"

Magda conceded with a nod for him to go on.

"There are those at the Keep who want a specific kind of magic invested in an object. They want me to do it."

Magda glanced around the room at all the strange objects lying about everywhere. There were things of every size and shape. Some were recognizable, some weren't. Some of the objects looked innocent enough, while others looked like they would snap shut and take off a finger if she were to touch them.

"What kind of object?"

He rubbed his palms on his knees as he searched for words. "Well, it's a kind of key to unlocking repositories of great power."

"A key? These people want you to make a key?"

Merritt waved a hand as if to minimize the impression. "I use the word 'key' loosely. It's only a key in the sense that it works to unlock the power. I'm trying to make it as simple as possible."

"Sorry I'm so dense."

His face turned red. "I didn't mean it to sound that way. It came out wrong. It's just that it can get awfully complicated to explain."

"So help me understand so that I can know the truth."

He took a deep breath before going on. "You see, it's not the specific key—the object itself—that really matters. The key, the object portion of it, could actually be a lot of different things. What matters is the specific magic invested in that object. The magic is what makes it a key that functions to unlock the power."

She didn't think that sounded all that complicated.

He was choosing his words carefully. It wasn't uncommon for wizards not to want to reveal details. Baraccus had sometimes done the same thing, even with her.

It could also be that Merritt was being evasive for some reason. After all, she had asked about men who died because of him. At least, that was what she'd heard. It could be hearsay. On the other hand, he might be trying to shift blame.

Magda decided to let him explain it in his own way and to be open-minded about what she heard.

"I've worked on this key, as it were, for years. It's a project that has long been close to my heart. These people, who have only recently come to be aware of the existence of this power, believe that it's very important that I go forward and complete the key, but for reasons of their own.

"The thing is, I can't complete the key because it's impossible to complete. More importantly, though, it's un-necessary."

Magda couldn't let that go. "If it's the key to opening great power, why is it unnecessary? Especially now, when we're at war? Couldn't this power maybe help us?"

"No, it can't."

"How can you be certain?"

"Because," he said, "I learned that the chests—"

"Chests?"

"Yes, the chests are the repositories of this power that these people want to be able to unlock. It's not actually the chests that the key unlocks, but the power contained within them. Like I said, I'm trying to make something extremely complex understandable."

Magda nodded for him to go on, but her mind was already reeling with worries. She reminded herself not to jump to conclusions.

"Anyway," he said, "I learned that the chests were taken away to the Temple of the Winds by the Temple team. I don't know if they were supposed to be taken there or not, but the simple fact remains that they were. Some on the team did say that they wanted to protect mankind from the tyranny of magic. Perhaps that's what they meant and why they did it. In any event, they're safe there, sealed away out of reach in the underworld."

Magda's heart felt like it skipped a beat. Her skin went icy cold with goose bumps.

Merritt frowned. "What's wrong?"

Magda swallowed. "Nothing."

"Your face just turned white."

"It's nothing. Probably the heat."

But it was something. The whole world felt as if it was crushing in on her. She knew that once a new First Wizard was named, she had to tell him what she knew.

She reminded herself that she might be jumping to conclusions. She wished she could slow her racing heart.

Merritt sprang up and went to a side table. He hurriedly poured a glass of water. He handed her the glass and then sat again on the stool in front of her, watching her with great concern.

"Take a drink. It will help."

"Thanks." Magda took a sip. "I'm fine. Please, go on with what you were telling me."

Merritt watched to make sure she took a few more sips before continuing the story. "Well, since the chests are safely locked away in the Temple of the Winds, there is no longer any point in me attempting to complete the investment of magic in the key to unlock their power. But even more importantly, even if I wanted to, it can't be done."

Magda needed time to think. She couldn't be sure, after all, that he was talking about the same thing. There were a great many things, important things, all dangerous, that had been sealed away in the Temple of the Winds.

"You mean it can't be done because of the rare rift calculations for creating a seventh-level breach that Baraccus couldn't give you?"

Merritt leaned back and blinked in surprise. "You know about that?"

Magda worked to keep her voice under control. "Baraccus told me about it some time back when you went to see him. I remember him saying that you had wanted the rift calculations for such a breach. Apparently, he thought a lot of you because he told me that he wished he could have given you what you needed, but he couldn't because the formulas were sealed away in the Temple of the Winds and no one could get to them."

Merritt was staring at her, so she knew that she had to say something.

"So, is that why you can't complete the magic for this key?"

"Yes, exactly."

Magda was struck by the sincerity of his frustration. She watched his eyes look away as he went on, almost as if talking to himself, opening again the wound of his disappointment.

"I've spent years working on the details of the conjured structure. No one else understands it the way I do. They don't understand its true purpose." He looked up. "You see, I don't believe that it was ever supposed to be just a key."

"What do you mean? Why not?"

He leaned in more intently. "I've come to believe that what is contained in these receptacles, these chests, is the only form of power known to exist that predates the star shift."

"You really believe that's what in the chests?"

"Yes. That's why I was so sure in the first place that there have to be formulas for a seventh-level breach. Baraccus confirmed their existence when he told me that they were locked away in the Temple of the Winds."

Merritt's gaze was locked on her eyes. "If I'm right, which I am, then this power is an order of magnitude beyond what anyone understands. If I'm right, it contains enough power to destroy the world of life."

Magda took a sip of water for the chance to look away from the intensity of his hazel eyes. She couldn't make her fingers stop trembling.

"Dear spirits . . . is that really even possible? Do you actually think such a thing could be true, that something could have that much power?"

"I do. I think the key was originally intended to contain the seventh-level-breach code in order to harness that power. That's why the breach code exists. It has no other purpose. Same with the rift calculations."

"You mean, as in a rift in the world of life? And the breach code cracks the egg?"

He betrayed what he thought of her analogy with a small smile before he went on.

"After years of tracking down everything I could about the origins of the power and what it really is, I think I have come to understand it as no one else does."

"And what have you come to understand?"

"Well, first and foremost, I know enough not to fool myself into thinking I know everything. But from what I do know, I believe that any number of people would have enough knowledge or ability to misuse it and cause great harm. What they likely don't understand, though, is that in pursuing their own ends, they could inadvertently annihilate all life.

"But that's if it's misused. I'm convinced that this power needs more than a simple key if it is to function properly. I've found bits and pieces in ancient texts that give me cause to believe that the key, in a way, also has to be a caretaker of the power, a kind of protector."

CHAPTER
49

T hat doesn't sound like a bad idea," Magda said, absently, as she tried to corral her galloping thoughts.

She had never felt so lonely. She didn't know what to do, who she could turn to. Merritt seemed the obvious choice, but there was too much she didn't know about him. If anything she'd heard turned out to be true, telling him could very well turn out to be the worst decision she could make.

Her only hope was if the new First Wizard was named soon. The new First Wizard would need to know what she knew. He would know what to do.

"After a great deal of research and work, I finally have every aspect of my theory worked out and in place," Merritt was saying. "I'm convinced that I know how to create this unique power for the key if only I could get my hands on the rift calculations and breach formulas. If I could, I could then make a key that would function as it should.

"This magic I would create with the help of the formulas, would at the same time function for something else of great importance that I came up with along the way."

That caught her attention.

He lifted an arm in a gesture of frustration, then sighed as it dropped back to rest on his leg. "But without all the parts, the magic can't be formatted and thus initiated."

"Are there no substitutes that would work well enough?"

"No. It needs the correct parts, and all the parts, simple as that."

Magda steered him back to the thing that had caught her attention. "So is this unique magic also what would allow you to create in a person the ability to pull truth from lies? Is that the other thing of great importance you wanted to create?"

He looked surprised. "Yes, as a matter of fact it is."

"So then the key these people want that you know how to make and the person you described to the council that you wanted to alter to be able to pull truth from lies, are linked with common elements and share some base form of this magic?"

"That's right—at inception, anyway. They differ as they develop, and in the end of course, but they do need to have certain base elements from the rift calculations in common."

"You mean they both need yeast to make the dough rise?"

Merritt frowned suspiciously. "For someone ungifted, you seem to have a knack for grasping the inherent logic in the nature of magic. And for someone who described herself as a nobody, you also seem to know a great deal about some of the most secret projects in the Keep."

Magda tilted her head, peering at him from under her brow. "You may think that they're secret, but Isidore knew about the person you want to alter with this magic. If she knew, then the dream walkers know. If the dream walkers know, that means Emperor Sulachan knows. If they know about the person, then they very well may know about the key you're trying to make. If they know about the key, they know what it is meant to unlock."

Merritt let out a troubled sigh. "I suppose that's all possible, but it can't do them any good. It would be impossible for them to reconstruct my work, and without those occulted calculations that are locked away in the Temple of the Winds, the magic that I was working on can't be completed.

"Besides, the key would do them no good because the power itself is sealed away and inaccessible."

Magda had to force herself to hold her tongue. She instead asked a question. "Why would these repositories containing this great power not have a key in the first place? What would be the purpose of creating something without a way to make it work?"

"Good question. Unfortunately I don't have a good answer. People take history at face value and assume it's accurate, but often it really isn't. Accounts of past events differ. You don't know the honesty or the motives of the person who wrote the chronicle. Accounts from antiquity may have been lost over time, leaving critical gaps that would change the picture. Some of what we do have may actually have been rumor or even false charges that over time were wrongly assumed to be true. Some historical accounts are biased or distorted viewpoints, while others were embellished along the way. It's a mistake to indiscriminately assume historical accounts are true.

"All that is meant to say that I don't know the truth about an original key. The repositories holding this power were a relatively recent creation intended to safeguard the power in its resting state. The key doesn't actually open them, it's actually meant to unlock the ancient power contained within them. For all I know, it may be that when the power was created it had a key

All I know for sure is that the power itself still survives today and there is no known key for it.

"That creates a problem because while the key doesn't exist, the power does and even without the key this power is still profoundly dangerous.

"That's one reason I've been working so hard to complete the key. Everyone else thinks the key is supposed to simply unlock the power, but from bits of surviving books and scrolls from before the star shift, I've come to believe that the key was an object intended to protect the power, not merely unlock it."

The word "protect" stuck out to her. He said it with a kind of natural ease. She remembered what the men down in the lower reaches of the Keep had been working on when they were killed.

Her gaze went to the object on the table.

"Protect. Like a sword," she said.

"Yes," he finally admitted. "The existing references and formulas we still have led people to believe that the key must be made in the form of a sword. So, those trying to make the key try to make it in the form of a sword.

"They don't know why, and they don't really care. They simply try to make the key in the form of a sword as is implied in the reference material in order that it might work to unlock the power."

"And you think," she guessed, "that there is meaning to the prescription that the key take the form of a sword."

"I do. That the magic is supposed to be invested in a sword implies its purpose, does it not? Besides working to unlock what it protects, I believe it was intended to have the power to prevent the wrong person from meddling with the power."

"So, if there's no key, and the power is that incredibly dangerous, that's why the chests containing the power were shut away in the Temple of the Winds in the first place?"

"Very likely so," he said. "The problem is, if anything should go wrong, the key would be the only chance to bring us all back from the brink of annihilation."

He leaned in and lowered his voice, even though there was no one who could possibly overhear him. "You see, the key I would create isn't simply coded to the power, it's coded to work with the person using it. It has to be the right person, for the right reasons, or it won't work. The magic can read not only the key, but the intentions of the one holding the key."

Magda knew from Baraccus that dangerous magic often had multiple layers of protection. Books of magic usually had wards and safeguards to protect them. According to Isidore, Merritt made just such bindings for books of magic. He was apparently employing that principle in his design for the key to the power.

"But all of this is only theoretical, since you can't make the key and prove your theories."

"Well, yes, I suppose that's true. The problem is," he said, "there are those here in the Keep—"

"You mean the council."

His mouth twisted as he finally gave in. "Good guess."

She was getting tired of dancing with shadows. "Not all that difficult."

He flashed a brief smile before turning serious again. "The council wants it done anyway. They want the key to be made."

Magda had to take another drink of water to compose her voice. "Why? If everyone knows that the power is locked in the Temple, why would the council want the key made?"

"They've given me a long list of reasons, none of which make a lot of sense to me, but they're very insistent.

They wish it to be done, period. Ultimately, they don't need to explain themselves. They wish it to be done so they command that it be done. But wishing and commanding doesn't mean that it can be done and they won't listen to reason."

"I'm well aware of how inflexible the council can be."

"They certainly are in this case."

Magda's mind was racing. "Which councilmen want it done?"

"All of them, but Weston and Guymer seem to be the ones forcing the issue most of the time."

"Weston and Guymer. It would be them," Magda murmured to herself. She looked up again. "I thought the council didn't want you to use this same basic conjuring to create this, this person who could pull truth from lies."

His hazel eyes again locked on her.

"The Confessor," he said.

"Confessor?" Magda asked.

"That's right."

She leaned forward, puzzled by the name. "Confessor?"

"Yes, that's what I call the person I would create because with the power I would invest in them, they could make anyone—anyone—confess the truth, no matter how abhorrent the truth may be, no matter how desperately they previously may have wanted to conceal it, no matter the lies they've told or hidden behind. The touch of a Confessor's power would change all that."

"So, the council wants you to make the key, for which there would be no use, but not this Confessor for which there could possibly be great use?"

"Ironic, isn't it?"

"To say the least." She wondered if something more than irony was involved. "I still don't understand why both the key and this Confessor could require the same base elements."

"Because at their core they both serve the cause of truth."

"How can the key serve the cause of truth? I get the Confessor, but not the key."

"At their root, the key and the Confessor both authenticate truth. The Confessor's power would force the subject to reveal the truth, while all of the coded alignments of the key involve proofing it against reality. Reality is truth. Therefore, both the Confessor and the key need the same formulas to initiate their ultimate function.

"In much the same way that a verification web authenticates a spell, the base elements of this new form of magic I'm trying to create gauges, or measures, matters at hand against reality. In the case of the Confessor, the subject is left unable to speak anything other than the truth.

"The key, as well, follows a verification sequence. By building in authentication routines, it prevents a person from using it, for example, if they are lying about their reason for unlocking the power."

"Maybe the council doesn't want you to create the Confessor because they fear the truth," Magda said.

"You may have just arrived at the heart of it."

"But they still want the key."

"Right," he said. "They want a simple key to make the power work, but I didn't think I could trust anyone with a key to that much power, even the council, so I intended to make the more complex key. That has been a great deal harder to devise, but if I ever get the chance to finally ignite the web, it will be worth the years of extra work.

"Yet neither the one I envision nor the simple one the council wants can be created because they both would need the information that is out of reach in the Temple of the Winds. Without those formulas, I can't make the key, or the Confessor. At least it doesn't matter about the key because the power, like the formulas, is safely out of reach."

Magda thought she might be sick. She gulped a drink of water. She wondered why the council would fear the truth. But more immediate questions sprang to mind as she stalled for time to think it through.

"How would this person, this Confessor, be able to force someone to speak only the truth?"

He looked uncomfortable as he searched for the words. "You have to understand, Magda, that a Confessor would be a last resort to get at the truth. For example, to get a killer to confess to murders he committed so that we would know the extent of his victims, know beyond a doubt his guilt. Or imagine if a man had snatched a child for ransom, or worse. A Confessor could pull the truth from his lies and deception."

She arched an eyebrow. "Or a traitor could be made to give a true confession?"

"Without question or hesitation."

Magda touched her fingers to her forehead, trying to grasp the enormity of what he was telling her.

"But how would this Confessor actually get the person to confess?"

"Basically," he said, "the magic I would invest in them, much like the key, would contain elements of both Subtractive and Additive Magic."

"So you would need a gifted person to create a Confessor."

"Actually, no, not at all. The person would be the vessel into which I would place this ability, this unique form of power."

"But if they aren't gifted—"

"Everyone has at least a small spark of the gift. It's part of our life force. Magic is merely a matter of degree. You are said to be ungifted, but that's not technically accurate.

"Life connects us all to magic, as illustrated through the design of the Grace. So, for a Confessor, I don't need a gifted person, just a living one."

Having spent a lot of time around Baraccus and a number of talented wizards, Magda was somewhat familiar with their world and what they considered to be within the working realm of possibility. She might not have fully understood what they did or how they did it, but she did have a general sense of the sphere of their capabilities. This was outside that sphere.

Her eyes widened with sudden understanding. She looked up at him. "You would alter a Grace."

"Of course," he said, as if it were a trivial matter.

This was one of the reasons people feared makers. They didn't think in terms of the impossible, only in terms of how something might be done. What Merritt was describing was unconventional thinking that, to most people, bordered on madness.

"But you could change the person you turned into a Confessor back, right? I mean, if—"

"Change them back?" He looked at her as if she had lost her mind. "Once I altered them, the power would become an integral part of the person, inseparable from who they become. Once altered in this way, they would forever be a Confessor. There could be no going back. Once done, it can't be undone."

Magda was feeling sick to her stomach. "So how would this power you would invest in a person actually work?"

"When a Confessor unleashes their power into someone, the Subtractive side of it would destroy who the person was."

"It would kill them?"

"No, not really, not in the conventional sense."

Magda leaned in with a frown. "What does that mean?"

"I mean, no, it wouldn't kill them." He gestured, seemingly reluctant to explain, but finally he did. "The way

I've created the web, it's narrowly targeted. Fine threads of Subtractive Magic would burn through the target person's mind like lightning crashing through a tree, all the way down through its roots, to obliterate their identity.

"So, in that sense, who they once were would be dead. They can never regain what is eliminated with the Subtractive side of the Confessor's power. They are alive, but who they were no longer exists. What it means to be that person is gone."

"So what would exist for them?"

"In place of who they were, in place of what the Subtractive Magic destroys, the Additive Magic would at the same time flow in behind, filling the void to create in them total, complete, blind devotion to the Confessor. The Confessor would become the center of the person's universe, the only thing that matters to them. The Confessor would become their identity, or the object of it, to be more precise.

"In that realm of total commitment and absolute compliance, they would feel the overpowering need for the object of their fidelity—the Confessor—to give them direction. That would be the only purpose of their life. It would be a terrifying emptiness in their existence to be without the direction of the Confessor who touched them with this power.

"The Confessor could at that point command anything and the person would be compelled to comply, no matter what the command was. If it is physically possible, they would without hesitation carry it out even at the cost of their own life. Even if it wasn't possible, they'd still try with every fiber of their being until told by the Confessor to stop, or until they died. The only purpose to their new existence would be to do as the Confessor commanded.

"So, as you can imagine, the Confessor would have but to ask and the person would, without hesitation, confess the truth.

"They would be utterly incapable of lying. That part of them, the desire, the need, the ability to lie, would have been destroyed and forever gone. Who they were is irretrievable. When the Confessor asks for the truth, telling the truth becomes the only thing that matters to the person touched by the power."

Magda was horrified. "How could you give that much power to anyone?"

Forearms resting on his thighs, fingers intertwined, he leaned toward her. "We give swords to soldiers, don't we? The gifted have children who through birthright inherit deadly abilities. The men chosen to serve as soldiers are at least subjected to some degree of scrutiny. The child is gifted with powers without qualification and in fact may grow up to use those powers to cause great harm. Look at what Emperor Sulachan's followers do with their abilities, abilities granted to them through no precondition except birth. They use their power to destroy innocent people.

"On the other hand, the person chosen to be a Confessor and invested with such power would have to be the right person, a rational person, a rare person who could be entrusted with such responsibility, as would the person entrusted to possess the key to the repositories of power. For the right person, either would be a tool. For the wrong person, either could be a weapon of evil. It is the mind behind that tool that matters."

She was beginning to understand why the council had originally refused his request. "I heard that the attempt to create this Confessor is dangerous and that it could even be fatal. You could very possibly kill a good person in the attempt to create a Confessor out of them."

He didn't look in the least bit daunted by the charge. If anything, he looked resolute.

"Yes, that's true. It's profoundly dangerous magic we're talking about here. I believe I can do it, but I can't be absolutely positive it will all work the way I think it will. Such a thing has never been attempted before. Dear spirits, as far as I know, such a thing has never been envisioned before. If I don't have every last little bit of it right, it could all go terribly wrong in a heartbeat and the person could be killed. There is that risk."

He leaned toward her again, searching her eyes. "But what is the danger of not trying? Despite all the efforts of our forces, towns and cities everywhere are being overrun. We are losing men by the thousands in battles. Yet the horde from the South continues to pour north, coming to destroy us all.

"You yourself said that there is something going on in the Keep, that you are searching for answers, that we are all in danger, that traitors are among us and very possibly plotting our destruction. We need to find those responsible. Do you think that the death of all our people is preferable to the risk to the person chosen to become a Confessor?"

Magda searched the depths of his hazel eyes, looking for some indication that he was misguided, or deluded, or even mad. She saw none.

She glanced to the graceful women he had carved from white marble. This was not a man who did anything without fully appreciating every angle of it.

"I admit that you may have a point," she finally said.

Magda had never liked the idea of magic altering a person. This was no different. It sounded horrific.

She changed the subject back to what she had wanted to know in the beginning.

"What about the other wizards who have died? The

ones people say died because of you. You haven't finished that part of the story."

The impassioned animation that had been so evident in his eyes when he had been talking about the key and the Confessor extinguished like a campfire in a downpour. He looked miserable to have to return to the subject.

Magda felt bad for bringing him back to something that was so obviously painful for him.

But all their lives were at stake. She needed to be able to find the truth.

51

W ell, the thing is, as I've explained and as I hope you can appreciate, without the required formulas that are locked away in the Temple of the Winds, trying to make this kind of magic function for even the simplest form of the key, much less to create a Confessor, is impossible. More than that, though, we're talking about very dangerous things, here, things that are not to be taken lightly. Without the needed components, the attempt is guaranteed to fail and very well might be fatal."

"I can grasp why it wouldn't work without all the parts you say it needs, but why is even trying to make the key so risky?"

With a grim expression, Merritt lifted his fist so that she could see the signet ring he wore.

On its raised center was a Grace.

The design of the Grace was deeply engraved into the ring so that it could be used to make an impression in sealing wax. Magda remembered seeing that particular design of the Grace left in the sealing wax of documents Baraccus had received.

"Even as an ungifted person, you must be aware of the power involved in the Grace when it is used by the gifted."

She was. The Grace represented the world of life, the world of the dead, and the way magic and Creation linked them.

The outer circle of the design represented the beginning of the infinite world of the dead. Inside that outer circle was a square, its points just touching the outer circle. Inside the square was another circle, just touching the insides of the square. The area between those two circles with the square represented the world of life. The inside circle was life's beginning, the outer circle its end, where souls crossed through the veil into the eternity of the underworld.

An eight-pointed star inside the smaller circle was the Light of Creation. Lines from that star's points radiated out across the inner circle, the square, and across the outer circle that also symbolized the veil to the world of the dead. The lines radiating outward from the Light represented the spark of the gift that journeyed with everyone from birth, through life, and on into death.

Magda imagined that those rays, those conduits of the gift, were what enabled Isidore, the living, gifted spiritist, to be able to connect with the spirit world beyond the veil.

The gifted drew the Grace when conjuring powerful spells in order to invoke specific forces. It added elements that nothing else could, but at the same time it was a dangerous tool and had to be treated with great respect.

A Grace was properly drawn from the outside toward the center—circle, square, circle, star—and then the rays back out across those elements. Everything inward and then back out. Drawing it improperly or in an improper sequence, when it counted, could cause magic to fail or even go terribly wrong.

Drawn in blood, a Grace could invoke alchemy of consequence.

It was said that a person with enough knowledge and power could alter the Grace and thus alter elements of it.

Though a Grace was a commonly used tool of the gifted, Baraccus had often said that, despite its seeming simplicity, it was rarely mastered.

Not many people would dare to wear a Grace. That alone said something important about his abilities.

Merritt stared down at his ring, burnishing the design of the Grace with the thumb of his other hand. He seemed lost in thought.

Magda touched his wrist, making him look up.

"You were saying?"

His eyes focused again on her face. "I was saying that the spell-forms in play to create a key are dangerously unstable in such combinations without the links from the rift calculations. You need those links to make the structure rigid. Only in that way can the various parts then fuse in the proper sequence. The council wanted us to try anyway. They wanted the key completed."

"What happens if you don't have those elements? What happens if you try it without them?"

"Without those rift and breach connectors you can't stabilize the verification web and hold the spell-form together. Without them, there is nothing to brace the various elements against, and those particular elements happen to involve both Additive and Subtractive Magic. As you can imagine, letting the two touch in the wrong way, much less combine, is highly reactive.

"Almost as soon as you bring the structure up in a verification web, with those opposing elements both so openly contained within the formation, and before you can begin to activate the generation process, it begins to collapse in on itself. The Additive and Subtractive components attract each other as it implodes, accelerating the reaction. Anyone nearby trying to hold it together in order to bind and fuse the components into the key would be seriously injured or killed.

"It doesn't matter how you try to construct the web, or what different routines or sequence you use. Without all the parts needed to complete it, there is no chance that it might work. None. As far as I'm concerned, it's insanity for anyone to think that you can put those particular Additive and the Subtractive components together in that way without the necessary bridging elements and expect them to coexist. The attempt is not merely pointless, it's suicide."

"Wouldn't others realize that?"

"Some do, but when people want something bad enough they tend to fixate on the prize and ignore the dangers. The first attempt went as I had predicted and men died. Some people saw the risk as the price of the prize and wanted to be the one to prove themselves better than anyone else. They think they will gain glory being the one to make it work. Yet more men died in subsequent attempts."

"But you do that same kind of thing," she said. "You're a maker. You don't accept that something can't be done. You figure out how to do things that are said to be impossible. So how can you fault them for wanting to make their attempts?"

"The things I do that have never been done before are different. I study the problem and rationally analyze if it is really possible. Then and only then I work on how to do it. I develop a plan based on facts, not wishes. I know each step, each element's nature, and I know where the lines are. To an outside observer it may seem that I'm attempting impossible things, but that's not the case."

He gestured across the room toward a statue. "It's like carving. Before you make a cut you know why, you know what to cut away. That's not what they're doing in this case. They are trying to carve, as it were, by hacking away without knowing what they're doing. They're substituting wishing for knowing.

"Some of the men, I know, understood the dangers involved and were worried about attempting to make this key. But the council insisted. Even in the face of deaths, they insisted that the effort to craft this sword continue. They've put all their hopes into wishing it to work. I refused to be a part of it."

Magda frowned. "I don't understand something. Is it a secret that the chests containing this power are locked away in the Temple of the Winds and no one can get to them?"

"No. Everyone involved in the attempt to make the key knows it. The chests were listed on the Temple team's manifest."

"Then why is the council so insistent that the key be made when they know that there is no use for it?"

Merritt lifted his hands in a gesture of frustration. "Exactly. I made the same argument. They didn't want to hear it. Elder Cadell offered that it was a safety measure should the power ever be returned to the world of life. He said that we couldn't wait for something to go wrong and only then find out that we are unprepared to deal with it."

"Elder Cadell said that?"

"That's right. The council wanted me to lead the team that was to make the key. I agree with their motive, but that doesn't mean it can be done. When I told them that it was impossible and would only get people killed, they became angry. They questioned my loyalty to the cause of the Midlands.

"They said that if I refused to help them and anyone was killed, it would be my fault. They thought that by putting me into such a position I would have to go along, and if I went along, then I would somehow find a way to make it work."

"They apparently have a great deal of faith in your ability as a maker," Magda said.

Merritt could sit no longer. He went to the table again, where he leaned on his hands as he stared down at the sword lying on red velvet. As Magda watched him, waiting for him to go on, his fingers lightly tracked the length of the blade's fuller.

"It's as if they want us to be able to fly," he finally said, "and so they command people to leap off a cliff, flap their arms, and fly, thinking that because they have commanded it to work, it will.

"But then when those people plummet to their death, I'm the one blamed because I'm the one who told them the truth that it wouldn't work."

CHAPTER

52

So you refused to lead them and they went ahead with the attempt anyway," Magda said when he had been silent for a time. "Then what happened?"

"What do you think happened? A lot of good men died for nothing, that's what happened."

"I see."

She remembered all too well the man down in the lower portion of the Keep, lying sprawled on the floor dead, with a large fragment of a blade jutting from his chest.

"Do you?" He shook his head without looking back. "You say that you think Baraccus died for something worthwhile, so you at least have that consolation. These men died for nothing. What consolation is there for those they leave behind?

"Do you know what it's like to face the widows of such men? Men whose lives were wasted? Can you imagine the grief of those women, knowing that their husbands are dead, hearing that I'm responsible, hearing that I could have prevented it had I not been 'selfish' and instead helped them? Can you imagine what it's like to hear their children, children I've given rides on my shoulders, crying for fathers they will never see again?

"Can you imagine what it's like to have the widows, mothers, sisters, and daughters of men who died lie at your door all night, wailing inconsolably, blaming you for the death of their loved one?"

"No, I can't imagine it," Magda said into the stillness.

She felt shame for being one of those who had so easily thought him guilty of the charge merely because she had heard it made. She had formed an opinion of him without ever meeting him. She felt a fool for so willingly embracing lies.

"How could I convince people in such pain that I tried to prevent such needless deaths? They wouldn't listen. They wouldn't hear it. They believed the council's word that had I helped it wouldn't have happened. It's easier for the families to blame me than to try to grasp the complexities of the issue. They can't understand that even if I had stayed and led the effort their men would be just as dead and me along with them. Easier for them to embrace lies than the truth."

Magda could hear children running up the street, playing a game as their barking dog bounded after them. She could only imagine the anguish of children very much like them losing a father. When they finally receded into the distance, the pall of silence again settled over the small, cluttered home.

"That's why you moved away from the Keep," Magda said aloud as the realization came to her.

His back still to her, he nodded. "That's why."

She could see how much it hurt him to be put in such an impossible situation and so unfairly blamed. She understood why Baraccus had said that he wished he could have helped Merritt.

Magda rose and crossed the room to lay a comforting hand on the back of his broad shoulder. She finally understood the depth of the compassion Isidore saw in him.

"Thank you, Merritt, for explaining it to me. I under-stand, now. I'm greatly relieved that what people say isn't true, but at the same time I'm ashamed that I blindly believed that you were to blame for those deaths."

He nodded his appreciation as he lightly touched the blade of the sword. "A lot of good people have died for nothing. I'm afraid that a lot more good men are going to die before they finally give up the attempt as impossible."

Standing beside him as he turned toward her, she saw then for the first time a full view of the magnificent sword lying on the red velvet. The fuller ran the length of a gleaming blade that flared beneath side notches near the top. An aggressive, down-swept cross guard tapered to sharp points. The hilt was covered in tightly wound, perfectly twisted, fine silver wire.

Gold wire woven through the silver spelled out the word *Truth*.

The beauty of the sword nearly took her breath.

Almost involuntarily, she reached out and touched the hilt, her fingers trailing over the word *Truth* standing out in gold. She'd never seen such a thing done before.

Merritt watched her for a moment; then, as he lifted the sword, her fingers finally, reluctantly, came off the word *Truth*. He laid the blade over his forearm and of-fered her the hilt.

Magda couldn't resist letting her fingers close around it. As she gripped the hilt, lifting the weapon, she could feel the raised letters of the word *Truth* with her finger-tips on one side, and the woven wire letters of the word *Truth* on the other side of the hilt pressing into her palm.

She knew a thing or two about using a sword, but she was by no means expert with one, as she was with knives. This sword felt magical in her hand. Its weight and balance were extraordinary. It felt light, swift, and remarkably right.

It also stirred something deep within her, called something forth in a way that she hadn't expected and didn't quite understand.

The only way she could interpret it was that it felt rather like righteous anger boiling just beneath the surface of her awareness, wanting release.

"This is meant to be the key," she whispered half to herself.

He was still watching her eyes. "Indeed it is, but as I've explained, I can't complete it."

"It all makes sense, now," she said, still speaking to herself as much as to him. "I understand what you meant about the magic of the key serving truth and at the same time protecting the power."

"The power needs truth to work. Truth is reality, the laws of nature. They're inseparable. That relationship is represented by the word woven into the hilt. That makes this a sword meant to serve more than just the power. It is also meant to serve truth."

She at last looked up into his eyes as the realization came to her.

"This is the Sword of Truth."

A warm smile softened his expression. "That's a good name for it. In fact, it's perfect. I don't know why I never thought of it myself. More than you realize, this sword serves truth on many levels and in many ways. I've always meant for the one who wields this sword to be a seeker of truth.

"Thank you, Magda, for the clarity." He gestured to the sword in her hand. "From now on, it will always be known as the Sword of Truth."

Magda lifted the blade upright, letting her eyes take in its graceful lines. Its fuller added not only lightness, which made it faster, but at the same time added strength to the blade. It was at once exquisite and deadly. Below the cross guard, the wire-wound hilt felt at home in her hand.

"Where did you ever get something this magnificent?"

His smile widened. "I made it."

She again lifted the sword in astonishment, watching the light flare along the length of the blade.

"You made this?"

Merritt nodded. "While any would serve the purpose, this is the sword I made with the intent that it be the key. It has always been the sword I intended to invest with the power."

"I feel . . . something. I can feel something stirring as I hold it."

By his reaction, he was not at all surprised. "Like I explained before, we are all born with a spark of the gift. Though you are not gifted, as such, you still respond to magic. This sword is invested with magic. That is what you feel."

Magda frowned. "What sort of magic?"

"In addition to preparing it to become the key, I also gave it abilities to help in its service to protect the power as well as to serve truth. Those are the elements you feel." His smile ghosted away. "But that was before I knew that what I needed to complete it isn't in this world any longer. I won't let others use this sword to try to make the key because such a fruitless attempt would destroy it. At least the power is safe."

Magda finally handed Merritt the sword. As his fist closed around the hilt, around the words *Truth* on either side, she closed both her hands around his, holding them tightly.

They were close as she searched his eyes.

"Answer a question for me?"

He shrugged, making no attempt to take the sword and his hand from under hers. "What do you want to know?"

"How many chests contain the power, the power that the Sword of Truth you hold is meant to protect?"

He seemed reluctant, but finally answered.

"Three."

Magda felt a tear well up and run down her cheek.

"The three boxes of Orden."

Something more than the gift alone shone in his eyes. "That's what the power was called before the star shift. How is it that you know that name? The name Orden is only used in the most ancient of sources. How is it that you know it?"

How could she tell him?

How could she not?

Merritt, I have to tell you something."

Concern creased his features. "What is it?"

Magda cleared her throat, hoping that her voice wouldn't fail her.

"When Baraccus returned from the Temple of the Winds, returned from the underworld, I was there in the First Wizard's enclave waiting for him. I was of course happy to see him, and he was happy to return safely to me. But he was strangely quiet. I asked him what it was that so troubled him.

"Baraccus told me that a great power, a very dangerous power, was no longer in the Temple of the Winds where it belonged. He said that it was supposed to be there, but it was gone. I asked him what he was talking about. He said that the three boxes of Orden were missing."

Merritt's face went ashen. "Missing?"

"He said that much was not right in the Temple of the Winds. When I asked what he meant, he just stared off and was quiet for a time. He finally told me about the boxes of Orden, and how important they were. I asked if he was certain they were gone. He said that the Temple of the Winds was a big place, but there was no doubt that the boxes were no longer there."

"Who else has he told about the boxes being gone?"

"He said that he could tell no one but me."

"The council doesn't know?"

"No. I'm the only one who knows. And now you. I was waiting for the new First Wizard to be named. I had planned to tell him once he is named."

One of her hands came off his holding the sword so that she could grasp his muscular arm to urge his gaze back to her eyes.

"But I realize now that you are the one who needs to know, Merritt. You are the one I needed to tell."

His face still hadn't regained its color. His gaze again drifted away to focus into distant thoughts. She couldn't imagine what he, having worked so long to create the protective key for the boxes of Orden, must be thinking.

"Thank you, Magda, for telling me. For trusting me."

She nodded as her other hand finally slipped away from his on the sword.

His expression abruptly turned expectant. "Did Baraccus say anything about the rift calculations for creating a seventh-level breach? Maybe he brought them back with him."

Magda shook her head. "I'm sorry, no. He didn't say anything at all about that."

His momentary eagerness faded, to be replaced by suspicion. "And the council doesn't know about this? You're certain they don't know?"

"Yes, I'm certain. Baraccus said that he could tell no one but me. I don't know why, but he was clear about it. He wouldn't have said such a thing unless he meant it."

"It makes no sense. How could the boxes of Orden not be in the Temple of the Winds?" Merritt stared off again. "I wonder if maybe someone else could go there to retrieve the formulas. I wonder if I could try it. I don't know how, but if I could—"

"No," Magda said with an emphatic shake of her head. "Baraccus told me that there was much wrong at the Temple. He said that it would be thousands of years before anyone again set foot there."

"That sounds ominous. I wonder why he said that?"

"I don't know, but if Baraccus said it he must have known what he was talking about. That means that you or anyone else wouldn't be able to get in."

Merritt thought for a moment. "The Temple was supposed to be brought back to this world after the war is over and it's safe again here."

Magda looked up at him from under her brow. "Baraccus was a war wizard. Part of that was his ability for prophecy. Maybe he meant that it wouldn't be safe in this world for thousands of years, and so it will have to remain banished."

"That's a grim thought."

"Maybe it's because of the other thing he said, though, that there is something seriously wrong there. Maybe it's not because of what's happening here in this world that it can't return, but because of the trouble there."

"I suppose that could be," Merritt said, deep in thought.

"That means that those things you need are never going to be within your reach."

Merritt's shoulders sagged in frustration.

"That still doesn't explain anything about what happened to the boxes of Orden. If they aren't there, then they have to be here, in this world."

"It would seem so," she agreed.

"The Temple team put the boxes there, in the Temple," he said as he reasoned it through out loud. "Lothain tried to get into the Temple to fix what the Temple team had sabotaged, but he couldn't get in. Then, when Lothain's attempt to enter the Temple failed,

Baraccus sent some of his best men to try to get in to find out what the Temple team had done. When none of them returned, he finally went there himself. He confirmed the trouble there."

"That's right," Magda said.

He gestured with the sword. "That would seem to indicate that the boxes of Orden were never actually placed in the Temple in the first place. That must have been part of the team's treachery."

"There has to be more to it than that."

"What do you mean?" he asked.

"If the boxes were never there, and no one else got in, then why did the Temple of the Winds turn the moon red in warning that something had gone terribly wrong there? After all, it was long after the Temple team had been tried and executed for treason. Something made the moon turn red in warning. Baraccus sent wizards who failed to return and then went himself to answer the Temple's call for help and find out what was wrong. Something had to have happened that made the moon turn red."

"I can't imagine what. Did Baraccus give any hint?"

Magda's gaze dropped. "He killed himself before I had a chance to really talk to him about it." She looked back up at Merritt. "Maybe the boxes really were there in the Temple all along, right where they belonged. Maybe someone else got in and took them, and that's why the moon turned red."

Merritt looked disturbed by the thought. "Someone else? Like who? You mean the enemy?"

Magda shrugged. "I don't know. But maybe someone got in and stole the boxes of Orden and caused the other trouble that Baraccus spoke of. Maybe that's why the moon turned red."

Merritt ran a thumb along his jaw as he considered. "I suppose that's possible."

"Maybe it was the enemy. Someone Emperor Sulachan sent."

Merritt looked over at her. "That's a troubling thought."

"Besides that troubling thought, as I told you, there are a number of troubling things going on at the Keep. I heard rumors of some of our wizards bringing the dead back to life. Do you know anything about such efforts?"

"I've heard that they're working to try to learn about the weapons Sulachan has developed," he said. "I think that Isidore was helping with just that sort of thing. She was dealing with matters from the spirit world."

"Other strange things are going on. Enemy forces are harvesting the dead. They took all the dead from Isidore's town of Grandengart. Reports I've heard say that they've taken bodies from other places as well, and from battle-fields. Why would they do such a thing?"

Merritt heaved a sigh. "I don't know."

Magda went to the wicker couch and retrieved the bundle she had brought along. "Take a look at this."

Magda unfurled the wispy cloth bundle and held it up so he could see it the way it had looked when it had hung in the maze of hallways outside Isidore's place.

Merritt set the sword back down on the red velvet and crossed the room, drawn by what he was seeing. She could make out his silhouette through the silky cloth as he ran his fingers over the spell-forms drawn on it.

"This is remarkable," he whispered.

"I certainly think so. It saved my life."

Merritt pulled the edge of the cloth aside to peer at her. "What do you mean?"

"The monster who killed Isidore came after me. He was no less intent on killing me than he had been on killing Isidore. He chased me through your maze. I was lost and trying my best to stay out of his reach. He finally trapped me in a dead end behind this cloth, but he couldn't pass it to get at me. This cloth somehow stopped him."

Merritt lifted the side of the cloth out so that he could examine all the symbols crudely painted on it.

"I can see why," he said as he studied the symbols.

"Isidore told me that the spells she drew were derived from her work as a spiritist, and that they were both powerful and significant."

He was still studying the drawings on the cloth. "There is no doubt of that." He shook his head as his gaze wandered from one symbol to another. "I taught her the basics of these spell-forms, but she has added some very peculiar elements to them."

"Isidore told me that the dead must heed them."

Merritt glanced her way but didn't say anything, so she did. "I can testify to the truth of what she said." Magda joggled the cloth. "This is what stopped that monster, that dead man, from getting at me. He wouldn't go past it. Isidore said that the dead must heed the things she drew. That's another reason that I believe that this man who killed her and was trying to kill me was actually dead. He heeded this warning."

Merritt glanced her way. "That might be true, but it's not necessarily the case." He took the cloth, draping it over an arm as he paced across the room, pulling folds aside one at a time as he considered the symbols lying across his arm.

"This is very disturbing, though," he muttered. "These are keeper spells, meant to ward the dead."

"Keeper spells? Merritt, why was Isidore worried about dead people? Why did she have these keeper spells drawn on hangings in the hallways around her that stopped the dead?"

He looked back at her a moment. "Perhaps because she had reason to fear them, or perhaps it was only a precaution. She was dealing with the world of the dead after all. That was her profession. Besides that, she was searching for spirits that are trapped in this world. Those spirits belong to the corpses that General Kuno took from Grandengart."

"But those are spirits of the dead. Not the dead themselves."

"What are you getting at?"

"What if what I've heard is true, and some of those wizards down there really are able to bring the dead back to life, or not really life, but, well, you know what I mean. What if they are creating monsters out of dead people? Mindless slaves to do their bidding?"

Merritt arched an eyebrow as he handed her back the silky cloth. "I have learned not to dismiss things that sound preposterous, but do you really believe that?"

She took the cloth from him and folded it back up. "I don't know what I believe." She lifted the bundle. "But I sleep under this."

She thought he might laugh at her. He didn't.

"Good girl," he murmured as he turned away in thought.

"Merritt, there are too many things happening that make no sense. I fear that something terrible is going to happen before I can figure it out, and no one but me seems to care."

"I care," he said quietly.

She was momentarily caught off guard. She hadn't expected him to say that. It was what she had hoped for, more than she had hoped for, in fact. It was why she had come to see him in the first place. But she hadn't expected it.

"Thank you," she whispered.

"You're right that there are too many unexplained things happening. Not only the things you mention, but others as well. In isolation, they each might seem innocent enough, or might be able to be explained away, but when you consider the larger picture, those things together become suspect."

"Do you know anyone who could help us get answers?"

He ran his hand back and forth along a curved iron piece of a strange, complex metal composition as he considered. It almost looked like a sculptural representation of verification webs she had seen before.

"I might," he finally said.

Encouraged, Magda stepped closer. "I'm listening."

He turned to face her. "Do you know about the defector?"

"Defector? No. What defector? What are you talking about?"

"Just within the last day or two, a sorceress from the Old World, a woman who it is rumored was close to Emperor Sulachan, arrived in the Keep seeking refuge. I heard that she told people she wanted to join our cause. If that's true, she might know something about the enemy's plans. We know precious little about what is going on under Sulachan's rule."

"I never heard of her," Magda said. "You're right, we definitely should talk to her. Do you know where we can find her?"

"In the dungeon."

"The dungeon?" Magda frowned. "If she defected and wants to join our cause, why is she in the dungeon?"

"I heard whispers that she was tried and convicted of being a spy, and that she is going to be executed."

Magda gaped at him. "I never heard about any such trial."

He lifted his brow. "Why should you? You're a nobody, remember?"

Magda's mouth twisted. "Before Baraccus died I used to know a lot more about the goings-on at the Keep than I do now." She folded her arms. "We need to go see her, find out if she can tell us anything."

"I already tried. They wouldn't let me talk to her."

"There have to be some people around who would be

willing to help." As she considered the problem, Magda went to the table where the Sword of Truth lay, gazing down at it. "Lord Rahl told me that some of the officers had given the devotion to him."

"Do you know which ones?"

"Officers Rendall and Morgan have," she said. "I trust them. Either would help me."

"They're both with their troops, somewhere outside of Aydindril."

"General Grundwall of the Home Guard swore the oath as well," she said. "I know him, although not well. He often came to Baraccus with reports."

Merritt nodded as he considered. "I've only met him once or twice, but commanding the Home Guard he could certainly get in to see a prisoner." He glanced her way. "Do you know him well enough for him to get me in there to see this sorceress?"

"I think I know him well enough for him to get me in there. I might be able to convince him to let you come along."

He smiled briefly. It quickly faded. "Let's hope they haven't beheaded her already, and that she would be willing to talk to us."

"We should do that first, then. Do you know anyone else you can trust?"

Merritt rubbed his jaw as he thought it over. "I know lots of trustworthy people but most haven't sworn the oath to Lord Rahl, so as trustworthy as they might ordinarily be, we can't trust that a dream walker isn't watching through their eyes. A lot of people don't take the threat seriously. That creates an opportunity the enemy can take advantage of."

"Then we dare not take a chance with any of them."

"I do know one person I trust, and he has sworn the oath."

"Who's that?" she asked.

"He's assigned to guard the sliph. I trust him, and I know that he's one of the gifted who believed in Baraccus. Since he is usually with the sliph, he sees a lot of important people coming and going. He also knows a great deal about the wizards at the Keep, who's doing what, that sort of thing."

"You mean Quinn?"

Merritt's brow furrowed. "You know Quinn?"

Magda smiled. "I grew up with him. When I was younger, I would sometimes go for walks with him in the forests around Aydindril out to an isolated pond that was home to loons."

"You were sweet on him?"

Magda could feel herself blushing. "No, nothing like that. I liked him, but we were just children. He was a couple years older, though, and that alone made him seem quite impressive. But Quinn was more interested in his journals."

"Ah yes, Quinn's journals. You certainly do know him, then."

"He pored through books all the time. He loved to study the past. He used to tell me that history shaped people's beliefs, and that one day he was going to be the Keep's historian and write about all the goings-on."

"He seems to be well on his way," Merritt said as he lifted the baldric off the chair and slipped it over his head. He placed it over his right shoulder with the scabbard at his left hip. "He has quite the collection of journals that he keeps down there with him as he guards the sliph."

"It keeps him busy," Magda said. "It's probably pretty boring being down there most of the time."

Merritt picked up the sword and slid it into the beautifully tooled silver and gold scabbard at his left hip.

"Let's go see if you can convince General Grundwall to take us down to the dungeon."

"You take the Sword of Truth with you often?"

"I never let it out of my sight. It already has certain conjured elements locked into it in preparation for the final process. I guess that's not to be now, but even with the powers it has, it's still a dangerous weapon. I wouldn't want it to fall into the wrong hands."

She supposed it made sense. Magda scooped the folded bundle off the wicker couch, tucking it under an arm.

On her way past the bookshelf, she paused, pointing at the tiny clay figures of people floating in the air just off the end of a small scroll sticking out from the shelf.

"Merritt, do you mind me asking what in the world this is?"

Merritt pulled the scroll off the shelf. The little figures floated along through the air, staying close to it.

"I call it a gravity well."

Smiling at the little figures hovering in the air, she turned back to him. "A what?"

"If you toss something in the air, it falls to the ground. In a way, we're all like these little figures, pulled to the ground by gravity."

He unfurled the scroll to show her that it had a spell-form drawn on it. She was a bit alarmed to see that part of the spell-form was made up of an altered Grace.

"You created gravity in a spell?"

"Not exactly. I created a spell that attracts specific things. I guess you could say that it only mimics gravity. In this case, I had it attract these clay figures, so they always are compelled to stay near the spell-form, like we must stay on the ground because of gravity. So, I call it a gravity well."

"What's it for?" She puzzled at the paper and its clay people drawn to it. "What is its purpose?"

Merritt shrugged. "Nothing, really. It's just something I came up with while I was working on something else more important. I've never thought of a use for it, so I guess that it's just for my amusement."

He folded the scroll up small enough to fit in his hand. The figures floated close. He took her hand and placed the small, folded paper in her palm.

"Here. A gift for you to make you smile."

Magda held the folded paper out in the palm of her hand, watching the small clay figures float around it. "Really? I can have this?"

"Sure, if you promise to smile that lovely smile you have when you look at it."

She couldn't help smiling. "I promise," she said as she gathered up the figures in her hand and put it all into her pocket.

With two fingers on the cross guard, he lifted the sword a few inches and let it drop back into place, making sure it was clear in its scabbard.

"Now, shall we see if we can go talk to this defector before they behead her?"

Magda nodded and hurried to follow after him.

For the first time since Baraccus died, Magda didn't feel totally alone. She had someone who believed her, who took her seriously, someone who was going to help her.

CHAPTER

55

On the stone bridge that spanned the vast chasm before the Keep, two women crossing, near the short stone wall on the opposite side, spotted Merritt and momentarily froze in their tracks. Both were in long gray dresses and both had short hair. One was a couple of years older than Magda, while the other appeared old enough to be the first woman's mother. Magda saw blood on the younger woman's dress. Both threaded their way through the throngs coming and going from the Keep to intercept Merritt.

"Mary, what's the matter," Merritt asked the younger of the two as she grabbed one of his hands. The older woman stood behind, expectantly wringing her own hands.

The younger woman's face was tearstained and she was in obvious distress. "It's James—he's been hurt. Hurt bad."

"Hurt?" Merritt asked, clearly alarmed. "How? What happened? How badly is he hurt?"

"He was working on an assignment from the council to make a sword of some sort." She had to pause to choke back a sob. "James never talked much about the work he does, so I don't know a great deal about it. But earlier this afternoon there was some kind of an accident down in the lower regions. Three of the men with him were killed outright by a massive explosion. Two others standing farther back were hurt but not seriously. James is in a bad way, though. He was closer and breathed in the inferno. They say it burned his lungs. He can't breathe. He's hurt bad, Merritt."

As she fell against him, sobbing, she clutched his black shirt in both fists. "What will I do if he dies, Merritt? What will I do?"

"It had something to do with magic gone wrong," the older woman added when the first succumbed to her tears, hoping that somehow the information might help him.

Merritt cast Magda a look as he circled an arm around Mary's shoulders. His big hand gently held the woman's head to his chest as she wept.

Magda knew what the look meant. Yet more men had just died and others had been hurt in a futile attempt to make the key to the boxes of Orden.

"Are they healing him?" Merritt asked. "Are there gifted working to heal him?"

"No. He wouldn't let them," Mary sobbed, barely getting the words out.

"What? Why not?"

The older woman placed a hand on his forearm. "James is asking for you, Merritt."

"But why? Why won't he let the gifted help him?"

"Apparently, he believes that you are the only one who knows enough about what they were doing, what elements are involved, to have a chance to heal him. The wizards with him are trying to keep him alive until you could be found, but they told me that they don't know enough to heal him and they need you. It's only chance that Mary and I spotted you on our way down to the city to look for you. Hurry. Please."

Merritt, with one arm around the younger woman, holding her as she cried against his chest, put his other hand on the older woman's shoulder.

"Of course."

He turned to Magda, concern shaping his features. "I need to help James. Wait for me?"

Magda nodded. "Hurry. Help him."

Magda put a hand on Mary's back. She knew what it was like to fear for a loved one. She knew the terror of it. She was getting tears herself at the sight of Mary's distress. At least this woman was not yet grieving her husband's death. Magda hoped that Merritt could prevent that from happening.

"Try to be brave," Magda said. "Merritt will help. Your husband will need to see you being strong for him."

The woman nodded as she reached out to squeeze Magda's other hand. "I'll try."

"Where will I find you?" he asked in a private tone.

"I'll either be in my apartments," Magda said, "or in the storage room next door getting my things ready to move so the new First Wizard can have the space."

"Wait for me, then, and I will come get you as soon as I help James."

His hazel eyes looked even more green in the late-day light, and they spoke more than mere words. He knew how important their business was, but at the same time he couldn't let a man barely clinging to life die if there was anything that could be done to save him.

Merritt reached out and briefly touched Magda's cheek, then let the two women lead him away in a rush.

Magda stood in the center of the massive stone bridge, still feeling the touch of his fingers on her cheek as she watched the three of them cross the bridge and race toward the gaping iron maw of the portcullis. It had been a small but rather remarkable gesture, she thought, as if to say that he understood the trouble they were in and to hold tight until he was back.

Magda knew that healing a seriously injured person could take quite a while. If everything went right, it could sometimes be done in a matter of hours, but it could also just as easily take days.

The man, James, was apparently a friend. He needed Merritt's help or he would certainly die. Merritt of course had to go help, to try to heal him. Magda would expect no less of Merritt.

But Magda didn't think the rest of them had days to wait.

The boxes of Orden were missing, dream walkers were haunting the Keep, traitors were among them, people were dying mysteriously, and dead men hunted among the dark passageways.

Magda knew that no one else but Merritt even believed her.

CHAPTER

56

As a jumble of thoughts fought for her attention, Magda gazed out over the stone wall at the side of the bridge and down into the vast chasm. The split in the mountain spanned by the stone bridge dropped nearly all the way to the very floor of the valley. Clouds frequently drifted by below the bridge, but not this day. This day a humid haze dimmed the details far below. A flock of birds passed beneath the arch of the bridge, and far below them trees clung in places to small ledges in the cliff. Far down at the bottom she could just make out boulders.

The boulders reminded her of the ones below the cliff where Baraccus had jumped to his death, and she almost had. At that thought she had to turn away from the dizzying drop.

The dark, soaring stone walls of the Keep caught the last warm rays of the setting sun. The humid air had gone dead still as the day neared its end.

Magda stood gazing out at the blue haze of mountains in the distance across the other side of the bridge, unsure what to do, unsure how long she dared wait for Merritt before she had to go without him down to the dungeon to look for the enemy sorceress. Someone coming across the bridge caught her eye.

It was Councilman Sadler. He looked grim as he strode resolutely across the bridge, head bent, watching the ground before him as if in a daze.

Magda stepped out and gently caught him by the arm. "Councilman Sadler, good afternoon."

His arm a captive in her grip, he looked up.

"Magda." He blinked at being so suddenly jarred from his thoughts. "Good afternoon."

As he started away, Magda held on to his arm, pulling him to a stop again and keeping him from leaving.

"What's wrong?" she asked.

He scowled unhappily. "Am I that obvious?"

"No, not at all. Just a feeling I had when I saw you. Is there anything I can do for you?"

He peered at her a moment. His clear eyes behind drooping lids finally looked away from her before he spoke.

"The council has made some decisions," he said. "You caught me thinking over the matter."

"And you don't like what was decided?"

"I can't say that I'm entirely in agreement with their determinations."

It was uncharacteristic for him to voice such personal feelings about matters decided by the council. He was usually quite stoic. With thoughts of all the trouble at the Keep still in her head, she decided not to let the matter go.

"May I ask what they have decided that troubles you?"

He pressed his lips tight for a moment, thinking it over, but then he finally relented.

"People will know soon enough. Won't be a secret for long."

"Have they named a First Wizard?" she guessed. "Is that it?"

He straightened and studied her face before finally letting out a sigh. He gazed off at the city far down in the valley.

"Yes. And more."

Puzzled, Magda was not about to let the matter go without more details. "I don't know what you mean. What more?"

He came out of his private thoughts and glanced around to see if anyone was close, then took her arm and led her over to the stone wall edging the bridge. Women carrying bundles hurried past on their way back from markets in Aydindril. Men walked before carts pulled by mules or rode in wagons piled high with supplies of every sort, from firewood to barrels of salted fish.

A double column of soldiers coming from the Keep rode past on big black horses. Their breastplates reflected the amber glow of the late-day light. Chain mail and armor jangled as the horses trotted past. People scurried out of their way. All the equally big men carried lances at a perfect upright angle. These heavily armed men, called the Black Lancers, were some of the most lethal soldiers in the Home Guard. Besides wearing black tunics beneath their armor and chain mail, they also proclaimed their identity with long black pennants as well as their beautiful black horses.

Sadler watched the Black Lancers gallop away once they reached the far side of the bridge. He waited until all the nearby people continued on their way again, waited until the two of them stood apart from everyone crossing the bridge.

"You're a good woman, Magda. Always fair and always well reasoned. So, I'll tell you before you hear it elsewhere tomorrow."

Magda tilted her head toward him so as not to miss his quiet words. "What is it, Councilman Sadler."

"Lothain has been named First Wizard."

Magda's mouth hung open. It was a moment before she finally found her voice.

"Lothain? Head Prosecutor Lothain? That Lothain? He has been named First Wizard? Are you serious?"

"Quite serious." Sadler's expression was grim. "His installation will be held soon—within a matter of a few days, I would expect, although I've not been informed of exactly when. With pressing matters of the war, the council wants to forgo the usual large, public event such as when Baraccus was named. They want it to be somewhat smaller than is customary in order to hurry arrangements along so he can get on with the business of First Wizard."

Magda was too stunned to know what to say.

"That's not all," Sadler added. He gestured down the mountain. "I'm moving down to my cottage in the woods. No need for me to live at the Keep any longer."

"But the council . . ."

His eyes, still as sharp as ever, flashed her way. "I won't be sitting on the council."

Magda blinked. "What do you mean?"

He looked suddenly uncomfortable, even embarrassed. "I have been dismissed."

Magda had to run the word through her mind again to be sure she had heard it correctly. "Dismissed? You can't be dismissed. Unless of course you have been convicted of—"

"No, no, nothing like that," he said as he waved with a gesture to indicate that she had gotten the wrong idea.

"Then what do you mean you've been dismissed? How can you be dismissed? By whom?"

"Lothain."

Magda stared a moment before again having to remind herself to close her mouth.

"I don't understand."

He grimaced a little as he looked away from her. "Lothain suggested, and the rest of the council agreed, that changes needed to be made so that decisions in such difficult times could be more easily reached. With six members on the council, we were often deadlocked."

"But it's supposed to be that way so that a majority can't run roughshod and dictate. Six members is meant to be more deliberative, meant to promote a measured pace in the council working toward the truth. It prevents rash decisions."

He gestured with a flick of his hand, as if he agreed with her, but could do nothing about it.

"It was thought that in wartime, with problems such as we now face, what the council needs most is the ability to reach swift rulings. Five members gives them that ability. Three members in agreement is all it now takes to pass a proposal."

Magda didn't know what to say. She had known Sadler for a long time. She had brought matters before him for several years. He hadn't always agreed with her, but unlike some of the others he had always listened with an open mind.

She reached out and laid a hand on his forearm. "I'm so sorry. Are you going to be all right?"

He again waved off her concern. "Don't worry for me. I'll be fine. I always wanted to spend more time in my quiet little cottage in the woods. Since my wife passed . . . well, I guess that I could use some time to reflect. Worrying about matters of war are probably too harsh a burden for me anymore. . . . At least, that was what the others said."

A slight breath of breeze pulled some of her short hair across her face. Magda pushed it back. "Can I come see you sometime?"

He grinned and pinched her cheek, something he had never done before. It was an extraordinary gesture that stunned her.

"I'd like that, Magda. I'd like that."

He seemed so much less reserved than, in her experience, he had always been. His weathered, wrinkled face looked tired. She thought it must be that he had believed he had to present a measured and resolute façade appropriate to being a councilman. Now that mask had faded away to reveal the man beneath it.

As he started away, she watched him turning his back on the Keep, on a life's work. He looked hunched and older to her than he ever had before. Magda suddenly thought of something and called out to him.

Magda took a step away from the stone wall at the side of the bridge.

"Councilman Sadler."

He stopped and turned. "It's just Sol, now. I am no longer a councilman. I am just Sol."

Magda smiled a sad smile. "I'm afraid that I could never in my life bring myself to call you anything other than Councilman Sadler."

He accepted the sentiment with a slight smile and a nod. "If you wish. I guess my ears are accustomed enough to the sound of it, and as long as we are alone I guess that there is no one to object."

Magda glanced around to make sure that no one was close. Everyone looked to be mostly concerned with their own business and in a hurry to get where they were going before it got too dark. They didn't pay the two of them undue attention, although people who did recognize him stared for a moment on their way past. Magda took another step, closing the distance to him so that there was no chance that anyone could overhear them. She again glanced around.

"Councilman Sadler, can you tell me anything about

a woman, a sorceress from the Old World, who defected and came here to the Keep to join our cause?"

He rubbed a hand back and forth across his mouth as he thought it over. He lifted a finger.

"Yes, as a matter of fact I do recall, now, that Lothain mentioned something about a woman coming over from the enemy side, claiming to want to change her loyalty. I think you're right that she was a sorceress. He said that she was a spy, though. Could that be the woman you mean?"

"Most likely. Do you know anything about her?"

"I'm afraid not. I never met her. Why do you ask?"

Magda didn't want to say. A councilman, of all people, would certainly be a prime target for a dream walker. For all she knew there could be a dream walker hiding in the shadows of his mind at that very moment, watching and listening to her every word. She had to be careful. She also had to think quickly. She lifted a hand in a casual gesture.

"I was hoping that maybe she might be able to help in our war effort. If she really did come from the Old World, I was hoping that maybe a woman like that would know something that could help us."

For the first time his expression turned suspicious. "You mean, like with information about the dream walkers, such as what tasks occupy their attention, and how far they've gotten?"

Magda showed a brief, if insincere smile. "Well yes, that had crossed my mind, but I was thinking in a more general nature. We could use all the help we can get."

He nodded. "Sorry, but I can't say. Not because I wouldn't tell you, Magda, but because I don't know anything."

"I see. Well, thank you anyway, Councilman Sadler."

She smiled again, but sincerely this time. "I'll try to visit you, soon, and see how you're getting along."

He smiled warmly in return. "I'd like that, Magda. I'd like that very much."

He took a step, but then paused and turned back to her. He laid a hand on her shoulder, his fingers tightening as he drew her a bit closer.

"Of all the people who came before us, Magda, you were the only one who always represented truth. I want you to know that."

She suddenly felt a bit guilty for being deceptive in her answer about the sorceress. But it was a pretense necessary to protect lives. The dream walkers, after all, could be anywhere.

"I came before you to represent those who have no voice."

He smiled a sly smile as he let the hand drop. "No, not exactly. You did not speak up for the deceitful, the covetous, the greedy who have no voice. You spoke only on behalf of the innocent, or those of principle, who have no voice. You came before us to represent truth. Others on the council may not have noted the distinction, but I wanted you to know that I always did.

"Though you are not gifted, there is power in a voice such as yours, power in truth. Our reasoning minds, after all, are where our greatest ability lies. Though you are not gifted, that ring of truth resonates with people more than you know.

"There are things going on at the Keep that I don't understand. Perhaps others do, perhaps even you do, but I don't. As a councilman I was in a way shut off from many of the real goings-on around us. I saw only what was shown to me. In that capacity I saw a great many people who came before us for a great many reasons.

"You, Magda Searus, were the only one who always came before us concerned only with the truth.

"We live in dangerous times. We may be living in the end of times. If we are to survive, we need truth more than anything else. Of all the people I have known, you are the only one who stood out to me as someone dedicated to finding the truth of things. I doubt you have any idea how rare that is.

"Don't ever give up on that calling, Magda. Know yourself, know who you are. Though few would admit it, even those on the council, I truly believe that we all need you."

Magda was stunned to hear him say such things. "But I'm not even gifted. I'm . . ." She almost said that she was a nobody. "I'm not able to do much on my own."

His smile returned. "Standing for truth is everything. Truth is power. Don't ever forget that."

"I won't. Thank you, Councilman Sadler."

He smiled at the title.

"Oh, and Magda, I want you to know that I took your advice."

"My advice? What advice?"

He lifted an eyebrow. "Your advice to give the oath to Lord Rahl to protect our minds from the dream walkers."

Magda stared at him. "You did? When?"

He smiled. "The night after you came to the council covered in blood. Like I said, I know that you are the only one who came before us concerned with nothing more than the truth. As soon as I was in my room that night, I went to my knees, as you had instructed, and gave the three devotions to Lord Rahl."

Magda hoped for his sake that he was telling the truth. "Did any of the other council members swear the oath?"

He shrugged. "I'm sorry, but I don't know. I would not 1 any of them, and I'm sure they would not tell me. I just wanted you to know that if you do come to see me, you can speak your mind without worry of a dream walker hearing it."

Magda grinned. "Councilman Sadler, you are a devious man."

He returned the grin. "How do you think I have managed to live this long? Be well, Magda Searus. And be true to yourself."

"I will. And please, take good care of yourself. You can never tell when the Midlands may have further need of you."

As Sadler once again started out across the massive stone bridge, mingling into the crowds, Magda felt a breeze kick up. She glanced to the horizon and noticed a black band of clouds. The hot, humid weather had been a harbinger of approaching storms.

Before passing under the iron fangs of the portcullis, she gazed up at the massive, dark walls and towers of the Keep rising up into the darkening sky. The silent Keep seemed to be waiting for her, waiting to swallow her up.

Magda was alone again. Even though she had only just met him, she missed Merritt being with her. There was something about him unlike anyone she had ever met. It felt easy, natural, being with him.

But now she was alone.

CHAPTER
58

Magda was just closing the heavy mahogany door to her apartment when she heard footsteps and then a knock. She thought it might be Merritt, even though she knew that it was too soon for him to be back—unless he had been unable to help James. She pulled open the door.

Lothain filled the doorway.

He smiled in that private sort of way he had whenever he looked at her. It was a lecherous look that always made her skin crawl.

After taking a quick appraisal of the room dimly lit by a half-dozen lamps, the man's black eyes again fixed on her. She could tell by the way he was looking at her that he was having some kind of private thoughts about her, thoughts she was sure she would not like.

Magda wanted to slam the door in his face, but she thought better of it. She had already pushed him to the edge once before. It would be risky to do it again now, when they were alone and he didn't have to worry about witnesses. The word of the head prosecutor would be taken at face value if she were to end up dead. Enough people already thought she was disloyal to the Midlands that anything he said would likely be believed.

He smoothed a hand over his short, wiry black hair and down the back of his bull neck. His shoulders and arms were as beefy as his neck.

Though he had more formal, dignified clothes that he often wore when conducting official business, such as during trials, this night he was wearing unadorned brown robes, a simple reminder of his high rank as both prosecutor and wizard. Lavish outfits were all too often worn as a pretense of status, since the poor could not afford fine clothes. Plain, modest robes were meant to be a humble reminder that even those of the highest standing were still mortal. More, though, they were a subtle statement to all that they were of such high rank that they didn't actually need to prove it with stylish attire. Their rank transcended fashion. Those seeking standing would only look silly should they try to mimic that standing with simple robes, since everyone would know they were pretenders. So they were left the middle ground of finery to scrap for standing.

"Good evening, Magda."

She didn't like the arrogance of his informality any more than she liked his greasy smile. She stuck to a proper address.

"Prosecutor Lothain."

His smile widened into a smug grin. "First Wizard Lothain," he corrected.

She bowed her head slightly with a single nod. "Congratulations. You come into a difficult role with the heavy burden of a terrible war. The people of the Midlands will wish you well with such responsibility, I'm sure, in the hopes that you might guide us safely through these troubled times."

She wondered if he was to also remain as head prosecutor. That would allow him to retain his private army, but she didn't want to ask and prolong the conversatio

"Yes, a grim duty and heavy responsibility has been placed upon my shoulders," he said in an indifferent tone, his gaze wandering beyond her to the apartment within.

It occurred to her that he was checking to make sure that she was alone.

He started to step past her into the apartment, then stopped. "Oh, I'm sorry, Magda. Where are my manners? Here I was, already thinking of the place as mine. Forgive me. May I come in?"

Magda stepped back, opening the door wider. As she did, she noticed his large contingent of personal guards down the hall.

"Of course. It's your place, now. Or at least it will be once I am able to have my things moved out. I will try not to delay you any longer than necessary."

She couldn't seem to make herself call him First Wizard.

"As a matter of fact, I'm here to discuss that very subject with you."

Magda didn't give him the satisfaction of asking what he meant. He wasn't at all a shy man. He liked the sound of his own voice. She knew that he would get around to it in his own good time. He didn't need her prompting.

He strode into the room, peering about, taking in all the furniture, the gold-fringed draperies, the plush, multicolored carpets, the richly plastered walls, and the layered cornices at the edge of the ceiling. He ran a finger over a sideboard of banded mahogany that was beautifully inlaid with silver stems and leaves. It had been a wedding gift from Baraccus, one of many.

She hadn't liked the idea of Baraccus getting such opulent furnishings. She didn't want people to say that he had only been able to win such a beautiful young woman into marriage because as First Wizard he was able to shower her with lavish gifts and provide her with a home like a palace.

He had gotten her the gifts anyway. When people thought what she had feared, he had laughed it off and said that he didn't care about gossip because he knew better. He had insisted that the place needed the warmth if she was to live there.

Magda had never in her life lived in such splendor. As beautiful as the surroundings were, though, they had never meant all that much to her. In fact, she preferred the small storage room because that was where Baraccus's workbench was. She had often sat on her throne of an old crate and watched him work.

"Nice," Lothain said, still looking around. "Very nice. You've obviously gone to a great deal of expense and effort adding a woman's touch to what used to be rather cold quarters."

"I can't take credit. It was all Baraccus's doing."

He glanced back briefly, looking like he didn't believe her. He strolled past a wall of books in arched bookcases. "Well, he created quite the comfortable home for you here."

"It's not my home. It is the First Wizard's home."

She moved to the door, hinting that now that he had seen enough of the place that would soon be his, she expected him to be on his way. She wasn't going to show him the rest of the apartment. He could see the other rooms once she was gone.

"I really should get to packing my things. The sooner I move out, the sooner you can move in."

He returned to stand before her. His burly build seemed all the more intimidating standing so close in front of her. She forced herself not to take a step back as she casually moved her hand closer to her knife hidden in the small of her back, beneath her dress. A small slit in the dress provided access to the weapon.

His smile was back as he fixed her in his gaze again. "That isn't necessary."

"I don't know what you mean," she said.

"Moving out," he said offhandedly. "It isn't necessary. You see, I think that it's time that we came to an arrangement."

Even though she was truly puzzled at his meaning, she didn't want to coax him into talking about it. She simply wanted him to leave.

"No arrangement will be necessary. If you will leave me to it, I will pack up my things and move out as quickly as I can so as not to inconvenience you. You are to be First Wizard, so this place is to be yours as well."

"No, I mean that we can make an arrangement so that you don't have to leave." He gestured briefly around the room. "It's such a beautiful home. This place really does fit you. I want you to stay."

"Stay? I don't need—"

"As my wife."

CHAPTER
59

Magda stared, unsure that she had heard what she thought she'd heard.

"What?"

"I have decided that it is socially appropriate for a man of such standing as the First Wizard to have a wife."

She was beginning to grasp more graphically the nature of the thoughts that had been so evident behind those black eyes.

"What in the world would make you think . . ." She checked herself, rethinking the wisdom of the insult she had been about to make. "What makes you think that I would in any way make an appropriate wife for you?"

His gaze drifted down her curves. "Oh, I think you will do just fine." When the calculating look finally made it all the way back up to her eyes, his tone turned a bit more serious.

"You see, you have already been the wife to a First Wizard. You know the protocols. You are familiar with the duties. You handled household matters admirably for Baraccus, relieving him of menial tasks, and you will do the same for me."

"There are maids and such assigned to hand

household matters. They come with the apartments. You will do just fine with their help."

"Be that as it may, there are larger issues at stake. You are a woman who also needs the protection of an important man."

Magda was getting the distinct feeling that there was a hidden agenda that he was working toward.

"Protection?"

He shrugged. "Of course. Your being the wife of the new First Wizard will bring an end to the questions about your allegiance. It would put to rest the whispers about your apparent loyalty to Lord Rahl over the Midlands. It would help disassociate you from the irregular matters Baraccus was entangled in. It would also bring an end to suspicions about all the strange things you have been up to, lately."

"Strange things I've been up to? What are you talking about?"

"You have been seen sneaking about, trying not to be seen, hiding your face."

"In other words, you have people spying on me. It so happens that as the former wife to the First Wizard I simply want to avoid undue attention."

"The fact remains that a virtuous woman, a woman with nothing to hide, would not do such things. It makes people wonder about you, wonder exactly what you may have been up to. Very unsavory behavior for someone of your standing." He glanced at her short hair. "Or should I say, former standing."

"If my loyalty to the Midlands and our cause is so suspect, why would you, as First Wizard, want to have a woman like that as a wife? More to the point, you are many things, but you are not stupid. You know what I think of you. Why would you be so interested in protecting my virtue?"

His smile widened. "Your virtue? You think I care about your virtue? I have use of you, that's all. Saving your reputation, and perhaps your hide, is merely a plum I offer in return."

"You have use of me? What use could I possibly be to you?"

He glanced back over his shoulder, then returned his gaze to her eyes. "Why don't you show me the bedroom, Magda, and I will make clear to you one of your many uses to me."

Magda could feel the blood rush to her face. She worked to control her voice. Yelling at him was not going to get her to the bottom of what this was really all about.

"You're a powerful man. You can have your pick of most any woman. A few of them might even be willing; the rest you can easily afford. You don't need me for that."

His grin remained in place. "That may be true, but I would rather have you. The most unobtainable of all flowers is the most desirable, don't you think? It would prove me the most worthy of any man at the Keep to win the widow of Baraccus as my wife."

"I wasn't aware that your self-confidence was so shaky."

His smile finally departed, leaving a grim expression. "Self-confidence is not my problem; how people perceive me is. You see, having you as my wife would give me credibility as First Wizard. It would put people in mind of Baraccus. It would put us on the same plane. I would be his equal, and as his equal, I would have the same woman at my side."

Magda gritted her teeth. "You are not the equal of Baraccus."

He chuckled. "My dear, you will reconsider that after our first night in bed together."

"Get out," Magda growled through gritted teeth. She pointed through the open doorway. "Leave."

His humor vanished as his pinched expression took on a vicious cast. He jabbed a beefy finger against her shoulder.

"Now you listen to me, Magda Searus. You've caused a lot of trouble here in the Keep, trouble that has spread down to the city. I don't know why, but there are a lot of people who believe in you. You got everyone in a fearful uproar with your bloody show before the council session when you put your wild theories about dream walkers out where people could hear them.

"Far worse, though, are your disrespectful and despicable accusations against me. Improbable as it seems, those insulting charges brought by a nobody have caught the attention of many. Those accusations have found support and created divisions within the Keep. They have disgraced and discredited me in the eyes of some. Your allegations have made people less willing to trust me, to follow me.

"We are at war and you have created speculation, divisions, and suspicion when we instead need to be united. Your theories and fanciful notions have shaken people's trust in the council's wisdom and especially in my authority. You have undermined faith in me!

"You, Magda Searus, have become a threat to order and therefore to our cause. If you care about the Midlands and the people, as you claim, then you would see that it is your duty to bring peace among them. You are the cause of the dissension and discord, so it is your duty to put an end to it.

"By marrying me, you will put to rest all the absurd theories flying around the Keep, absurd theories started by you. The gossip and speculation will end. You becoming my wife will calm fears and bring suspicion to an end. It will show people that your behavior was only your grief playing tricks on your weak, feminine mind.

"Marrying me will put an end to the whispers, about you, and especially about me. Marrying me will silence the dissent that is brewing. It will restore unity to the people.

"You are going to marry me in order to restore faith in my unquestioned authority, faith you undermined. You are going to do this for the good of the Midlands."

"I am not going—"

"This is not a matter open to debate! It is for the good of our people and you are going to do it!"

He smoothed a hand back over his bull neck and calmed his tone.

"Now, I will give you a chance to think it over. It's a big step, remarrying, but it will do you good and give you a renewed purpose here at the Keep. I hope that you don't make it any more difficult for yourself than it needs to be.

"Either way, I can assure you that, in the end, one way or another, you will be married to me and serve me as a good and loyal wife should serve her man and her leader, the First Wizard."

He leaned close, his teeth clenched, as he jabbed his fat finger into her shoulder over and over, punctuating his words.

"That is the road of life you are going to travel. Don't make that road any harder than it needs to be."

Magda ignored the throbbing pain from his finger jabbing her shoulder.

"I told you to get out."

He flashed her a cold, patronizing smile. "So you see, since you will be marrying me, you will be remaining in your apartment—or I should say, our apartment— surrounded by the luxury to which you are accustomed, living the privileged life of the wife of the First Wizard. Fears and doubts about the leadership of the Midlands will soon be forgotten when people see you faithfully at my side."

"I asked you to leave."

Magda's heart was hammering so hard with rage she couldn't think straight.

He gestured. "You will have to let your hair grow out, of course. It's only fitting for the wife of the First Wizard to have long hair."

"I told you—"

"Is there a problem, here?"

Magda turned. Merritt filled the doorway.

Merritt had Lothain fixed in a dangerous glare.

"No, there's no problem," Magda said. "Prosecutor Lothain was just leaving. He had a minor issue to ask me about, but as it turns out, I'm afraid that I'm unable to help him with it."

Lothain stared at her for a moment, as if to say that it was already decided and he would have his way, before letting his icy look move to Merritt.

"What are you doing here, Merritt?"

The two men glared at each other like two stags unexpectedly encountering each other in an open meadow. She knew that she had to do something before one of them decided to.

"I asked him to come," Magda said into the dangerous silence.

Lothain's brow twitched as he looked over at her. "You asked him to come? Why?"

Before Merritt could say anything, Magda replied, in an offhand manner, "Baraccus was a maker."

"What does that have to do with anything?" Lothain asked before Magda had a chance to explain.

"Well, when the council told me that they needed the apartments for a new First Wizard," she went on, "I told them that I would find a new place and move my things out. I'm in the process of packing them up. But I have no use for Baraccus's old tools. I heard that Merritt is also a maker, so I offered him the tools. They aren't of any use to me. I thought they not only might be of some use to Merritt, but it would save me the trouble of moving them. Besides, I won't have the room for them in my new quarters."

Lothain smoothed a hand over his head as he considered what she'd said. "I see."

Lothain's legendary temper was balanced on a knife edge, and she knew that it could go either way. She was overwhelmed by what he had told her and she needed time to think, but if she didn't do something to cool him off, or at least move him into another direction, there was going to be trouble.

With Lothain's private army filling the hall, she knew that Merritt didn't stand a chance.

"I'm glad that I was here and had the chance to show you the quarters," Magda said before he could say anything. She gestured to the door. "If you're finished inspecting them, then I will see to getting rid of Baraccus's old tools and moving the rest of my things out as soon as possible."

Magda had always thought of Lothain as a sizable man, but next to Merritt he looked almost puny. Still, one man was no match for all the soldiers in green tunics.

For whatever reason, Lothain took the opportunity to pass up an ugly confrontation. He flashed her a cold smile and a meaningful look.

"Of course." He bowed his head slightly. "Thank you, Lady Searus, for listening with an open mind to my . . . proposal. We will be coming to an agreement on it very soon, I assure you."

Lothain let his gaze turn to take in Merritt, from his long, wavy hair to his boots and back up again. It was a condescending examination.

"Didn't anyone ever tell you, boy, that real wizards don't need swords?"

Magda expected the trouble to begin, but Merritt instead did something that surprised her. He grinned. As he leaned against the doorframe he shrugged with his other shoulder.

"I'm compensating for my many inadequacies."

Lothain arched an eyebrow as he bulled the taller man out of his way. "I imagine you are."

Merritt looked back over his shoulder, watching Lothain and the prosecutor's private army depart.

"What did he want?" Merritt asked, his grin gone.

"A wife."

"What?"

Magda waved off the question. "I'll tell you later. What about James?"

Merritt sighed. "I got lucky. He was having a lot of trouble breathing. They thought his lungs had been burned when he inhaled the illumination from the explosion of the collapsing web. They just didn't understand the reaction caused by the combination of spells involved. Those spells were still stuck together, I guess you could say, still reacting and suppressing his ability to breathe. Once I decoupled the elements of the spell-forms to cease the reaction, he could breathe again.

"He's still hurting, but the others can heal him now. We have more important things to worry about."

Magda let out a sigh of relief. "Thank goodness."

Merritt didn't look to share her relief. "There are still three other wives mourning the deaths of their husbands."

Magda nodded. "Let's go next door, to the storage room, just in case Lothain comes back. I told him that you were here for Baraccus's tools. Let's not give him any excuse to think we're up to something."

CHAPTER
61

As they walked into the storage room, Merritt swept an arm out to ignite the lamps. Since he was gifted, his presence also lit the half-dozen heavy glass light spheres in iron brackets on the walls. The closed shutters held back the night and the distant flickers of lightning at the horizon.

"So what's this about Lothain wanting you as his wife?"

His tone betrayed his displeasure.

"We have trouble," Magda said without answering his question.

"More trouble than Lothain wanting you as his wife?"

"Lothain has been named First Wizard."

Suddenly speechless, Merritt stared at her, not unlike the way she had stared at Councilman Sadler when he'd first told her the news. The only sound in the storage room was the hissing sputters of the freshly lit lamps.

Merritt finally found his voice. "That is trouble. I've never trusted the man. He's not half the man needed for First Wizard."

"Believe me, I have a far lower opinion of him than you do, but he's apparently a man with enough power to get himself named as First Wizard."

"That's true enough. A lot of people support him. His reign as head prosecutor has seen a lot of formerly respected people brought down. Many people hold him in high regard for so vigorously going after criminals and traitors. You have to admit, he has been able to prosecute a lot of traitors." Merritt leaned toward her as they crossed the room. "I have to confess, though, that I've always had my doubts about the guilt of some of those he has prosecuted."

Magda frowned over at him. "Like who?"

Merritt pressed his lips tight before finally giving in. "I knew some of the wizards on the Temple team. I'd always thought favorably of them. I can see that many on the team turned against our cause and betrayed us, but all of them? I wonder if some of them might not have been scapegoats. Charging someone and beheading them ends the investigation. It makes Lothain look like he successfully prosecuted all of the guilty. But I wonder."

Magda was a bit surprised to hear Merritt say such things. She had thought that she was the only one. Being ungifted, she had assumed that she didn't know enough about the whole thing to judge. She didn't know that wizards had doubts about the guilt of the Temple team. Maybe Merritt was the only one.

She looked back over her shoulder at his eyes. "I've wondered as well.

"That's not all of it," she said as she reached the familiar workbench. "Right after you left me to go help James, I ran into Councilman Sadler as he was leaving the Keep. Besides telling me that Lothain was to be named First Wizard, he also told me that Lothain dismissed him from the council."

"Dismissed him?" Merritt leaned in. "Can he do such a thing?"

"Apparently. Sadler put on a brave face, but I could tell that he was heartbroken about it."

Merritt scratched his cheek as he considered it. "Why would Lothain get rid of Sadler?"

"In order to reduce the council's number to five so as to make it possible to carry any motion with three votes. There were six members, before, so the vote could be split three to three, preventing action. Now, with five members, the council can't be evenly split anymore, as happened with difficult decisions. Now, no matter what, they are always guaranteed to have a majority to decide up or down on any matter."

"That is troubling. I've never really had much to do with the higher powers running the Keep, but this doesn't sound good to me. What I'm more worried about, though, is what does Lothain know about running a war?"

"He has his own private army."

Merritt arched an eyebrow. "That doesn't make him a general, it makes him a petty tyrant with muscle behind him."

"Well, if I'm right about him, he may now become a bigger tyrant."

Merritt considered silently for a moment, and then folded his arms. "All of this news is troubling enough, but what's this about you marrying him?"

Magda took a deep breath. She hated the whole subject. "Well, Lothain says that I'm causing all kinds of trouble in the Keep. He says that the Keep has become divided and filled with discord and distrust. Apparently, a lot of people besides us don't think he is the right man to be First Wizard.

"Lothain thinks that his problems with credibility are chiefly my doing. He thinks that because of the things I said about him I've undermined his authority and have made people doubt him."

"You said something about him? What did you say?"

"When I was in front of a crowd in the council chambers, he accused me of making up the story about the dream walkers in order to get people to switch allegiance to D'Hara. I, in turn, accused him of chasing phantoms just to make a bigger name for himself. I said that he sees conspiracies lurking in every shadow, spies hiding around every corner, traitors behind every door. I said that he cared only about inventing wrongdoing in order to advance his own personal fame and power."

Merritt let out a low whistle. "You said that? Publicly?"

"I'm afraid so. In front of everyone I accused him of coming up with conspiracies that were only meant to promote his own status. I said that in order to elevate himself he was deliberately ignoring the truth about the dream walkers."

"No wonder he blames you for tarnishing his credibility."

"He also says that I've given birth to wild speculation about dream walkers. He says that my groundless accusations have turned people in the Keep against him. He says that such divisions are harmful to our cause."

Merritt paced a few steps away and then returned with heat in his voice. "Then why in the world would he want to marry you?"

"His solution to people's doubts about him, doubts that he says I created with what he calls my baseless accusations, is to have me marry him. He thinks that if I were to marry him, it would convince everyone that I've reconsidered my views, views shaped by my grief and not any true failing on his part. He says that my consent to marry him would show people that I'm putting my faith and trust in him, and so they should as well. He thinks that it will banish any lingering doubts. He thinks that only in that way will people unite behind him and the war effort. He says that I need to do it for the good of the Midlands and our cause."

Merritt, arms still folded, stared at her with an unreadable look.

Magda finally leaned toward him and said, "I'm not going to marry him."

He let his arms drop. "Oh. All right, then."

Magda turned to the familiar, worn workbench. She knew how angry the very idea of marrying Lothain made her, but she was a little surprised to see how upset it made Merritt. It made her feel good, though, that he cared that she didn't make the mistake of marrying Lothain.

Shadow jumped out from the darkness among crates and supplies stacked on the floor and up onto the workbench. The silky black cat came close and rubbed against Magda's hand.

As Magda stroked the cat's back, Shadow lifted her hind end, hoping to have it scratched. As she enjoyed the attention, her tail curled around Magda's wrist.

"Who's this?" Merritt asked.

"This is Shadow. Isidore told me that cats have some small capacity to see between worlds. She said that black cats catch glimpses of the spirit world."

Merritt held his hand out so that Shadow could get to know him. "Isidore would know." Shadow inspected each finger in turn.

"Shadow detected the presence of that dead man that attacked us before we knew he was there. She definitely didn't like him." Magda smiled. "But I see that she really likes you."

Shadow was rubbing against Merritt, purring in response to his touch. With his black shirt, the cat matched him, looked almost part of him. Magda wondered if

Merritt, too, could detect the presence of spirits. The limits of the gift were often a mystery to her.

"I now sleep with the cloth from Isidore's maze as a blanket, and Shadow curled up beside my pillow." Magda scratched the cat's head. "Don't I, little one? But now you need to move."

"I'm glad to hear it," Merritt said. "For someone ungifted, you seem to know how to use the things of magic at your disposal."

Magda smiled as she lifted the cat and set her to the back of the workbench, where she lay down on her side, curled a paw under, and settled in to watch as Magda pulled a piece of wood out that covered a secret compartment in the bench top.

"I have something to show you."

CHAPTER

62

"This is the note Baraccus left for me," Magda said. "You asked before about its exact wording. I thought we had better check. I know how important such little details can be to a wizard."

Suddenly alert, Merritt stepped closer. "Would you mind if I knew what the whole note said? Context can be important in such matters. Besides that, I might be able to pick up on something you missed. I mean, only if you'd be willing. . . . Would you mind?"

Magda smiled. "No, of course not."

She carefully unfolded the piece of paper and then held the note up in the light so that she could read it aloud.

"'My time has passed, Magda. Yours has not. Your destiny is not here. Your destiny is to find truth. It will be difficult, but have the courage to take up that calling.'" She looked up. "I was right. It doesn't say 'find the truth.' It just says 'find truth.'"

Merritt was frowning, deep in thought. After a moment, he gestured to the note in her hands. "Is there more?"

Magda nodded and went on. "'Look out to the rise on the valley floor below, just outside the city to the left.

There, on that rise, a palace will one day be built. There is your destiny, not here.' "

She had to swallow and compose herself before she could read the last part. " 'Know that I believe in you. Know, too, that I will always love you. You are a rare, fierce flower, Magda. Be strong now, guard your mind, and live the life that only you can live.' "

The only sound was Shadow's tail slowly, softly, slapping the top of the workbench.

"It's a beautiful note, Magda," Merritt said in a soft, compassionate voice as she stood staring down at the paper in her trembling fingers. "It's clear how much you meant to him."

Magda wiped a tear from her cheek. She hadn't realized how shaken she would be to read it again. It brought back so much, and at the same time reminded her of how distant it had all become. Baraccus was gone. The world of life had moved on.

Magda cleared her throat. "Do you have any idea what he could mean about a palace, and my destiny being there?"

"Sorry, but I don't. Baraccus was a prophet, though, so he must know something about the future. A possible future, anyway. Our free will makes the future sometimes uncertain, even for prophets. I think that what he means is the future is yours to decide and he is hoping you will make the right decision."

Magda's arm lowered. "When the dream walker was trying to kill me, I remembered what he said in this note. Alric Rahl told me that the devotion he created—the one you helped him create—is meant to guard our minds from dream walkers. When a dream walker had me, and was trying to kill me, those words in the note made me realize that I had to give the devotion to Lord Rahl in order to guard my mind and save my own life. Baraccus's words made me choose my own future, choose life, and as a result his prophetic words proved true."

"Prophecy is often like that," Merritt said. He seemed to surface from deep thoughts. "It also says your destiny is to find truth, just like you said, not *the* truth, as I had thought when you first told me."

"Does that mean something to you?"

Merritt gave her a meaningful look, then drew the sword at his hip. As it emerged from the scabbard, the blade made a soft ringing sound that filled the quiet storage room. Magda could see something besides the gift in his eyes when he held the sword. It was a kind of deep, distant rage, something almost alive with its power.

Merritt carefully laid the sword on the workbench. Shadow gazed with drowsy green eyes at the blade he laid before her. Merritt finally looked at Magda in a way that told her he expected something from her.

She looked from Merritt to the sword and back again. "What?"

Merritt gestured to the sword. "What does it say?"

She knew very well what it said. She hadn't been able to get it out of her mind. Still, Magda's eyes turned to the hilt. She let her fingers lightly glide over the raised gold letters.

"It says 'Truth.'" She lifted a brow at Merritt. "Are you saying that Baraccus's words in his note—'Your destiny is to find truth'—are meant to say that my destiny is to find the Sword of Truth? You really think that's what he meant? You really think it could be that obvious?"

Merritt shrugged. "I don't know. I'm a maker, not a prophet. But I made the word *Truth* on the hilt, and you came to me and found the sword with that word crafted into it. You are the one who named it the Sword of Truth."

A jumble of thoughts tumbled through Magda's mind.

Was Baraccus saying that her destiny was to find Merritt and the sword with *Truth* on it?

Or was he saying that this was the beginning of the path to her finding truth, and that path had taken her to Merritt?

CHAPTER

63

M agda again ran her fingers over the letters as Merritt stepped up beside her at the workbench. His gaze scanned the tools off to the side.

"This is where Baraccus made things, then? This room, this workbench?"

Magda nodded as she gestured to the side. "I used to sit on this crate, here, and watch him work."

Magda glanced to the ornately engraved silver box to the side of the table that held treasured memories. Baraccus seemed so distant, now. In some ways it was all like only yesterday, but in other ways it all seemed so long ago in her life. She missed him, but even that pain was gradually fading as she worried about all the immediate problems.

"Did he make that as well?" Merritt asked, gesturing to the silver box.

Magda nodded as she pulled it closer to show him. She ran her fingers over the top, much as she had done with the letters on the sword, and then opened the lid.

"It just holds some small memories of things he gave me."

Magda lifted out the white flower to show him.

Merritt looked somewhat surprised. "That's pretty rare. I've only seen one of those once before."

Magda twirled the flower between a finger and thumb. "You know what this is, then? Baraccus said it was rare, but never mentioned the name."

"It's called a confession flower."

Magda frowned. "Really? A confession flower? Why would it be called that?"

"Because a confession is a revelation of the truth. Truth is pure. White is pure. Thus the name."

"That's a lovely name, for a lovely flower," she said as she replaced the flower and closed the lid.

"Maybe you could come watch me make something, someday."

Magda smiled. "I'd like that." She hopped up onto her seat on the crate and pointed at the well-used collection of exquisite metalsmithing tools, semiprecious stones in divided wooden trays, assorted supplies, and the small books filled with notes that had belonged to her husband.

"I was making an excuse at the time," she said, "but I think Baraccus would like you to have his tools."

Merritt's eyes lit up. "You really think so? Me, have the tools that belong to a First Wizard?"

"I guess that they're my tools now. I know that I would like you to have them. I really do think that Baraccus would approve. He would want them to go to a good use, to a good person."

Merritt reached out and reverently touched some of the small tools in the collection. They really did seem to mean a great deal to Merritt. He respected their value.

"These are some of the finest tools I've ever seen."

"I'm glad you like them and that you can put them to good use," Magda said with a smile.

He pointed, then, at the little books beside the tools.

"What are those?"

Magda lifted her head to see where he was pointing. "Oh, those. Notes he took, I guess."

Merritt gestured to the books. "May I?"

Magda's smile widened at seeing how excited he was by such simple things as tools and notes. She leaned forward enough to slide the stack of little books closer to him. "Of course. Maybe they can be helpful to you."

Merritt picked up the one on top and opened it, slowly turning the pages, taking a look at what was written there. She watched his hazel eyes move as he scanned the pages.

As he read, his smile vanished. His eyes grew wide.

And then the blood drained from his face.

"Dear spirits . . ." he whispered.

Magda frowned. "What is it? What's wrong?"

He began rapidly turning the pages. He studied each briefly, then turned to the next page.

"Celestial calculations," he whispered to himself.

"That makes sense," Magda said. She didn't understand why he was so excited. Baraccus was forever writing down celestial calculations and measurements. He would take distances and angles from stars to stars, or from certain stars to a distant spot on the horizon, or sometimes to the moon. "I often heard Baraccus speaking to other wizards about celestial calculations, measurements, and equations. I thought all wizards knew about those kinds of things."

"No, you don't understand." He tapped the book as he held it before her face, as if maybe she, too, should be able to decipher the tangle of lines and numbers and formulas. "These are celestial calculations."

"You said that before. I'm sorry, Merritt, but I can't make sense of them."

"Magda, these are the rift calculations for creating a

seventh-level breach." His voice broke. "Dear spirits, these celestial calculations are the measurements and formulas from before the star shift. These are the formulas that I knew had to exist, but had never been able to find. These are the formulas that Baraccus said he couldn't give me because they had been taken away and hidden in the Temple of the Winds."

Magda felt goose bumps tingle up her arms as she hopped down off her crate. "Are you sure? Are you sure that these are those formulas?"

"Yes. Yes, the very ones." He tapped the book excitedly again. "This is them. These are the occulted calculations and templates for creating a seventh-level breach. It's all right here."

As Merritt dropped heavily into the chair at the bench, Magda looked down at the small open book he was holding. The lines and writing looked like nothing but a bunch of angles and numbers to her, the same kinds of measurements Baraccus took all the time from his own observations. It was like a foreign language to her, but it was a language that Merritt, like Baraccus, understood well.

It came to her, then.

Merritt was still staring at the open book.

"I understand, now," she said in little more than a whisper.

With a finger, Magda lifted his chin until his gaze met hers. "I understand."

"What do you mean? Understand what?"

"Baraccus knew that you needed these. He must have brought them back with him from the Temple of the Winds." She felt the goose bumps on her arms crawl the rest of the way up to the nape of her neck. "Remember what I told you before? That when he went there he found out that the boxes of Orden were gone and he could tell no one but me? He knew they'd been taken. Do you see? He must have brought these back so that the key could be completed."

Merritt could only stare at her.

Magda swallowed past the lump in her throat. "He brought them back for you, Merritt. He knew what you were making, and he knew that you needed these. He wanted you to be able to complete the key, hoping you could use it to protect the boxes of Orden. He said that my destiny was to find truth. That led me to you, so that I could bring you to what Baraccus wanted you to have to complete the key."

He put a hand to his forehead. "You're making my head spin, Magda. Do you grasp the enormity of what you're saying? It's all so hard to believe."

"The truth is there in your hand, in that book."

"It certainly is. These formulas are staggeringly valuable. Some believe that their existence was only gossip and rumor. Some believe they never existed and were only a myth. But some of us knew from our work that they had to exist. And here they are, sitting on the First Wizard's workbench."

"They've been here ever since he returned from the underworld with them. He hid them in plain sight."

Merritt's eyes filled with tears as he stared up at her. His voice broke with emotion. "Do you know how many good men have died trying to re-create these formulas? Died making wild guesses in the dark?"

"And now you have what you need to finish the Sword of Truth?"

Merritt reached out and touched the blade. He lifted the little book. "With these I do. I believe that I now have everything I need to complete it."

"You should be able to get some of the other men to help you finish the sword. The key will be complete."

He went silent for a moment as he considered her words.

"I've already done all the preliminary work, and I did that by myself. No one helped me. I don't really need any of those men to complete it."

"Then why are the people trying to make the key always working in teams?"

"The council ordered the key made, but they didn't know how to make it. They assumed it would take teams of wizards. A lot of things do."

"Didn't you tell them?"

"Every chance I got." His face twisted with frustration. "They wouldn't listen to anything I was telling them about how I thought the key needed to be made. Since it was such a complicated task, they guessed that a team would be needed just like they guessed about everything else. They wouldn't listen. They thought that with more men they would be able to cover more ground, overcome the difficulties, and figure it out. But all that did was get more men killed."

"But shouldn't you have someone you trust help you?"

He regarded her with a meaningful look. "Yes, but with all that's happening at the Keep, I don't dare trust anyone. After all, you didn't trust even the council with the news that the power of Orden is back in this world."

"I guess you're right about that."

"Worse, though, the more people who know that the key has been completed, the more we risk word leaking out to whoever has the boxes of Orden. Baraccus didn't trust telling anyone but you. If I do it by myself, no one will know that a key exists. Then I can work to try to find the boxes and protect them."

Magda looked from the sword back to his eyes. "Are you sure that you should finish the Sword of Truth? I mean, if the key doesn't exist . . ."

"Whoever has the boxes very well might try to access the power without the key. That intoxicating temptation has always been the danger. By doing so, and if they do certain things wrong, they could unintentionally destroy the world of life. If that happened, the key would be the only way to control the power and walk us back from the brink."

"Then I guess it's better to complete the sword and then we can try to protect the boxes."

"We?"

"We're the only two people who know all of this. Baraccus trusted me with the information about the missing boxes for a reason. The people who have the boxes don't know about the formulas that Baraccus brought you. We're the only two people who know the whole story. We need to work together."

Merritt mulled over her words. "You're right about that much of it, but I don't know if I like that idea. It's too dangerous for you to be involved."

Magda cocked her head. "Too dangerous? Merritt, I'm already at the center of this whole thing. What unexpected threat might come after me next? The only true safety is to figure out what's going on and put a stop to it."

He wiped a hand back across his face as he let out a weary sigh. "I don't like it, Magda, but I have to admit that you very well might be right. No matter which way you turn, you seem to always be at the center of the storm, whether it's dream walkers, or dead men trying to kill you, Baraccus's prophecies in his note to you, or the boxes of Orden."

Magda was glad he understood. "That's the way I've always looked at it. I have to find out what's going on at the Keep before it's too late. It's something that maybe only I can do."

Merritt closed his fingers around the hilt of the sword

and lifted it off the table. Shadow's green eyes followed the blade. Merritt's own eyes were filled with iron determination.

"I need to do it right now, before anything happens."

"What about going to the dungeons to talk to the sorceress who defected? We have to do that, too. We need to get to her before they execute her."

He placed the sword's point in the scabbard and slid the blade home. "If she is still alive they aren't going to behead her at night. They usually do beheadings in the afternoon, so we have at least until tomorrow. That gives me tonight to complete the key."

"That's true, I suppose, but that's for public executions. This may be something different." Magda didn't want to lose the opportunity to find out if the woman could tell them anything important about the enemy's plans. "Are you sure, Merritt? What that woman knows could be important. We may never get another chance to learn about secrets from the Old World."

"I understand, but this is more important." With a thumb, he tapped the hilt of the sword. "We need to do this first, then we can go to the dungeons and see if we can find her. For all we know, she may not even still be alive. This is more important."

"All right, then, let's head down to the lower reaches of the Keep and finish the sword."

With his palm resting on the pommel, Merritt drummed his fingers on the cross guard as he considered. "I think it best not to do it in the Keep. I don't know for sure how big a reaction the release of that much power will create, but I expect that it will be pretty violent. It's sure to attract the attention of anyone nearby. Besides, I need water. Lots of water."

"Water? Why?"

"To cool the reaction."

Magda brightened. "I know a place like that out in the woods—the pond I used to go to when I was younger."

"The one you went to with Quinn?"

Magda nodded. "That's the place. It's not too far and it's not only secluded, it's deserted. We should go now. At night we wouldn't chance anyone being out for a stroll in the woods."

Merritt paced for a moment as he considered. "Even though I have what I need, it's still profoundly dangerous. Such a thing, with the real elements, has never actually been attempted before that I know of. I think it would be better if you waited here."

Magda waved the note. "Baraccus said that my destiny is to find truth. I named it the Sword of Truth. It's not complete yet and it needs to be. I think my destiny is to be there with you when you complete it. Besides," she added, "you said you needed help. Who else can you trust?"

He watched her eyes for a moment. He finally succumbed to a smile.

"I'd like that, Magda. I'd like that very much. Besides, like I said, I do need another person to help me."

"But I'm not gifted," she reminded him. "What are we going to do about that?"

"I don't need you to be gifted."

"Then what do you need me for?"

"I'll need your blood."

CHAPTER

64

Magda glanced toward the call of unseen creatures echoing out from the darkness. She had
little chance of seeing anything, of course, but
she couldn't help looking every time she heard a strange
sound. The hoots, yelps, and howls coming from the distance in the deep woods, even though she was familiar
with many of the animals that made them, were unnerving at night, and especially a night such as this one. The
lightning and thunder didn't help, either.

The dark shadow of Merritt behind her felt like she was
being haunted by a spirit. After leaving the Keep, they
had walked for quite some time through the blackness
of the dense woods that stretched away in all directions
from Aydindril.

She often thought of that thick carpet of forest as
nearly going on forever, because it seemed to touch the
most distant of places. The roads and trails through
those forests connected Aydindril with the rest of the
world.

She had traveled the vast wilderness too many times
to count as she journeyed to visit distant peoples of the
Midlands. She had followed woodland trails through
mountains to small kingdoms to the north, the routes off

to the distant settlements to the west, the woods roads to cities in D'Hara in the east, and the nearly trackless stretches all the way down to the peoples that inhabited the open grassland of the wilds, far to the south.

Beyond the wilds, farther south, lay the boundless mysteries of the Old World. Though there were well-traveled trade routes down into the Old World, she had never had reason to venture to the distant empire. By some of the trade goods brought back from there, it seemed like it must be an exotic land.

Not wanting to distract Merritt's mind from what he needed to do, she hadn't said much since they had left the city of Aydindril. He had considered the task that lay ahead in silence as Magda had guided him along the little-used path in the deep woods.

She couldn't imagine what Merritt must be feeling. He had worked toward this moment for years, only to come to believe that the goal was out of his reach. Men had died trying to do what he was now about to attempt. But now, because of Baraccus, he had a real chance to complete the key.

While it had been years since she had been on this particular trail, she used to walk it often enough that it was still familiar, although it seemed more overgrown and narrower to her now than it had as a young girl. The lantern Magda carried lit only a small patch of the trail close around her, but it lit enough between the flashes of lightning for her to make her way without difficulty. Since they had left Aydindril, the clouds had built and the lightning had taken on a kind of stormy urgency.

Magda recognized a forked tree and then a particular jumble of granite ledges that abruptly loomed up out of the darkness. She knew that the rock led up and over the spine of a long, descending ridge. Without having to think about it, she took the correct footholds in roots and cracks to smoothly make the brief but tricky switch-back ascent. She noticed that Merritt followed in her footsteps, taking the exact same route, so as to be able to make the climb without any trouble.

He looked at ease in the dark woods. In his dark clothes, he blended right in. Being used to traveling herself, Magda could tell by the way he moved through the woods that he was used to being in the wilderness. A lot of wizards weren't. A lot of wizards rarely left the confines of the Keep. That contrast, too, made him stand apart from other wizards.

With rain imminent, Magda wanted to finish their business as soon as possible and get back to the shelter of the Keep. Since her encounter with Councilman Sadler, just before sunset, the clouds she had seen at the horizon had moved in to lower the sky into a brooding mass seething with flashes that revealed a menacing green cast deep inside. That color, she knew, often foretold especially violent weather. The arrival of the clouds had pushed out the hot, muggy air, replacing it with chill, gusty breezes.

The sudden bursts of lightning lit the towering pines all around in flashes of harsh, white light that cast bizarre shadows, making the journey through the dense forest unsettling. When the lightning abruptly cut off, it suddenly plunged the woods back into blackness. It made for alternating glaring light and then total blindness. The loud crack of thunder that followed each flash was equally unsettling. Sometimes a bright flicker of lightning and the loud bang were quickly followed by deep, rolling thunder that shook the ground.

Unlike most storms, this lightning became ever more incessant. As they made their way between the towering trunks of pines and occasionally followed the trail as it tunneled through thick foliage, the lightning flashed relentlessly in a nearly continual display of crackling intensity. In fact, the lightning was often so closely stitched together that she could almost, but not quite, have made her way without the lantern's light. The intervals of darkness between flashes were surprisingly brief, but without the lantern it would have been like being blind as they went from brightly lit to darkest night.

The air smelled like rain was imminent. Magda was resigned to getting wet. She could also smell the dry pine needles matting the ground, along with the occasional balsam trees or swaths of cinnamon ferns beside the trail.

"How much farther?" Merritt asked as they descended the back of the low ridge.

Magda stopped and pointed off to the right. "If it was light, I believe you could see the pond through the trees, down there."

Merritt cast out his hand, as if he were tossing a pebble. A flare of light, not unlike a tiny, solid bit of the colossal light show overhead, sailed out in the direction she had pointed, illuminating the dark trunks of trees as it passed. She saw the water reflect the light before it touched down on the rippling surface and was extinguished.

"That's too steep and wooded here down to the shore," he said. "We need to have some open space."

"Just up here ahead is the place I told you about," she said. "The trail just ahead will take us to the open area at the pond's edge."

Magda led him onward until she reached a familiar, ancient oak. She passed just beneath a fat, low limb and warned Merritt to watch his head. He ducked under as he followed after her. The trail wound its way down across a band of open ledges and then through a narrow cut in a screen of cedar trees. Dropping down a steep but brief slope, they arrived at a broad, flat, open area with scattered tufts of grass. In the spring it was often flooded at the windward end of the pond, but by high summer it was dry and open.

Lightning flashes revealed the pond before them and the towering stands of trees to the sides that sheltered them somewhat from the wind. In the flashes of lightning, Magda could see that to the right the surface of the pond was thickly layered with lily pads riding the choppy surface. Off to the left stood a band of rushes bending and whipping with each gust. Stretching out from the gravel shoreline was the black expanse of the pond, with a short cliff backing it at the far side.

"It's perfect," Merritt said as he looked around.

A bright, crackling flash of lightning, followed by booming thunder, silenced all the night creatures. When the thunder rolled away into the distance it left an interlude of quiet in its wake. The only sound was the wind in the trees and the small waves lapping the shore. The quiet was quickly broken by yet more rolling thunder.

When Magda turned back, she saw Merritt down on his knees, smoothing the sandy dirt among clumps of long grass. Once he had a clean, flat area, he stood and brushed his hands clean.

"Set the lantern down over here on this rock," he said, pointing beside the area he had just smoothed out.

As Magda was setting down the lantern, the chilly air rang with the sound of the sword being drawn. The blade coming out of the scabbard made a uniquely menacing sound that sent a chill up her spine. In the faint lantern light she could see Merritt standing with his feet spread and the sword in one hand. A bright flash of lightning cast his shadow across the area he had prepared.

"You know how to draw the Grace, right?" he asked her as he lifted his fist, showing her the ring he wore with the Grace engraved on it.

"Merritt, I'm not gifted."

"I told you, it isn't necessary. I will be the one doing what is needed with magic, but you will have to be the one to draw the Grace. That's all I will need you to do."

"Well, since I'm not gifted I never had reason to draw the Grace, but I've seen it often enough. It's not that complicated. I shouldn't have any problem at all drawing it."

"It needs to be drawn in blood."

She had expected as much and nodded.

He had that serious look again that had a way of making her brow bead with sweat. "The sword needs to taste the blood as well," he said. "The blood connects the sword to the Grace."

Magda eyed the sword. She didn't know what he meant about the sword needing to taste blood. She folded her arms against a chill gust.

"How much blood will it take?"

He stepped into the center of the flat area and, using the sword to point, gestured in a circle around him. "The Grace needs to be big enough to surround where I'm standing. It has to be enough blood to complete the whole thing. All the lines you draw have to be complete. They can't be a bit here, and another bit there. It has to be fully drawn with complete lines. I'm afraid that it will take quite a bit of blood to do that."

She pulled strands of windblown hair back off her face. She had known it wasn't going to be easy. She had insisted on being a part of it. She had to be the one to do it. She wasn't about to back out now, no matter what it took.

"I understand," Magda said. "I'll do my best."

65

Merritt stepped closer. He swept his hair back. Lightning cast his handsome features in stark light and black shadows.

"Listen, Magda, for the last time, you don't have to do this. It's dangerous. There are wizards on the teams who would—"

"Wizards we can't be sure we can trust," she reminded him. "Especially not with something this important."

"I know, but you need to understand that this particular sort of conjuring requires the use of blood in order to power certain elements. Your blood would link you to the event. It ties you directly into the elements involved. Those elements contain not just Additive Magic, but Subtractive. The mixing of those elements is what got a lot of wizards killed while trying to do this very thing."

He had told her all that before—several times—when they had been crossing through the city as he began having second thoughts about her being a part of finishing the key. She hadn't let him dissuade her then, and she wasn't about to let him do so now, but she also hadn't asked for explanations of some of the things he'd said. She'd figured that what was necessary was necessary, and she would find out what she needed to know when the time came. That time had come.

"You said that before, but I don't know what it means, actually, to be linked to the event."

Merritt looked sympathetic. He stepped closer still, gazing down at her as he lifted his fist to show her the ring he wore.

"The Grace represents the interconnection of everything, the world of life and the world of the dead, Additive and Subtractive, as well as the spark of the gift that runs through it all. The Grace does more, though, than simply represent Additive and Subtractive magic, Creation and obliteration, life and death; it connects them into a cohesive whole.

"By using your blood to draw the Grace, you are the one providing those living elements, that cohesive whole, to the completion of the key. What was missing before was the breach formulas that are supposed to guard those new links in the sword while the combination routines allow the elements to coalesce. Those breach formulas are meant to keep the whole thing stable while the Additive and Subtractive parts are fusing. They do that by actually breaching the nature of the Grace long enough for the elements to fuse into the target—in this case the key.

"That's how the others were killed; there was nothing breaching the Grace until the two sides could combine in a stable fashion. That's what happens in life, when a wizard with both sides of the gift is born, both sides are fused into him, but we're trying to do that same thing artificially, and we didn't have the formula to create the breach that would allow it to take place. Now, with the breach open, the whole process can draw what it needs from you, through the Grace drawn in your blood, as it uses both sides—life and death—that are inherent in your existence."

Much to her amazement, Magda was actually beginning to understand the principles involved. That wasn't making it any easier to work up the nerve to do it, but at least she was grasping the true nature of the danger.

"So I would be providing the power of death as well?"

"Yes. We all will die one day, so I think that we also carry latent death within us from the moment we come into existence. Your spark of life is what powers the Grace you draw with your blood. That Grace thus contains both the power of life and the power of death because you do.

"The power of Orden deals with life, death, and the whole nature of existence, so the key also needs to have both sides. It needs both Additive and Subtractive, life and death, to be complete.

"Through the Grace, you would be providing those forces. As I invest those elements in the sword, with the breach open, it will draw strength from your life force.

"But if something goes wrong because the formulas I use have flaws, or I make a mistake in conjuring spellforms, or if the seventh-level breach doesn't open and then close properly, you could be caught beyond the veil to the underworld, just like those wizards Baraccus sent to the Temple of the Winds in the underworld. They were caught beyond the veil and never returned."

Magda twined her fingers together. "I trust you, Merritt. You've been working on this for a long time. No one knows more about it than you. If it can be done, you can do it. I could be in no better hands."

"And what if I'm wrong about some part of it?" He gestured vaguely. "Look, Magda, you don't need to do this. I can get a wizard from one of the teams to try it first. This kind of thing is their job. They've devoted their lives to creating such dangerous things. I'm not so sure that you should—"

"We've had this argument already and it's settled. This is more important than my life and you know it. This is the only life I have and I don't want to lose it, but there are profoundly important things at stake here this night, things I care deeply about, things I believe in, like not letting harm come to all our people.

"The boxes of Orden are here, in the world of life. Someone stole them. They obviously must want to use those boxes and when they do they will intentionally—or even unintentionally—bring all of our lives to an end. Stopping that from happening is what matters. What good will it do to worry about a possible danger to me tonight, at the cost of all of us tomorrow?

"Who else but you can stop that from happening? Who else but you can complete the key? Who else but me can we trust to help you?

"I have to do this, Merritt. I trust you to take care with my life, but if I lose it in the attempt, then I will have died trying to save all life and I don't want you to blame yourself. This is worth doing. I'd rather die trying to preserve the value of life than watch it all end because I failed to do what only I can.

"Trust in yourself, Merritt. Do what no other but you can do. Use me for what you need to complete the key."

He watched her eyes for a long time as lightning flashed and thunder boomed.

"You're something else, Magda Searus." He slowly shook his head. "You really are."

She realized that she was glad he was having a difficult time putting her life at risk. She wouldn't want him to be indifferent.

Merritt finally held out a hand, palm up. "Give me your arm."

Magda held her arm out for him. Merritt closed a big hand around her wrist and held it in a firm grip.

"Be still, now," he said. "I don't want you to jerk or I might cut too deep."

Magda took a deep breath and let it out slowly, trying to steady her racing heart. It wasn't the blade she feared as much as the unknown of the ordeal that was to follow. She glanced around, briefly wondering if she would ever see the world of life again. She met Merritt's gaze.

"I'm ready. Do it."

Without preamble he drew the blade across the inside of her forearm, close to her wrist. She felt the razor-sharp edge bite into her flesh as he dragged it across her arm, carefully controlling how deeply he cut. It sent a shock of pain through her. Blood immediately began gushing down her arm. He had cut deeper than she had expected. She felt faint. She fought the feeling. She knew that she had to remain conscious.

Magda watched the blood flood down her arm, her wrist, down over her palm, to finally engulf and run off her fingers. She was shocked to see how much blood there was.

"Hurry, now," Merritt said, "before you lose too much blood."

Feeling like she was watching herself in a dream, Magda took a couple of steps away to begin drawing the outer circle, the one representing the beginning of the world of the dead.

"No," Merritt said, holding her shoulders as he guided her back, "I need you to start in the center. You need to draw the star first."

She looked up at the shadow of his face. "But I thought—"

"I know what you thought and ordinarily you would be right, but it can't be drawn the way you were taught. This is for something entirely different than the Grace is

usually used for. We're altering the elements involved."
He nodded his encouragement. "Draw the star first."

Magda had been taught that a Grace was always
started with the outer circle, then moved inward through
the square to the inner circle to the central eight-pointed
star, and then finally the rays of the gift were drawn from
the star to cross that inner circle, the square, and finally
across the outer circle out into the underworld. She had
always been told that the Grace was never to be drawn
in any other way, not even casually. The Grace was a serious device that carried great importance as well as
powerful magic if done by the right people, and especially if done by them in blood.

Worried about the implications, Magda nonetheless
did as Merritt asked, letting the blood drip in a steady
line across the sandy ground he had smoothed out. She
was careful to go slow enough that the lines of blood
were unbroken.

"Good," he said. "Now draw the beginning of the
world of life around it, touching the points of the star."

Lightning flashing all around, thunder booming, Magda
followed his instructions. Wind whipped her hair across
her face and she had to pull it back to see what she was
doing. What the lightning didn't light for her, the lantern
did. After the circle was completed, he had her draw the
square, and then the outer circle, where ordinarily a Grace
was begun.

"Now," he said, "draw the rays. But you need to begin them out beyond the outer circle, in the world of the
dead, pulling the lines inward through the whole thing
until they touch the points of the star, until they touch
Creation."

Magda stared at him. "Merritt, are you sure? I've
never heard of a Grace being drawn that way. I've never

heard of anyone daring to draw the rays inward from death toward the Light of Creation. It seems a sacrilege."

He was nodding. "I know. But that's what I need you to do. We're mixing elements, remember? This is what the rift calculations are for. This is why I need the seventh-level breach formulas. Hurry, before you lose too much blood."

By the time she was finished, she was feeling decidedly light-headed. She tingled all over, except for her fingers. They had gone numb.

Magda realized that the dim world all around her seemed to be tilting at an odd angle. Merritt caught her in his arms before she hit the ground.

He set her down, leaning her against a log off to the side. He placed a hand over the cut. "You did good, Magda."

She felt the heavy warmth of magic flowing into her arm.

"This will stop the bleeding so that it can start to heal," he told her. She could hardly hear his voice. "While I'm working, I want you to sit right here and rest. Be strong for me, now. I need you to be strong for the next part."

Magda nodded, but he was already rushing back to the Grace drawn in blood.

Her blood.

CHAPTER
66

Magda lay back against the log, watching the lightning flicker deep in the clouds overhead, turning them a greenish color deep inside. The lightning danced from place to place, running in jumping, jagged lines as it ripped across the sky, causing a great cracking, booming sound in its wake. She could feel the deep rumble of thunder through the sandy ground.

Something about that greenish color tickled at the back of her mind, but she couldn't seem to bring it forth.

When Magda realized that not all the lightning, not all the rumbling roar, was coming from the sky, she used her elbows against the log to push herself a little more upright. Standing near the center of the Grace, Merritt was using a finger and thumb to pull a line of light through the air, as if he were pulling yarn from a skein. Before him stood a structure of hundreds of thin lines of light all connected into a complex scaffolding. It was a verification web beyond the complexity of any she had seen.

Lightning crackled around it, jumping around from point to point on the framework or coming down from the darkness above to connect with it, touching here and there, testing, almost as if the threads of lightning were tasting it.

In the center of the armature the Sword of Truth floated in the air, a goodly distance above the ground. It stuck halfway out of the top, turning slowly as if turning on a spit. As it turned, the blade reflected flashes of the colored light from the glowing lines in all directions out across the Grace.

As Merritt added more lines, and yet others spontaneously sprang on their own from various points to establish new junctures, the structure grew ever taller, with the sword continuing to rotate inside. Merritt circled around the outside of the lighted framework, adding bits of lines here and there, pulling some of them in arcs from intersection to intersection, as if reinforcing areas he deemed weak.

As the structure began building more rapidly on its own, Merritt raced to the points of the star of the Grace and began drawing spell-forms in the sandy ground. He used his finger and drew each line with swift precision until the form was complete. He moved from point to point on the star, adding a complex and exacting drawing at each of the points. Each spell-form looked different to her.

When all eight had been completed, he returned to the glowing structure, pushing at it here and there with his palms, testing, then carefully adding a line of light here, another there, to stiffen the whole thing.

Magda's head felt as if it were in a vise. The pressure was painful. She didn't know the source of the pain. She wondered whether it was her connection to the Grace and the spells, or simply the loss of blood. She didn't know what to expect as she watched the framework continue to build on itself, growing ever upward, growing broader at the base. Legs of light grew from the side of the skeleton of lighted lines to anchor themselves at places along the lines of the star drawn with her blood. She saw blood being drawn up along the beams of light.

Merritt put a finger and thumb together at a spot in the structure and as if pinching the air itself pulled a radiant line all the way from the glowing scaffolding out and down across the Grace until he attached it at the end of one of the rays from the star where it crossed the circle representing the world of the dead.

Magda gasped as she flinched. She gritted her teeth against the stabbing pain. It felt like someone had pushed a knitting needle through her left side and taken a big stitch. She struggled to breathe against the pain bearing down on her.

Merritt quickly returned to the opposite side of the structure and pulled another line of light from the scaffolding to the end of a ray on that side, where it crossed over into the underworld.

Magda gasped again as she felt another stitch at her waist, but this time on the right side. When Merritt pulled the next line of light across the Grace, Magda felt yet another stitch of pain sear through her in the small of her back. She put her hands to the pain, urgently wanting to make it stop, but it didn't.

Overhead dark, cloudy shapes had begun to swirl around the glowing structure of the verification web. Threads of lightning flickered from the framework to the shapes moving in a circle high above it as Magda felt yet more stitches of pain knitting around her waist coinciding with Merritt pulling lines of light out past the veil on the Grace. She felt as if she were being sewn to the ground. She could hardly move, hardly breathe.

Above them, the lightning in the clouds had the whole sky boiling with a writhing greenish light that seemed to be spreading through the firmament.

She saw, then, that the sword had begun to glow with a soft light that pulsed between a warm yellow and a green color not unlike that green light deep within the clouds overhead.

Merritt dropped to his knees, drawing yet more spell-forms at various places in the Grace. Magda couldn't move and could barely pull each shallow breath through gritted teeth. She felt as if she were being torn in half.

The rotating dark mass over the structure grew in breadth as it revolved until it seemed like the entire sky was moving above her. The farthest-out parts rotated more slowly. The closer in toward the glowing web, the faster they spiraled around. At the center a point of intense greenish light flared.

Magda realized that the green color was not merely in the clouds. It seemed as if the very air itself was becoming the same strange tint of green.

She remembered then what had been at the back of her mind. Baraccus had told her that the veil to the world of the dead had glowed a strange green when he had passed through it. He had told her that when he had gone through that green wall, that was how he knew that he had crossed over into the underworld. He had called it the green meadow of the spirits.

Magda gasped when she thought she saw a face in the rotating clouds over the structure. In the billowing green light, she saw another, and then another. Each had its mouth wide open, releasing a terrible scream. Each face was distorted in pain and terror. The howls filled the air so that they all joined together into the sound of the roaring wind.

Before long, it seemed as if thousands of vague, filmy corpses were fluttering through the spinning air above the glowing structure.

The sound they made was unbearable. It was terror, misery, and pain all melted together into one long, ripping howl. The green air seemed packed full of writhing, diaphanous figures like so many swimming, squirming, twisting souls all fighting for space. None of them seemed real, none of them seemed alive, and yet they moved with frenzied purpose.

Magda wondered if she had died and was being swallowed up into the spirit world, or if she was suspended, barely alive, beyond the veil in the world of the dead. She wondered if this was what it had been like for Baraccus.

The air above the sword ignited with a massive jet of flame that shot upward. Even at the distance she was, the heat of it felt as if it might burn her flesh from her bones.

The sword heated to white hot. It glowed brighter than anything else, even the bolts of lightning. It was so bright it hurt her eyes. Above it the sky burned with reddish orange flame that turned and churned, blackening as it rolled away, replaced by yet more bright orange fire continually boiling forth.

The ground around the glowing verification web seethed with a carpet of bluish flame that flickered and jumped.

In the center of it, Merritt raced through the walls of flame to pull more lines and draw yet more spell-forms. The world seemed an inferno, while forms in the greenish light howled in fury and agony.

Magda could feel waves of heat off the white-hot, glowing sword rolling over her. The blade glowed incandescent.

Magda thought that surely the heat was burning her lungs. The air above them was a rotating, turning, churning ceiling of flame. The noise of it was deafening.

Black lightning, as dark as death itself, crackled through it all as it arced from the fire above to the hilt of the sword. Every time the black lightning touched it, the blade went momentarily just as black. Magda knew that she was seeing Subtractive Magic called to life before her.

Black lightning erupted from points of the Grace outside the outer ring to arc to the pommel of the glowing sword. Every crackling, twisting streak of it felt as if it was born in her very soul.

At the same time, blinding flashes of bright lightning grounded at the pommel of the sword exploded skyward with earsplitting booms. The blade looked as if it might explode from all the heat and the mix of lightning from different worlds.

Merritt stood then and lifted his arms. As he drew his arms upward, over and over, great columns of water erupted from the pond, pouring up and over the sword. As the waves of water broke over the sword and the structure, she could see the glowing sword through the water.

Clouds of steam billowed up as more and more water funneled up from the pond in a twisting column that cascaded over the sword.

The flashes of white-hot and inky black lightning hurt her eyes. The thunderous noise hurt her ears. The sword smoked and steamed with a howling sound that matched that of the spirits twisting through the greenish air.

Magda's head felt as if it might explode. The stitches of pain in her side hurt so much she couldn't draw a breath. It felt like a great weight was crushing her chest, preventing her from drawing air into her lungs.

Everything began to dim. Even though she knew that all the sight and sound was still going on, it seemed ever more distant.

And then, the Sword of Truth suddenly plunged straight down toward the ground.

Magda screamed. As the sword fell, it felt as if an iron spike were being driven down through the top of her head, through her insides, and right into the core of her soul.

Like a great iron door slamming closed, the world went from green to black.

Magda was dimly aware that she was lying on something soft. She slitted her eyes, squinting. The light hurt her eyes.

She was shivering all over. She realized that for some reason she was not simply cold but also soaking wet. She remembered, then, that it had started raining fat drops of icy rain when they had been out in the woods. She didn't think that she was still in the woods, but she was having difficulty, between bouts of shivering, trying to figure out where she was.

She saw the hazy figure of Merritt moving about not far away. It was comforting to see him.

Her vision wouldn't focus but she could make out a table and a chair. There was a bit of red on the table. She saw statues, stacks of books, scrolls, bones, and all sorts of strange devices sitting everywhere around the floor. There were lit candles around the room, too, some on low tables, some on the tops of short pillars, some on the table.

As the room came more into focus, she realized that she was on the wicker couch in Merritt's home. She had no recollection of how she had gotten there.

Merritt came closer and quietly bent over her a little,

moving his hands in the air above her, sweeping them from her head downward. As his hands moved, she felt her frigid, soaking-wet dress turn dry. By the time he had worked his way down to her feet, she was completely dry. The bone-chilling cold melted away as a calming, radiant warmth seeped back into her bones.

But she still hurt everywhere.

"Am I still alive?" she managed.

Merritt turned to look at her. He smiled.

"Quite alive. We're at my place, in Aydindril. It was closer than trying to make it to the Keep. I wanted to get you in out of the rain. It was quite the storm. You were in trouble. The reaction of all the elements combining was greater than I had hoped, but not as bad as I had feared. The breach held."

His fingers touched her shoulder. "You were strong, Magda. You did good. But I was afraid to try to make it to the Keep."

"You carried me?"

He nodded. "I didn't think . . . well, I thought it best to get you in out of the rain here, and see to making sure that you're all right as soon as possible."

"The sword," she said, licking her cracked lips.

"What about it?"

"Did it work, Merritt? Were you able to complete the key?"

His handsome smile widened. "Thanks to you, yes. Thanks to your strength and determination I was able to do it."

"You did it . . ."

"We did it." He squeezed her hand. "I've healed you, but more than anything you need to rest, now. I can't use magic to give you that, and you desperately need it."

In the dim recesses of her memory, she recalled him holding her head in his hands as he worked to save her.

She had been healed before, so she had known what he had been doing. His touch, though, felt different from any healing she had felt before. It had fierce intensity, yet a warmth to it that calmed her and let her relax so that he could do as he needed.

She could remember only bits and pieces of him bent over her, holding her head, as the rain poured down on them. She did remember, though, how much she hurt, and how terrified she had been that she would die there in the dark woods.

Magda didn't know what had needed healing, but she was aware that for a time she had been on the other side of the veil of life.

Merritt had come after her and brought her back.

"Is it still night?" she asked.

"No," he said. "It's morning."

"Morning?" Magda tried to push herself up on her elbows, but she couldn't seem to muster the strength. "Merritt, we have to go. We need to get to the dungeon. We need to find that sorceress who defected. If she's even still alive. If she is, they could execute her at any time."

Merritt's hand on her shoulder gently pushed her back down. "I know, but right now you have to rest. I healed you, but if you are to recover, you still need to rest. I can't do that part for you, and you can't do anything if you don't finish getting better, first."

There was something serious about his tone. She looked up to his face. His eyes revealed the level of his concern. The look in his hazel eyes gave her a ripple of terror.

"Am I going to be all right? Am I going to live?"

A touch of his smile returned. "If you rest. Your body needs sleep to fully recover."

Magda narrowed her eyes, peering, trying to focus her still-blurry vision to see the sword at his hip. Trying to focus her eyes gave her sharp pains in her temples. She didn't see the scabbard there at his hip.

Merritt saw where she was looking and gestured. "It's hung on the chair."

"Please," she managed past the pain in her throat. "Can I see it? I want to touch it."

Merritt scratched his temple. "Sure."

He went to the chair sitting before the table with the red velvet where the sword used to lie. When he drew the blade from its scabbard hanging on the chair, the room filled with the clear ring of steel. It sounded the same, yet somehow different. The ring had a nature to it that resonated with something deep inside her.

He brought the sword to her, holding it out in both open hands. Magda reached up and touched the hilt, running her fingers over the raised letters of the word *Truth*.

She stretched both hands toward it, wanting it, needing it. Merritt let her lift it from his hands.

Magda laid the blade down the length of her body, feeling the satisfying weight of it against her. The hilt rested on her chest just beneath her chin. At that moment, after all she had been through, it was more comforting than any blanket. Knowing that it was now complete was gratifying beyond words.

She held the hilt with both hands, letting the deep satisfaction of knowing that they had done it seep through her.

Merritt had accomplished the near impossible. The key was complete. Magda had managed to do her small part to help him and as a result the Sword of Truth was now complete.

Though she was ungifted, she could clearly feel the power of the magic the sword now possessed. It was power unlike anything she had ever imagined. It churned the way the storm had. It held more power than the storm had. It was fury and rage and love and life all folded together, over and over, blending them into the finest layers of something new, something remarkable.

This was now a weapon unlike any other, more than any other.

It felt so good holding it, knowing that they had done it, that she never wanted to let it go.

Magda let out a deep breath of contentment and, with the Sword of Truth held in both hands, lying down the length of her, listening to the steady drumming of rain on the roof, she allowed herself to succumb to sleep.

Are you sure that you're all right?" Merritt asked in a quiet voice as they made their way up the broad hallway. "I know I would feel more confident in your recovery if you had gotten more rest. You've been through quite an ordeal."

This section of the Keep was reserved for the Home Guard. The hall was simple stone block walls, beamed ceilings, and plank floors. There were barracks, dining halls, and assembly rooms down various corridors. As they passed intersections, she saw that some of the halls were filled with soldiers. Iron brackets held torches with flames that flapped in the breeze as they passed. The hall smelled musty, punctuated with the heavy aroma of pitch each time they passed a hissing torch.

Two soldiers in polished armor breastplates over blue tunics, their heads bent close in a confidential conversation, were walking swiftly toward them. Magda waited until they passed and were out of earshot before she answered Merritt.

"I'm fine," she said. "Really. Stop asking me, would you?"

As they marched down the long corridor Merritt glanced over with a skeptical expression but didn't answer. From time to time he looked over at her out of the corner of his eye, as if checking to make sure she was still upright.

Magda wished it weren't so late. She had slept the entire day, and on into the night. No matter how much she might need rest, she didn't want to sleep any more. She was strong enough to do what had to be done. That was all that really mattered at the moment.

"Don't I look fine?" she asked.

Merritt finally smiled. "Yes, you certainly do look fine." His face reddened. "I mean, you look like you've regained your strength."

Magda smiled at his look of embarrassment.

Truth be told, she didn't feel at all fine. She was so exhausted that she could hardly put one foot in front of the other, but she was more concerned that the sorceress from the Old World might be executed before they could get to her. It might be their only chance to get information about what the enemy was up to. She couldn't afford to worry about how tired she was when there was so much at stake.

Despite the late hour, she expected General Grundwall to still be up. She knew him to be ferociously dedicated to his duty of protecting the Keep and those who lived and worked there. She remembered Baraccus often reminding General Grundwall to get some sleep or he wouldn't be good for anything. The man rarely took the gentle reminders to heart.

By the clusters of men crowded around the archway to the Home Guard's headquarters, she was sure he would be there. Some of the soldiers in blue tunics and light armor clutched papers or scrolls, waiting to give the general their reports. Other men were gathering for their patrols. The dozens of reflector lamps along the stone walls outside the archway reflected sparkles of light off polished armor and weapons that all the men carried. It was a decidedly male environment that made her feel out of place.

As Magda and Merritt made their way up the corridor, past soldiers coming and going as well as clusters of men discussing their work and their plans for the night, she spotted the general coming out of the arched opening to his headquarters. He was average height, but built like an oak tree, with thick arms and a neck that started flaring right from his ears down into his broad shoulders. She thought that he looked like a man who could shove a mountain aside if it was in his way.

He spoke to various people with brief, direct orders, sending men on specific types of patrols, or telling officers how he wanted watches run, or taking papers with reports from waiting men even as he was talking to others. He scanned each report and thanked the man giving it. Before long he had a sheaf of papers in his big fist.

When General Grundwall spotted Magda weaving her way through the swarm of soldiers, his face lit up with a big grin.

Magda instantly went on alert.

The general smiling like that was out of character. He was a serious soldier, healthy and fit despite the gray at his temples. He often rode with his men or walked miles and miles of patrols through the Keep with them, up and down countless stairs as he checked that his people were safe. He was focused and serious. He was not a man to smile casually.

Since the strange deaths at the Keep, he was, if anything, short-tempered. He felt that the murders reflected poorly on him personally. That the deaths continued put him continually on edge.

But here he was grinning as if he were at a ball and full of wine.

"Lady Searus! So glad to see you," he said as he rushed up to her.

Merritt, standing beside her, made the general look not nearly as big and muscular as she had always thought of him.

"General Grundwall, can we speak privately? I need to ask you something."

"Of course, of course," he said, still grinning as he gestured expansively, urging her into an alcove to the side that held several statues of famous soldiers from history.

Before she could say anything, the general, still grinning, did.

"I must congratulate you, Lady Searus."

If Magda had been on alert before, now she was alarmed. Again, the general spoke before she had a chance to ask what he meant.

"It's wonderful news, simply wonderful. Just what the Keep needed. It lifted the gloom."

Magda was not merely bewildered, she was becoming ever more apprehensive. She thought it best to be as careful as possible.

"And how did you hear the news, General?"

He straightened with a proud grin and hooked his thumbs on his weapons belt. "Prosecutor Lothain told me himself."

Magda had to force herself not to act startled. "He did?"

General Grundwall nodded. He glanced around to make sure no one was close enough to hear him.

"I have to say, I've been worried about matters here at the Keep, but now, with you to marry our new First Wizard, I have been put at ease." He held up his hand as he glanced around again. "Don't worry, I haven't told my men yet that Lothain is to be named First Wizard. I know that the news is supposed to be saved for an announcement at the council session.

"But the biggest news, as far as I'm concerned, is that you will once again be the wife of our First Wizard. I can't tell you how relieved I am at that news."

Out of the corner of her eye, Magda shared a look with Merritt.

She couldn't help herself. "Why are you relieved?"

His brow lifted. "Lady Searus, you are widely respected. You may not be aware of it, but your word is widely listened to and valued. People know of all the times you have spoken with measured reason before the council, oftentimes being their conscience. You have always spoken for those who have no voice before the council. That has earned you the quiet respect of many people in the Keep.

"A lot of people had doubts about Lothain, and what you had to say about him before, and, well, your words put voice to the concerns of many. At the same time, though, there are others who believe in Lothain, believe that he is our savior for going after all the traitors among us. Those people, who believe in Lothain, would like to cut your throat. I have worried greatly for your safety because true believers are often quite vicious.

"But Lothain explained it all to me. He made it clear how your grief over Baraccus's suicide weighed terribly on your nerves, that's all. As he says, such deep grief can make even good people act out in misguided ways and so they must be forgiven.

"But by your marrying him, it will settle the matter and end any misgivings about Lothain being named First Wizard. People will be very pleased to have the reassurance of your confidence in him. After all, you're marrying him!" He thumped his chest with a fist. "I'm reassured and pleased! I have to tell you, it will really quiet things down in the Keep. I can't tell you how happy I am for you, and that you once again are to be wife to the First Wizard."

Magda did her best to conceal her rage.

"And who have we here?" the general asked as his typical suspicious gaze turned to Merritt.

"I'm Merritt," Merritt said with a pleasant smile, a smile that she could see was forced.

Merritt held out his hand. General Grundwall, still looking suspicious, shook the hand.

"Merritt is a maker," Magda said, drawing the general's attention back to her. "Since I have no use for them, I am giving Baraccus's tools to Merritt, here. He will be able to put them to good use."

"Ah," the general said with a nod indicating that his suspicion had been allayed. "Well that's a nice thing to do. I'm sure that First Wizard Baraccus would have wanted that."

"That's what I thought," Magda said.

General Grundwall leaned close. "Now, what was it you wanted to ask me?"

Magda was taken off guard, and her mind suddenly raced for an answer.

If this man was now on the side of Lothain, she couldn't very well trust him to take her to see the sorceress that Lothain was intent on putting to death. She momentarily considered taking him into her confidence and telling him that she had no intention, under any circumstances, of marrying Lothain. She was furious at Lothain for having the audacity to tell people that she was going to marry him.

As he stared at her, waiting for her answer, she reminded herself to focus. She couldn't take the chance of trusting him.

"Well," she said, "I was taking Merritt to show him

Baraccus's tools, like I said. We were passing nearby, and I hoped to run into you. I wanted to ask you if you had found the man who had murdered Isidore, the spiritist."

"Oh, the spiritist." The general frowned. "No. We've not been able to find anything at all. Even more disturbing, she is not the only one to be murdered in such a horrific fashion."

Magda let out a disappointed sigh. "I'm sorry to hear that the killer is still on the loose in the Keep. I was hoping he would have been caught by now."

The general nodded grimily. "A number of wizards working in the lower parts of the Keep, and even a few a bit higher up, have been murdered."

"Murdered. By 'murdered,' do you mean . . . murdered like Isidore was murdered? In that same fashion?"

"That's right. Ripped apart. They aren't the only ones. I've had two patrols killed as well."

Surprised, Magda leaned in a little. "Patrols? You mean soldiers? Armed soldiers?"

He folded his meaty arms. "That's right. One of the patrols had three men, then several days later a patrol of four men was also attacked and killed. They were torn apart. Blood, guts, and brains everywhere in the hallway where their remains were found. We didn't even know which body parts went with which men. We couldn't even identify the remains, and only determined who they were when we took a head count."

"Dear spirits," she whispered. "That's terrible. I'm so sorry to hear about this. And you have no suspects?"

"None. None at all." His gaze had turned abruptly penetrating and uncomfortable. "And you say the man who did it, the man you saw kill Isidore, was a dead man?"

Magda shrugged, trying not to be argumentative. This

was not the time or place. There were more important considerations.

"He looked dead to me. That's all I can tell you. I suppose that maybe he was just disheveled and filthy. Maybe he used magic. Maybe that's why he appeared so strong and could do what he did."

"Ah." The general nodded thoughtfully. "That makes sense."

"It's quite frightening to hear that no one has been caught."

He peered at Merritt for a moment and then again eyed Magda carefully. "Are you all right? You look . . . I don't know, tired."

"I am tired, I'm afraid. A lot has been going on in my life recently."

His grin returned. "I understand."

Magda could feel her renewed flash of anger heat her face.

"Well, I must be going. Merritt here wants to pick up his tools and be on his way. I probably should get some rest."

"Of course, Lady Searus," the general said with a bow of his head. "Once again, my congratulations on your imminent marriage to our soon-to-be new First Wizard. I'm sure that everyone else at the Keep will be just as happy and relieved at this news as I am. People think a great deal of you, and will be encouraged by your decision."

Magda nodded. "Thank you, General Grundwall."

Before he could say anything else, Magda turned and headed away. Merritt jumped to quickly follow after her and stay at her side.

CHAPTER
69

Magda fisted her hands in fury as she marched away. She and Merritt passed groups of soldiers coming in the other direction as she resolutely made her way down the stone corridor.

"What was all that about?" Merritt finally asked. He sounded about as angry as she felt.

"Isn't it obvious? There must have been opposition to Lothain being named First Wizard. Apparently, he's trying to quell dissent, shore up his support, and win people over. It appears to be working. Grundwall thinks it's going to be good for the people of the Keep. Lothain is no doubt counting on just that attitude.

"He probably thinks that when I see how pleased everyone is, how it eases tensions and reassures people in a time of crisis, I will have no choice but to go along with his plan. He knows that I care about the people here. He's trying to shame me into doing it for the good of the Keep."

"But you're not going to actually do it," Merritt said.

It didn't sound like a question. Magda frowned over at him. "Are you out of your mind?"

He heaved a sigh of bottled exasperation. "Where are we going, anyway?"

"To the dungeon."

"The dungeon?" Merritt grabbed her arm and pulled her to an abrupt halt. He checked both ways to make sure none of the soldiers coming and going from the Home Guard headquarters were close enough to hear them. "Are you crazy?"

Magda squared up to him. "Look, Merritt, we're running out of time. If that woman is still alive, we have to get to her before they execute her." She threw her hands up. "I already wasted the entire day sleeping, we can't afford to waste any more time."

"It wasn't a waste," he said in a tone meant to calm her down. "It kept you from dying."

Magda took a breath, trying to calm her anger over the things the general had said. She didn't want Merritt to think she was angry with him, or blamed him for what they'd had to do. Merritt was the only one who believed her and he was trying to help. She lowered her voice.

"I suppose, and I'm grateful, I really am. You healed me, and I'm better. I know I need more rest to be back to myself, but right now it doesn't matter how exhausted I am. We may never get another chance. We have to get to that sorceress."

Merritt nodded as he visibly cooled off. "I understand and I share your sense of urgency. After all, I'm the one who told you about the sorceress defector in the first place, remember?"

"I remember."

"So, how do you propose we get in to see her without General Grundwall? They don't simply let people in to see prisoners."

A group of soldiers hurried past, eyeing the woman in the midst of their domain. She flashed them a brief, polite smile of greeting. Most of the men returned the smile.

Once they were past, Magda pulled the hood of her cloak up over her head and started out once more. She peeked around the edge of the hood at Merritt.

"You heard the general. I'm respected. It's news to me, but maybe not to the men down in the dungeon. They certainly won't be expecting a woman—the wife of their dead First Wizard—to show up in their midst in the middle of the night."

Merritt looked to be getting agitated again. "And what good is that going to do you?"

"Surprise is sometimes the best advantage a warrior can have."

He eyed her suspiciously. "Where did you hear that?"

"Baraccus told me."

"He's right, but this is different from what is typically meant by that saying."

"That's why this surprise will work to our advantage."

"And if it doesn't?"

Magda took his arm, leaning closer to him as they started down the stone steps of a broad stairway. Their footsteps echoed through the stairwell, so she kept her voice low.

"Merritt, we have to try. Time is working against us. If they haven't executed her before, or even today while I was sleeping the day away, they will surely behead her soon, maybe even tomorrow. We can't delay. If they've tried her and condemned her to death, they're not going to keep her alive down in the dungeon for long—a few days at most. Every day we don't get to her adds to the odds that we never will. Maybe she doesn't know anything and can't help us, but what if she does know something about what's going on here at the Keep, or Emperor Sulachan's battle plans?

"By the way she was tried without the public knowing about it, someone must have a reason to want to get rid of her. After all, why wouldn't Lothain want to try her publicly so he could add another executed traitor to his list of heralded accomplishments? Could he be doing a favor? Or protecting someone? Maybe even protecting himself? Why was the trial conducted out of the public eye?"

"I was wondering those same things." Merritt looked both up and down the stairwell to make sure no one was near. "What we really have to ask ourselves is why they've let her live this long."

"What do you mean?"

"If they charged her with being a spy and sentenced her to death, maybe it's because someone has a reason to want her dead. Maybe it's to shut her up. So if that's true, and they want to shut her up, then why didn't they just put her to death immediately after finding her guilty?" Merritt leaned closer and arched an eyebrow. "If they want her dead, then why have they kept her alive for this long?"

It dawned on her what Merritt was implying. "You mean you think they're torturing her? You think they haven't killed her yet because they're torturing information out of her?"

"Wouldn't any spy in the Keep want to know if she has any companions defecting with her, and if she does how much they know about the people Emperor Sulachan might have secretly slipped in here? Nor will killing her solve their problem if she's already spoken with people here at the Keep and given them names of traitors working on behalf of the emperor. They would need to know that before they killed her, don't you suppose?"

Magda glanced over at him. "For a traitor, worried about being discovered, finding out how much she knows would be reason enough to torture her."

Merritt waved a hand. "But this is all speculation. For

all we know, maybe she really is a spy, or even an assassin, posing as a defector, intent on using her gift to kill our leaders. Maybe they wanted to keep the trial out of the public eye in order to find any accomplices. Maybe they did a good thing by uncovering her plans. For all we know, they may very well have beheaded her right in the beginning—right after convicting her. We don't know that she's even alive."

"All the more reason to get down to the dungeons as soon as we can. We may never get another chance to find out the truth. Maybe she is an assassin, but maybe she really is a defector who wants to help us. And if they're torturing her, she may soon enough be as good as dead as far as helping us is concerned."

Merritt considered her words as they continued down the broad stairs leading to the lower levels. The stairwell was a core passage used by the Home Guard to move quickly between different areas of the Keep. As they kept taking flight after flight down, several patrols passed them going up.

"I don't like it," Merritt said after a group of half a dozen soldiers, climbing the stairs two at a time, were far enough above them not to be able to overhear, "but I have to admit that what you say makes sense. We won't know the answers to any of it—if she's still alive and if she is, is she in any condition to talk to us—unless we get down there and see for ourselves."

"The thing that worries me," Magda said, "is that these dungeon guards might not necessarily be the reasonable type."

"Likely not, actually. That's why they're chosen for the task in the first place. Some very nasty criminals and killers are kept down there before being put to death. Those guards need to be tough men."

When they reached the bottom of the stairs, Magda

headed to the broadest corridor. It led to the immense chamber down in the heart of the lower Keep. Their shadows from the torchlight rotated around them as they moved swiftly down the simple hall.

"That's what I mean," Magda said. "I'm not sure they will have any desire to let us in. But, on the other hand, they are liable to be so surprised to see me down there that we may be able to bluff our way through."

"I'd prefer that to having to kill them," he said under his breath.

Magda blinked in surprise. "Kill them? They're on our side, Merritt. They're our men."

"How do you know that? What if the traitors in the Keep had those men placed there to keep the likes of you and me away from their dirty work. You said yourself that something terrible is going on at the Keep and there seem to be a number of people involved. This woman might have some answers about that and that's why she's in the dungeon. So who are we up against? Who's keeping her there? Who is involved in wanting her dead?

"We're at war. We can't afford to fail or we could easily end up dead, along with all the innocent people of the Midlands.

"Those guards down there may be our men, or they very well may be working for a traitor—for the enemy. With what we're doing, we've already crossed a lot of lines, here.

"And don't forget," Merritt added, "we're probably dealing with an enemy who stole the power of Orden. This sorceress may know something about all that. She may know who has the boxes or where they are. If we're really serious, then we can't be halfhearted. We dare not let this chance slip away, no matter who gets in our way. If we go down there and those guards won't let us in to see this woman, we may have to end up killing them."

Magda sighed in frustration. "You're right. If we don't discover the enemy's plans before it's too late, everyone could die. The risk is too great. We're going to have to do what is necessary." She looked over at him as they turned down a carpeted corridor. "Let's hope it doesn't come to that."

"Hope isn't a plan. We have to get in and to do that we may need to kill the guards."

"I'd rather bluff my way in."

"If it works, I'm with you. But I need to be ready to have your back."

"Magic doesn't work in the dungeon," she reminded him. "The dungeons are shielded to prevent any gifted prisoner from using magic to escape, or from any gifted ally of a prisoner from getting in and using their magic to break them out. Down in the dungeons, it's muscle that matters. That's why they have the kind of guards they do down there."

Without looking over at her, he said, "The sword will still work down there. When they crafted the shields, they didn't shield against the magic I invested in the sword."

"How do you know?"

"Because it didn't exist at the time. No one had ever thought of the kind of power I put into the sword until I did. It never existed until I created it, so it's impossible for them to have shielded against it."

"So if you have a way to defeat our shields, it would be foolish to think the enemy didn't as well."

"That thought had occurred to me."

Magda nodded, already thinking about the journey down into the lower reaches of the Keep, into the place of the dead.

CHAPTER
70

Magda's legs ached from the long descent down into the place of the dead. She was so exhausted that at times she thought she might fall over. She knew that what she was feeling was more than normal fatigue. She hated to think about the eventual long climb back up.

Magda knew that Merritt was telling her the truth about needing rest to complete her recovery from the ordeal of creating the key. Healing alone hadn't been enough. From little things he had done at the time, to hints in the way he had acted, she suspected that the use of her blood and life force in the effort to create the key had come close to costing her her life.

Before she could rest, though, they needed to get down to the dungeon. That was the prime concern. If the sorceress was still alive, they had to talk to her.

The deserted corridor they hurried through, carved from banded, tannish sandstone, created a maze of twisting passageways. None of the walls were square or straight. For the most part, the passageways were little more than a warren of tunnels gouged out through the stone.

She hadn't been in these particular underground

passages the last time she'd come down into the catacombs. This area was considerably deeper beneath the
section she'd been in before, where not only were there
resting places for the dead, but rooms where wizards
also worked. That level was also where Isidore's place had
been.

Over time, as ever more people had died, the available
space in the catacombs had been filled to capacity. The
living then had to dig even deeper to create more room
for the newly deceased. That meant that some of the areas they were entering were not nearly as old as the places
above that she had seen before. Up above, some of the
tombs were centuries old. Some were said to be thousands
of years old. Magda didn't know if that much was true
or not, but it was clear enough that some sections of the
catacombs higher up were ancient.

This part, though, was newer. In fact, it was repulsively
new. The stagnant stench of death hung in the air down
in this place. Even the scent of the stone all around and
the smell of burning pitch from the occasional torches
stuck in holes drilled in the soft rock of the walls as well
as pots of aromatic oils was not enough to mask the
smell of death. In spots, some of the rooms they passed
with the recently dead reeked so strongly of rotting flesh
that it gagged her and spurred her to hurry past.

As they made their way through the tunnels, Magda
couldn't help glancing off into the dark recesses where
the dead were laid to rest. The light sphere Merritt carried
cast a greenish glow into the hollowed-out chambers.
In the tunnels, the light sphere helped fill in shadowy
stretches between torches.

In that greenish light, Magda could see countless
corpses lying in niches. Some of the dusty finery was
filled with bones and nothing more. In other places, the
dead were desiccated, with mouths hanging open and eye

sockets staring up at nothing. In some of the rooms they passed, the places that smelled the worst, the bodies had grotesquely swollen tongues protruding from gaping mouths and eyes bulging out of sockets. It was a natural process that bodies went through as they rotted, but it was horrifying to see. It was one of the reasons she was glad that they had reduced Baraccus's remains to ashes.

Magda speculated that the sights they passed were also one of the reasons the dungeons were down below the catacombs. As prisoners were brought down through the place of the dead, the rotting corpses would be a demoralizing spectacle meant to be a disturbing preview to the living being taken to the dungeon of the fate awaiting them if they caused any trouble. Or a reminder to those condemned to death of what they would soon look like.

Magda only hoped that those condemned really were guilty. If they were guilty of murders, then they deserved their fate. But such an end was too horrifying for her to contemplate if the condemned were actually innocent. She knew that guilt was not always clear-cut, and there were instances where people wondered if the true guilty party had avoided paying the price, and an innocent person was instead being put to an unjust death.

It seemed like an endless spectacle of corpses as they made their way down the tunneled hallway. It was numbing to see so many dead people.

Magda missed a step and then jerked to a halt. She stood frozen in place. The realization ran an icy shiver up between her shoulder blades to the nape of her neck. With the sudden comprehension, she could feel her hands begin to tremble. Her heart started beating faster.

Merritt turned, holding the light sphere up to better see her face and to look into her wide eyes.

He leaned down a little. "What's wrong?"

Magda glanced around at all the niches carved out of the stone, all filled with remains of the dead.

"General Grundwall said they hadn't found the man who killed Isidore."

"That's right," he said.

Magda met his gaze. "That night, when I was lost in the maze outside her quarters, a lot of men—wizards, wizards with gifted abilities to sense the living—came to see what the commotion was all about. They fanned out and searched the maze. They didn't find anyone. General Grundwall says that they haven't found those responsible for the murders."

"I'm listening."

"How is that possible? I mean, really? How in the world is that possible? How could a killer like that vanish? The Keep is a big place, and there are tunnels everywhere down in the lower reaches as well as down here in the catacombs, but still, they've had a lot of soldiers searching day and night. Think about it. How could the killer evade all those searchers? How did the killer manage to vanish so easily each time he struck?"

"Well, I don't know but even with all the soldiers—"

"What if the killer really was dead?"

Merritt stood staring at her. He glanced to the rooms filled with the dead. "You mean, like these dead, here?" he finally said. "Dead, dead?"

Magda gestured to one of the rooms beside them. There were dozens and dozens of desiccated corpses lying inside in various degrees of decay, some with hands crossed over their chests, others with arms at their sides, all with dead eyes staring at nothing. Some had been reduced to almost nothing but bones. Yet some, dark and dried-out, didn't look at all unlike the man Magda had seen murder Isidore.

"Yes. What if," she said, lowering her voice, "what if the killer was one of these dead men. What if, after he killed, he simply went back to his resting place down here and, well, resumed being dead? He would have vanished in our midst. How would anyone find him? How would anyone know who it was?"

"They would have the blood of the victims on them," Merritt pointed out.

"No one searched all the dead to see if they had fresh blood on them," Magda scoffed. "No one believed me that it was a dead man who killed Isidore."

"That's true. After the murders, the soldiers searched for a killer, but no one checked all the corpses, looking for fresh blood."

"If it wasn't discovered soon enough, any evidence of fresh blood would soon deteriorate. In many cases, it might just look like natural decomposition and fluids seeping from the dead. The blood of the victims would become part of the dead." She gestured to a nearby room. "I mean, look at them. Yes, some are neat and tidy, but with a lot of these bodies looking like they do, it would be hard to spot fresh blood on them. Within a short time, you couldn't see it even if you were looking for it."

Merritt slowly shook his head as he peered in rooms. "Dear spirits, Magda, I wish that didn't make so much sense."

"You told me that the shields wouldn't stop your sword because they weren't made to stop the magic it contained."

"That's right."

"There are shields everywhere in the Keep. Think about it, what are the shields made to stop?"

"The enemy," he said.

"What enemy?"

Merritt grasped her meaning. "The living enemy. The

shields work by detecting life. They can't detect something that isn't alive, something dead."

"With the war going on and the attacks in the Keep, as a safeguard the council ordered new shields placed all over. I've had to make detours to get around shielded areas." Magda lifted a finger. "Yet, it hasn't halted the murders, has it? Or helped soldiers trap the killer. The shields wouldn't stop a dead man. The shields wouldn't even be able to detect one, would they?"

"No, they wouldn't. Something dead wouldn't even set off any of the alarms, much less the shields. After all, why would an alarm need to be set off to warn of the dead?"

"What do shields do to intruders?" Magda asked.

"Some of the shields are set to kill any unauthorized person who tries to pass." He arched an eyebrow. "But you have to be alive to be killed."

"What is it that Isidore was searching for, looking into? What were the wizards that she was helping trying to do?"

Merritt showed her his ring with the Grace on it. "They are trying to interfere with this. They are altering the natural order of things, the flow of life and magic and death. I haven't heard a lot of specifics about what they were doing, but I assumed they were looking into what Isidore was so worried about—the dead the enemy took and their missing spirits."

"From rumors I've heard," Magda said, "wizards down in the lower reaches have been working to try to bring the dead back to life. Or an imitation of life, anyway.

"I wonder if it could be that some of those experiments have gone terribly wrong. I wonder if that is the source of the murders."

Merritt stared at her for a long, uncomfortable moment before he gestured with the light sphere. "We'd better get down to the dungeon."

The chiseled stone of the narrow passageway cut through the granular granite bedrock of the mountain beneath the Keep was not only darker but much harder than the extensive vein of fine, tan sandstone of the catacombs up above them. This was not a place that had been so easily carved out, as were the subterranean galleries for the dead higher up. This place had required a great deal of muscle, sweat, and effort to construct.

All to confine evil. At least, that had been the original intent.

The smell of stale sweat and acrid rat droppings permeated the dark, dank tunnel just above the entrance to the dungeon. Magda wrapped her cloak tighter against the chill air and wrinkled her nose at the stink. When they reached the iron stairs at the end of the single shaft she started down without hesitation. Gritty rust and crumbled bits of remaining paint from the iron railing stained her hands.

At the bottom of the long, steep descent, a pair of burly men waited. They had clearly heard the visitors to the dungeon approaching. Both were shirtless, and as round-shouldered and hairy as bears. In the illumination of the light sphere Merritt carried, their white eyes peered out from dark, grimy faces stained by soot from torches. They were clearly surprised to see a woman and suspicious of Merritt.

An oil lamp sitting off to the side on a small, simple plank table provided the only light. It wasn't much, and so the men, used to the near darkness, squinted in the relatively bright light Merritt was holding. They were as filthy as a pair of moles.

Before the men could speak, Magda did. "You have a woman prisoner, a spy. We're here to see her."

The two guards shared a look, surprised that it had been she and not Merritt who had spoken.

"Prisoners don't get to have visitors," the first guard said in a gravelly voice.

"I'm not a visitor," Magda told him. She kept her voice cold and unfriendly. "I am here to question her."

In ill humor, the man planted his fists on his hips.

"Prisoners don't generally answer questions, either." He grinned as he glanced over his shoulder at the second guard. "Unless it's under torture."

They both chuckled.

Magda knew that she had to be bold in her bluff if it was to work. She had convinced Merritt to go along with her plan and follow her lead, so he was letting her do the talking. She reasoned that it would be unexpected and thus more convincing coming from her than from a man. Although he had agreed, Merritt stood ready if it didn't work. Not speaking, resting a palm on the hilt of his ever-present sword, towering just behind her left shoulder, he looked quite forbidding.

Magda leaned toward the grinning man, putting her face close to his, looked him in the eye, and gritted her teeth. "Then I will have to torture the bitch, now won't I?"

He blinked in surprise. He opened his mouth to say something, but before he could, Magda again spoke first.

"Do you know who I am? Do you have any idea who you are talking to?"

His thick brow drew lower. "Yes, I'm talking to—"

Merritt, off to the side and just behind her, gestured from side to side with his fingertips across his throat, a warning to the man not to say anything to make her angry. It apparently looked convincing, because the man paused and reconsidered what he had been about to say. He poked his tongue out between missing bottom teeth to swipe at his lower lip, unsure what to do.

The second man, picking up on Merritt's warning, spoke up instead. "I'm afraid that, no, we don't know who you are. You have us at a disadvantage."

Magda pushed the hood of her cloak back off her head. "I am Magda Searus."

The first man's brow came up a little. "Wife to dead First Wizard Baraccus?"

"Well, yes," she said as she flicked her hand, dismissing the importance of that much of it. "But more to the point, as far as you gentlemen are concerned, I am soon to be the wife of our soon-to-be new First Wizard."

"New First Wizard." His brow drew back down. "What would you be talking about?"

She turned to Merritt. "Don't they tell the guards down here anything?" When Merritt shrugged, she turned back to the guard and again leaned toward him. "I'm talking about Prosecutor Lothain."

Both men backed away a bit at the name. They clearly knew who Lothain was, and they were afraid of him.

"Prosecutor Lothain is to be named First Wizard?" the second man asked.

Magda planted her fists on her own hips. "Who else? Do you have a suggestion for the council as to who would make a better First Wizard? Shall I tell the council and my soon-to-be husband that the two guards down here in the dungeon have someone better in mind?"

Both men held out their hands. "No," they said together.

"No," the first repeated. "We have no better suggestion. You misunderstood. Lothain will of course make an excellent First Wizard."

"And husband," she said in cold correction. "Like I said, we're soon to be married. He will be First Wizard and as such he wants me to serve beside him as his wife." Again she leaned toward them. "Unless, of course, you two gentlemen have an objection?"

The second man leaned in a little around the first. "Congratulations, Lady Searus. He could have chosen no better woman for his wife. Everyone will be delighted by the news."

She bowed her head once, acknowledging the proffered praise with a brief, deliberately insincere smile.

"Now, gentlemen, when my betrothed sends me to question one of his prisoners, he fully expects me to return with what he sent me for. Don't you suppose?"

"Well . . ."

"If you would like, I will wait right here for one of you two to trot on up to his office, interrupt his important work, and question him. Or better yet, we can have him dragged down here just for you two, so that you both can question his wishes and intentions. I'm sure he would be only too happy to explain it to you." She grinned wickedly as she glanced back over her shoulder at Merritt. "I think that would prove quite entertaining, don't you suppose?"

Merritt chuckled. "Indeed it would."

Both guards shared another look. "I don't think that will be necessary, Lady Searus, as long as—"

"Then open the door!"

They both flinched.

"Of course, Lady Searus," the first said as he nodded vigorously even as the second was pulling out a big key as he turned to the door.

As Magda started for the door, the first man held up a finger. "Ah, if I might inquire, Lady Searus? I can understand Prosecutor Lothain sending you to see the prisoner, but . . ." He gestured to Merritt. ". . . what would be the purpose of this fellow you have with you?"

Magda glared at the man as if she were having difficulty believing how stupid he was. "Do you really expect me to torture the prisoner for information myself?"

He straightened in relief at the explanation. "Oh, I see what you mean." He glanced at Merritt's stony expression and then bowed quickly. "Of course, Lady Searus. I mean, no, of course not."

The man with the key in his beefy fingers fumbled at getting it into the keyhole. The first man backhanded the side of his meaty arm and told him to hurry. Once the man got the key into the lock, his mouth twisted with the effort of turning it. He strained to turn the key, and it finally threw the bolt back with a loud clang. Both men seized the iron handles. Together, they pulled and tugged. The door appeared to be too heavy to be opened by one man alone. Rusty hinges protested as, inch by inch, the door was jerked open.

When they finally had an opening wide enough to pass through, the first man gestured to the second and under his breath ordered him to get a torch and take the two visitors in to see the prisoner they were interested in. It was obvious that he was eager to be out of Magda's sight and away from her sharp tongue.

The second man nodded at the instructions and snatched up a torch from a pile at the side against the wall. He bent over the table to quickly light a splinter in the lantern and then set flame to the torch. As soon as he had the torch lit, he gestured for Magda and Merritt to follow as he ducked under the low opening and stepped through the doorway.

Magda hiked up her skirts and stepped over the high threshold. She and Merritt followed the hunched guard into a twisting maze of narrow tunnels that in places were no more than what looked like cracks in the bedrock. They took the second passageway to the left, down a split in the rock that was so narrow they had to turn sideways to pass through it. In places they had to walk through ankle-deep, stinking, stagnant water. To the sides, at intervals, were small iron doors set into places carved out of the solid rock. The fist-sized openings in the doors were all dark.

"Here it is," the guard said, lifting a finger to the door.

When Magda only stared at him he jumped to stab the key into the lock and turn it. As the bolt clanged back the sound echoed through the cavelike tunnels. Holding the torch in one hand, he used his other to tug the heavy door open. Neither Magda nor Merritt made any move to help him with the difficult task.

When the door was opened enough to pass, Merritt cut in front of the guard and stepped through the doorway first. Magda followed close on his heels. The guard followed them in.

She could see by the light of the glass sphere Merritt was holding that there was a second iron door. The outer room they were in had a ceiling so low that she and Merritt had to stoop over lest they hit their heads. She knew that the cells for the gifted had double doors with an outer room as an extra layer of protection. Besides the iron doors, the small outer room, as well as the inner room, would be heavily shielded.

"Give me the key," Merritt said to the guard. "You can wait for us back at the entrance."

The squat, burly guard hesitated. Merritt snapped his fingers and held out a hand, palm up, wiggling his fingers impatiently. The guard reluctantly placed the key in his palm. Seeing the two of them silently waiting for him to leave, he fidgeted a moment, scratched a hairy shoulder, and then stepped back out the first doorway.

He ducked his head back in. "If you need anything, yell. Sound echoes down here, so we'll hear you."

"Well, if you hear the woman screaming, that doesn't mean we need you," Merritt snapped as he gestured a curt dismissal. "It only means we're questioning her."

As Magda watched the torchlight disappear into the distance outside the first door, Merritt unlocked the second. As she waited anxiously, he put his weight into pulling open the inner door. It was so cold down in the dungeon that she could see her own breath rise slowly in the still air.

Finally, the greenish light penetrated into the inner darkness.

There hanging by chains from manacles attached to the wrists of her spread arms, was a bloody, naked woman.

CHAPTER
72

The woman in the center of the inner room hanging by her wrists appeared to be nearly unconscious. She barely slitted her eyelids to see in the dim greenish light from the light sphere who was entering her cell. Only her eyes moved to take in Magda and Merritt.

She wasn't older, as expected, but instead looked closer to Magda's age. Her disheveled, straight, jet black hair was shoulder length with bangs that came to just above her eyes. She was so beautiful, even with strings of blood across her face, that Magda found herself pausing for an instant to stare.

Magda's heart ached at the sight of what had been done to this poor creature.

The woman, even though she was only half conscious, still managed to level a black look at the two people entering her cell. She obviously expected more torture. Even though she was chained and helpless, Magda sensed that this was not a woman to be trifled with.

Magda reached out and gently touched the woman's cheek. "We're not here to hurt you. I promise."

"She tells the truth," Merritt said in a compassionate voice as he looked around, trying to see if there was a simple way to get her down.

The woman watched Magda's eyes but didn't answer.

Magda turned to Merritt. "Get her down, will you?"

"The chains are pinned into the rock. The key is the only way." Merritt stretched up, fitting the key into the lock in the manacles. Despite how he tried, the key wouldn't turn. "It doesn't work," he said.

"It's probably rusty," Magda said. "Try harder."

"No, it's the wrong key. I can feel that it doesn't fit the lock properly. If I try any harder it will just break off in the lock and then we'll never be able to get them open."

Magda started to turn away. "I'll go get the right key from the guards."

Merritt caught her arm, stopping her. "I have the right key."

Magda frowned at him. "What are you talking about?"

As the Sword of Truth came out of its scabbard, the blade sent a clear, distinctive ring through the small prison chamber that had been hollowed out of solid bedrock. The steel looked as menacing as the greenish light flared off it as it sounded.

The woman's eyes widened, expecting the worst.

"They're heavy iron," Magda said. "You can't cut iron with a sword."

Merritt flashed her a private, one-sided smile before turning to the woman hanging before them. As he lifted her a bit by her forearm and held her steady, he carefully slid the blade of the sword under the iron manacle around her wrist.

"Don't move," he told the woman. "I'm going to get these off you. The blade won't cut you. But just to be sure, don't move."

It appeared to be too much effort for the woman to turn her head to see what he was doing. Instead, only her eyes turned to look at his face as he cautiously worked the sword under the iron band. She seemed puzzled; her smooth brow twitched slightly.

"Hold still, now," Merritt said.

With a mighty effort, the muscles in his neck straining, Merritt pulled the sword.

A loud crack rang out as the metal band shattered. As the blade of the Sword of Truth erupted from under the iron manacle, bits of metal ricocheted off the stone walls and clattered across the floor.

With one arm suddenly freed, the woman's weight dropped. Her bare feet were finally able to touch the ground, but she was unable to hold her weight and her knees buckled. She hung limp by her other wrist.

Magda could see that her weight hanging in the manacles had cut up her wrists. With the sudden added weight on just one wrist, fresh blood started flowing and running down her arm. Magda swept an arm around the woman's middle to try to take some of the weight off the bleeding wrist. The woman let out a small moan.

Magda pulled off her cloak and wrapped it around the woman, covering her as best she could even though the woman still had one arm trapped and hanging from the chain pinned in the ceiling. The woman's lips moved as she whispered her thanks. It was a voice as gracefully feminine as the rest of her.

Merritt tried to work the sword in under the other manacle, but it wouldn't go. "Can you lift her any? Her weight is pulling her hand into the top of the shackle and I can't get the sword through."

Magda nodded and strained to lift the dead weight. "Can you help at all?" she asked the limp woman. "Can you use your legs to lift just a little? For just a moment?"

The woman strained to put weight on her legs. It was just enough of a help for Merritt to start to get the sword through. Magda could feel the woman shaking with the effort.

As soon as Merritt was able to get the blade fully under the manacle, he immediately gave the sword a mighty yank. The iron band shattered with a loud bang. Pieces of iron clanged against the stone walls. One piece hit Magda's arm. The metal felt hot when it hit her skin and bounced off, but fortunately it didn't cut her.

The woman collapsed into Magda's arms. Controlling the descent, Magda went to the ground with the weight of the woman, keeping her from falling hard and hurting herself. Once safely down on the ground, Magda hugged the woman close and pulled the cloak around her, trying to cover her and begin to warm her icy flesh.

"Who did this to you?" Magda asked, unable to contain her anger. "Who put you in here and ordered this done?"

The woman looked up and shook her head. "I don't know them. Men. Some men." She squeezed her eyes shut for a moment in a stitch of pain. "I came to help. They wouldn't let me. They hurt me instead. They said they were going to send me back in pieces to show others what would happen to them as well if they tried to do the same as me."

"I'm so sorry," Magda whispered.

Looking rather mystified, the woman frowned as she reached up and touched her finger to a tear rolling down Magda's cheek.

Magda quickly wiped her cheek. "We're going to get you out of here," she told the woman.

The woman laid a hand on Magda's shoulder. "Thank you, but you can't help me."

"Yes, we can," Magda insisted. "Do you think you can stand?"

"You don't understand. You must not help me. I am lost. You must leave me. You don't know what you're dealing with. The dream walkers will tell their contacts here and then they will do this to you as well."

Magda shared a look with Merritt.

"We have a way to stop dream walkers from doing that," Magda said.

"Dream walkers are powerful." The woman turned her eyes up. "Are you so sure?"

"We're sure," Magda said. "Now, can you stand, just until we can get you out of here?"

The woman nodded. "If it kills me I want to walk out of this place."

Magda had to smile at that. She could easily understand the sentiment.

"I'm Magda, by the way. This is Merritt. He's gifted. As soon as we get you out of here we'll protect you from the dream walkers so that they can't enter your mind, and then when you're safe, Merritt can heal you."

The woman reached out and squeezed his hand.

With a finger, Magda lifted some of the jet black hair back off the woman's face. "What's your name?"

"Naja Moon."

It was a name as exotic as the woman's looks.

"Well, Naja, can you tell me why you came here, to the Keep?"

Naja looked up at Merritt and then back to Magda. "I came because Emperor Sulachan must be stopped or he will destroy the world of life."

Magda straightened a little as she glanced up at Merritt standing over them with the light sphere. She leaned in again toward Naja.

"How do you know this, Naja?"

"I was his spiritist."

CHAPTER
73

Before Magda could ask anything else, Naja's eyes winced closed as she endured a shudder of pain. When the stitch of agony eased up, she struggled to catch her breath as she rested, huddled in Magda's warm embrace.

Steam from her labored breathing rose into the still air of the small stone cell. Instead of asking anything else for the moment, Magda rubbed the woman's hands, letting her rest while working some warmth into her icy fingers. The chill of being deep underground was an insidious killer, over time sapping a person's energy and eventually their life.

Magda knew that the woman needed to gather her strength after having her arms freed. No longer hanging from the ceiling, she was at last able to breathe properly. Her wrists had finally stopped bleeding, but she had other, more serious wounds that Magda knew needed tending as soon as possible.

Merritt was impatient to get out of the dungeon—to be away from the shields so that he could heal her, but also to get them all away from the ever-present threat of the guards. By the way he kept checking the corridor outside the outer door, it was clear that he was concerned that the longer they waited, the more suspicious the guards would get.

They also had to worry that someone else might show up, possibly even those who had captured Naja, had put her in the dungeon, and had been torturing her. Getting trapped down in the dungeons would be the end of them all. No one knew they were there, and if they were locked in, no one would be coming to help them.

After catching her breath for a short time, Naja, without being asked, started to try putting weight on her legs. She looked to be even more impatient than Merritt to get out before the guards returned.

Naja finally stood to her full height. The woman's clothes were nowhere to be found in the cell, but fortunately Magda's cloak was big enough to wrap around her. Naja was thankful to have it, and clutched it to herself as she stood, testing her legs. She was proving to be stronger than Magda had expected.

The cloak would have to do for the time being. She was close to the same height and build as Magda, so Magda would be able to give her some of her own clothes. First they needed to get out of the dungeon.

"How is it that your blade did not cut me?" Naja asked Merritt as she moved her arms about, working the circulation back into them.

He looked back after checking out the doorway. "It has magic that prevented it from cutting you."

"Magic does not work down here. I tried. I tried very hard."

"This magic is not obstructed by the shields down here. It's somewhat similar to the way the magic of the light sphere isn't blocked by the shields. It's complicated, and I don't want to oversimplify it, but basically the sword's magic won't harm an innocent or a person believed to be a friend. I don't consider you the enemy, so the sword didn't cut you. I hadn't tested that aspect of it, though, so I had to be careful. It appears to work as it should. It also appears, by the way it cut through those iron manacles, that the other side of its magic is working as well."

This was news to Magda. He hadn't told her the part about its magic not being able to harm innocent people. Merritt was full of wonders.

"Why are you two helping me?" Naja's voice was clearly laced with pain, and justifiably, some suspicion.

"We're actually hoping that you can help us," Merritt said. "I heard that you wanted to join our cause. When we found out where you were, we knew we had to get you out."

"I thought that the people here did not want my help. I thought I was wrong about the New World and the wizards who live and work here. Instead of my help, they chained me up in this awful place. They said that I was a spy and I was to eventually be put to death."

"We believe that there are traitors, here, in the Keep," Magda told her. "I think they had you put down here to keep you from helping our people."

"I thought that I had made the worst mistake of my life in coming here," Naja said, shaking her head. "I'm glad to learn that what I believed really is true, that there are good people here, as I had heard. But maybe it is not that there are traitors here."

Magda frowned. "What are you talking about? Why would the men who captured you put you down here, if they weren't collaborators with those in the Old World?"

She looked from Magda, to Merritt, and back to Magda. "Maybe dream walkers possess them and made them do it."

Merritt stiffened. "Do you think that could be what is really going on?"

"It's possible. Dream walkers can make people do terrible things."

Magda let out a sigh. "We don't know what is really going on. That's why we came down here looking for you. We hope you can help us learn the truth."

"If this place is shielded," Naja said, "then maybe in here we are safe from the dream walkers hearing us."

"That's possible," Merritt said. "The dungeon is heavily protected with some of the most powerful suppression shields ever created."

"Your sword has a newly created form of magic," Magda said. "It works down here in spite of the shields. The dream walkers were likely also created after these shields, so the shields may not be able to protect us from them."

She cast a meaningful look at Naja.

Naja caught her meaning. "If one of them found me and was in my mind, watching us, I wouldn't know it."

Magda looked up at Merritt. "We can't trust that the bond will work through the shields. We only know for sure that it works when not shielded. We dare not take a chance. Before we talk, we'd better first get her out of here and then get her protected from the dream walkers."

"She's right," Naja said. "If you have a protection that works, then we need to get out of here and use it."

Merritt lifted his sword a few inches and then let it drop back into its scabbard, making sure that the weapon was clear.

"As soon as you feel strong enough to go, we're ready. We're glad to have you on our side in the war, Naja. And we do need your help," Merritt added. "Just as soon as we heal you."

"If there are traitors in the Keep, spies who are working for Emperor Sulachan, and not merely dream walkers using people, then you need my help more than you realize."

Magda didn't like the sound of that.

Before she could say anything more, Naja started sinking again toward the ground. Both Magda and Merritt held her up.

"We need to get out of here," Merritt said to Magda. "I think that she's as recovered as she is going to get until I can heal her. We can't wait any longer. We need to get her out of here, bonded, and healed. She's strong, but her injuries are serious. It can't wait any longer."

"He's right," Naja said through gritted teeth from a stitch of pain. "I'm able to stand, now. Let's go."

Magda nodded. "We'll help hold you up as best we can, but it's narrow and you'll have to be strong for a little bit longer. Merritt can carry you once we're out of the dungeon."

"Thank you both," Naja managed between gasps of increasing pain.

74

Now that the surge of excitement from being cut down from the chains was wearing off, it was clear that Naja's strength was flagging. By the twitches of her brow, Magda could see that even though she didn't complain, she was enduring increasingly serious waves of pain. Her determination was keeping her moving better than Magda would have thought possible.

Naja had difficulty trying to make it out through the small doorway of her cell. It was proving easier to stand than to bend. Merritt held an arm on the outside of the doorway while Magda, still in the inner cell, held her other arm. After Naja was through, Merritt picked the woman up in his arms and carried her across the outer room. He stopped before the outer door, still holding Naja in his arms.

He gestured with a tip of his head. "Check outside," he whispered to Magda.

Magda carefully stuck her head out of the doorway and peered into the darkness.

"It's too dark to see," she told him.

"Take the light. I'll carry her."

Magda lifted the heavy glass light sphere from his hand. Merritt rearranged his hold on Naja while Magda stuck the light out into the passageway, checking. She signaled to Merritt that she didn't see anything.

Naja wrapped her arms around his neck to help hold on as he bent low to pass through the slightly larger outer doorway and follow Magda into the narrow tunnel. Merritt was easily able to carry the woman, but in places it was so narrow that he had to turn sideways and even then it was a tight squeeze.

"How are we going to get her past the guards?" Merritt asked as he followed behind Magda.

Magda looked back over her shoulder without slowing. "I guess we bluff our way out the same way we bluffed our way in."

Merritt looked more than a little skeptical. "You really think they'll go for that with us trying to leave with her?"

"I'll tell them that we have to take her to my soon-to-be new husband because he personally wants to question her."

Merritt let out a sigh as if to say how unhappy he was with such a sketchy plan, and that he didn't think for a minute that it was going to work.

"Unless you have a better idea," she said.

"We can try it. You know my backup plan."

Magda hadn't liked his backup plan of killing the guards, but now that she'd seen the condition Naja was in, Merritt's suggestion that they might have to kill the guards was not sounding like nearly such a bad idea. She still didn't know, though, if the two guards actually had anything to do with what had happened to Naja. They might be nothing more than they seemed: guards who didn't know what was really going on.

Before they reached the outer doorway to the dungeon entrance, where the two guards would be waiting, Merritt came to a halt.

"Do you think you can walk?" he asked Naja in a quiet voice. "Just until we get past the two guards? I may need to get at my sword."

She nodded. "I'm getting some of my strength back. Put me down."

He set her on her bare feet. For a moment Magda wondered if the woman was going to be able to stand, but she steadied herself and with an effort straightened her back.

"I'll go first and do the talking," Magda whispered. "Naja, stay close behind me. We're going to try to walk you right out of here before they have a chance to argue."

The three of them made their way silently the remaining distance down the stone tunnel toward the light coming from the outer door. The lamplight from the doorway was a relief, because that meant the heavy iron door was still standing open. Magda hiked up her skirts and boldly stepped over the raised threshold out to the area where the guards waited.

Naja's hand lightly touched Magda's back for guidance as she stayed close behind.

The two burly men stood waiting, one a little in front of the other, blocking the iron stairway up out of the dungeon. The big man in front had his thumbs hooked on his belt. The men were close enough that she could smell how badly they stunk.

There wasn't a lot of room to maneuver. Magda hoped that Merritt had enough room to use his sword if needed. If he did have to go for his sword, Magda intended to pull Naja out of the way and protect her.

"Well, well," the guard in front said. A depraved grin widened as he spotted Naja in Magda's shadow. "Look who we have here out in the light."

"We need to take her for further questioning," Magda

said in an icy voice, not wanting to discuss anything with the man. "Stand aside."

"Well, the thing is," the man said, scratching the stubble on his chin and no longer looking the least bit cowed, "you forgot what I told you."

Magda glared at him. "What are you talking about?"

"I told you that sound carries through these tunnels. We heard what you said. 'We're going to try to walk you right out of here before they have a chance to argue,' I believe is the way you put it. Did I get it right?"

Magda felt a quick touch, a light pressure, at the small of her back. Before she could fully make sense of it, Naja flew past her.

Naja had Magda's knife.

The woman struck like lightning. The blade slashed the first guard's throat open from the side of his neck under his right ear clean across his windpipe. Blood erupted in great throbbing gouts from a severed artery at the side of his neck. His open windpipe blew clouds of red mist as he struggled to breathe.

As Naja twisted around, completing the powerful, slashing strike, the second man's big hand clamped down around her other wrist where the manacle had been.

Without pause, Naja used his hand holding her wrist for leverage to spin herself around. Using his hold on her wrist, she deliberately yanked herself forcefully toward the hulking guard. As she flew toward him, she whipped the knife in her other fist around in an arc and hammered it straight into his heart.

His eyes opened wide in shock.

The first man hit the floor with a heavy thud. Blood from the severed artery in his neck pumped out into a spreading pool. His last breath gurgled from his lungs. The man with the knife in his chest toppled back. The back of his head hit the stone floor with a loud crack.

Blood oozed out from under his greasy hair. He was as still as the stone that had cracked open his head. He stared with wide-open, dead eyes.

It had happened so swiftly that only then did Magda even realize that she'd heard the sound of steel being drawn. Merritt stood with the sword in his hand and rage in his eyes.

Magda had to catch Naja when she stumbled back a few steps. She weakly got her balance and then straightened herself to stand tall and glare down at the bodies at her feet.

In the lamplight Magda could finally see that Naja's eyes were as blue as the sky on a bright summer day. Her jet black hair and bangs made her blue eyes all the more dazzling.

Now, though, those blue eyes were filled with fiery rage.

"They both took turns having their way with me," Naja said defiantly. "If I had had the time, I would not have given them the mercy of a swift death."

Magda couldn't blame the woman. She would have felt no differently. The surprising strength she had shown reminded Magda again that Naja Moon was not a woman to be trifled with, or underestimated.

"Then you have carried out justice," Magda told her. "You'll get no condemnation from me."

Naja smiled with triumphant satisfaction.

"Well, that simplifies things," Merritt said under his breath. He slid the sword home into its scabbard. "No one knew we were coming down here. No one else but these two knew that we were in here, or would be aware that we freed Naja, and they aren't going to do any talking."

"Right now we're anonymous," Magda said. "Let's get out of here before someone shows up and identifies us."

Naja bent and yanked the knife from the man's chest.

She carefully wiped it clean on his pant leg. She flipped the knife and caught it by the point, then offered Magda the hilt. "I apologize for borrowing your weapon without permission. Had my gift worked down here, I would have handled it without needing to use your knife."

"I don't blame you. The men got what they deserved," Magda said as she replaced the knife in its sheath under the slit in her dress at the small of her back. She headed for the iron stairs. "Now let's get out of here."

Naja smiled and followed her up.

CHAPTER
75

Magda carefully slid the flimsy door aside just enough to peek through the small opening. At the moment she didn't see anyone out in the passageway through the catacombs, but a few minutes earlier she had seen two wizards, deep in conversation, hurry by. Across the way she could see one of the nearly countless chambers filled with the dead. At least this upper area didn't smell as bad as the lower levels.

She didn't know how long Merritt was going to take with Naja, but Magda hated to have to spend any time in the small catacombs library near where wizards worked, because it was not all that far from the dungeon. The library was utilitarian, little more than a small space hollowed from the soft rock. It was only large enough for three short rows of simple plank shelves for books. Between two of the shelves sat a simple bench. There was not even any room for a table.

Naja lay on the bench, Merritt kneeling beside her, working as quickly as he could to heal the wounds that required the most urgent attention. He had said that the library was seldom used, but Magda worried that this night someone might come looking for a rare volume and happen upon the three of them. She couldn't think of a plausible story as to why they were there, who Naja was, and what had happened to her.

They'd had to stop somewhere, though. Merritt wouldn't have been able to carry Naja far before someone saw them and started asking questions. The small library was the first place they could find that Merritt thought would be somewhat safe for a brief time.

Naja had a number of injuries, including torn muscles in her legs, a few broken bones in her feet, and most concerning, a serious abdominal wound that threatened her life. Killing the two guards might have been satisfying retribution, but it had ruptured her abdominal wound and it needed to be closed.

Before they'd done anything else, though, even before healing her or addressing any of their other problems, as soon as they'd gotten out from the influence of the shields down in the dungeon, Naja had gone to her knees and given the devotion to Lord Rahl. She was so eager to be protected from the dream walkers that she ignored the pain long enough to say the devotion three times and gain the protection of the bond. Magda ached to have the woman healed, but more than anything she had wanted to know that they would be safe from the view of dream walkers.

When they had finished with the devotion, they had immediately turned to the problem of finding a place to tend to her injuries. Merritt had said that healing the sorceress was going to take some time, hours at least, possibly all night. Since they knew that they couldn't risk staying in the catacombs library that long, he had decided to use the place just long enough to get her out of imminent danger of dying and able to walk on her own so they could get her to a safer place.

Once they were able to move from the little library to a safe place, Merritt would then be able to take the time to heal the rest of her serious injuries without the risk of being interrupted at a critical moment. In the meantime, he would do what he could as quickly as he could.

Magda was nervous, though, about getting caught in the catacomb library. She knew that if someone went down to the dungeons and found the two dead guards, they would raise an alarm and the whole place would soon be crawling with soldiers. They would look in every corner. Magda didn't know if they would know who Naja was, or be aware that she had been in the dungeon and had escaped, but if Merritt and Magda were discovered in the library healing an injured woman, the soldiers would certainly ask a lot of questions and they would expect answers.

Merritt had worked down in the area on occasion, so he was familiar with this part of the catacombs. He had known of a storage cabinet where wizards and sorceresses kept supplies. There, he'd found a spare sorceress's robe and some clean rags. The flaxen robes were decorated at the neck with red and yellow beads sewn in the ancient symbols of the profession.

Merritt had then taken them to the little library and stood watch at the door while Magda cleaned Naja up enough so that she wouldn't draw suspicion if anyone saw her. After using a damp rag to gently wash some of the blood off the face of an only half-conscious Naja, Magda had managed to get the robe onto her. While only partially responsive, Naja had been aware enough to be grateful to have the robe to wear.

After that, Magda had let Merritt hurry and get to work healing the woman while Magda stood watch.

Merritt finally stepped up behind Magda. "Anyone out there?"

"No, not for a while." Magda looked back and saw

Naja standing close behind him. "How are you?" she asked the sorceress.

"Merritt helped me enough for now. He is very talented. I think I will be strong enough to walk to a safer place where he can finish."

"Your house?" Magda asked Merritt.

He pressed his lips tight as he considered it. He glanced back briefly at Naja.

"I wish we could get there. We'd be secluded and alone. But I really think it needs to be someplace closer. She can walk for a short while, but I'm afraid she wouldn't make it that far and then we'd be in trouble."

Naja looked past Magda to peer out the crack in the door. She abruptly stepped back in surprise.

"There are dead people out there."

Merritt nodded. "This is the catacombs, down under the Keep, where the dead are laid to rest. We're just a ways above the dungeon where we found you."

Naja was clearly alarmed. "We need to leave, now."

"They're dead," Merritt said. "They can't hurt you."

"Yes they can," Naja said.

Magda slid the door closed and turned to the woman. "What do you mean?"

"Emperor Sulachan uses the dead."

Both Merritt and Magda stared. Magda, having fought a dead man, was not all that surprised by Naja's claim.

"Uses them how?" she asked.

"To serve him."

"How can the dead serve him?" Merritt asked.

"For Emperor Sulachan, the dead can serve him as well as the living. In some cases, better."

"Better," Merritt repeated as he stared at her. "They have no heartbeat. They have no life in them. How can they do anything?"

"Chickens can move and flop for hours after their

heads are cut off. They have no heartbeat, either," Naja said, "and that doesn't even involve any magic.

"The emperor has rare, gifted people called makers," she said, leaning in, speaking in a quiet, reverent tone. "I never met any myself, but I do know that makers have remarkable powers of originality. They imagine what others never envisioned before, and through that mechanism are somehow able to create what others never could."

Magda glanced up at Merritt. "We understand. We have makers as well."

"Then you understand the wide range of the totally new and unexpected creations they can sometimes come up with. Most people's minds travel along the same road traveled by everyone else, never straying off the route of conventional wisdom. Makers know no such boundaries. They have a rare ability to make their own roads of thought. Their minds venture through the wilderness of all that exists, combining random bits of knowledge in ways that have never been imagined before."

"We understand that much of it," Magda said. "What does this have to do with making the dead walk again?"

"The emperor's makers have created new forms of magic, new spells, that function in part by altering the nature of the Grace. Through the new forms of power envisioned by the makers, along with the help of the emperor's many gifted, they have learned to use magic to control the dead."

"How do you know all of this?" Merritt asked.

"I know because I was one of the gifted who helped them. Through the manipulation of the spirits of the dead in the underworld, and investing powerful magic into the corpses that those spirits came from, the dead are made to respond. That was the secret that the makers unlocked, using the spirits of the dead from the spirit world, linking them back to corpses they came from, using that connection in the Grace, the spark, that runs through Creation, life, and into death, connecting it all. With the new spells designed by our makers, the dead are made to serve the wishes of Emperor Sulachan."

"Against their will, then?" Magda asked.

Naja shook her head. "They have no will. They are dead. They are like a raw material which, through the methods dreamed up by makers, is crafted to serve as the emperor wants."

"Serve? How do they serve?" Merritt asked. "What purpose would the dead have that could serve Sulachan better than the living?"

"The dead never get weary, they don't know hunger, or pain, or pity. They don't need to eat, or sleep, or rest, or stay warm, so they don't need any supplies. They have no ambition but the one given to them. They have no capacity for fear so they act without hesitation."

"Act how?" Magda asked. "What do the emperor's forces use these dead people for?"

"For all those reasons I mentioned, they make perfect assassins." She gestured beyond the door. "They can be right there, in your midst, and you never know it. You walk by them and never see them for what they are.

"The dead can be animated as needed. They are then given a single-minded purpose. They never stop trying to carry out that purpose.

"For these reasons, they also make the perfect warriors. The dead have their limits of service, though. There are things for which Emperor Sulachan cannot use them.

"When he needs the same sorts of things done that the dead do well, but with some intelligence behind them, he uses the half people."

"Half people?" Magda leaned in. "What are half people?"

"Living people he has stripped of their souls."

76

Merritt folded his arms across his chest. "How much, exactly, do you really know about all of this? How complete is your understanding of it?"

"I told you, I was Emperor Sulachan's spiritist." Naja heaved an impatient sigh. "Must we discuss this now? Can we please go and talk about it later?"

"We need to know some things, first," Merritt said.

Naja gestured toward the door. "What you need to know is that any one of those dead could be a servant of the emperor. You wouldn't know it until one of them sat up, grabbed you by your throat, and ripped your arms off. If the emperor or his minions knew we were in here, they could set one or a dozen of the dead on us to tear us apart."

"She's right," Magda said, recalling the horror of what had happened with Isidore. "We should get out of here."

"How could he get any of those dead people down here to do his bidding?" Merritt asked, not ready to leave before he had a better grasp of it all and exactly what they faced. "He may be powerful, but he's all the way down in the Old World. How could he do a thing like that from such a great distance?"

"Easy. One of those loyal to him prepares a dead body, here, at the Keep or in Aydindril, and then has it laid to rest out there in your catacombs among the other dead people. How would you know? How would you know that the body that was being laid to rest down here wasn't one of the ones that had been prepared to serve Sulachan's purpose? Any of his people hidden here as spies or traitors at the Keep could then bring the dead out of their death sleep"—she snapped her fingers—"as quickly as that."

Magda had to remind herself to breathe. "Dear spirits, I never thought of that."

"I hadn't either," Merritt admitted. "Is there a way to check the dead, to know which have been prepared in this way?"

"Before they are called into service, they are nothing more than a corpse. There is no way to tell, unless you were to find a way to contact their spirit in the underworld. As a spiritist I can tell you that would not be an easy task. I could probably venture into the spirit world to probe for the spirit of a dead body, but that could take days of searching, and that's for one dead body. You have thousands out there. Do you have thousands of spiritists who could be assigned such a monumental task?"

"We might have a handful of such gifted," Magda said, "but I'm afraid that the only one that I actually know of was killed by one of the emperor's dead servants."

"Then you have no way to test a corpse being laid to rest even if you wanted to. Worse, though, those seeking to use the dead wouldn't even have to go to that much trouble. Do you have guards who check the people who come and go from the catacombs? Escort them to see what they might be doing?"

Merritt arched an eyebrow as he grasped her meaning. "No. There are wizards who work down here on countermeasures to Sulachan's weapons. They come and go all the time."

"Exactly," she said. "Any of those wizards could be a spy, secretly working for Emperor Sulachan's cause. They would have their pick from thousands of dead. They merely find a suitable corpse and prepare it to be awakened from death. The spells have already been well developed by Sulachan's makers to use on the dead. Such spies would also be able to identify important targets among the gifted and set the dead upon them to cripple your efforts."

Merritt wiped a hand back across his face in exasperation. "Naja, this is all pretty hard to take in. I need to have an idea of what, exactly, it is that we're up against—the larger picture. Not just about some traitors assassinating people here, but how it all fits together in Sulachan's larger purpose. It's important for me to be able to grasp the totality of it."

Naja took a deep breath as she nodded. "I understand. It must be difficult to hear this all for the first time."

"It certainly is," Merritt said.

"Well, you see, Emperor Sulachan is old and sickly," Naja said. "He fears that he will not live to see the Old World unite all people into his vision of a just world. He calls that vision the People's Alliance. He wants all people ruled under that alliance.

"Emperor Sulachan sees this as a just cause that transcends his life, as a larger cause for the good of all existence—the world of life and the world of the dead as one interconnected entity, one whole, just as the Grace is one whole, interconnected concept. To that end, he believes that all people must have common rule for that greater good of all, both the living and the dead."

Merritt looked incredulous. "The living and the dead?"

"That's right," the sorceress said.

"Setting aside for the moment the issue of thinking he can rule the spirit world," Merritt said, "how does he think it's going to be possible for him to accomplish this merely with the world of life if he's dying? He won't be around to carry out his plans."

"He seeks to continue to exist and function without life in the conventional sense, so you can't separate the issue of ruling the spirit world. They're interconnected. You said that you wanted the larger picture. The larger picture is that he seeks an alternate form of existence, you might say, so you have to understand it in those terms.

"What he seeks is a way to remain connected after his death to a functioning form in this world, in the world of life, so that he can rule it all. He believes that if he rules the spirit world, he can not only rule through his spirit in that world, but rule this world as well through his spirit's connection to his reanimated body. In that way he unites it all."

"It's madness." Magda shook her head as she let out a deep sigh. "We stand at the twilight of everything we hold dear, not only our liberty, but our very existence."

Merritt looked stymied by a thousand questions he wanted to ask all at once, so Magda asked a question instead. "How do the dead fit into this plan of his?"

"As I said, he uses them for assassins and is preparing to use them as warriors. They are mindless at that task, once set to it. They are very difficult to stop. If you cut them, they don't bleed. If you chop off an arm, they don't feel it and will attack with the one they have left. If you cut off their legs they will use their arms to continue to pull themselves after you. They don't rest. They are tireless, bloodless, relentless, remorseless killers. More corpses can be animated as needed. The dead are plentiful."

"They just keep going forever?" Magda asked.

"Well, no, not forever, I don't suppose. The dead rot away, but the magic that possesses them forestalls that process as part of its function, but the magic that has been invested in the dead is not a perfect solution. It has limits. It decays with time, much the same as a corpse would decompose. As the magic breaks down, so does the effectiveness, and so do the dead it possesses."

"Well there is that," Merritt said. "Maybe there is a way we can attack this magic." He rolled his hand for her to continue.

"The army intends to start using them at the front line as they advance in battle. Arrows and spears are of little use against the dead. Stabbing them over and over is futile. They can't really be killed because they are already dead. The soldiers on your side will waste their energy trying to kill them, trying to hack them apart, trying to stop their advance. The dead will keep coming, wearing them out.

"Sulachan intends his forces to sweep in after the waves of the dead have exhausted your soldiers and cut them down. Their corpses will be recovered and end up serving Sulachan's side in his lifeless army.

"When the dead are no longer needed, no longer have a use at the time, Sulachan's forces simply sever the links of magic and leave them as they would any of the dead. They are thus returned to what they were: corpses. They are of little value, individually. They are just a supply to be used. If he needs more, his gifted can provide them."

Deep in thought as he listened, Merritt pinched the bridge of his nose. "How can they be stopped?"

"I am not really all that familiar with their use in warfare. I didn't deal with the army officers, command structure, or strategists. I dealt with the gifted who created things, not the people who used those things.

"But I can tell you from my general knowledge and familiarity that there are only a couple of ways to stop them that I know of, other than cutting off the magic that drives them. One way is to rip them to pieces. Not as easy as it sounds, because the magic also hardens them to an extent. It's not intended to create a better weapon out of the dead person. Its purpose is rather straightforward. It's meant to counter the decomposition of the body that would otherwise allow tissues to break down.

"Even then, if a disembodied arm is close, it will try to grab you, try to attach itself to your leg to slow you down, or if it managed to use the fingers to pull itself across the ground into camp at night, it might clamp on to a sleeping soldier's throat to choke them to death. But as you might expect, body pieces don't have much of an ability to come after a person, so they aren't nearly so serious a threat.

"Your forces will try to use shields, but I can tell you from experience that shields don't work. Shields key off life. They have nothing to latch on to with the dead."

"That's true enough," Merritt said, still deep in thought as he listened. "Keying a shield to things that aren't alive would paralyze the shield because it would try to ward the world around it." He looked up. "What about fire. That would have to work."

Naja nodded. "That's the second way to stop them. Fire, any kind of fire, is effective because it can reduce the dead to ashes. That certainly would be one sure way to stop them.

"Wizard's fire would obviously work because it would stick to them and keep burning, but as you can imagine, the effectiveness of using it would degrade over time because Sulachan's gifted can send endless ranks of the dead into the face of the wizard's fire.

"I can also tell you that his gifted are working on ways to shield the dead they send in from wizard's fire. I don't know if they have perfected that sort of shield, or if they ever will, but you need to be aware that they are trying. Even if they don't come up with a counter to such conjured fire, it's not a significant setback because they don't care about losses.

"Eventually, the wizards summoning such fire would begin to tire. It takes effort to keep up such conjuring. That is the advantage of using the dead. As I said before, they don't tire. Enough of the dead would eventually make it through.

"Through the process that animates them, some of the dead will be dedicated to the task of going after specific targets, such as your gifted. If it takes a hundred, or a thousand dead to take out one wizard on the battlefield, what does Sulachan care? If it takes ten thousand he wouldn't care."

Magda thought that Merritt was looking numbed by such horrifying accounts. It was overwhelming and she could see the despair in his eyes.

"What about these others," Magda asked when Merritt fell silent. "The half people?"

Naja ran her fingers back through her black hair, clearly unsettled by the mention of the half people.

"The half people are worse. Far worse."

W hat do you mean, the half people are worse?"
Merritt asked. "How are they worse?"

"They were actually created to control and guide the dead. They are living people who are stripped of their souls, so the dead and the half people share certain things in common."

"Things in common?" Merritt asked. "Like what?"

"They are not alive, at least not in the accepted sense."

Merritt let out an angry breath. "What do you mean by accepted sense?"

"The accepted sense of life means having a soul. That is part of existence as we understand it, part of what it means for us to be in the world of life."

Naja reached out and lifted his hand with his ring and with her finger tapped the Grace on it. "Creation, life, death, with the Light of Creation running through it all. The half people are a perversion of the Grace. They are separated from that spark of the gift that is their soul, that spark they are supposed to carry through life and then after death into the spirit world.

"But these souls from the half people did not pass through the veil in the normal manner, didn't carry that spark through the veil themselves. They have been ripped asunder. They are neither dead, nor alive. Though they are alive in the sense that they breathe, eat, even talk some, they are not really alive because they have no soul, no connection to Creation and the Grace. It is a living body that is just a vessel that has been torn away from the conventional sense of the Grace.

"If Emperor Sulachan dies before he can complete his grand scheme, he will be reanimated to be an extension of his soul in the spirit world. But the emperor is hoping that when the method is perfected, if he is still alive, his soul can be sent on to the underworld, while his living form remains here to rule the world of life as one of the half people, or should I say, what is left of the world of life. It is his way of achieving a form of immortality."

"How can that make him immortal?" Merritt asked, his impatience growing by the moment.

"He wants to create a race of half people, with him as their ruler. He would no longer have to fear being old, fear being sickly, fear dying. His soul would be safe in the spirit world, leaving his temporal form to carry out his wishes in this world, thereby uniting the world of life and death in purpose.

"He and his race of half people would live indefinitely, largely unaffected by the afflictions of the living because they aren't living people. They are, to an extent, animated in the way the dead have been animated, with magic having quickened their corporeal form.

"And, of course, the world of the dead is eternal, so there is no such thing as death for spirits. Spirits are by definition dead. Some of the spirits he has stripped from both the living and the dead still haunt this world. Having lost their connection they are unable to pass through the veil.

"The half people wouldn't live forever, but through the process of sending their souls to the underworld and investing this vitalizing magic in their bodies, they also alter the way the body that is left behind would age. Changing the Grace changes the way time passes for them. Time doesn't touch them in the same way it does us. Without the soul and with what they do to the husk of the living person, that person ages very slowly. I don't know much of the details. I'm not sure anyone does, yet.

"Emperor Sulachan wants to convert as many people as possible into this new race of humans, these half people, living in this altered timeline. He plans to eliminate any opposition to his grand scheme by first eliminating the gifted who would oppose him—that would be you here in the New World—so that there will be no one with the ability to stop his plans."

"That's what the war is about," Magda said out loud as the full realization came to her. "He wants to unite everyone under the rule of the People's Alliance, but his main goal in attacking the New World is to first eliminate magic so that he and his followers are the only ones with the power of the gift."

"That's right," Naja said. "He never says that, though. He promotes his goal as 'eliminate the tyranny of magic from mankind.' He makes people think that magic is their oppressor, and he is fighting for them by fighting to eliminate magic from the world of life."

"But in reality," Merritt said, "by eliminating the magic we have, he is eliminating the potential for opposition."

Naja nodded. "Then he plans on eliminating life itself."

Merritt's arms came unfolded and dropped to his sides. "What?"

"He seeks to destroy the world of life as we know it, purging it of those people with souls. That would leave only the dead which he can control and the half people, who, as I said, aren't really alive in the conventional sense. Then, the lifeless half people would rule a lifeless world.

"With his soul safely in the underworld, Emperor Sulachan would be the ruler of the world of life, but the world of life would no longer contain life as we know it now. There would be plants and birds and beasts, but the people here would no longer be the race of man as we are now. The people would be nothing more than animals, really.

"The world of life, as we know it, would no longer exist. There would no longer be any purpose in life, no ambition, no initiative, no accomplishment. No joy. No love."

Magda and Merritt shared a look. She could see in his eyes what he was thinking: the boxes of Orden. In wordless confirmation, a private message to Magda, he lifted the Sword of Truth a few inches and let it drop back into its scabbard.

"That's insanity," Merritt finally said. "There is no other word for it. It's hard to even grasp the very idea of it."

"Whether you can grasp it or not, whether you believe it will work or not, whether you think he has a chance to succeed or not, what matters is that he intends to try to carry out his plan, insane as it is. He intends to try to destroy the world of life in order to create this vision of a perfect world where people do not think for themselves.

"That is why I defected. That is why I want to join your cause of stopping him. I, too, think it is insanity. I don't want any part of it. I don't want to live in his idealistic version of an ideal world. I don't want to be a slave to his purpose, to his deluded vision. It's my life to live, not his to take for his ends."

Merritt smiled for the first time in a while. "Then you

have come to the right side. That is our feeling as well. That is what we believe in and what we are fighting for. The right to the joy of life. The right to our own life. The right to love."

"The problem is," Naja said, "I believe that even if he doesn't succeed at his plan for the perfect world, he very well may succeed at destroying the world of life in the attempt. He is a technically intelligent, resourceful, and determined man and he is tampering with the very nature of what the Grace represents. Even if what he believes he can accomplish is utterly impossible and he doesn't succeed with his ultimate plan, he will kill untold numbers trying. Even if he doesn't succeed, even if he is insane and he fails to do what he thinks he can do, I fear that he may very well accidentally destroy the world of life in the process.

"Either way, the result is the same. Everyone is dead in the end."

"Are you certain about all this," Merritt asked in a careful tone. "Were you close enough to him to know this to all be true? To really believe all this half-people talk?"

Naja Moon lifted an eyebrow over a cold blue eye. This was the dangerous sorceress Magda had recognized from the first moment she had seen her.

"I know how the half people were created because I helped create them. I am a spiritist. I speak with the dead. I also manipulated the spirits of the dead in the underworld to create for Emperor Sulachan an army of the dead. I helped show him how it could be done."

Even though she had defected, Magda suddenly wanted to strangle the woman. "Why would you do such a thing? How could you do such a thing? How could you help put all the innocent lives everywhere in such mortal peril?"

Naja leveled a grim look at Magda. "What was being done to me down in your dungeon is a fate I would have prayed for, had I not done as Sulachan commanded. You could not begin to understand what life is like in the Old World, and especially in the halls of power there.

"Though he may be old and sickly, Emperor Sulachan is still a wizard of great power. Defying his wishes earns a person unimaginable torture. He keeps those he tortures alive for a very long time to serve as a reminder to others of the fate that awaits them should they, too, disobey his wishes. You would be surprised what you would do when living every day of your life in such terror."

"If he is so powerful, then how did you manage to escape?" Merritt asked.

Naja let out a deep breath as her gaze drifted away. "There was a brief window of opportunity created by an unexpected calamity. While people were distracted, I saw my chance and was able to slip away. I ran and I kept running. I didn't want Sulachan's vision to come to pass. I didn't want people to die to fulfill his plans. I didn't want innocent people to be visited by such horror as I knew was coming. I hated that I'd had a part in it all. I was ashamed that I hadn't been brave enough to have chosen torture and death instead of the things I did to help him.

"I thought that maybe this was my chance to do something to try to stop the world from falling into such darkness. After all, if not me, then who? What was my life to mean, if I did nothing and let this happen? What kind of person was I, knowing what was coming, if I stood by and didn't try to stop it?

"I saw my chance and chose to act. Because I am gifted, I was able to fight my way through some of our forces standing between me and the free parts of the New World, and because I am a spiritist I understood how the dead and the half dead function, so I was able to avoid them along the way."

Magda laid a hand on Naja's arm. "Thank you for being brave enough to take up the cause of life."

"Yes, we appreciate it, Naja," Merritt said. "Your help will be invaluable. So what was the calamity you mentioned?"

"An unexpected complexity developed in the emperor's plan. The half people he created took to eating humans."

Merritt and Magda both leaned in together and together they both said, "What?"

"At first, there was no evidence of the behavior, but then without warning the half people began attacking and eating the living. I had warned the emperor of that possibility, but he wouldn't be dissuaded. He wouldn't listen to any warning that went against what he wanted."

"Why would they start eating people?" Magda asked. "What would make them do such a thing?"

"I believe that the half people crave the soul they no longer have. That emptiness drives them with a form of insanity that compels them to eat living people in a futile effort to try to pull a soul into themselves. It doesn't work that way, of course, but you can't exactly talk sense into the half people. It rapidly became a kind of madness infecting all of them, an obsession, that overrode everything else.

"They tear living people open, believing the soul they crave is inside. They eat the insides first, where they think the soul resides. They drink the blood, fearing the soul might leak away. When they aren't satisfied because they haven't gotten what they want, they strip all the meat from the bones, devouring it, trying to find and consume the soul in the still-warm flesh.

"If a group of them catches a living person, they will all tear into them, competing for the soul. A cluster of half people will reduce a living person to bones in short order. It's horrifying. The dead are not even able to be identified because the half people will use their teeth to peel the face right off the skull and eat it. They even suck the brains out of the skull."

"And no one anticipated this?" Merritt asked.

"I did, but like I said, no one would listen. When it didn't happen at first, and everything seemed fine, they were all the more convinced that I was wrong.

"The evolution in their nature took a little time, but when it happened, it happened quickly. They attacked people in the palace, feeding like wolves off the living who were trying desperately to control them. It was chaos for a time.

"That was when I saw my chance and escaped. For all I know, those in charge may believe that I was eaten, as were a number of the gifted involved in the project. It was a terrifying and very bloody time."

"And this is still going on?" Merritt asked.

"Yes, but I think they've managed to gain some degree of control over the situation. They would have been able to do that, to some extent at least, because they have altered the Grace in order to use the spirits of these people."

Merritt frowned. "Use their spirits? How can they control spirits in the underworld beyond the veil?"

"When they take the souls of living people to create the half people, those souls are not allowed to go to the spirit world. The spirits of the dead they also use are pulled back from the world of the dead as well.

"These spirits are kept trapped between realms. Unable to get back to the underworld, they sometimes drift back in this direction and haunt this plane of existence.

"When I left, the gifted were attempting to channel the need to eat the living into the need to instead eat the flesh of the enemy. That way, rather than having to try to find a way to counter such a powerful drive, they instead redirected it to serve their objective. That makes them an even more terrifying weapon. The half people are hard to put down, and if they get near your people and get the chance, they will rip them open, eating them from the inside out, trying to consume their souls."

"Why are they hard to put down?" Merritt asked.

"Because they still have a functioning brain. They can think, plan, scheme, plot, hide, evade, and then attack."

Merritt let out a sigh. "Great. Just great."

Naja spread her hands. She was starting to look worse again.

"I hate to sound ungrateful to you both, and I want to help—that's why I'm here—but I think that you need to get me to a place where you can finish healing me."

Magda looked up at Merritt. "She's right. We need to get out of here. We can talk more later."

Merritt circled an arm around Naja's waist as she started sagging. "I know just the place."

CHAPTER
78

As they passed through the opening off the walkway around the inside of the immense circular stone interior of the great tower and into the sliph's room, Magda saw Quinn sitting at a table across the room, writing in one of his journals. Dominating the center of the room, under a domed ceiling, sat the sliph's stone well.

"Merritt!" Quinn called. He leaned over in his chair to peer past Merritt, helping Naja walk into the room. "And Magda!" Quinn skidded the chair back from the table and rushed to meet them. "So good to see you both!"

The young wizard was about Magda's height, and of average build. His ready smile matched his good nature. But it was his brown eyes that were so riveting. They had a quality well beyond his years, an incisive grasp of all they took in, and despite the intellect behind that astute gaze, the man was always modest when others would have been cocky in their knowledge and accomplishments. They were the eyes of a wise advisor.

"Good to see you, too, Quinn," Merritt said.

Quinn's gaze finally settled on Naja. "Who have we here?"

With one arm around Naja's waist, steadying her, Merritt held his other out in introduction. "Quinn, I'd like you to meet a friend of ours. This is Naja Moon."

Grinning, staring at the woman for an instant, Quinn remembered his manners and gestured into the room. "Please, Naja, won't you come in and have a seat. I'm afraid that there is only the one chair, please take it. You look like you may need to sit down. Let me get you some water."

"She needs more than water," Merritt said, getting right down to business. "She needs to be healed."

Quinn regarded the sorceress with a more appraising look. "Yes, I can see that."

Naja showed a brief smile of greeting to Quinn, but declined the offer to sit.

"To tell you the truth, Merritt, I don't think any of you look all that good." Quinn laid a hand on the side of Magda's shoulder. "What's wrong. You look ashen. You don't look well at all. Maybe you had better sit down."

Magda gently waved off the concern. "Thank you, but we don't have time for that at the moment."

"Some things have happened," Merritt said. "Magda has been healed, but she needs rest to complete the process or she is going to soon go downhill and then she's going to be in trouble."

It was more a warning to Magda than an explanation to Quinn. Magda got the point, but it wasn't really needed. She knew that she was nearing the end of her strength. It was only her worry after what she had learned from Naja that was driving her on at the moment. Her stomach felt like it was in a knot.

"I can see that," Quinn said, a look of concern creasing his brow as he leaned in toward Magda, looking into her eyes for any sign of the trouble. "What happened? How were you hurt?"

Magda smiled to dispel his concern. "That's not important at the moment. We have more urgent business right now." She looked toward Naja, signaling what she meant. Quinn got the message.

Naja had turned, transfixed by the liquid silver hump of the sliph rising up out of the well that contained her. The swelling bulge of what looked like nothing so much as polished, highly reflective, liquid silver began to rise up until it formed into a head with the aspects of a human face.

The quicksilver features resolved fluidly into those of a beautiful woman. A pleasing smile formed in the expression of what looked like nothing so much as a silver statue that was the sliph, except that it always seemed to be moving.

"Do you wish to travel?" the sliph asked, her silvery voice echoing around the round room.

"No," Magda said in a blunt tone. "We don't wish to travel."

"You will be pleased," the sliph said.

"Thank you, but not now," Merritt said on his way past as he helped Naja toward the chair.

"I've heard rumors of such a creature, but I never imagined she was real," Naja said as she dragged Merritt to a halt in order to stare at the silver face watching her.

Quinn cast a rather fond look at the creature in the well. "She's real, there is no doubt of that. She likes to watch me record things in my journals as I watch over her."

"May I touch you?" Naja asked the sliph as she stepped close to the waist-high stone wall of the sliph's well.

"If it pleases you," came the haunting reply.

Naja reached out and carefully touched her fingers to the gently rolling silver surface. The sliph watched. Feeling no ill effects, Naja submerged her entire hand below the surface.

"You have both sides," the sliph said with a satisfied smile. "You may travel."

"Thank you, but I don't wish to travel right now," Naja said. "Maybe another time."

"When you are ready, I will take you where it pleases you."

Naja looked back over her shoulder at Merritt and Magda. "This is remarkable."

Magda folded her arms. "That's one way to put it."

Magda held no favor with the sliph. Not only had the sliph often taken Baraccus away, she took him away as she cooed to him and made gentle promises that he would be pleased.

Baraccus had told Magda that it was just the nature of the sliph, that it didn't mean anything, and that in any event, there was nothing that could be done about it. Magda still hadn't liked the manner in which the perfect quicksilver face had spoken so intimately to her husband. Of course, the sliph talked to everyone that way. Baraccus was right, it was her nature. That didn't make Magda feel any better about it.

The sliph had even talked to Magda the same way when Magda had needed to travel. She wasn't gifted, as was required, but Baraccus had instilled in Magda some bit of magic that enabled her to travel. Traveling was at once a wildly exhilarating and a terrifying sensation. She hoped never to have to experience it again.

Naja withdrew her hand and stepped away from the well. "No, you don't understand. What is remarkable is that this creature has been altered in a similar way to the half people. Her soul has been fragmented."

Quinn swept his sandy blond hair back. "Half people? What are half people? What are you talking about?"

Merritt held a hand up. "Listen, Quinn, we have problems."

Quinn's features took on a serious cast. "So then you've heard the rumors that Prosecutor Lothain is going to be named First Wizard? Is that the trouble you mean."

"That's not the problem I was referring to," Merritt said.

"And it's not a rumor," Magda told him. "It's true."

Quinn's serious expression turned worried. "Is it really going to happen tomorrow, as some say?"

"Tomorrow? I haven't heard that part of it," Magda said. "What have you heard?"

"There's a lot of rush planning going on. Something big is in the works for tomorrow afternoon in the council chambers. I don't know what, but it only makes sense that it would be the naming of the new First Wizard." As he gestured to Naja, his eyes again took on that discerning look that Magda knew so well. "Now, what's this about half people? What are half people?"

Before Naja could speak, Merritt did. "Quinn, we don't have time to explain it at the moment. Right now I need you to listen and do something for me."

Quinn shrugged. "Sure, Merritt, you know I will. Just tell me what you need and consider it done."

Merritt pulled Naja forward by the arm. "I need you to heal Naja for me. You've always been better at healing than me anyway. I have some important things to do that can't wait. Once you've healed her, she can explain why she's here, about the half people, and the trouble we're in."

Quinn glanced at Naja's face briefly and back to Merritt. "Well, I've never seen her before. Can you at least tell me who is she? And how she's involved in what's going on?"

"I was Emperor Sulachan's spiritist," Naja said before Merritt could explain. "I came here to help your people stop him."

Quinn's brow lifted. "You're the defector I've heard rumored? I could never find out anything about you. People said that it must be gossip and nothing more."

"Not gossip, real."

"Did you get injured escaping, then?"

Naja fixed Quinn a serious look. "When I came here I was captured. Men said that I was a spy and sentenced me to death. They tortured me. That is how I was hurt."

"Who did such a thing?" Quinn demanded, looking from one face to another. "What men?"

"She doesn't know who they were," Magda told him.

"They were torturing her to find out if she knows who the traitors in the Keep are and if she has others with her," Merritt said. "They must be worried about being discovered."

"And do you know?" Quinn asked Naja.

Naja looked genuinely downcast. "No. I'm sorry."

Quinn ran his fingers back through his hair as he walked off a few paces, considering what he'd been told. "This is the very thing I've been worried about. I'm convinced that there are traitors, or at least spies in the Keep."

Magda and Merritt shared a look.

"Do you have any information about such traitors?" Merritt asked. "Have you heard anything from all the wizards and important people who come through here to use the sliph?"

Quinn turned back to them. "No, no one knows anything. I have my suspicions, but I don't have any evidence to base it on. With the war going badly people are making a scapegoat of Baraccus. You know me, Magda, and you know that I believe that Baraccus was our greatest champion, but people are beginning to believe Prosecutor Lothain's contention that Baraccus was responsible for conspiracies that have harmed our war effort. He thinks those conspiracies are the source of the murders at the Keep. Lothain has been asking a lot of questions about Baraccus, trying to find out if he was working with enemy agents."

"I know," Magda said. "I've heard the accusations."

"A lot of people are starting to listen to Lothain's theories because he has been right so often and so successful at uncovering traitors no one would have suspected. Fortunately, there are still a lot of people who don't believe it. It seems the whole Keep is in turmoil over the discord. From what I've heard, that friction is beginning to become a problem."

Feeling momentarily faint, Magda had to lean against the side of the sliph's well. Merritt saw her fading.

"Look, Quinn, we have to go. After you heal her, Naja will explain about the walking dead and the half people. She can fill you in on everything."

"Walking dead?" Quinn blinked. "Does that have to do with the murders down here? Is that what you're talking about?"

"That's right," Merritt said. "The enemy is animating the dead with magic and using them to assassinate important wizards. If you see a dead person walking, use wizard's fire."

Quinn wiped a hand across his mouth. "This fits with some of the pieces I've already put together."

"You hear a lot of talk from wizards and officials using the sliph," Magda said. "Have you heard anything that would give you any idea who the traitors or spies might be?"

Quinn gestured toward the table at the back of the room. "Let me go through some of my notes and entries.

I've talked to a lot of people. Now that I have a better idea what I'm looking for, I might be able to pull out some important details. After I heal Naja, of course. I'll let you know tomorrow if I find out anything meaningful."

"Good." Merritt stepped closer to his friend. "Listen to me, Quinn, this is all very dangerous. We're not sure who was torturing Naja, but they are surely the same people responsible for killing so many of our friends and fellow gifted. I don't want you taking any chances. You need to keep this all secret for now."

"I understand," Quinn said as he gestured out the doorway. "There are empty rooms up off the tower. My relief watch is due down here soon. I'll take Naja up to one of those rooms right now to keep her out of sight. As soon as my relief shows up I'll go heal her. From the look in her eyes, it will likely take all night."

"Thanks, Quinn. You've got it all right. Naja will fill you in after you heal her. We're going to need your help, then, to get to the bottom of things and catch the traitors before they kill us all. There are a lot bigger things going on than you realize."

"I'm glad you came to me," Quinn said. Magda could see in his eyes that he meant it.

Merritt turned to Magda, putting a big hand under her arm. "I need to get you up to your room. You need rest to recover."

"Recover from what?" Quinn asked. "I meant to ask what happened?"

"We'll tell you tomorrow when we talk again," Merritt said as he started Magda toward the door. He obviously was getting concerned by her fading strength.

On the way to the door, Naja stopped them. She squeezed Magda's arm. "Thank you both. I'm going to return your confidence in me, I swear. I'm going to help you."

Magda smiled and touched Naja's cheek. "Thank you, Naja."

Out in the immense, round tower outside the room with the sliph's well, only a few torches burned higher up on iron landings at intervals in the stairs curving up around the stone walls. The openings at the top revealed a night sky clouded over to hide the stars and the moon. Magda looked up at Merritt in the near darkness.

"What is it that you need to do? You told Quinn that you needed to work on something."

"I need to work on a way to stop the dead and the half people. We don't have any time to waste. When I get you to your room I need to have another look at the cloth hanging that you took out of Isidore's maze. I need to see the specific alterations she did to the keeper spells."

"Because it stopped the dead?"

Merritt nodded. "Because it stopped the dead. I need to do some experiments and try some things."

CHAPTER
79

Shadow meowed and came running when Magda opened the door. The black cat rubbed against her leg, and then against Merritt. Magda leaned down and briefly scratched the cat's back.

"Have you been a good girl, little one?"

The cat answered, as if she had understood the question, with a long mew.

"I guess that neither one of us has had dinner."

"You need to eat," Merritt said as he waved an arm, lighting the lamps in the apartment, "but it can wait until tomorrow. Right now you need to sleep more than you need food."

Magda put a hand on his shoulder. "Thank you, Merritt. As terrifying as everything seems right now, it's comforting to have you on my side in all of this."

Merritt smiled. "Thanks to you, we now have the key. That's a monumental achievement that is going to be a great asset, and I couldn't have done it without you. It's all the better for having your strength."

Magda let out a sigh. "It certainly did seem to have taken my strength. I can't believe how weak I feel."

"It's the sword borrowing your life force. As soon as you get some sleep to finish your recovery you'll feel a lot better, I promise." He gestured off into the apartment. "Before I leave you, I need to see the cloth from Isidore again so that I can work on some things tonight while you're resting."

Magda nodded and went back through the white, carved double doors into her bedroom. The bed looked inviting. She retrieved the silky cloth and hurried back out with it. Merritt was gazing around at the place in wonder. She often forgot what a beautiful retreat the apartment really was. She was eager to move, though, because it was going to be Lothain's place, now.

"Do you want to take it with you?" she asked as she handed him the folded fabric.

Merritt unfolded the long cloth, holding it up to get a good look at the symbols. "No. With you in a deep sleep, I'd feel a lot better knowing that you have this over you, warding off any of the monsters Naja told us about."

"So far as I know, all the murders have been down lower in the Keep. Do you really think that the dead would come all the way up here?"

Merritt stretched the cloth out, looking at it as he spoke. "Your life isn't worth the risk. I'm the one who gave Isidore the basic keeper spells. I just need to check some minor details about the modifications she did to them—make sure I have it right in my memory. With something this critical, I don't want to get it wrong."

She put her hand over his, drawing his gaze. "Merritt, what are we going to do about all this? How are we going to go about putting a stop to it?"

Satisfied with his inspection, Merritt handed her back the cloth as he showed her a brave smile. She thought that it was a nice gesture of him to pretend for her sake.

"Tomorrow, Magda. Sleep, get the rest you need, and tomorrow we'll worry about it. You'll be able to think more clearly after you get the rest you need to finish healing. We have Quinn working with us now. He'll be a big help, as will Naja."

Magda smiled at the memory of the stunning sorceress.

"I don't think I've ever seen a woman that beautiful."

Merritt's eyes searched hers. "She's not nearly as beautiful as you, Magda," he said in a quiet voice that surprised her with not only the words themselves, but the sincerity in his tone.

Merritt caught himself and looked away. "I'm sorry, Magda. I should never have said that. You are wife to Baraccus."

She laid a finger along the side of his jaw, turning his face back to hers. "Baraccus is dead. We're not."

"Still . . ."

"It's all right, Merritt," she said as she took his arm and walked him to the door.

Merritt bent and scratched the top of the cat's head. "You watch out for your mistress, will you? Watch over her."

Shadow pushed her head against him as she squeezed her eyes closed in contentment. Magda was glad to see that Shadow liked him. The cat was a good judge of character.

"Where will you be?" she asked. "Where will I be able to find you?"

"I'm going to go back to my place down in the city. I have some ideas. I need to try some modifications to Isidore's spell-forms and then I want to run some integrity checks on them."

"You're going to try to make something to keep the dead in their place?" Magda guessed.

"It's not that simple. Sleep. I'll come back to the Keep tomorrow. I'll wait for you with Quinn. When you're rested we can talk about it tomorrow. Maybe by then we'll know what the big event is for tomorrow afternoon.

By then Naja will be healed, too. She'll be able to help. We'll start fresh in the morning."

Magda held the edge of the door and leaned against it. "All right." As he started away, she called out to him. "Merritt, who do you think is responsible for all the trouble at the Keep?"

He turned back and looked at her for a long moment. "I have my suspicions."

Magda did as well, but she couldn't be positive. She didn't want to make a mistake in something so important. Getting it wrong could cost all of them their lives.

"Sleep," he said, pointing back at her in command before starting away down the dark hallway. It made Magda smile.

She went to a cupboard and checked inside. She was thankful to find some pieces of salted, dried fish in a jar where she thought she remembered seeing them. She was so sleepy that she could hardly stand, but she was also starving and feared that if she didn't have a bite to quell her grumbling stomach she wouldn't be able to fall asleep. She tore a piece of fish off with her teeth and chewed as she went to a sideboard that held a pitcher and a washbasin.

Shadow followed her, looking up, tail high in the air, meowing the entire way. Magda sucked the salt off a chunk of the fish for a moment and then bent and gave it to the cat. Shadow looked as ravenous as Magda felt. While the cat crouched over her meal, Magda poured a glass of water and washed down the salted fish. She drained the entire glass. It felt good to have some food in her stomach, even if it wasn't much.

When she looked up at herself in the mirror, she was mildly horrified by what she saw. Her face was dirty and her hair, even though it was short now and easier to manage, was still a mess. She hadn't realized that Merritt had seen her looking so disheveled and dirty. He must have thought she looked like an urchin. But he had said she was beautiful. Such a compliment felt good coming from a man as handsome as Merritt. Still . . .

Magda dunked a washcloth in the basin and wrung it out. Her face felt grimy from her trip down to the dungeon. She saw that her hands were dirty with rust from the iron railing down there. She reminded herself of Naja's condition and then felt rather foolish for worrying about the way she looked.

As she washed her hands and face, Shadow jumped up on the sideboard, hoping for another handout. Magda smiled and after sucking the salt off, gave the hungry cat another piece of the fish.

Sitting on the sideboard, Shadow hunched over her second helping. In the middle of chewing the fish, she jerked her head up. She dropped the fish as she stared at the door.

The cat rose up on her tiptoes, back arched, tail puffed up. Fangs showing, Shadow hissed.

Magda stood frozen, eyes wide.

Someone knocked.

Magda stood frozen at the sideboard. Her heart pounded. The black cat was still hissing.

Magda couldn't remember if she had thrown the bolt on the door. When the handle turned and the door started opening, that answered her question. She backed up a few steps, wondering where she could run. There was the balcony in the bedroom. It was several stories off the ground, though.

When he strolled into the room, Lothain swept out an arm, lighting a few more of the lamps, all the better to see his bull neck, short wiry hair, and his black eyes as they fixed on her.

Fists at her side, Magda stormed toward where he stood at the door. "How dare you enter without permission?"

"I knocked," he said casually, dismissing her objection.

Out the doorway, in the hall, Magda could see a large contingent of his personal guard in their green tunics. She was puzzled to also see about a dozen women in their midst. Magda realized that they were some of the staff.

"This is a poor time to come to claim your apartment," she said. "I told you, I would move as soon as I could."

With his eyes still fixed on her, he smiled. "I haven't come to claim my apartment, I have come to claim my wife."

"Your wife?" Magda's jaw clenched as she felt her rage build. "Get out!"

When Lothain gestured, two of the big guards stepped into the room and seized her by the arms, one man on each side. Magda struggled only momentarily, quickly realizing that it was only liable to entertain them all to watch her struggling, helpless to do anything about it.

"In here," Lothain said to the women out in the hall. "Bring your things in here."

Magda was surprised, when the women filed in, to see all the women carrying things: sewing baskets, small chests, rolls of lace, and dozens of bolts of cloth of every color.

"What do you think you're doing?" Magda asked Lothain.

He followed Magda's gaze to the women. "Seamstresses. They're here to make your wedding dress for tomorrow's ceremony. I'm to be named First Wizard, so I thought that would be the appropriate moment for us to be wed. It will settle matters, reassure people, and bring everyone together in support of me."

"You're crazy if you think—"

"That's enough," Lothain said in a dangerous tone. "It's time you learned your place." He gestured with a tilt of his head to the two men who were holding her as he turned and went out into the hall. When he was sure that they had her well in hand, he marched off down the hallway without further word.

Magda had to walk swiftly to keep from being dragged by the men who had her arms in a firm grip. At least another dozen soldiers followed behind them, while even more waited back at her apartment.

"Where are you taking me?" she demanded to his broad back.

Lothain glanced back over his shoulder. "I'm taking you to a place where we can discuss my marriage proposal. I need you to see something before you say no to my offer of marriage. I think it will put you in mind to be agreeable. Our marriage will be for the good of the Keep and the good of our cause. I'm going to show you one of the great benefits of your agreeing that it is best for all if you agree to marry me."

Magda decided not to waste her energy telling him that there was nothing that could make her agree to marry him. She tried not to fight the men dragging her along. Several times she stumbled but it didn't slow them.

She didn't fight them. She needed to conserve what strength she had. If she could ever get to her knife, she was going to need her strength.

Lothain took several turns as he led them down a series of halls to a service area. A utility room where supplies and provisions were kept in the back also had a space for staff to gather for instructions before going about their duties. Without pause, Lothain opened a door and went inside, going through an outer gathering room where more of his guards in their green tunics waited. He went through an open door in the back into a darker inner room.

There, tied in a chair, sagged a weeping Tilly. She was a bloody mess. Guards towered all around her.

"Tilly!"

Magda broke from the guards and rushed to the woman, falling to her knees before her. Tilly's terrified gaze met Magda's.

"Tilly, what's going on? What have they done to you?"

Before Magda could say another word, or Tilly could answer, the men snatched Magda's arms again and hauled her back up and away from the woman in the chair.

Tilly's hair was matted with blood. It looked like some of her teeth had been knocked out when her face had been pounded. Her nose looked crooked and her eyes were blackened. Blood dripped in thick strings from her chin, soaking the front of her dress.

Filled with rage, Magda turned her eyes to Lothain. "What is the meaning of this outrage?"

A humorless smile widened his mouth. "The meaning of it is to help you make up your mind to do the right thing."

"The right thing? You do this and talk to me of the right thing?"

The last piece of the puzzle had just fit into place for her. She now knew.

"Yes, the right thing. You see, whether this friend of yours lives or dies is up to you, Lady Searus. If you make the right choice, then she lives. If not . . . well, I believe you get the point."

Lothain turned and gestured to one of the guards. Without hesitation, he pulled Tilly's arm out straight. She screamed "No! No! No!" over and over, but to no avail.

With one powerful blow, the man broke Tilly's arm.

Magda jumped in shock at the loud crack when the bone snapped.

Tilly screamed and struggled wildly. "Please! Please! No more! Mistress! Please! Make them stop!"

The guard stuffed a wadded rag in her mouth to silence her.

Magda panted in fury, tears streaming down her face as she struggled in vain against the muscle holding her.

"Now," Lothain said, "this is the way it's going to be. If you agree to go through with the marriage tomorrow afternoon before the council and gathered dignitaries as I am installed as First Wizard, and don't in any way cause a scene, but rather act in a gracious manner that will help bring our people together under the rule of their new First Wizard, then Tilly here will be freed."

"And if I refuse?" Magda asked, already knowing the answer.

His smile returned. "Well, of course you know that it will go very badly for her until she eventually dies. I will take you to visit her every day as she is tortured. And then . . ."

When she didn't ask what he meant was next, he leaned a little closer. "And then, there are a number of your other friends who are going to pay the same price. We have a whole list. Your friend who used to be on the council? Sadler?" He arched an eyebrow as he held out a hand and folded a finger down. "Sadler will suffer a similar fate, all because you refuse to do the right thing.

"Your friend Quinn? The young man you grew up with?"

Lothain folded another finger down as he watched her eyes. He went on to name other longtime friends, folding a finger down each time he spoke a name. When he ran out of fingers, he opened his hand and started over naming people she knew and folding over a finger with the mention of each one.

"We know where each one of them is, and we have men standing by, keeping an eye on them in case they are needed," he said. "I have but to give them the word and every one of those people will be suffering just like Tilly here by the end of tomorrow. Each one of those people will know that it is because you have demonstrated through your selfishness, your unwillingness to help the people of the Midlands, that it is because you are a traitor and you have brought the same fate down on them, since they, too, must be part of your conspiracy.

"Like you, they will be charged and found guilty of treason against the Midlands. Under torture, they will all eventually confess. They will all go to their eventual deaths cursing your name.

"You will be able to hear them cursing your name because you will be chained up close enough to hear their every scream. And then, when every one of them passes beyond the veil into the world of the dead, we will start in on you, and I can assure you, for being the leader of such a vile conspiracy against the Midlands, we will save the best till last. And I promise you, when we are finished with you, you will confess. Publicly."

Magda swallowed. She was trembling all over.

"Now, Lady Searus, we have seamstresses standing by, back in the apartment of the First Wizard, my apartment, waiting to make you the wedding dress of your choice. I'm a generous man. The choice is to be up to you. They will make any dress you wish to be wed in. You see? I wish you to be pleased. Now that I think of it, though, I guess I would prefer that it not be white, because, well, you have been married to a First Wizard before.

"We have food and drink being prepared for tomorrow afternoon's grand event. We have people from far and wide coming to attend the momentous gathering, everyone hoping to see the Midlands brought back together under a new First Wizard, hoping to see Lady Searus leading the way by giving her hand in marriage to the new First Wizard, showing that she places her trust in me, and thus, so can they.

"So, you see, the choice is yours."

Magda tried to think, but listening to Tilly's muffled

cries was making it impossible to think. She couldn't figure out what she could do. She couldn't come up with a way out of it.

And then she realized that there was nothing to think about. There was no choice.

Magda swallowed again. "All right."

"All right, what?" He smiled a wicked smile. "If you accept my proposal of marriage, then say it."

With Tilly's life hanging in the balance, this was no time to tempt his temper. Magda had never felt so low, so humiliated.

"Yes, First Wizard Lothain, I accept your proposal of marriage. I'll do it. I'll do as you say."

"And exactly as I say. With grace and dignity."

"Yes. Just as you say. I promise. Now let her go."

Lothain smiled at Tilly's wide-eyed terror. He turned back to Magda. "In due time, my dear. In due time."

"What does that mean?"

"It means that after you keep your word, after everyone sees that you are recanting all the accusations you made against me in the depth of your mindless grief, and after you prove to everyone your sincerity in that retraction by becoming my wife to show your support of me and your belief that I am the man to be First Wizard, then we will release her. But not before.

"If you carry out your part with a smile and gracious good cheer at my appointment as well as our marriage, all your other friends will never know how close they came to suffering a terrible fate. Their lives will be in your hands. If you do as you have promised, then they will celebrate in your joy at being the new wife to the new First Wizard."

Magda was nodding. "As long as you promise to keep your word."

"My word? My dear, my word has nothing to do with

it. You carry out your part, do as you are told, and I will see if you have been cooperative enough to warrant me granting mercy to Tilly here, and to all the rest of your friends. But I can tell you that if you do it all correctly, and make everyone believe in your sincerity, then I will be in such a good mood that I will be far more interested in the pleasure you will bring me on our wedding night than harming anyone. Do we understand each other?"

Magda swallowed back her rage. "Yes."

"Good." He smiled. "Good." Lothain turned and patted Tilly on the cheek. "She is a good person, is she not?"

Tilly, tears of pain and terror streaming down her cheeks, nodded. Magda doubted that Tilly even knew why she was nodding.

"Don't worry, Tilly," Magda said. "I will do what I have to do to keep you safe."

Tilly's eyes squeezed closed as she wept. Magda could just make out her muffled words of gratitude.

Lothain lifted Magda's chin. "You know, I was going to kill you for all the trouble you've caused, but then it came to me that it would be much better to subvert you instead and have you undo all the harm yourself. Much better solution all around, don't you think? Better that you live to see it, than to be dead and unaware of my triumph."

"You had better let her go after I do what you want."

Lothain chuckled. "I don't care about this scrub woman. She means nothing to me. I have no need to kill her. It's all up to you what happens to her."

"I told you that I would do as you say."

"Indeed you did. And I believe you mean it." He leaned back a little as he took her in with an appraising look. "You are so weak that you would do it to save a handful of lives. You foolishly value the life of an individual over the greater good.

"You don't have the courage it takes to be a part of such an epic struggle.

"That is why you are a nobody."

He gestured to the guards. "Take her back to her room so that she can have the women there make her wedding dress. Stand guard out in the hall tonight. No one goes in or leaves but the seamstresses."

The men saluted before yanking Magda away.

She could hear Tilly weeping behind her.

The corridors she was dragged through were empty. The Home Guard had apparently been dismissed by the prosecutor's private army. The men's bootsteps echoed through the halls. The Keep was gradually being subverted by Lothain's looming rule. His influence, his control, was tainting everything and everyone.

In the depths of her despair, as the men were dragging Magda down the hall, in a crystal-clear instant of inspiration, it came to her.

Magda knew what she had to do.

More clearly than anything she had ever known before, Magda knew what she had to do.

Are you sure, Mistress?" The seamstress stretched her arm out to indicate all the choices that had been laid out. "Wouldn't you like something a little more resplendent? After all, this is a big occasion, a big moment in your life in front of so many people. Wouldn't something with more dazzle be appropriate?"

Magda smiled her assurance to the concerned woman. "Thank you, but I believe that my choice is quite striking. Adding layers of lace, needlepoint, and beads isn't necessarily an improvement. There is power in simplicity."

The woman's face was a tapestry of worry lines. "If you say so, Mistress."

"I do." Magda, driven by an overriding purpose, made an effort to sound pleasant. "Please, make it exactly as I have shown you I want it done."

The seamstress nodded reluctantly. "Yes, Mistress."

It was clear that the women were concerned that they would be blamed for less than a masterpiece of layered glamour.

"And I don't want any of you to worry," Magda said to all the women watching her. "I will let it be known that the dress was my choice, and my choice alone."

That seemed to ease the tension in the room somewhat.

Having forced herself to set aside her outrage and horror, Magda had managed to gather her senses as she had been dragged back to her apartment. She knew that she had to think everything through clearly and deliberately. If she gave in to panic, or worse, resignation, she would be unable to act effectively.

Magda held no illusions about Lothain's potential for cruelty, so while she was worried for Tilly, she knew that she had done everything she could for the moment to give Tilly the best chance. She couldn't dwell on it.

With a firm plan in mind, she had felt a resolute calm come over her. She knew what she had to do.

"And which material, Lady Searus?" the seamstress asked.

Dozens of bolts of cloth were laid out on two of the couches. There were beautiful prints as well as a wide variety of colors and exotic tone-on-tone fabrics. In addition there were yards and yards of lacework of every sort.

But Magda had spotted the right one the very first moment.

As far as Magda was concerned, there was only one choice among the wide assortment. She wanted no other.

She pointed to a simple, silken material. "This one."

The woman looked up. Worry returned to etch itself back into her expression. "Are you sure, Mistress? Master Lothain said he didn't think it should be white."

"I'm sure that he was referring to a bright white. This isn't exactly a brilliant white. I'm sure he meant that he didn't want it to be a glaring white, that's all.

"Besides, my future husband is not the one who will be wearing the dress. I am. This will be my day. I want to look my best." Magda smiled warmly and sought to make it clear that she would not be dissuaded. "I think this one, this slightly off-white material, is absolutely beautiful for the purpose, don't you agree? I love the sheen of it. It's the most elegant of all the material here. There is none its match. It's beautiful. I love it. It's perfect for the purpose."

"The purpose?"

"My rebirth."

The woman blinked. The others, getting out shears and preparing all the needles and thread, shared furtive looks but said nothing.

"Rebirth, Mistress?" the first woman asked.

"Yes," Magda said, her fingers leaving the lustrous material as her gaze returned to the woman staring up at her. "This will be my rebirth into a new person. Marriage is changing from a single woman into a woman devoted to her husband's wishes, is it not? So, since I am about to be reborn into a new person, this fits the purpose."

The seamstress smiled, even though she still looked anxious. "I see your point, Mistress."

"You have all my measurements, then? You're finished with all that? You have everything you need?"

"Yes, Mistress."

"Good. I've had a very trying day. I need to get a good night's sleep to be ready for the big day tomorrow. For my rebirth, as it were."

The woman, still unsure, held up a finger before Magda left. "Mistress, about the cut. Master Lothain was very clear that he wanted the dress to show a lot of cleavage. I don't mean to contradict your wishes, but—"

"Then don't. My future husband, in his eagerness, is simply getting ahead of himself. He can wait." Some of the women tittered. "Please make the dress as I have drawn it out."

The seamstress's smile widened. "Yes, Mistress. Of course. We have everything we need. The dress will be exactly to your design, I swear. We will finish it and leave it out here for you, and then close the doors on our way out so that you may get your rest. We will not disturb your sleep."

Magda made herself smile. She touched the woman's shoulder in gratitude.

"Thank you, ladies. Good night then."

On her way toward the back bedroom, Magda found the folded pieces of paper in her pocket, along with the collection of small clay figures. It was the gravity spell that Merritt had given to her.

She stood staring at the paper in her hand, the little figures floating in the air above her palm, thinking.

She finally stuffed it all back into her pocket and went through the open double doors to her bedroom.

"Good night, ladies," she said again as she closed and bolted the white double doors into the bedroom.

CHAPTER
82

Lothain had told his men that they should remain in the hallway outside the apartment all night to make sure that no one went in and that she didn't leave. The guards all knew, of course, that they were several stories above the surrounding portions of the Keep. The soldiers in green tunics who had brought her back to the apartment all knew that the only way she would be able to leave was back out through the doors into the corridor where they stood guard.

Since they knew she couldn't sneak past them, it seemed to her highly unlikely they would have any reason to come into the apartment, much less her bedroom. Lothain was covetous of her. They weren't going to want to give the man cause to be suspicious of what they might be doing with her. Magda was relatively confident that they would stand guard but not want to come into the apartment without direct orders.

In any event, she couldn't worry about the off chance that they would come in and check on her. She would simply have to be quick about it. She had to do what was necessary, or she was going to find herself the wife of the new First Wizard Lothain.

Without delay, Magda went to the big maple wardrobe

that had belonged to Baraccus. His clothes still hung where he had left them. Magda hadn't known what to do with them, so she had simply left them there. Before he had killed himself, he had left his war-wizard outfit in the First Wizard's enclave. The wardrobe held a variety of other clothes, everything from old pants and shirts he wore when working at his workbench to elaborate ceremonial robes. She pushed the ceremonial robes aside to reach in on the side as far as she could.

Magda pushed in the right spot, and the door over a hidden compartment slid open. Baraccus had made the hiding place himself. Reaching inside, her fingers found the knotted rope hanging from a peg. She pulled it out, relieved that it was still there.

There had been times when Baraccus had to meet people under cover of darkness, and for the safety of the men he was meeting, those meetings had to be kept secret. Had he left the apartment by the front door and gone out through the corridors, all kinds of people would have known about it. Whenever he went out in the Keep there were always eyes watching him. He'd said that he never knew the motives of the people who saw him.

If he had been seen leaving the Keep in the middle of the night, word would have eventually gotten around. People would have wondered what he was doing, where he was going, who he was seeing. As it was, as careful as Baraccus had been, it seemed that Lothain had found out about at least some of the late-night meetings.

In an attempt to keep such meetings secret, Baraccus had kept a knotted rope hidden in his wardrobe so that he would be able to leave from the bedroom balcony. It was a drop of several stories, so people would not be expecting him to leave that way.

The rope was exactly the right length to make it safely all the way down to a shallow slate roof. The roof led to a rampart where there were old, unused exterior stairs that were hidden from view. Magda knew how to make her way from there without being seen.

She grabbed a clean, black, hooded cloak and threw it around her shoulders. She went to a cabinet and pulled her shielded travel lantern out by its wire handle. With a long splinter that she lit in one of the reflector lamps on the wall, she set flame to the wick of her travel lantern. Once the wick was adjusted low, she shut the curved metal door and latched it so it wouldn't give off any light until she wanted it to, then hooked it on her belt.

Magda went to the bedroom doors and carefully checked the bolt to reassure herself that the doors were locked. Across the bedroom, she went out the leaded-glass door onto the balcony. It was heavily overcast and black as pitch. Fortunately, there were a few lights around the Keep that let her see what she was doing.

Magda knelt at the edge of the balcony and slipped her hand out through the balusters, feeling over the edge for the heavy hook that Baraccus had sunk into the stone with the aid of magic. Her fingers found the hook. She slipped the loop on the end of the rope over the hook, then fed the rest of the rope out between the balusters.

Once she was confident that it was secure, she climbed over the railing and was able to lower herself down and get ahold of the rope. She started down, catching the knots between her feet for support as she carefully descended hand over hand. She had never used the rope before, and it was frightening hanging in midair in the darkness, but she kept her mind on the task and before long she touched down on the slate roof.

She was glad that it was a dark night so that no one would see her leaving.

She followed the rooftop until she reached the rampart, then ran until she found the small opening for the stairs. With no time to waste, she took them down two at a time.

CHAPTER
83

Magda staggered to a stop. She put her hands on her knees as she caught her breath. Her legs ached. In fact, her whole body ached. She knew that Merritt was right about her needing rest. That inexorable requirement after giving herself over to the completion of the sword was rapidly catching up with her. Her lungs burned, making her cough.

She knew that if she didn't get rest, and soon, she ran the risk of collapsing. But she couldn't stop, not yet.

She'd walked the Keep road down to the city countless times, but the low, threatening clouds hid the moon, making it hard to see. At least they reflected some of the isolated lights down in the city of Aydindril and it was enough for her to be able to make out roads when they came in from the sides. With those landmarks she knew where she was.

This part of the road coming down the mountain from the Keep to Aydindril wound its way through dense forests. She knew that the trees would soon thin out and then she might be able to see a little better. The thing that she had to be careful of was that to her left, around some of the turns in the road, there were steep drop-offs. Carelessly taking a step too far off the edge of the road in the darkness would likely be the last step she ever made.

From time to time on the way down, she had stopped and cracked open the door on her lantern to be sure of her surroundings and where she was. Each time, as soon as she got her bearings, she quickly closed the lantern door. With the danger of spies in and about Aydindril, the Home Guard was on the lookout for any suspicious activity. She didn't want any patrolling soldiers to spot her and come to see who she was and what she was doing.

As she panted, catching her breath, a few fat, cold drops of rain splattered against her head and shoulders. She hoped it didn't start coming down in earnest. Her breath back, she started running again.

Before long, as she entered the city, the reflected light off the clouds was enough for her to make out the road and the buildings to the sides. A little farther into the city the street narrowed because it passed between buildings that were shops on the first floor, with living space above. They were all dark.

It was still quite a distance to Merritt's house, so, head down, she ignored her burning leg muscles and drove herself on at a quick pace. When she heard some odd noises up ahead, she stopped cold and looked up.

Ahead in the darkness, still off a ways on the narrow street, she saw a group of men coming toward her. They weren't carrying any lamps, so it was hard to tell how many there were, but the bunch of them looked to be a goodly number. She stared with wide eyes, trying to tell who they were.

And then, as they passed a shop with candlelight coming from a window, she saw the glint of light off swords at their hips. Several men had upright pikes.

They were soldiers, probably a patrol of the Home Guard. There looked to be maybe eight or ten of them.

Before the patrol saw her, Magda quickly ducked into the alleyway to her left. She ran a map of the city through her head and realized that, rather than following the route she'd been planning on taking, she could actually take a shortcut to Merritt's house and probably save some time, as well as stay out of sight from the patrol. She didn't know why she hadn't thought of it before. She guessed that she was so drained of strength that it kept her from thinking straight. She reminded herself that her survival depended on thinking clearly.

She hurried up the alley, trying to put distance between her and the end of the alley where the soldiers would pass by. She knew that patrols sometimes took gifted with them to sense people who might be hiding. When she heard them approaching the intersection where she had gone into the alley, she slipped into the narrow space between two buildings to hide. She held the lantern behind her in case there was any crack in the metal door that might be spotted if one of the soldiers looked her way.

Magda peeked out with one eye. She could see them, off in the distance, as they passed by the end of the alley. It was hard to tell, but she was pretty sure that she was right, that there were eight to ten of them. She hadn't thought that patrols were typically that large.

She saw, then, that one of the men in their midst appeared to be restrained with some kind of device around his neck with a bar in front. It looked like maybe his wrists were manacled to the end of the bar.

That explained the number of men. They had taken someone into custody. Soldiers typically took a larger contingent when they went to apprehend a criminal. She supposed that it was easier to catch a man in his bed than to try to run him down in the day.

Once the soldiers and their prisoner had gone past the

alley, Magda cautiously emerged from her hiding place and checked in all directions for any sign of other soldiers. When she saw nothing and everything was dead quiet, she rushed off up the alley. She trotted to cover ground as quickly as possible. She didn't think she had it in her to run anymore. At least the brief sprinkle had stopped, but she worried that the clouds still threatened rain.

When she reached a cross street with a two-story brick building that she remembered, she squinted in the darkness across the road. She saw a sign hanging over a door. It was the right size, but she couldn't tell if it had a blue pig painted on it. Around the corner, though, she could see the narrow street following rolling, uneven ground. It was the right place. She turned up the street toward Merritt's house.

When she at last saw a forked plum tree in the front of the little porch, she let out a sigh, thankful to have found the place so quickly in the dark. Light came from the window to the side of the house, so she knew that Merritt was still up working.

She knocked just loud enough that she thought he would hear her but the neighbors wouldn't. She hoped that dogs didn't start barking and rouse people.

When Merritt didn't answer the door, she knocked a little harder. When she knocked harder, the door swung in a little. It wasn't latched.

"Merritt?" she called out in a quiet voice. "Merritt?"

She thought that maybe he was out back, so she slipped inside. She pushed the door closed behind her as she looked around. She didn't see him. A few lanterns were lit in the room, but Merritt wasn't there.

She went to the back, looking out, but it was pitch black. She went to a dark doorway and opened the metal cover on her lantern, throwing light into the dark bedroom. The bed was empty. She couldn't imagine where he could be.

On the way back through the house, weaving her way through the assortment of objects lying about all over the floor, she froze in midstride. In front of the table with the red velvet cloth, the chair was lying on its side.

The Sword of Truth, in its sheath, still hanging from the back of the chair, lay on the floor.

Magda righted the chair. She stood staring at the sword.

Merritt wouldn't leave the sword. He had never left it before, and he certainly wouldn't leave it since completing its transition into the key to the boxes of Orden.

And then she saw a small piece of green cloth snagged on one of the metal objects standing nearby. It was the same wool material and the exact same green color as the tunics worn by the soldiers of the prosecutor's office. The same soldiers in green tunics who were guarding her apartment. The same soldiers in green tunics who had brutalized Tilly. The same soldiers in green tunics that were Lothain's private army.

She remembered, then, the soldiers with a prisoner she had seen only a short time before. They were headed toward the Keep.

It was too much to be a coincidence.

Magda pulled off her black cloak and threw it on the table. She slipped the baldric over her head, laying it on her right shoulder, placing the scabbard with the sword at her left hip. Once it was securely in place, she put her cloak back on, hiding the sword, and headed for the door.

In her mind, she swiftly plotted a variety of routes through the city. All the times when she had been a young girl, running with friends through the city, were paying off as she considered the fastest way to intercept the soldiers.

She needed to get out ahead of them and cut them off.

She wondered briefly what she thought she was going to do to make them release Merritt.

As she ran out the door of his house, she knew only that she had to get Merritt away from those big soldiers in those green tunics.

CHAPTER

84

Magda raced down dirt alleyways, jumped fences, and cut through yards, taking a diagonal course through the city rather than take the easier but longer route along the streets. In places along the way, she dashed down the narrow spaces between buildings. Once, she encountered an impassable barrier of stacked junk at the end and had to retrace her steps, going around the other side, only to be stopped by a tall fence. She managed to pull herself up and over the fence so that she didn't have to find another route.

As she ran past houses, dogs in the yards charged toward her, barking and snapping. Fortunately, the ones she encountered were tied on ropes, or inside, and couldn't get to her. Their barking made other dogs nearby bark, though. Soon, it seemed that half the dogs in the city were all barking. Here and there Magda saw lamplight brighten in windows as wicks were turned up.

She knew that if the soldiers heard the sounds of dogs barking coming ever closer to them, they would get suspicious.

Magda stopped just shy of an intersection and leaned back against the short stone wall for a moment, gulping air and catching her breath while still out of sight of the street. She opened the door on her lantern a crack and carefully peeked around the corner. She had been running with such abandon that she wasn't sure of exactly where she was.

As she held the lantern out around the corner, light fell on closely spaced buildings that she recognized. Signs hanging out front advertised several small businesses: a cobbler; a seamstress; and a carpenter's shop. Just up the street to the right, she knew that there would be a road coming down off the lower parts of the mountain that intersected the street.

That was the one road she needed. It made a loop past a few homes and a number of storehouses that held grains and dry goods. A little higher up, the side road reconnected back with the main road going up to the Keep.

Without taking time to finish catching her breath, Magda shut the door on her lantern and raced off up the street. If she got there too late, she had no chance. Without pause, when she reached it, she took the road that angled off up the hill and curved up along the skirt of the mountain. She could just see the lights of the Keep high above.

It was harder running uphill. Her legs burned from the effort. She feared that they might give out at any moment, but she knew that she dared not slow. If she didn't get out in front of those men before they made it up to the Keep, she knew that she wouldn't have a chance. If they got past her, she'd likely never be able to find where they took Merritt.

The Keep was immense. There were places all over the Keep where they could hide him. For all Magda knew, they might take him to an obscure room like the one where they had taken Tilly. There were thousands of rooms in the Keep. She would never be able to find him.

And if they took him to the prosecutor's offices, with his private army headquartered there, she would never get in.

In all likelihood, though, they would take him down to the dungeons where Naja had been. Magda didn't think that she would have a chance to make it in there again. After the two dungeon guards had been killed, not only would the men down there be on alert, they would probably double or triple the guard.

The smell of pines and fir trees got stronger the higher up the road she ran. Magda could at last hear a small brook off in the darkness. She knew the brook and where it was located above the buildings. Finally out of the city, she found herself running past the dark shapes of towering trees.

Abruptly, she came to the intersection with the main road up to the Keep. Magda was terrified that they might have already passed by. She feared being too late.

As she stood in the center of the intersection gulping air and catching her breath, trying in vain to see in the darkness, she heard voices in the distance. They were deep voices interspersed with fragments of laughter. She was relieved that they were coming from down lower on the road, in the direction of the city.

Magda rushed up the road, toward the Keep, around a sharp bend to a spot were the road narrowed. She wanted a place that wasn't open to the sides so that the men couldn't spread out and easily get around her. The voices were getting closer.

She found a place that looked about as good a spot for her purpose as she was liable to find on short order. Besides, she didn't have any time to spare. She set the lantern down in the center of the road, placing it so that the closed door aimed in the direction of the approaching men.

Magda didn't want to consider the wisdom of her hasty plan too carefully because it was the only plan she had. She could think of no other idea, and besides, there simply was no time left. She had no choice but to try.

If it didn't work, she would likely die. If she didn't try, they were all going to die anyway.

She crouched behind the lantern, waiting. Her hammering heart was making her rock on the balls of her feet.

She briefly thought that she must be crazy to think it would work. She had no choice. Either it worked, or they were all dead anyway.

She could hear the sound of gravel crunching under the boots of the men coming her way as they rounded the bend a short distance down the hill. They weren't talking any longer. She couldn't see them. Only the sound of their boots told her where they were.

When she judged that the group of men was as close as she dared let them get to her, she threw open the door of the lantern. Light fell across about a dozen startled faces. They blinked in the sudden light. They weren't the Home Guard. They wore the green tunics of Lothain's private army, as she had expected.

Magda stood and backed a few steps behind the lantern so that she would be in darkness and the men wouldn't be able to see her.

In the lantern light, when a couple of the big men spread out defensively, she spotted Merritt in their midst.

He had an iron collar around his neck, with a short iron bar coming out from the front of it. His hands were shackled to the end of the iron bar. His ankles were hobbled with a length of chain short enough to prevent him from running.

Blood ran down the side of his face. He looked groggy.

Magda focused her rage. It didn't take an effort.

"You are surrounded," she said in a loud, clear, commanding voice. "Let the prisoner go or you will all die."

One of the men stepped forward. In the light coming from the open door of her lantern, she could see that he was not a soldier. He wore simple robes. She could see the deep scowl twisting his features. Even though it was dark, she thought that she could see the gift in his eyes.

When he lifted his hand and fire ignited in the air above his palm, Magda knew.

It was a wizard.

"Magda Searus?" he said. "Magda Searus, is that you?"

CHAPTER

85

The man in the robes was not half a dozen strides from her. Magda had seen him before. He worked in the lower regions of the Keep. She didn't know the wizard's name, but he knew hers. Most likely because when she had been with Baraccus he had stopped briefly to talk to the man a few times, as he had talked to a number of wizards. A lot of people knew her because she was Baraccus's wife and they saw her with him, but she hadn't known the names of all those people he spoke to.

"Let him go and your lives will be spared," she said. "You are surrounded. Do as I say or you will all die. I'll not warn you again."

Worried, the soldiers peered around into the darkness. There was a brief moment of silence, and then the grim-faced wizard spoke.

"I sense no one but you," he said in a surly voice. "You are all alone out here. There is no one with you."

In the lantern light she could see the soldiers grin.

Almost without thought, Magda slipped her hand inside her cloak, tightly wrapping her fingers around the hilt of the sword. The word *Truth* pressed into her palm. Through that connection, she could feel something stir and seem to come alive. It seemed to be coming neither from the sword nor from her, but came alive through that connection.

She felt the promise of something powerful and merciless in the connection.

Without warning, the wizard flicked his hand toward her. In the lantern light Magda could see the air waver.

The bolt of power just missed, flicking her hair as she dove aside and drew the sword.

The clear ring of its blade filled the night air with a haunting threat of violence.

With the blade freed, Magda felt a storm of power surge from the hilt and up through her. As it inundated her, it made her flesh tingle and took her breath.

Exquisite rage thundered through every fiber of her being.

The men all drew weapons.

The wizard, angry that he had missed, pulled his arms back to conjure yet more magic. He looked more annoyed than angry that she had not fallen to his first strike. She knew that this time he would not be so timid in what he called forth.

A roiling ball of fire ignited in his palm. The liquid flames rolled and burned with a sinister bluish light.

Indeed, he did not intend to take any more chances. He was intending to loose wizard's fire against her.

Magda knew that she had to act fast or she would die. The sword reacted instantly to her intent, unleashing a surge of fury through her that charged her muscles.

Even as the wizard was cocking his arm back, Magda was already flying toward the man, closing the distance, trying to get to him before he was able to send the deadly fire toward her. As she ran, the blade swept around with lightning speed, whistling through the air.

Her glare was locked on the wizard's murderous

scowl. She was only dimly aware of the sword's tremendous momentum. She knew only that it felt right. It felt good. She guided its track through her intent as the blade made its way inexorably toward where her eyes were fixed.

She wanted this man dead. She focused all her rage at everything that had happened into her need to end this traitor's life.

It seemed to take forever to close the distance.

She could see the wizard frantically working with both hands to expand the wizard's fire between his palms, to make it more deadly and ready to kill. She could see the indignation in his eyes that she would dare to come at him.

She intended far more than merely to come at him.

For both of them, it was a race to kill or be killed.

The blade won the race. With a loud crack it intercepted the side of the wizard's skull.

Fragments of bone and gore filled the night. In the lantern's light she could see the cloud of blood and brain matter explode away from where most of his head had been only an instant before. Only the base of his skull and his jaw remained. A trail of blood followed the arc of the blade.

The wizard hadn't even had time to scream.

But Magda heard herself screaming, screaming with ferocity that was a match for the sword's.

The killing strike thrilled her, filled her with wild joy. It was nothing short of a sense of magnificent completion.

As the blade came around, his headless body was still falling. Parts of his head still sailed away into the night. His arms were lifted out at his sides, the wizard's fire smothered by his instant death and massive loss of blood.

Behind the wizard, the soldiers were momentarily frozen in shock at the sight. That shock broke all at once. With weapons raised, they screamed as they charged in toward her.

Magda sidestepped the first man to rush in. As she did, she came around, bringing the blade with her in a circle to split his skull from behind. The strike took off the top of his head. A clump of dark hair flew off into the darkness. His forward momentum drove him face-first into the hard ground.

Magda ducked under a mighty swing of another man's sword. He wasn't used to fighting someone as small and fast as Magda. His method was mighty blows, not swift, precise strikes. As Magda came up, she drove her sword straight through his heart.

She heard men roaring in rage as they came after her. She didn't have time to think. She acted on instinct acquired in part from learning to use a knife to fight and in part out of the single-minded drive to kill them. She struck without hesitation or pause as they got close enough, using her smaller size to move faster than they did and to stay out of the way of their reach and weapons.

She didn't try any clever moves, any fancy tricks. With every opening she saw, she simply went in for the kill.

She kept moving, ducking, rolling, and twisting to avoid their blades. Not being a soldier, she didn't move the way they expected. There was no time for her to plan her moves. As they swung, she followed up with a strike of her own, allowing them no time for another try.

She pulled back as a man's arm shot past her, his stabbing move narrowly missing making contact. Still in the grip of rage, Magda whipped the sword around with a scream of power, taking off the arm he had thrust out toward her. As the man fell to the ground screaming, she let the swing of the sword follow around, bringing it up behind her to run it through a man rushing in with his sword raised to chop her from behind. As he was collapsing to the side, she yanked the sword free and brought it around in a circle, gripped the hilt in both fists, and drove it straight down into the armless man writhing on the ground. She hammered it down so hard that the blade stuck in the ground.

Before she could yank it free, another man charged her, his sword flashing through the night air. She knew instinctively that she wouldn't be able to get out of the way fast enough.

At the last instant, just before his blade made it to her, Merritt crashed into him from the side, knocking him off balance. The big soldier stumbled from the impact and fell to a knee. Before he could get up, Magda brought the sword down from above, splitting him all the way from the top of his head to the center of his chest.

The man toppled, hitting the ground with a wet thwack that spilled organs out the gaping split and across the ground.

The night was suddenly still. There were no more men coming at her.

CHAPTER
86

Magda, on her knees, sword gripped in both hands, eyes wide, ready to defend herself, gasped for breath. The night was silent. There were no men screaming battle cries. There were no more blades coming at her.

Her head swiveled, looking everywhere, scanning for threats. She was surrounded by bodies. Blood and gore and unrecognizable bits of flesh lay scattered all around her.

There were no men left standing to come at her.

Not far away, Merritt, in the iron collar and hand restraints, struggled to get to his feet. Once up, he rushed to stand over her, a small, proud smile lighting his face.

With the threat ended, the Sword of Truth dropped from her hands.

And then, searing torment started like a spark deep inside, quickly expanding into an inferno of pain, burning through every part of her. Magda doubled over. She cried out as she collapsed onto her side, arms crossed over her middle, trying to quell the torture that felt like it was consuming her. She desperately needed air, but try as she might, she couldn't draw a breath. The weight of suffering pressing in on her wouldn't allow it.

Merritt knelt beside her, but with his wrists shackled into the device locked around his neck he couldn't reach out to her. He was helpless to do anything, but it was a relief to simply not be alone with the terror of the suffering.

As quickly as it came, the pain released her.

As the agony lifted its grip, Magda flopped over onto her back. Tears rolled down her cheeks as she gasped, getting her breath. She looked up at the concern on Merritt's face.

"I don't know what's wrong," she finally said between panting breaths.

"It's the sword's magic," he said. "It extracts a price when you kill with it. The first time is by far the worst. You're fortunate. The sword's power was derived from your life force, so it was already somewhat familiar with you."

Magda rolled onto her side and pushed herself up off the ground to sit back on her heels. "I'd hate to experience worse."

"Anger is a shield for the power of the sword's magic, so that helped, too."

"Then I was well protected." She reached out and turned his head to see the wound. "This doesn't look so good."

"I'm all right now. I'll be better when I get this thing off from around my neck."

"Can you use your gift to break it?"

"No," he said. "It's shielded to prevent a gifted person from using magic to escape."

"Shielded," she said. She remembered the shielded shackles on Naja. "I think I might have a key that would work on it."

She retrieved the sword and worked the blade under one of the iron cuffs. She turned her face away. With a mighty pull the iron exploded in a shower of pieces. Merritt held the bar to stabilize it for her to break the collar. In short order she had the rest of the immobilizing apparatus off him.

Once he was free, she threw her arms around him. "I was so afraid. I thought you were lost. I was so afraid that they would kill you."

He pushed her away for a moment. "'You are surrounded. Do as I say or you will all die.' That was your plan? Are you out of your mind?"

Magda winced self-consciously. "It was the best I could come up with on the spot." She frowned. "And it turned out to be true, didn't it?"

"It certainly did," he said with a smile as he pulled her back to hold her tight in a grateful hug. "Thank you, Magda. I have to tell you, that was quite something to behold."

She felt shaky in the wake of the fear from the fight, but it felt good to have his arms around her. "It was the sword," she said. "Your creation is magnificent."

"The sword is just a tool. The one wielding it has to be the right person. That's what matters most."

She cast him a skeptical look as he stood. "If you say so."

The clouds were beginning to break up and the moon had emerged to cast light over the landscape.

"We need to get rid of these bodies," Merritt said as he surveyed the area. "If they're found it will bring the whole army looking for who was responsible. They'll look for the missing men soon enough as it is."

"It's quite a drop over there," Magda said, gesturing. "We can roll them over the edge. No one is likely to spot them, at least not for a time. That should buy us a day or two at least."

In short order, with the aid of Merritt's gift, they had

all the bodies in green tunics and their body parts moved to the side. Arms and legs flailing, the big men rolled and tumbled and bounced down the steep drop, vanishing into the dense underbrush. No one would be able to see anything from the road, and unless they noticed a lot of scavengers no one was likely to climb down looking for the men. Merritt then used his gift to eliminate any trace of blood from the fight. With his foot, he smoothed the gouges in the ground. In the moonlight, the road again looked completely normal.

"We have to get off the road," he said. "There could be more of Lothain's soldiers about. With the moon out, we could easily be spotted out in the open like this."

Magda looked around in the moonlight, getting her bearings. She pointed, then, to the dark wall of trees on the opposite side.

"There's a trail over there coming up the mountainside. It passes by near the road not far off through there. It's steeper and tougher going in places than taking the road, but it's also shorter. No one is likely to be traveling the trail at night. The forest is pretty dense, so we can use the lantern in places if we have to. If a patrol passes, they won't be able to see us from the road."

Merritt nodded, and after a check of the surrounding area one last time to make sure they weren't missing anything, they quickly headed off the road, through the dense undergrowth, and in a short while found the trail. The ground was covered in a layer of pine needles, so it made for silent passage. With the moon out, enough light made it through the trees to the forest floor and the trail so that they could see to make their way.

"Now," he said after they had moved deeper into the protection of the trees, "not that I'm unappreciative, but what are you doing here? I told you that you must rest. I'm surprised that you have enough strength to stand up, and after that battle you're lucky you can still breathe on your own. You're in more trouble than you realize, Magda. You—"

"And we're in more trouble than you realize. Lothain is being installed as First Wizard tomorrow afternoon. He forced me to agree to marry him at the ceremony."

"What!"

Magda didn't let him launch into a rant. "Listen to me. I had no choice. He said that he would start killing everyone I know if I didn't agree. He had Tilly and had done terrible things to her just to show me that he was serious. Had I said no he would have killed her on the spot. As it was, she was in a bad way. She was just the first of many he would start in on if I didn't agree. I couldn't allow that."

"Dear spirits," he said under his breath.

"Here," Magda said as she pulled the baldric off over her head and handed him his sword back. "I have a plan, though. I've figured it out. I know what we have to do."

After Merritt had put the sword on, he gripped her arm. "You may have a plan, but I can clearly see in your eyes that you're at the end of your endurance. That battle and running around out here is only making you worse. I can't heal you further. You must rest to complete what I've done."

"This wasn't my choice, Merritt," she said impatiently.

He sighed. "I suppose not. But I'd better get you back to the Keep. We can talk about your plan after you rest."

"We don't have time for that," Magda insisted as she pulled her arm away from his grasp. "We have something much more important to do and it has to be done right now. I know that I need rest. Do you think I don't know how weak I am? But we don't have any choice. This can't wait."

He appraised the resolve in her eyes. "What are you talking about?"

"Merritt, we're in a lot of trouble. Lothain obviously intended to get rid of you so he must suspect that you're working to find the truth of what's going on. You were surely being taken back to be tried and executed, and you can bet that they would have tortured a confession out of you, first.

"Lothain needs to end the doubts about himself and subvert any opposition as a last step to seize rule at the Keep. He's consolidating his power. He was able to dismiss Councilman Sadler so that he can more easily control the council. He already has his own private army.

"By marrying me he gains the confidence of the Home Guard and a number of key officials, as well as a lot of wizards who believed in Baraccus. Were I to refuse, he would then need to discredit me. He'd simply throw me in the dungeon, torture a confession out of me, and have me executed for treason. It isn't all that hard to get people under torture to confess.

"I'm in a box. The way it is right now, no matter whether I go along with him or not, I can't change what is going to happen. It still all ends the same way. My word alone against Lothain's won't sway enough people. He will be First Wizard. He will rule the Midlands.

"By agreeing to marry him during the ceremony tomorrow when he is named First Wizard, that at least keeps people from dying tonight. But that's all the time it buys. If I refuse, a lot of innocent people are going to die immediately, but I hold no illusions; once he uses me to win the popular support in the Keep and has an iron grip on rule, he will purge the army and the officials of anyone who doesn't fully support him and then I will encounter an unfortunate end. I am only an expedient means to his ends, and my value to him is very short-lived.

"If we don't do something, and do it now while I'm still useful to him, then we and a lot of our people are going to die. I now know the truth about him, but half the Keep doesn't.

"Many people believe that Lothain is fighting for the good of mankind by prosecuting those he says are traitors. They think he is our savior. If I tell them otherwise, that he is often prosecuting people who can reveal his true intent, like Naja, most people won't believe it. They will believe the lies Lothain tells them.

"People aren't going to believe me if I try to tell them what is really going on. They believe the word of Lothain, an important man, the head prosecutor. When Lothain makes the accusation that Baraccus conspired with those in the Old World to defeat us, they believe him. No matter what I say, they would think I am the real traitor for siding with Baraccus.

"People need the truth. I'm the only one who can deliver truth. But I'd be dead before I could finish making the accusation.

"The way things stand, I don't have any way to stop him."

Merritt eyed her suspiciously. "But you said that you have a plan."

"Yes, I have a plan. It's true that I'm so exhausted I can hardly stand. I understand that. But we have only one chance. We have to take it. I came looking for you for a reason."

Merritt's expression turned unreadable. "What reason?"

Magda gathered her resolve.

"I want you to use me to create a Confessor."

CHAPTER
87

Merritt tilted his head toward her as his eyes narrowed. "You want me to alter you into a Confessor?"

"Yes," she said. "We don't have a lot of time. We need to hurry."

Merritt walked off a distance to stand beneath one of the enormous limbs spreading from an ancient oak. With his back to her, the moon cast cold light over his broad shoulders.

Looking grim, he finally turned back.

"Please don't ask that of me, Magda."

She stepped closer under the massive limbs of the oak. "I had always thought that changing a person's nature with magic was a cold, calculating, callous thing to do for the sake of creating a weapon. I could never understand how people could allow wizards to alter them. I thought that it was a perversion of our existence.

"Isidore taught me that it isn't always the case. She taught me that if it's done for the right reasons it can actually be a chance to make the best of ourselves. Done in the right way, it is adding to who and what we already are and what we already believe. In that way it's not altering a person's nature, but adding to it. Such a purpose can be the moral thing to do.

"Even more, though, you're not only a wizard. You're Merritt. You may not see the difference in that, but I do. Though we haven't known each other for long, it has been long enough for me to know you, to know your heart."

"That's reassuring to hear, but knowing me isn't enough."

"I realize that, but I've thought this through. You may not believe that, but I have. It's not just that this is the only way, it's that it's the right thing. While creating weapons out of people can be a terrible deed, done in the right way by the right person and for the right reasons, it can be a wondrous thing.

"You envisioned the idea of a Confessor for the right reasons. Life is truth. Truth is life. You wanted a way to seek truth. Such a cause, in the promotion of life, is noble.

"Killing is a terrible thing, too. I hate killing. But killing isn't necessarily wrong." She gestured back down the trail. "Killing those men tonight was the right thing to do, for the right reasons. It was done for good. It was done to preserve innocent life. In this instance, not killing would have been immoral.

"You intend the Confessors to stop evil, just as my killing those men stopped them from doing evil. That makes both the right thing to do.

"Merritt, I want that person, that Confessor that you create, to be me. I understand the nobility of purpose in the creation of a Confessor. I know precisely what to do with that opportunity. Please, give me the chance to do what only I can do. Give me the means to help stop evil and preserve life. Don't let me fail to do what only I can do.

"It's my life. I want it to have this purpose."

"There's more to it, Magda. We need time to consider all the implications."

"Ordinarily, that would be the right thing, but we have no time. It has to be now. It has to be tonight. I have to use that Confessor power to expose the truth. I wish it could wait, but it can't. This is our only chance.

"Baraccus told me that my destiny is to find truth—"

Merritt threw an arm up, gesturing angrily. "Life is not about fulfilling a destiny. Your life has no destiny but what you make of it."

"And this is what I want to make of it. Baraccus also told me to live the life that only I can live. He told me to have the courage to take up that calling. He was asking me to choose my destiny. Prophecy is not only about destiny, but the balance—free will. Becoming a Confessor is my calling. But it's not preordained. It's a chance, a fork in the road of my life. I have to have the courage to take it on of my own free will. In that way, the balance of prophecy and free will is the magic of the future."

He looked to have calmed down considerably. "I have to admit, you have that much of it right."

"Merritt, this is the life that only I can live. I've always been the person trying to uncover the truth of things.

"I found you for a reason. Destiny brought me to you so that the choice could be laid before me to make. I rejected any such choice for my life until I came to know you and to understand the real nature of what such a choice means. I found you because I need to make that choice for my life. Since then I've come to understand that I need this mission for my life.

"I am that person, Merritt. I've made the choice.

"I am your Confessor."

Merritt looked down and turned away.

After a moment he cleared his throat. "Magda, you don't know all that is involved, all that it means. You don't know what you're asking."

"Then tell me, and tell me now, because we are rapidly running out of time."

He turned to look her in the eye. "This would alter the nature of who you are. The Confessor power would become part of you, much as eyesight and hearing are part of your nature. You would be a Confessor in much the way I am a wizard.

"That means that just as any child you have would carry other traits from you, such as sight and hearing, they would also carry this trait. Any child you bear would be a Confessor. Their children would inherit the same power, and theirs, and so on. Once created, the power is part of you, it is you."

Magda paced off a short distance, chewing a thumbnail, thinking. "It would be part of them by birth?"

"Yes. You would be deciding not only for you, but for them as well. In a way, you would be creating their destiny."

She turned back. "No more than giving them the destiny of eyesight. I would be giving them a different kind of vision."

"But if—"

"Merritt, if we don't do this, I will have no chance to have any offspring because I will be dead. If I live, I will only be able to bring a child into a tortured existence of half people crafted to fit Emperor Sulachan's deluded notions for the world of life. I may even be changed into one of those half people, giving birth to a soulless offspring. Is that better?

"Don't you see? I'm not deciding their destiny, I am giving them the possibility of a life, a life worth living."

Merritt squeezed his temples between the thumb and

fingers of one hand. "Look, Magda, even if I wanted to do this, I can't."

Running out of patience, she folded her arms. "Why not?"

He took a deep breath before explaining. "The process is similar to what we did to invest power in the sword. The difference is that the sword has no life force of its own, so it needed to borrow a life force to help in its creation. You provided that with the Grace drawn in your blood.

"Creating the Confessor power is similar in purpose and in many ways in the methods involved, but there is a crucial difference. You have your own life force. You can't be given someone else's life force to turn you into a Confessor the way we turned the sword into the key. You need to use your own."

Magda shrugged. "All right. I can draw another Grace with my own blood."

He was shaking his head. "Ordinarily that would be the first step. But you have already given your strength to the sword. I don't think that you understand the true depth of what you so willingly gave over to create the sword. Right now you don't have enough strength to be able to do it for yourself."

"I think I do. We can try. We have to try."

"Do you think I'm guessing about this?" Merritt stepped close and leaned toward her in an effort to make sure she grasped his point. "It's not simply that it wouldn't work, Magda. It's that the attempt would kill you."

She let out a sigh. "Are you so sure, Merritt? I'm pretty strong. You just saw me fight those men."

"This is a different kind of strength." He gestured in frustration. "You saw the forces involved when we created the sword. Don't you recall how violent it was?

Don't you understand how close you came to dying? And you came close to dying when you were well and in perfect shape.

"Trying to unleash such forces on you tonight would kill you. Not maybe. Not possibly. I'm not saying that I'm worried, or fear it might harm you. I know what I'm talking about. I'm telling you without a doubt that it would kill you. You can't hope to help us if you're dead."

"What if we used another person to help, like I did with the sword? What if you were the one to lend me power? Or maybe we could get Quinn. He'd help us. We can trust him."

Merritt laid a hand on her shoulder. "Unlike the sword, the unique ability of a Confessor's power requires that the person to become a Confessor must be the one who provides the life force. Another person cannot be a part of that. Another person cannot loan their life to you in such a way. It must be you, and you alone who gives yourself, your life force, into becoming a Confessor. The process would alter you. Another person can't do it for you."

Magda walked off a ways, clasping her hands.

She felt her world, everything she cared about, slipping through her fingers. All because she was too weak.

She wanted to tell Merritt that he was wrong, that she was strong enough. But she knew that he was right. She could hardly stand, hardly pull each breath. She remembered how she nearly died in the ordeal to create the sword. At the moment, she had nothing left to give of herself.

Merritt was right. She wouldn't survive the attempt.

"Isn't there another way?" she asked without turning back to him.

"The wizards who wanted to create the sword died trying to do it without what was required. The process to create a Confessor requires a prodigious amount of your strength. You don't have it to give right now. You gave that strength to the sword. Just as those wizards died, you would die trying it without the required strength."

"I see."

Magda felt as if her heart was breaking. She'd thought it through and had it all figured out. She'd made the decision. It was already done as far as she'd been concerned. She needed only the formality of the magic to complete it.

In her mind, she'd gone over what she would do once she was a Confessor. She'd gone over it at least a hundred times. She had envisioned every detail until it was almost real.

And now it was ashes.

"I wish there was something I could do, Magda," he said in quiet sorrow. "If there was one person in the world I could choose to invest with the power of a Confessor, it would be you, I swear."

Magda nodded, turning away to hide her tears.

"Thank you, Merritt. I know you mean that."

"I do."

Not only was her world ending, the world of life was going to end. She had lost her chance. She had no way to fight Lothain and those helping him. He was too powerful.

She had given her strength over to the making of the Sword of Truth.

And now they were all going to die.

Magda turned back suddenly. "Merritt, when I used the sword, I felt the power of it surging through me. It was unlike anything I've ever experienced."

He nodded. "I know. I'm the one who created the thing, remember? It holds immense power, in part because of what you gave it during its creation. As long as you live, you will always share a connection with the sword. I guess you could say that as long as it exists it carries some of you."

Magda stepped close to him. "So investing my life force into it made its creation possible."

Merritt shrugged at the obvious connection. "That's right."

She watched his face lit by the moonlight. "What if we used the sword, had it loan some of that power back to me, in turn giving me the strength I need to get through the ordeal of becoming a Confessor? It's my life force, after all. You said that it couldn't be from someone else. Coming from the sword it wouldn't be."

Merritt's gaze searched her eyes but he didn't answer.

"I'd just be borrowing some of my own life force," she added.

He had that odd frown again. "I already thought of that."

"And?"

"And it's too dangerous. Creating a Confessor is dangerous enough in and of itself. It's a process that has never been attempted before and very well could be lethal, and that's if there weren't any other complications involved. Trying to do it the way you're suggesting is theoretically possible, but it would be an order of magnitude more perilous."

"Are you saying you don't have the skill, or that it's dangerous for me."

"My skill has nothing to do with it. It's too dangerous for you for a variety—"

"We don't have a choice. We have to try."

He shook his head. "Magda, please don't ask me to do that. You have no idea at all what you're asking."

She leaned toward him in the moonlight. "Merritt, I know exactly what I'm asking. I'm asking for a chance at life. Without trying, I'm going to die, you're going to die, our people are going to die.

"You heard Naja. Those in power in the Old World seek to end the world of life. Even if their ideas are crazy, even if their plans are completely unworkable and impossible and they fail at accomplishing their ultimate aim, they are still slaughtering our people just the same. They still intend to rule the world of life one way or another. Untold thousands of innocent people will die in their attempts, and even more will die if they succeed in winning the war. If they win, at the very best, the people of the New World will be enslaved.

"And what if they really can succeed at what Sulachan wants to accomplish? What if he has the boxes of Orden and he uses them to end the world of life as we know it?

"The war is going badly. I believe it's because the Keep

is infected with spies and traitors helping the enemy. That's what Baraccus wanted me to uncover. I now know who is at the center of it, anyway. It's Lothain. He's been hiding right under our noses, posing as our champion, prosecuting traitors.

"But if we kill him, his secrets die with him. If we capture him instead and he gives other names under torture, how would we ever know if they are really his accomplices? He might hold back the names of important spies, or accuse innocent people. How could we be sure? With something this important, how could we be sure that we have rooted out the entire nest of traitors and spies?

"If we don't get all those who are helping him they will still be able to work from inside the Keep to undo our cause, still activate the dead to assassinate key people. If we kill the man at the head of it, we'll never know who the rest are until it's too late.

"But if I can get a confession out of Lothain, a true confession, and we can expose the extent of the subversion within our ranks, then we might have real a chance to counter it. We would have a chance to save the Keep.

"Think of what is going to happen to us and our people if we don't stop the enemy wizards among us. They will breach the Grace. We won't merely die. Our souls will be kept from crossing over into the underworld.

"We'll be like those people of Isidore's town of Grandengart. Our bodies will be used by the wizards from the Old World while our spirits are trapped between worlds. Our spirits will wander, lost, in this world. How many innocent people will be doomed to such a fate?

"So, are you trying to tell me that you think such a grim fate would somehow be better than the danger of trying, even if it means I die in the attempt? How? How is that better?

"Isn't this the very purpose for which you developed the concept of a Confessor? Isn't this the reason you believed so strongly in it that you argued before the council to be allowed to create a Confessor? Wasn't it you who said that the risks were so great that we had to try?"

He stared at her from under a lowered brow without answering.

"Please, Merritt, don't condemn me to a brief life of watching all that is good end because we lack the courage to try. Please don't do that to me. Please don't condemn us and our friends and our people to the horrific fate that Emperor Sulachan has chosen for us all."

His gaze finally fell away. "Magda, you don't know what you're asking me to do. I just can't."

Tears trailed down her face. "Then it is you who has chosen our destiny, and that destiny is endless suffering, all because you are afraid of harming me. But the safety you want for me is an illusion. In trying to protect me, you are only bringing me to even greater harm."

Gritting her teeth, she seized his shirt in her fists. "Well I'd rather die trying for life than endure the destiny you want to condemn me to. If you won't help me then at least give me the Sword of Truth so that I can kill the bastard. Give me the sword and let me die fighting for what I believe in."

His big hands closed around her wrists as he looked into her eyes for a long moment.

"All right," he said at last. "All right, I'll try. I'd rather die, too, than see you have to be a helpless witness to the end of all we hold dear. I'll try, Magda."

She threw her arms around him in gratitude.

After too brief a time, he pushed away, looking into her eyes again. She had never seen him looking so grim.

"Don't be so eager to thank me. Doing it this way is nothing like the process when we created the sword.

What I have to do now is very different from the method I originally developed to create a Confessor. We can't do it through that process. You can't really help me this time. You have to leave it to me to do."

The sobering look in his eyes gave her pause. "What do you mean? What do you have to do?"

"You have to put your trust in me. No questions. You will have to put your life in my hands and let me do as I must."

Magda swallowed back her rising sense of alarm and nodded.

"We really have no choice. We're running out of time. Do it."

He touched her cheek. "I wish there were another way, Magda, but if we're to do this now, there is no other way."

With a hand on her shoulder, Merritt gently eased her back against the trunk of the massive oak. Dark, crooked arms of branches stretched out overhead like some great monster about to embrace her in its clutches. The moon cast a cold, eerie light across the angular features of Merritt's handsome face.

Magda heard a rustling sound and looked up to one of the great branches of the ancient oak. There, perched in a crook on the limb, a raven ruffled its feathers.

She looked into the raven's black eyes as it sat quietly watching her. The last time she had seen a raven had been down in the maze when the dead man had been chasing her.

Merritt slowly drew the sword. The sound of the blade rang through the night, drawing her gaze back to him.

Magda wet her lips. "What are you going to do?"

"Use the Sword of Truth to help you be reborn a Confessor."

Magda's concern was growing by the second. "Reborn? How? What are you going to do with it?"

He almost seemed to be looking out at her from a distant world. "Do you trust me?"

She wished he wouldn't keep asking her that. "I told you that I do."

"Then please, Magda, don't ask."

She nodded. "I'm sorry. Tell me what you need me to do."

With one hand, Merritt pressed her shoulders back against the tree. "I need you to let me do what I must."

With the sword in his other hand, he placed the tip of the blade in the center of her chest.

She could see so much more in his hazel eyes than merely the glow of his gift. His eyes were gentle, yet at the same time they were charged with fierce intensity. More than that, though, she could see wisdom, integrity, competence, and the sort of rage she'd never seen before. Some of that, she knew, was coming from the Sword of Truth. Some, though, was all his.

She had seen the hint of that rage when she had first met him and told him that Isidore was dead. His was a temper that had the potential to be devastatingly violent, and yet at the same time he was also a man able to control it and focus it.

He was focusing it now.

Combined with the rage from the sword, such fury was frightening to behold.

Magda glanced down and saw the blade glowing white.

"Merritt . . ."

The blade turned from a white glow to an inky black that was like looking into the depths of the underworld. The air around her crackled with threads of light, both the pure white light of Additive Magic, and the sinister void of Subtractive. They wrapped her in a cocoon of magic that dimmed the world.

Magda couldn't seem to stop herself from trembling. "Merritt . . ."

"Are you sure about this, Magda? Are you certain?"

Behind the shadow of quiet sorrow, she could see love in his eyes.

"Yes. With all my heart and soul. Who I was, who I will be, is in your hands."

"Tonight, Magda Searus, you are reborn a Confessor." A tear ran down his cheek. "If I fail, may the good spirits take me, for I would not want to live in a world without you."

She blinked in surprise at his words.

Glowing white light and inky black darkness rolled up the length of the blade in dizzying, undulating waves.

"Now you must trust me," he said with finality.

Magda wet the roof of her mouth with her tongue. "I do, Merritt. I trust you with my life."

And then, as he held her shoulders back against the tree, he pushed the sword straight through her heart.

Thunder without sound silently shook the world around her.

Oak leaves and pine needles rained down in the forest all around as dust rose in a rapidly expanding ring spreading away into the night.

Magda's eyes went wide in shock at what he had just done.

She let out a last scream as she died.

P eople had gathered in great numbers. They crowded around the towering, polished black marble columns to each side of the gallery leading toward the council chambers and gathered beside the statues of robed figures, leaning around the people in front of them, rising up on tiptoes, all trying to see.

The soft rumble of their collective voices echoed from the vaulted ceiling hung with a procession of long, red silk banners meant to represent the blood that had been shed in defense of the people of the Midlands. The carpet, with the names of battles woven along the edges, was also red, meant to be a reminder of the struggles fought and the lives laid down so that others might live.

This day was no less a battle for the survival of the Midlands, a battle for the survival of all innocent lives in peril. Before the day was done, there was a good chance that more blood would be shed in that seemingly endless battle for survival.

Magda wore a blank expression, showing no emotion as she strode in a measured pace past the gathered throngs.

The drone of voices and light laughter withered to

whispers before falling silent as she passed, leaving a hush in her wake.

People gawked as she marched past them, stone-faced, her eyes fixed ahead, looking neither left nor right. None of the people staring could have imagined the charge of power seething somewhere deep inside her.

It had at first been an alien power, a terrifying monster within. At first, when she had again become aware after that terrible, timeless voyage through darkness, she hadn't known what to expect and didn't know what she was supposed to do. Since she was ungifted, she had never experienced any power at her control, at her beck and call, much less a power like this.

Somewhere, at some point, that inner force had ceased to be a stranger to her.

Somewhere in the night, it had become a part of her, as if it had always been there and she had merely become aware of it.

It was no longer an alien force within her. It now *was* her.

She was also aware from the first that it was a power that sought release. It required her to master it continually, to restrain it. Merritt had assured her that as time went on it would become easier and feel natural, like breathing. But at that moment it had ached to be set free and she'd had to keep a tight rein on it. As he had promised, that need had eased.

She had never felt such a thing before, and had no idea what to expect when she eventually did release it. Merritt had offered some advice based on some of the component elements, but to a large extent he didn't know either.

As she entered the great rotunda not far from the council chambers, Magda saw spectators crowded all through the enormous room, all hoping to get a glimpse of the grand event, a look at the arrival of the future wife of the future First Wizard.

Afternoon sunlight flooded in through the high windows around the lower border of the golden dome, making the towering reddish marble pillars around the edge of the room glow. Between the columns, against the stone wall, along with the throngs of people, the imposing statues of past leaders watched her pass.

The great mahogany doors to the council chambers stood open, flanked by rows of the Home Guard in spotless uniforms and polished armor, all standing at attention. Through the open door Magda could see even more people crowded into the vast council chambers. Bluish shafts of hazy sunlight slanting into the room gave the inner chamber a kind of reverent glow, an anticipation, to the impending ceremony.

Magda marched alone through slanting streamers of sunlight and down the runner of blue and gold carpet leading off toward her waiting betrothed and the council.

With her thumb, she turned the ring Merritt had given her, feeling the raised ridges of the design, a symbol of strength and a reminder of what was at stake.

The balconies below the windows were packed full with observers, all dressed in their finery. The open floor beneath the shadow of the balconies was likewise packed with important people as well as military men in dress uniforms accompanied by clusters of staff, officials in dignified robes with color-coded bands to denote rank and position, wizards and sorceresses in simple robes, and aids accompanying well-dressed, important women. A beaming General Grundwall stood at the head of his officers. Commanders Rendall and Morgan were there as well.

Troops in green tunics, the soldiers under the authority of the prosecutor's office, stood at attention at regular intervals around the room. It was unusual that there were no Home Guard standing guard in the council chambers, as there had been all throughout the gallery and the great rotunda.

Magda, her face expressionless, marched onward through the room, down the long blue and gold carpet and through isolated patches of sunlight. Quinn stood near the front of the room watching her approach. Magda spotted Naja, partly hidden behind Quinn, wearing a hooded cloak that did a good job of shadowing her face and concealing her black hair. Councilman Sadler was closer to the front. He smiled and gave Magda a meaningful look when he saw her. Though she saw both out of the corner of her eye, she returned neither. Her face was a mask that showed nothing.

Emotion did not play a part in truth, only reality did.

A Confessor was about truth, not emotion.

In the distance, atop the dais, the council sat at the long, curved, ornate desk. Staff and assistants sat close by. Even more people stood behind. As Magda approached, she could see Elder Cadell sitting in the tallest chair in the center, as well as the rest of the council, minus Councilman Sadler.

Merritt was nowhere to be seen. Since the troops from the prosecutor's office had arrested him, the sight of him in the council chambers was likely to spark a battle, so he was remaining hidden. But Merritt hadn't wanted to be too far away.

She saw the glint of steel in the deep shadows between the pillars behind the council. Magda expected that it was the Sword of Truth she was seeing. At least, she hoped it was.

Lothain, in his elaborate, silk brocade ceremonial robes of office, stood in the center of the dais where everyone could see him. The desk of the council framed him in its half circle. His black eyes watched her approach.

As Lothain stepped to the left side of the dais, several officials in gold robes intercepted Magda. She was surprised to be stopped by them. Not knowing what was going on, she let them guide her to the right side of the dais, where they directed her to turn to face Lothain. One of them whispered to her that she was to stand there for the ceremony.

This wasn't what she had expected. She needed to be closer to Lothain. She had expected to be standing at his side. She needed to be close. She needed to be able to touch him.

She wasn't far. She considered trying to run at him in order to touch him, but Lothain was acting unusually cautious, which was making her suspicious. He had forced her to agree to the marriage. He was well aware that she was not happy about it. She guessed that he might fear that she would try to assassinate him with a knife. But she had no knife on her. There was no place for it in the dress the seamstresses had made for her overnight. Other than her power, she was unarmed.

Lothain wouldn't know that, though. If she ran toward him, he was likely to fear an attack and use his gift to drop her halfway there. He was so close, but he was far enough away to kill her if he wanted and she would never get her chance.

Magda didn't know what to do. If she couldn't touch him, she couldn't use her power. If she couldn't use her power, her entire plan was dead.

She had the growing sense that something was very wrong.

Lothain's smirk seemed to confirm her suspicion.

CHAPTER
90

Magda did her best to curb her anxiety and tried not to let herself be distracted by worry that her entire plan was unraveling. She reasoned that as the wedding ceremony began, perhaps after Lothain was installed as First Wizard, the council would have to bring the two of them together to be married. That had always been the procedure. She reasoned that it only made sense that he was to be installed as First Wizard before he took his wife. She would just have to be patient.

Still, she had the sense that something wasn't right.

"Why are you in a white dress?" Lothain asked in a low voice from where he stood watching her from a dozen feet a way. It was clear that he was not pleased but he didn't want the crowd to hear him. "I told you to pick any color but white."

"This is the day of my rebirth. White is perfect for the occasion."

When he glanced deliberately from her face to her chest and then back up again, he did not look pleased. She knew that he had ordered the neckline to show ample cleavage.

"It looks awfully plain," he grumbled. "And . . . modest for such a grand event."

"Are you more interested in the dress than what is in it, then?"

Lothain's gaze drifted down the length of her again, at the way the dress was cut to fit her every curve. The sight brought his own private, unreadable thoughts behind his black eyes.

The dress, made of the satiny white material she had selected, was unadorned. The women who had made it had followed Magda's instructions perfectly in every detail. It hugged her curves in a way that gave it a feminine elegance no amount of lace and needlework embellishment could have matched.

The neckline was cut square. It complemented the cut of the dress perfectly and added to the grace of the design. It was a dress unlike any Magda had ever seen. For that matter, it was unlike anything anyone in the room had seen, and that was just what Magda had wanted to accomplish. Rather than draw attention to itself in an attempt to define beauty, it instead revealed the underlying beauty of the woman wearing it.

But it was meant to be more than simply an unexpected look for a dress. It was meant to be a lasting symbol.

It was a Confessor's dress.

Lothain flashed her a sly smile before turning his attention to the crowd.

"This was to be a joyous occasion," he said in a voice loud enough to carry across the sprawling room. The crowd quieted, looking unsure at what he meant. "I'm afraid that while I am to be installed as First Wizard, and that will go forward, there will be no wedding."

Their unspoken question answered, the crowd erupted in chatter. Much of it unhappy at the news. Magda stood as stunned as everyone else. Lothain held his hands up, calling for silence.

"I'm sorry to have to inform you of this at this late moment, but I have only just learned the truth a short time ago, learned that Magda Searus had ulterior motives for agreeing to marry me. In truth, she harbored a monstrous reason.

"Her deadly plan was devious in its simplicity. It turns out that she only wanted to marry me so that she could bed me as her husband."

Lothain let the scattering of chuckles spread, only to die out when he didn't join in. Magda could sense, more than she saw, soldiers closing in behind her. There was nowhere to run.

"She wanted to bed me as her husband," he said in a clear voice that everyone could hear, an accusatory tone honed as head prosecutor, "because she planned to stab me to death in the night. She only wanted to marry me to be able to get past those brave men who protect me, get close enough so that she could assassinate me as I slept beside her."

He lifted an arm toward her as he gazed out over the crowd. "You see, Magda Searus is a traitor. But she is no ordinary traitor. She is the architect of all the strange murders that have been taking place here at the Keep."

He held up a hand, forestalling the questions. "I've thoroughly investigated her nefarious activities. Multiple witnesses have come forth. They testified to having seen her sneaking around in the night, hiding her face, meeting with mysterious people in the shadows."

Magda stared toward the man. Two of Lothain's private guards seized her arms from behind, preventing her from getting closer to Lothain.

"You accuse me of treason because I was seen outside

at night? Where is your proof of such a charge!" Magda called across the dais.

"Proof? You would like the proof?" He cast a glance across the stunned crowd watching in rapt attention. "Yes, I think proof is in order."

He gestured off over the heads of people standing behind the council desk, and men dragged someone forward out of the shadows. It was Tilly. The woman was covered in filth and blood. Her bloodied face hung nearly lifeless, as did her broken arm.

"This woman," Lothain said, "is a worker here in the Keep. Perhaps many of you have seen her, thinking nothing of her comings and goings. It turns out that she was a clever criminal, but we were finally able to get her to admit to her part in the crimes Lady Searus has committed against the Midlands. She long helped Baraccus with his schemes and then later Lady Searus in her plans. She guided Lady Searus through the lower reaches of the Keep, where together they murdered our spiritist."

The crowd gasped. People had heard the terrifying stories of Isidore's murder. Whispers broke out, swelling to fill the council chambers.

Magda said nothing. She knew it was useless. No one was going to listen to her, and besides, Lothain would simply use his gift to silence her. She could release her power on the men holding her, but that would waste it. Merritt had warned her that using the Confessor's power would sap her strength and she likely would need to rest for hours, possibly days, before being able to summon it again.

She didn't want to waste her one chance with her only weapon on the soldiers holding her. That would accomplish nothing. She looked to the shadows, wondering if Merritt would do something. With all the gifted and armed men in the room, it would be foolish to try just then, but knowing Merritt that didn't mean that he wouldn't.

Lothain held up a hand again, calling for quiet. "This woman confessed the entire plot." He turned to Tilly and lifted her chin. "Isn't that right?"

Tilly's fearful eyes turned from him to Magda. Tears started coursing tracks down through the dirt on her face.

"Say what he wants you to say," Magda told the woman in a quiet, confidential voice. "It is useless for you to speak the truth right now. Tell him what he wants to hear."

Tilly looked shamefaced. "But . . ."

"I know what they've done to you," Magda whispered, "and I don't blame you. Don't throw your life away for nothing of value. Tell them what they want to hear."

"The truth has value," Tilly whispered.

"It will," Magda assured her, "but not from you, not right now. Do as I ask. Say what he wishes you to say."

Tilly looked out at the crowd, tears streaming down her face. "What Prosecutor Lothain says be the . . ." She couldn't say the word. "It is as he says. We both be traitors."

"Traitors," Lothain added in a loud voice, "that she admitted have killed a number of our most valuable people. There is no just verdict for such crimes except execution!"

Some in the crowd lifted fists, shouting their anger that this was the source of the mysterious murders, the war going so poorly, and all their other troubles, echoing the sentiment that both Tilly and Magda should be executed immediately.

Others in the crowd, though, looked disheartened, distraught, and confused by what was happening. This was to have been the day of a joyous wedding, of the Keep coming together in unity, a reason for hope in the midst of troubled times.

A few people broke out in tears. Others turned their faces away. They had believed in Magda as well as Baraccus, and now that confidence was shaken or even shattered. Magda could see in the tormented expressions that some people felt that their faith had been betrayed.

"Why would Lady Searus do all this?" Elder Cadell asked from behind the desk, his voice carrying out over the crowd.

"You see," Lothain explained, "her plan all along was to discredit me." He turned from the elder to the audience. "She knew how effective I've been as head prosecutor. I've ferreted out, prosecuted, and executed a number of her fellow conspirators. I was getting too close to the heart of the plot and she feared I would uncover her deadly plans. She wanted to stop me from exposing the rest of the traitors here at the Keep so that they could continue to sabotage our efforts, so she made wild accusations about me, hoping not only to throw me off track but to damage my ability to do my duty to our people.

"When so many of you good people maintained your steadfast faith in me, that plan failed to work out as well as she had hoped. She became impatient and decided to use her feminine wiles to worm her way into my life, taking the route of my heart. I believed her sincerity at first, as did so many of you, but in the end I came to see through her schemes."

Some in the crowd shouted angrily for Magda's head.

Magda maintained the mask that showed nothing.

Even though the soldiers were holding her by her arms, she managed to lift her hand out enough that the crowd could see that she meant for them to see the ring she was wearing.

"The symbol on this ring is at the heart of what is happening," she said to the people watching. "Lothain and those he is loyal to seek to breach this. If they succeed, you will all die, but that will not be the end of your suffering. If they breach this, your souls will never be able to join the good spirits. They will instead wander between worlds, forever lost."

The wave of worried murmurs started in again. She knew that none in the crowd could see what was on the ring, but it succeeded in stirring their curiosity. Lothain couldn't help but notice.

"What is that you have, there?" he demanded.

"Something you fear," Magda said with a defiant smile.

When Lothain saw the smile he stormed across the dais.

"Let me see that." He gestured to the soldiers to release her arms so that she could show him the ring. "You heard me, let me see what it is you have there."

Magda lifted her hand to show him the ring with the Grace, but she kept it just out of his reach.

"This? Merritt gave it to me."

He had given it to her when she had come back from beyond the veil. She had traveled the lines of the Grace and returned. She had lived what the Grace represented.

She'd told him that she knew she was safe in his hands, that she knew he would protect her. That was when he had given her the ring. He said he wanted her to have it as a symbol of his protection.

It meant more to her than anything she had ever been given.

It meant everything to her.

"Merritt? Merritt is a traitor and has been arrested as well," Lothain said out toward the crowd before turning back to Magda. "Why would he give such an important and sacred object to you, to a nobody?"

Magda arched an eyebrow. "A nobody? He gave it to me because I am a protector of the Grace." She pulled her hand back out of his reach when he grabbed for it again. "Because I am a champion of truth."

"Champion of truth? You're a nobody!"

"If I was a nobody you wouldn't be so eager to see me dead. Just like these people here, you know that I am devoted to the truth. That's why you want to eliminate me."

"You are a nobody! Worse than a nobody, you're a traitor devoted only to murdering our people and you will be executed for your crimes! Now give that to me!"

Lothain charged forward like an angry bull that was being repeatedly taunted. He reached out again, snatching for her hand.

Magda again pulled the hand back, drawing him onward in a rush. Then, in an instant, she reversed her retreat and stepped into his charge.

Magda planted her hand in the center of his barrel chest, becoming a wall against his full weight.

In that instant, he had made the last mistake of his life: he had let her touch him.

Magda knew that it was not necessary for her to invoke the power within her. It was hers, now, always there. She had but to release her restraint of it.

She felt no pressure of his advance against her hand because the world had already stopped in the instant that she made contact. Lothain might as well have been a feather coming at her.

Time was hers.

This was the man who, along with his fellow spies, directed the dream walkers toward the minds they wanted to sneak into and snatch. This was the man, along with his fellow spies, who awakened the dead and sent them out in the night to kill people. This was the man who had sent one of the walking dead to tear Isidore apart.

This was not the prosecutor who protected the people of the Midlands from those doing evil, this was the vicious enemy who plotted against them, who planned their demise, who served evil.

And now he was hers.

The inner violence of her power's cold, coiled force slipping its bonds was breathtaking. Unleashed, that power exploded through her, surging up from the depths of the dark core deep within, obediently inundating every fiber of her being.

It was a dead silent, pristine instant of the ignition of a fierce new power unleashed into the world for the first time. Nothing would ever be the same—for Lothain, or for Magda.

She contained no hate, no rage, no horror, no sorrow . . . no mercy. In that infinitesimal spark of time, her mind was a void where there was no emotion, only the all-consuming rush of her power through the void of time suspended.

He had no chance, none at all. He was hers.

Time was hers.

Magda could see beads of his sweat suspended in air. She could have counted every dark hair of his stubble before he moved half the width of one of those hairs.

She could see the first hint of terror in his black eyes.

She could see that, while he didn't yet comprehend how, he was beginning to realize that he had just made the biggest mistake of his life. Even as he wanted to draw back from her touch, there was no chance. He might as well have been carved from stone.

Magda could see the gift in his eyes, too, but it would do him no good. His mind would be gone before he had time to begin to form a thought of how to defend himself.

Like a room of thousands of mute statues, everyone watched, but Magda was focused on this man who had done so much harm, who intended so much more. Behind her, the soldiers were also frozen in place even as they reached for her, but they, too, had no chance to close the distance and make it to her.

Magda was in a silent world of her own.

In that spark of time, her power suddenly became all.

Thunder without sound jolted the air around her.

The violence of it was magnificent, immaculate, glorious.

As the world came crashing back, the heavy concussion raced outward in a ring, knocking the soldiers near her off their feet. People close to the dais screamed as they toppled back from the impact of the power exploding outward in an ever-expanding circle.

When it ended, the people who had been closest were on the floor, rolling around, crying out in pain, clutching their aching joints. Those not quite as close staggered back but were able to stay on their feet and weren't in as much pain. Those farther back fared better yet, showing little sign of being hurt.

Lothain, showing no signs of pain at all, dropped to his knees before Magda, looking up with new eyes, eyes that revealed only the wish to please her.

"Mistress, command me."

The two closest soldiers, still struggling to recover from the pain, managed to get to their feet. They both drew weapons as they lurched toward her.

Merritt, having appeared from the shadows not far away, thrust his left arm out, palm up. At the same time as he was launching magic with his left hand, he was drawing his sword with his right. The bolt of power he hurled streaked across the dais, the air wavering in its wake, and slammed into the two men with the force of an avalanche. Both men disintegrated in blackened bits of flesh and bone. As they hit the floor, unrecognizable, gooey, sooty fragments spilled out from their uniforms and across the floor in the direction they had been running. There was nothing recognizable left. The air smelled of burned flesh and hair.

It was a staggering demonstration of power that stopped a few of the men in green tunics in their tracks. Magda had never seen the gift used in such a shocking way. She wasn't sure if anyone in the room had.

Other soldiers, though, off to the sides and farther away, big men, angry and eager to fight, raced forward to take out the threat that had felled their fellow soldiers. Merritt was already spinning, sword already arcing around. When the blade caught the men, the air exploded with a fog of blood. Bone fragments hit the columns with a sickening sound. Merritt was in a full rage unleashed.

Battle erupted in the council chambers, with men falling to Merritt's sword or bolts of power as fast as they went after Magda. Merritt didn't let any of them get remotely close to her. The attempt brought a swift death.

In the calm at the center of the chaos, at Magda's feet, Lothain put his hands together. "Please, Mistress, command me."

Magda glanced around at the battle, then back down at Lothain. "Tell your men to stop. Stand up and command them to stop."

Lothain jumped to his feet. "Stop!" he called out. "All of you who served me, I command you to stop!"

Magda could see men of the Home Guard pouring in the doors at the rear of the room, weapons to hand, as the men in green tunics came to a confused halt on Lothain's command.

"Tell them to lay down their weapons and surrender to the Home Guard," Magda told Lothain.

"Soldiers of the prosecutor's office," Lothain screamed, "lay down your weapons and surrender!"

Bewildered, many of the men looked around and cautiously began following his orders. Others who didn't were overpowered by the soldiers of the Home Guard and disarmed. The few who wouldn't listen and fought on were cut down. Soon, all of Lothain's private army were either dead or subdued.

The men in green tunics who had been holding Tilly likewise unbuckled their weapons belts and let them drop to the floor as soldiers with swords drawn closed in. With no one holding her up, Tilly collapsed.

Magda gestured to a young sorceress she knew standing close to the front of the spectators. "Please, Davina, can you help Tilly?"

The sorceress nodded, lifted her skirts, and rushed up onto the dais to see to helping the woman.

Elder Cadell shot to his feet. "What is the meaning of this outrage! Magda, what do you think you're doing!"

"Sit down," she said in a deadly cold voice. "Prosecutor Lothain is about to confess so that everyone can know the truth."

"The truth? What do you think—"

"I said sit down," she repeated through gritted teeth.

When he saw the look in her eyes, he sank back down into his tall chair.

N ow," Magda said to Lothain as a winded Merritt joined her at her side, "I want you to tell everyone here who you are loyal to."

The crowd, never having seen the likes of such an event and not understanding what was really going on, inched closer. The sea of faces stretched away as far as Magda could see. Everyone tried to crowd in closer in order to hear.

Lothain again fell to his knees, again clasping his hands as he gazed up at her with wide eyes filled with the desperate need to please her.

She had always thought of the prosecutor as a bull of a man, a commanding figure feared for his dogged pursuit of his quarry as well as his intimidating presence. Now, he looked weak and powerless. She supposed that he was. The man that he had been, was no more.

Now, he was a man who suddenly appeared to be in great distress as he hesitated. "I'm not sure what you mean, Mistress."

Magda frowned as she looked down the length of her white dress at him. "It's a simple question. Who are you loyal to? Answer the question."

"To you, Mistress! I am loyal to you and no other!"

Magda shared a look with Merritt.

"That's not the right answer," she whispered.

"You have to be more specific," Merritt whispered back. "He is trying to follow your instructions exactly."

Magda understood. She looked back down at the concern on the stocky face peering up at her, waiting expectantly.

"No, that's not what I meant—"

Lothain cried out in anguish at hearing that he had displeased her. He fell to the floor, grasping the hem of her white Confessor's dress.

"I'm sorry, Mistress!" he sobbed. "Please, forgive me! I'll tell you whatever you want to hear!"

"I want to hear the truth. I meant that I want to know where your loyalties used to lie before you became loyal to me."

Relief washed over his creased face at understanding what she wanted, relief that he now knew how to please her. He sat back on his heels.

"I was loyal to Emperor Sulachan, Mistress. I was a spy for him. I did his bidding."

The crowd gasped. Some of the people were still helping those in pain on the floor as others were pushing around them, trying to get in closer to be able to hear.

"How can that be?" one of the older wizards near the front asked. "How is it possible for our prosecutor to be loyal to Sulachan, and even if it was, why would he admit it to you?"

Magda gestured to Merritt, for the first time really noticing how much blood was all over him. She paused momentarily to take him in, then turned to the watching faces.

"This is Wizard Merritt. He is a maker."

That sent ripples of whispering back through the crowd. Some people, she knew, thought that makers were a myth. Other people had known that Merritt was gifted, but hadn't known that he was a maker. A number of the gifted, though, nodded knowingly, some even with pride.

"I want you all to understand what has happened, and why this traitor is confessing. You see, with his gift as a maker, Merritt created an entirely new form of magic never conceived of before."

Excited whispering swept back through the crowd at the news. Magda waited for the crowd to quiet down. Wanting to hear what she would say next, they quickly did.

"That magic was crafted specifically to get the truth from a person. Touched by this power, anyone will reveal the truth, no matter what the truth may be, no matter how guilty they have been, no matter what evil they have committed.

"Once touched by this power, anyone, no matter how much they may have wished to hide it before, is changed forever and they will reveal the truth.

"This is not the time to go into a detailed explanation of how it works. That doesn't matter right now. Right now, the important thing for you to understand is that this powerful magic is infallible at what it is designed to do. A person touched by this power confesses the truth about anything they are asked. They cannot lie."

"What kind of power were you using for this?" a wizard in plain robes standing in the front of the crowd asked. "I've never heard of such magic."

"In part, I used the calculations for a seventh-level breach," Merritt explained with casual finality.

Eyebrows around the room lifted. Wizards shared grim looks.

Merritt stepped up closer beside Magda. "You've seen the terrible weapons that have been created out of people, things such as the dream walkers. This one was created to help us. This power creates a new kind of weapon that serves the cause of truth. That's what matters.

"Lady Searus volunteered her life to the attempt. It was a perilous journey she undertook for our sake, for the sake of being able to know truth from deception and lies. I guarantee you that none of you can imagine the sacrifice she made to do this, or the personal risks she took for our cause. In the end it worked, and she has been reborn with this new power."

Merritt held a hand out in introduction. "Please meet Magda Searus, the first Confessor."

CHAPTER
93

Magda could hear the word "Confessor" whispered over and over, repeated countless times back through the mass of people watching. Lothain, still on his knees, continued to gaze up at her, patiently awaiting her further instructions.

When Magda signaled, Quinn brought Naja forward. Naja pushed her hood back so that Lothain could see her. Rage reddened her face. Magda could see the dangerous aura of the gift shimmering in her icy blue eyes.

Naja pointed at Lothain. "This is the man who put me in the dungeon. This is the man who tortured me and—"

Quinn grabbed her and pulled her back as she lunged, trying to kick him between his legs. "We need him to be able to talk," he whispered in Naja's ear. "Magda needs to get all the truth out of him. Let her do it."

Naja, her breast heaving in rage, pressed her lips tightly together as she looked into Magda's eyes. Magda could see that the sorceress was on the edge of unleashing enough violence to reduce Lothain to a smoldering corpse.

"I know," Magda whispered to her. "I know."

"I owe you both my life," Naja said to Magda and Merritt. "Everyone here does. My trust is the least I can offer in return." At last, she pulled back from the brink and gave Magda a nod to continue.

"Who is she?" Magda asked Lothain as she gestured to Naja. "Tell everyone here who this woman is and what her duties were before coming here to the Keep. Tell us what you know about her."

Lothain looked out at the crowd watching him and answered without hesitation. "She is a defector from the Old World. She came here to help the cause of the Midlands. She was Emperor Sulachan's spiritist. She knows about the ways of the wizards in the Old World. She knows how they have been able to use the dead to serve the ends of Emperor Sulachan. She knows how we are able to control the souls of the dead in order to use their corpses to do our bidding. She knows, too, about the half people and how we steal their souls as well."

Cries of terror broke out as near panic washed back through the people watching. The true dimension of the threat from the Old World was sinking in. Most of these people had never heard of such things.

"And what did you do when she defected and came here to help our cause?" Magda asked him.

"I had her chained in the dungeon and tortured."

"Why did you put her in the dungeon?" Magda asked.

He leaned in eagerly at the question, happy that he was able to answer her, to be able to please her. "To make sure that she couldn't help the wizards and sorceresses here at the Keep who work to defend the Midlands and counter the weapons being created in the Old World. We didn't want her to stop what we were secretly doing with the dead, or with assassinating important people." Tears welled up in his eyes. "I'm sorry, Mistress. I meant you harm, too." He fell to his knees again, clutching at the hem of her white dress. "Please, forgive me!"

"Stop that and look at me."

He immediately came to attention on his knees.

Magda suddenly went cold with dread.

She had forgotten to take it into consideration.

She looked down at Lothain. "You know about the dream walkers?"

"Yes, Mistress."

"Are there dream walkers here, now, secretly hiding in people's minds, watching us right now?"

"Yes, Mistress."

She hadn't considered that. She had been so worried about getting Lothain to confess in front of everyone, so determined to expose his treason, that she hadn't thought about dream walkers watching along with everyone else.

A man, his eyes wild, his hands clawed, screamed with murderous intent as he ran toward the dais, toward Lothain.

Merritt, grasping what was happening, thrust his hand out just in time, sending a charge of power into the man flying in toward Lothain. The man shuddered when the power hit him and he fell dead at Magda's feet. He had been one of their own, not a traitor, but a dream walker had turned him into an assassin.

As a couple of soldiers dragged the body away, Magda looked up at the shocked faces. "That was a dream walker taking control of one of our people to try to kill our witness, here."

People backed away, gawking at the dead man being dragged past their feet, one of them, used by a dream walker to become a killer. It was suddenly becoming all too real to people who hadn't been willing to believe that it was possible dream walkers were already invading the minds of people in the Keep.

Screams broke out as several wizards in the crowd suddenly covered their ears, writhing as they were stricken out of the blue with terrible agony. Some of the people around the victims backed away as blood began to run from the ears and noses of wizards gasping for breath, pressing their hands to their heads, trying to suppress the unbearable pain. They began choking on blood and coughing it out in thick gobs.

Magda understood all too well what was happening. It had happened to her. She rushed to the edge of the dais, close to the crowd.

"Listen to me!" she screamed out loud enough for all to hear. "Listen to me or some of you will die! You have to listen to me and do exactly as I say!"

Pleading faces turned toward her. Others tried in vain to help the stricken.

"Dream walkers are taking your minds!" Merritt yelled from beside Magda. "They intend to murder you! You only have one chance to live! Listen to her if you want to live!"

"Lord Rahl created magic to protect people from dream walkers," Magda called out. "Giving the devotion to Lord Rahl bonds you to him through links to this magic. It will protect you from the dream walkers. You have no time to waste! Drop to your knees! Do it now!"

A good many people did as she had commanded.

"How can such a thing be possible?" one of the confused-looking wizards asked. "There is no way for a remote bond to accomplish something like that."

"Yes there is!" Merritt answered. "I know because I helped him create it. Just as a dream walker can function remotely, so can the bond to Lord Rahl. I know because I ran the integrity check myself, from inside the verification web. It works. I tested it with a dream walker. Now listen to Magda and do exactly as she says or the dream walkers will be able to steal into your minds."

"But I don't see—"

"There is no time to debate this! I'll give you details

later!" Merritt pointed at a man in front, crumpled forward on his knees, bleeding from his ears. "If you want to be vulnerable to dream walkers just like that, then ignore her!"

All the people still standing, including the wizard, dropped to their knees.

"Everyone!" Magda shouted. "Bend forward, put your forehead to the ground, open your mind to the words, and repeat them after me! You must do it three times! Repeat the words after me if you want to live!"

The vast room reverberated with people shouting that they would do it, or crying, or begging her to hurry.

"To be protected, you must swear as follows," Magda called out in a clear voice. "Repeat the words after me. *Master Rahl guide us.*" The voices echoed as the crowd repeated them. "*Master Rahl teach us,*" Magda said into the tense quiet. Those stricken, bleeding, and in agony gasped the words of the devotion along with everyone else, as she had once done herself. "*Master Rahl protect us.*" With each phrase she called out, everyone repeated it in unison. "*In your light we thrive.*" She waited for the echo to die out so they wouldn't miss her words. "*In your mercy we are sheltered.*" She paused, then went on, "*In your wisdom we are humbled.*" They repeated together. "*We live only to serve.*" She looked out at all the bowed heads as she spoke the last of it. "*Our lives are yours.*"

The echo of the last words of the devotion spoken in unison finally died out. For good measure, Magda had them all repeat it two more times.

When the three devotions were finished, the people stricken had collapsed in relief. They nodded to those attending them that it had worked. The news that doing as Magda had said had saved the lives of those in the grip of dream walkers spread like wildfire through the packed rooms.

"Congratulations," Magda told the crowd, "you have taken an important step in successfully protecting the Keep from dream walkers. You must tell everyone who was not here today. They must all give the devotion to Lord Rahl in order to be protected by that bond. We cannot allow anyone unprotected to be among us."

CHAPTER
94

I'm afraid," Magda told the people who were now more than eager to hear what else she might reveal, "that besides the dream walkers, there are other dangers among us here at the Keep."

She gestured to the man still on his knees before her. "Lothain, here, has long been a traitor acting to damage our ability to defend ourselves. He has been working to see to it that our countermeasures are betrayed and our weapons are ineffective so that our forces will be weakened and defeated by Emperor Sulachan's invading army. His intent was to seize the rule of the Keep, here, today, by being named First Wizard so that he could hand control of the Keep over to the enemy.

"We were at their mercy and they have none. Without even being aware of it, we were on the brink of defeat, about to be slaughtered or enslaved."

She turned her attention to the former prosecutor waiting on his knees. "Isn't that right?"

"Yes, Mistress."

"But you weren't doing this all alone, were you?"

"No, Mistress. I had help."

"So you have others, here at the Keep, working with

you?" she asked. "Wizards and others working under you to help subvert the Keep?"

Lothain was nodding. "Yes, Mistress. A number of others."

In the distance, Magda could see people trying to slip out of the council chambers. Soldiers of the Home Guard crossed their lances to bar the doors. Gifted working with the Home Guard stood, prepared to use whatever means necessary to prevent any resistance.

"Tell us all gathered here," Magda said, "who are these other traitors working here at the Keep."

Lothain began rattling off the names of wizards first. Some of them were the men who had just been detained trying to leave.

Lothain named a half dozen gifted that Magda knew worked down in the lower reaches of the Keep, and another half dozen she didn't know. He named other, lower-ranking people who were helping him with various tasks and murders. He named the captain of the prosecutor's private guard and in a rapid ramble named off a good thirty names of soldiers loyal to the Old World who were helping him take control of the Keep.

Magda had to stop him and have him repeat names because in his eagerness to answer her questions, they couldn't easily understand him. Lothain burst into tears that he had displeased her. She ignored the tears and told him to continue, but to do it slower so that they could get all the names.

General Grundwall stood grim-faced nearby, listening to all the names. Aides worked feverishly to scribble down each one. Even as he was listening to the list of names, General Grundwall was giving instructions to his officers to find and capture all the men named and put them in the dungeon. He ordered the outer portcullis closed to seal the Keep until they were all caught.

"And those wizards took orders from you?" Magda asked once he finished the names.

"Yes, Mistress. I was the one commanding the efforts here."

"And those men working down in the lower part of the Keep, what were they to do?"

Lothain again looked overjoyed to be able to answer her question. "Some were helping wizards who work on defenses against Emperor Sulachan's weapons so that we would know what countermeasures the people of the New World had developed. Others worked with those developing weapons for the Midlands.

"When the people here went to great lengths to come up with a weapon and deploy it before a battle, they won't know that Sulachan's forces were ready and waiting with a trap. We also learned how you are able to defend against our weapons so that we can circumvent those countermeasures."

"What else did your spies do here at the Keep and down in Aydindril?"

"They identified targets, letting me know who the most valuable and important people were. Then, I had others send the dream walkers to take them out, or else I would have them animate the dead down in the catacombs and send them out to kill those targets in order to spread terror in the Keep."

Again the crowd gasped and whispered at all the horrific news they were hearing. A lot of these people had friends and loved ones who had been murdered mysteriously in the Keep. Now they knew not only how, but who was responsible. They wanted Lothain's head. Some people, angry at the level of treason Lothain was revealing, surged forward to try to get at him.

Merritt quickly gestured to soldiers of the Home Guard. They understood and rushed in to hold back the angry crowd.

"Are there others working with you?" Magda asked after the crowd had settled down and was listening again. "Other officials or people higher up in the Keep?"

"Yes," he said, pointing a meaty finger back toward the council. "Guymer and Weston. When they traveled in the sliph to meet with officials in the Midlands, they would also secretly travel to places close to the Old World in order to go on to meet with Emperor Sulachan and his inner circle of wizards. There, they reported on the progress of wizards here, handed over secret information about weapons as well as countermeasures, and brought back orders. The sliph never reveals anything about people who use her, so no one ever knew that Guymer and Weston were carrying important information to the emperor's forces."

Both councilmen, red-faced, shot to their feet.

"This is the most preposterous story I've ever heard!" Weston shouted. "You can't believe the product of such wicked magic!"

"It's all lies!" Guymer added. "You can't believe this man's delusions!"

Magda ignored them as soldiers surrounded the pair. "Anyone else?" she asked Lothain.

"Of course." He began to lift his hand to point.

Elder Cadell thrust out his arms. With a thump, a tumbling ball of wizard's fire ignited and shot across the dais. The sphere of liquid flame rolled through the air as it roared toward them, expanding into a deadly inferno that hissed with menace. The hot yellow glow of it lit the faces of the stunned people watching.

The room erupted in panic.

Merritt dove on Magda, driving the wind from her lungs as he knocked her out of the line of deadly flames flying across the dais. The wizard's fire lit everything and everyone in the fierce glow of its orange-and-yellow flames. Quinn, Naja, and the general dove the other way just in time.

The wizard's fire hit Lothain with a sickening thump that Magda could feel deep in her chest. The liquid inferno exploded over Lothain as it hit. Blobs of the deadly fire splattered and sailed on past him to splash down among the crowd. People everywhere screamed, some in panic, some in mortal pain.

There was nothing that burned with the deadly ferocity of wizard's fire. It had a thick consistency that stuck to victims, burning down to bone. People with bits of it on them screamed as they tried without success to extinguish the fiery blobs.

Lothain briefly struggled in agony, his movements rapidly slowing to a stop, as the inferno consumed him. The fire was so intense it hurt her eyes to look at it. His arms, like brightly glowing torches, disintegrated as the man crumpled to the floor, turning into an unrecognizable burning black mass.

Out in the crowd, gifted rushed to do their best to quench the droplets of fire that had splashed out into the crowd. Others bent close, helping those injured. There were a number of victims who were beyond help. People everywhere were screaming.

"He's a liar! This is all lies!" Elder Cadell cried out as he stood in front of his taller chair at the center of the council desk. "This Confessor power is a curse that brings forth nothing but terrible lies. The council forbade Merritt from creating such a power because we knew it would become a tyranny of magic controlling us all!"

Naja, her ice blue eyes as cold as anything Magda had ever seen, pointed at the elder as she addressed the crowd. "The term 'the tyranny of magic' is the excuse Emperor Sulachan uses to go to war. It is a cover for his true aim of disarming all those who oppose him. He wants to eliminate magic to keep anyone from fighting back effectively."

"She's a liar! And so is she!" Elder Cadell screamed as he pointed at Magda. "She's a traitor! They are both traitors! This is the tyranny of magic right before our very eyes! This sham of a Confessor power is an evil contrivance of an unscrupulous wizard meant to thwart the common good and control our lives!

"Arrest her!" Elder Cadell yelled as he gestured wildly at the soldiers nearby. "Lady Searus is a traitor! Lothain proved it! She must be put to death. She must be—"

The elder's words were cut off when a frightening blast of power from Councilman Sadler slammed into him. The elder staggered back a step, his hands clawing as his flesh blackened and boiled. He only had time to let out the briefest of cries before his shriveling flesh melted and sloughed away, leaving the top of his skull exposed. His eye sockets opened up as his eyes liquefied. His shriveled lips fell away, revealing a skeletal grin.

Elder Cadell collapsed dead across the council desk, a smoking corpse.

Grim-faced Councilmen Clay and Hambrook both watched as soldiers wrestled Weston and Guymer under control and dragged them away.

"I'm ashamed at how easily we were deceived by Elder Cadell, Weston, and Guymer," Councilman Hambrook said, "to say nothing of Prosecutor Lothain."

"How do we know that you two weren't part of it?" General Grundwall asked as he suspiciously eyed the two remaining councilmen. "Lothain is dead. He can't tell us if you were in on it, too."

Clay gestured at Magda. "From what I know of this Confessor power from when Merritt came before us before, there is no limit to it. She can use this power to get Councilmen Weston and Guymer to confess all that they know, just as Lothain was in the process of doing. Under the touch of a Confessor they will reveal the truth and the rest of the story. That will confirm that I wasn't a traitor."

"Nor I," Hambrook said.

"Councilman Clay is right," Merritt said. "We will not only be able to confirm if there are any more traitors among us, but also who is innocent.

"That's the beauty of having a Confessor working with us. She will be able to burn through the deception and lies.

"As a Confessor, Magda will for the first time reveal for us the truth."

Councilman Clay watched as the two treasonous councilmen were led away. "At least Magda can use her power on them and discover if anyone else is involved."

"We'll have to move quickly," General Grundwall said, "before any of them can cause trouble before they are caught."

"How did this nest of traitors come about?" Councilman Clay asked. "How were they able to work so effectively right under our noses?"

Magda stepped away from what was left of the smoldering remains of Lothain. She had never trusted Lothain, but she had believed in Elder Cadell. She was angry that he had fooled her for so long, and that he had betrayed them all.

"Naja was forced to help Emperor Sulachan with his twisted objectives," Magda said. "I don't think that any of us could have imagined what was going on down in the Old World while we were going about our lives. Everyone needs to know the truth about what they have been doing."

Magda drew Naja closer. "Please explain it. Give these people a picture of the true horror that the enemy has in store for us. Tell them how Sulachan uses the dead, and how his wizards rip the souls from the living."

Naja looked out at the faces watching her. "If there is a tyranny of magic, it is what Emperor Sulachan and those who rule with him would impose on all of you."

Everyone quieted to listen to her story.

"Hold on a moment," Merritt said as he caught Magda under her arm as her knees started to buckle.

Magda was beginning to realize how seriously exhausted she was from using her new Confessor power. The sword had given her the strength she had needed the night before, but the use of her Confessor power had drained that strength.

Magda gestured. "I need to sit down."

Merritt guided her around the desk. He seized the robes at Elder Cadell's back and heaved the corpse aside. He gave quick orders. Soldiers rushed up and dragged the body away.

Merritt held out the tall chair for Magda. When she sat, he stood behind her, resting a hand on the carved top of the chair.

"The council has lost members. We need a council," Magda said from behind the chair in the center of the council table. "As a start, I hereby reinstate Councilman Sadler."

No one objected. When Magda gestured to him, Councilman Sadler smiled and took a seat to her left. Clay and Hambrook sat on her right again, at their traditional places.

Magda nodded for Naja to go on, then sat quietly listening to what she already knew as the sorceress revealed those terrors being hatched by the rulers in the Old World.

Wide-eyed people listened as Naja explained what they had never heard before, and told them what they really faced.

When Naja finished her brief summation, Magda, having regained a bit of strength, stood.

"When you hear the words 'the tyranny of magic,' as we heard from Elder Cadell, you will know that it is the calling card of killers. Don't be fooled by their platitudes that it is for the common good. Their real purpose is to strip us of our abilities so that they may more easily conquer and rule us.

"If we are to survive, we need magic now more than ever to defend ourselves from those in the Old World. We need to learn, discover, create. We need to use our reasoning minds and truth.

"You have now heard the confession of the traitor Lothain and how he subverted the Keep. You have heard from Naja what Sulachan has planned. We now know the real nature of the war that is upon us.

"If we lose this war, we lose more than our lives, we lose more than the future for our people. We will lose our connection to all that is good." Magda lifted her hand, showing them the ring with the Grace on it. "We will lose our connection to the very nature of Creation, life, and our souls.

"We did not choose this war, but if we don't defeat Sulachan's forces, these thieves of souls, then we and future generations will live in a half world of the half people and the enslaved dead, disconnected from the Grace forever. We will be ruled by Sulachan, who will be nothing more than the embodiment of the Keeper of the underworld."

Her gaze carefully moved across everyone in the room. Every eye was on her. People listened in rapt attention. Every face was serious. Everyone knew that they were hearing the truth.

"To win, we must have the truth," Magda said. "Today, the true war for our survival begins. I intend to help see to it that we win this war, that our people not only survive, but thrive. The Midlands is my home. I promise you all that I will not abandon you, our cause, the Midlands, or truth."

As she looked out from her seat at the tall, center chair, the crowd erupted in cheers.

The first thing we need to do," Magda said when the crowd had finally quieted, "is to seal the catacombs."

Councilman Sadler frowned. "Seal the catacombs? But wizards work down there."

"The dead also work from down there," she said. "The dead hide in their resting place, only to come up in the darkness and murder us. We don't know how many of those dead down there have been prepared by the enemy to be able to be awakened. We don't know how many of the dead that have been laid to rest there were really being placed by spies.

"We have no way of knowing which corpses might sit up and strangle us. How would we find them? The wizards will have to be moved to other work areas."

"But seal the catacombs?" Councilman Hambrook sounded incredulous. "That's sacred ground. The people of the Keep have been laying loved ones to rest there for centuries. Visiting ancestors is a deeply valued tradition. Are you sure there isn't another way? Maybe it isn't necessary. Maybe our gifted could find a way to reveal the dangerous bodies and remove only those so that we wouldn't have to take such a drastic step."

Magda looked out at all the faces watching. "Do any of you feel comfortable risking having the dead walk the halls of the Keep at night, looking for more victims to rip limb from limb? I know that I certainly don't."

The crowd assured her they did not like that idea one bit.

She looked back at Hambrook. "I understand your concerns. But we are fighting for the survival of the living, not the dead. They are gone. We have to let go of those who have died and move on to devote ourselves to the living."

Magda's own words abruptly hit a painful place deep within her. She still could not let go of Baraccus. As much as she knew that he was gone, and as much as she realized that she had to move on with her life, she couldn't seem to let him go.

"Magda is right," Merritt said. "Even if we thought that we had come up with a way to detect the dangerous dead from all the rest, how would we ever know for sure that we were right? A day could come when we tragically learned that we had only been fooling ourselves. Aren't the living what really matter? Would any of us want to lose the life of a loved one on such a risk? Would anyone here want to lose a mother? A father? A child?"

None in the onlookers indicated that they would.

Councilman Hambrook sighed in resignation. "I have to admit, that makes sense. I wouldn't want to risk loved ones."

"Nor would I," Councilman Clay added.

Councilman Sadler nodded. "We have a responsibility to life. The living should be our only concern."

"Then seal the catacombs," Magda said with finality.

"We will need to use magic to be sure," Merritt cautioned. "We'll need some of those keeper spells that

Isidore developed. They will ensure that none of the dead can escape to hunt us."

"Please advise our wizards what they will need to do," Councilman Sadler said. "General, please assemble a team as swiftly as possible."

General Grundwall clapped a fist to his heart in salute. "At once."

"And let it be done before Lady Searus's nightmare comes to life," Sadler added.

"Confessor Searus," Merritt corrected under his breath.

Councilman Sadler lifted a finger and addressed the onlookers. "I meant to say, 'Confessor Searus.'"

The crowd seemed to like the title.

98

As Magda and Merritt made their way from the walkway around the inside of the great tower and into the stone room with the sliph's well, Quinn heard their footsteps and looked back over his shoulder. Seeing who it was, he set down his pen and stood. Smiling, eager to see them, he flipped his journal closed and put it back with all the others.

"Magda, how are you feeling?" he asked as he came past the sliph's well to greet them.

She smiled. "A night's rest did me wonders."

She glanced at the well, but the sliph didn't emerge to take a look at the visitors. Magda couldn't say that she was unhappy about that. The sliph was probably off traveling.

"How are things going?" Quinn asked.

Merritt rested the palm of his left hand on the hilt of his sword. "I talked to General Grundwall this morning. Overnight the Home Guard captured most of those named by Lothain. They should soon have the rest in hand. Magda will have to use her Confessor power on some of the worst of them in order to get them to confess the details we otherwise would have gotten from

Lothain had he not died. That will enable us to be sure we've rooted out all of the traitors and collaborators."

"What about the councilmen, Weston and Guymer?" Quinn lifted a finger toward the sliph's well. "Lothain told us that they used the sliph to travel to the South to collaborate with Emperor Sulachan and his officers."

Quinn's task was to guard the sliph to make sure that the enemy didn't use her to secretly slip into the Keep to do them harm. It had been Baraccus who had asked Quinn to take up the duty after they'd had some unfortunate penetrations by dangerous people. Now anyone unauthorized and not a friendly force would not live long enough to climb out of the sliph's well after using it to try to sneak into the Keep.

In the beginning, Quinn had killed a number of the enemy gifted who had thought they could slip into the Keep through the sliph. After a while, they realized it would no longer work and such incursions ended, but Quinn or one of several others always stood guard over the sliph to make certain they didn't decide to try it again, especially with a weapon created out of a person.

It was a personal outrage for Quinn, who guarded the sliph to prevent the enemy from using her, to know that two of their own people, trusted councilmen, were actually traitors who had used the sliph for a deadly purpose and no one knew it.

Magda leveled a meaningful look at Quinn. "I am looking forward to hearing the truthful confessions of those two. They have caused great harm. A lot of innocent people died because of them. I'm sure they have a lot to tell, and they are going to tell it all."

Quinn smiled. "Having a Confessor is going to be a tremendous help in our efforts, just as Merritt had always argued before the council. How ironic that the two men who so steadfastly stood against the creation of a Confessor are now going to be confessing the truth about their treason because of that power." He turned his attention back to Merritt. "What about the dream walkers?"

"The general told me that a few of the men he captured, hoping for leniency, are cooperating and have confessed to directing the dream walkers to key people. The dream walkers had been watching what those people were working on, and in several cases they had exerted their control to force the sabotage of important projects. We've been systematically compromised on a massive scale. It's frightening to grasp the extent of it."

Merritt smiled at her. "Magda was right from the beginning about there being a great deal wrong in the Keep. Without her determination to discover what was behind it all, we wouldn't have known about it until it was too late. We all owe her our lives. All of the Midlands owes her a debt of gratitude."

"There is no doubt of that," Quinn said, adding his smile.

Magda didn't really feel that it was necessarily her doing, so much as Baraccus's. It was because of his death that she suspected something was wrong at the Keep in the first place. It was because of him ending his life the way he did that she began her search for answers. She knew that he had to have had a purpose that was motivated by wanting to save the lives of the rest of his people.

She still wasn't entirely sure, though, what was behind him ending his life. She was only certain that it had been for a good reason. She still wished she knew what that reason was.

She still couldn't let him go.

"The Home Guard has gone through the gifted and

then the rest of the Keep to make sure that everyone has given the devotion to Lord Rahl," Merritt was telling Quinn. "In a couple cases, we were too late. Several wizards were found dead, obviously killed by the dream walker they were unwittingly hosting. As I said, the extent of the infiltration is shocking. None of us realized how close we were to losing the Keep. We were only days away from the end.

"The Keep will soon be as close to completely sealed off from penetration by dream walkers as we can make it. Anyone wanting to enter will be stopped at the portcullis and not allowed in until they go to their knees and give the devotion. Of course, while we think this will end the threat, we can't be absolutely certain. People entering could be deceitful about the devotion they give. I suppose that's why we have a Home Guard. But the dream walkers will no longer be able to use innocent people to secretly penetrate the Keep and sabotage our efforts."

Quinn shook his head in wonder. "Frightening. At least we've now halted it all and we can move forward to begin to rebuild all of our efforts on a solid footing rather than the rotted foundation created by traitors and spics. Unfortunately, in the meantime, the enemy has gotten way ahead of us."

"We have a lot of catching up to do," Merritt agreed. "The wizards working down in the catacomb areas are being moved as we speak. Then we can go to work on sealing off the entire area. I've already prepared some spell-forms for them to use."

"How is Naja doing?" Magda asked.

"She is already hard at work helping the gifted." Quinn let out a troubled sigh. "After some of the things she talked about with me, they are going to have a lot of work to do. She's incredibly intelligent, though, and she's going to be an invaluable help. She understands things that I don't think one in ten of our gifted entirely grasp."

As Quinn was talking to Magda, Merritt selected a journal from the row standing on the desk. "Do you mind?" he asked.

Quinn looked back and then gestured. "No, please, go ahead. I've always intended my journals to one day be read by others. I'm hoping that it will give people in the future an insight to these troubled, historic times, much the way I've gotten insights and knowledge from old books I've read."

Merritt, already engrossed in reading through one of the journals, made a sound deep in his throat in answer.

Quinn returned to what he had been telling Magda. "As a sorceress and a spiritist, Naja has remarkable talents and abilities. She can more than fill in for the work that Isidore was doing helping the gifted. Isidore was only working at the fringes of a lot of things, trying to understand them. Naja was at the center of them. In some cases, she helped originate what Isidore was only starting to investigate.

"It's possible that she will be able to unravel the mysteries of the spirits trapped between worlds. She's hoping that maybe she can find a way to guide them through the veil.

"We're more than fortunate that Naja came over to our side. It will accelerate our understanding of how to catch up with what those in the Old World are doing to defend against us, and losing her specialized assistance will be a blow to the efforts of Sulachan's gifted." Quinn lifted his brow as he tilted his head toward her. "But more than that, I would hate to have to fight against that woman. Having grown up in such a strange and exotic place, she is, well, she is unlike anyone I've ever met."

"I know what you mean," Magda said. "From the first

moment I saw her, I knew this is not a woman to underestimate." Magda glanced toward the sliph. "Have you heard from Lord Rahl, yet?"

"A couple days back, when we thought Lothain was going to be named First Wizard, I sent an urgent message to him through a journey book." Quinn gestured to the well. "He should be on his way."

"Quinn," Magda said, gathering her thoughts to move on to their reason for coming down to the sliph's room in the first place, "Merritt and I need to tell you about some important matters."

"Very important," Merritt said, lowering the journal he was reading. "But the things we have to tell you about must be held in strictest confidence. Once we tell you, only the three of us will know about it, and it has to stay that way. Forever."

"Of course," Quinn said as he nodded with an earnest, if worried, look. "You both know that you can trust me. What is it? Has something else happened?"

"Yes," Merritt said on his way back from the table, "and we need your help."

CHAPTER
99

My help?" Quinn shrugged. "Of course. What is it? What's happened?"

"We need you to know that I completed the key," Merritt told him.

Quinn blinked. "What?"

"The magic used to complete the key has a great deal in common with the magic I used to create the Confessor power."

"But you always told me that you had to have the seventh-level-breach calculations to complete the key."

"Baraccus left the formulas for Merritt to find," Magda told him. "With the calculations he needed, Merritt was able to complete the key."

Quinn stared at her. "The key to the power of Or—Or—" he stammered.

"Orden," Merritt finished.

Quinn squinted at him. "You completed the key? It's done?"

Looking him in the eye, Merritt lifted the sword a few inches and let it drop back into its scabbard.

Quinn wiped a hand across his face as he sighed. "The teams will be relieved."

"You can't tell them," Magda said. "You can't tell another soul. You can't tell anyone."

"What?" Quinn was clearly perplexed. "Why not?"

Magda gripped his arm. "Quinn, listen to me. There's more to it. There are complications. What we have to tell you requires the utmost secrecy."

"All right." He took a breath to compose himself. "What else?"

"When Baraccus came back from the Temple of the Winds, he told me that the boxes of Orden were gone. Someone took them."

Quinn's eyes widened as his face went white. "Dear spirits. Do you have any idea what—"

"I know about the power they contain," she said. "Baraccus didn't tell anyone but me for a reason. I've only told Merritt and now you know. No one else can know about this."

"This is important, Quinn," Merritt added in a grave tone, holding the journal closed with a finger marking his place. "We don't know who stole the boxes of Orden. We don't believe that Baraccus did either. He was obviously very worried about the boxes being gone. We think that's why he brought the rift calculations back. He hid the formulas. We think he wanted me to find them and complete the key."

"Why would he hide them? The key is the safeguard for the power. The key may be the only thing that could control a release. Why wouldn't he want the teams trying to create the key to have the necessary formulas?"

"Think about it," Magda said. "Think of how the Keep has been compromised by traitors, spies, and dream walkers. If anyone had access to the formulas necessary to complete the key, then whoever has the boxes would be able to get hold of those formulas and complete the key themselves and unlock the power."

Quinn gazed off in thought. "That's true . . ."

"When Baraccus brought those valuable seventh-level-breach formulas back," Merritt said, "he knew how important they were. He hid the calculations so they wouldn't fall into the wrong hands."

"Where were they hidden? How did you discover them?"

"He wrote down the calculations in his notebooks that he left on his workbench. Right there in plain sight the whole time. People who saw those books didn't even know what was in them, because they were not the right people. When Magda gave me his tools, I discovered the formulas in his notebooks.

"He didn't tell anyone but Magda about the boxes being gone. I think he left a trail that took her to me. I think he wanted me to find the rift calculations because he knew that I was working on the sword alone. I was the right person. He didn't want anyone else to know about the existence of the formulas to keep whoever has the boxes from making a key.

"That completed key is now the most important object in the world, other than the boxes themselves, because the key can access the power. If whoever has the boxes knew that the key is complete, they would come after it, so we can't let a word of this get out."

"Of course," Quinn said, waving a hand as if to dismiss any concern that he failed to grasp the gravity of the situation. "No one even knows the true purpose of the power of Orden. We know some of its potential, some of its dangers, but we don't even know for sure its original purpose. Not much is known about the time before the star shift.

"But one thing is certain. If Emperor Sulachan is the

one who managed to obtain the boxes of Orden, he would do anything to get his hands on the key."

"Exactly," Merritt said. "That's why we need to hide it."

"Hide it?" Quinn shook a finger at the sword on Merritt's hip. "Bags, Merritt! You're wearing the thing in plain sight!"

Merritt leaned closer and lowered his voice. "Sometimes, the best way to hide something important is to hide it in plain sight. Baraccus wanted to show us that with how he hid the formulas."

Quinn threw his hands up in frustration. "But there are lots of people who have worked on creating the key out of a sword. A sword is the first thing someone searching for the key would suspect, the first thing they would look for."

"Not necessarily," Magda said.

Quinn's gaze shifted between the two of them. "I'm listening."

"They only think the key needs to be a sword because that was the theory gleaned from ancient books. I'm the one who came up with it, remember? I'm the one who told people it needed to be a sword."

"Well there you go. That's what I mean. Everyone believes it has to be a sword."

"That's why we need you to create a more inviting belief," Merritt said, "something more convincing, something that will cause people to shift their thinking to a better theory of what the key would have to be."

"A better theory?" Quinn looked intrigued. "You mean send them off track so that they aren't looking for a sword?"

"Exactly," Merritt said. "The boxes of Orden were stolen from the safest place anyone could think of to put them. So why were they vulnerable?"

"Because people knew where they were," Quinn answered. "If you know where something is, you can work on how to steal it no matter how difficult it may be to get to."

"You're getting the idea," Magda said. "What makes the key, in the form of the sword, vulnerable, is that if people know it exists they will look for it. That's why secrecy is so critical. People won't look for something if they don't know it exists."

"So in place of the sword," Merritt told him, "we have to give people something else more inviting to look for."

Quinn lifted a finger. "A diversion."

Merritt smiled in answer. "It needs to be something they will come to believe is the key to the boxes of Orden. Then we'll hide it—to make it look all the more important—when in actuality it will be carefully planted, not hidden. Hiding it makes it all the more enticing. If people are all looking for the diversion, they won't be looking for the real key."

"In the meantime," Magda told him, "we'll have the real key."

Merritt smiled. "Magda named it the Sword of Truth, so that's what it will be—a tool, a weapon, in its own right, as its own end. It has powerful magic designed around truth in order to protect the power of Orden, not just unlock it, so it will have a purpose—seeking truth— that will give it a purpose, a life of its own, a reason to explain its existence.

"Since it is the Sword of Truth—a weapon created to fight for truth—people won't have reason to expect that it could also actually be the key to the power of Orden."

Quinn slapped his forehead. "I never knew that my two old friends were this devious."

Merritt smiled with one side of his mouth. "In the meantime, with the sword at my side, I'll search for the boxes of Orden. If I can find them, we'll protect them. With no one knowing about the existence of the true key hiding in plain sight, then hopefully the rumors of our diversion key will entice whoever has the boxes to look for that fake key instead of trying to use the power without it.

"We have to understand, though, that the power of Orden has existed for longer than any of us knows. It's ancient. We have to realize that this search, this struggle to protect such an ancient power, may be a struggle and a search that is part of mankind itself, and very well may stretch beyond our lives. It may go on for centuries, or even for thousands of years. This is something more important than the three of us. It is our struggle right now, but we have to keep in mind that we may in the end be passing this struggle on to future generations.

"If we never find the boxes, then in the future, as the Sword of Truth is passed on to the right sort of person who can protect it, that person will have his own mission—seeking truth. In that way, the true power, the true purpose of the sword as the key, will be hidden in plain sight until the right person eventually comes along."

Quinn stared at Merritt. "This is a heavy responsibility we're taking on."

"It is," Merritt agreed.

Quinn put his fingers to his forehead as he paced around the room, thinking it through. He came back to stand before Magda and Merritt.

"So you two want me to create a fake key of some sort?"

"Yes, as a diversion for the real key," Magda said. "Then we'll hide it. If it's hidden well enough, but we leave hints to its location, then people will come to believe that your fake key has to be the true key."

"This is getting awfully complicated," Quinn said as he dry-washed his hands. "We have to get a long list of things right for all this to work."

"That's why we came to you," Magda said. "You're the only one who could pull it off."

Merritt regarded him with a sobering look. "Quinn, you know how dangerous the power of Orden is. Used in the wrong way, it very well could breach the veil and destroy the world of life. We have to do everything in our power to see to it that such a thing never comes to pass."

Deep in thought, Quinn flicked a hand. "Yes, of course you're right. How will we hint at this diversion key?"

CHAPTER

100

Merritt waggled the journal. "We'll hint at it in books of magic, information, records, and history. That's how I came to the belief that the key had to be a sword. You're always recording history of the Keep. You need to create a false history, for the false key. Create a better idea of what the key should be, one that makes more sense to people, so that they believe in the diversion we create."

Quinn nodded thoughtfully. "Wizard's First Rule."

"Right," Merritt said. "Emperor Sulachan has been able to amass information because he is a student of history. He gleans all he can from records and accounts. According to Naja, that's part of the way he uses dream walkers.

"So, in order to help hide the real key, we need to make some parts of history more muddled. We need to obscure what I learned about the key needing to be a sword. We don't want it to be easy for Sulachan, or anyone who might get their hands on the boxes, to be able to so easily learn the truth through history.

"If people see the muddled history you create, they will repeat it. Those accounts you create will take on a life of their own. They will become the conventional wisdom.

As they do, the truth will be blurred, at least until we find the boxes or, if not us, then the right person eventually comes along.

"So, while you're down here with the sliph, writing your journals and histories of the Keep, don't make clear what is happening now. Don't make it easy to understand what has taken place here in the Keep, or to grasp what we know, what we have discovered, and how we solved the plots against us. Don't let people know how Magda uncovered Lothain's plots, or how we unmasked the traitors and collaborators and spies. Don't let the enemy know how we did what we did. Mix it up."

"Of course. Disinformation," Quinn said. "I can do that. I'll leave out critical events, then I'll put in false information and twist everything that has happened around into a kind of vague, shadowy history that obscures what really took place."

"Good," Merritt said with a firm nod.

Quinn snapped his fingers. "And what if I made the diversion for the key, be a book?"

"A book . . ." Merritt gazed off as he considered it.

"Yes, kind of like the books with the complex rift formulas that Baraccus brought back from the Temple of the Winds."

"That would be fitting," Magda said.

Quinn shook a finger as he thought. "I could even use some calculations from the rift formulas to give it legitimacy. Not enough to make it function properly, of course, but enough star azimuth angles and such to make it appear legitimate. If it was complex enough, and if some of the magic in it actually functioned, that would make the false key look real."

"What kind of book would it be?" Magda asked.

Quinn leaned in. "A book of instructions. After all, isn't that what people expect? They will want to know how to use the power of Orden. An instruction book meets their expectations."

"The power of Orden predates the star shift," Merritt said. "Information about it is sketchy, at best."

"Exactly," Quinn said. "So they will want to know how it works. They start out invested in wanting a book of magic that will tell them how the power works. So why not give them one?"

"Create a fake instruction book as the key to the power?" Magda asked.

"Yes. It would be a book on how to use the boxes of Orden, full of legitimate formulas that predate the star shift to add legitimacy, but altered just enough so that they wouldn't be of any value as a real key. Who would know they're false? There would be no way to check them, nothing to check them against."

Magda was intrigued. "And you think that you could create a book that would appear real enough that people, even if they found it and looked at it, would believe it was real?"

"The power of Orden is ancient," Quinn said. "How would they confirm anything in it? I can make it look real and fabricate a verification process within the book itself, but this book would actually be nothing but shadows. Along with the muddled history I create, that would further add to the sense of authority of this shadowy book."

"You could even call it that," Merritt said. "Name it *Shadows*, or something."

"That's too simple," Magda said. "Sounds like my cat's name. It would work better as a diversion if it sounded like it functioned as a key. Like it contained methods for unlocking answers. It needs a more mysterious title."

Quinn frowned. "Like what?"

Magda thought a moment. It came to her, then.

"How about *The Book of Counted Shadows*."

Quinn's brow lifted in delight. "I like it."

"It's brilliant," Merritt said, grinning at her.

Seeing him smile at her like that lifted her heart. But the shadow over her heart dimmed her bright, momentary pleasure.

"I'll get started on it right away," Quinn said. "I'll also create some historical sources to make it look like the key to the boxes can be found in *The Book of Counted Shadows*. I can even come up with some fragments of text and make them look like they survived from before the star shift as well.

"If we let some of these accounts slip into the wrong hands and they get back to Emperor Sulachan, he will be sent off chasing shadows, so to speak."

Merritt pinched his lower lip in thought. "You could create some fake documents about recent events, with tantalizing bits of ancient knowledge talking about the key to the power of Orden, hinting at the book as the key, and then we could plant this documentation on a dead man dressed as a courier." Merritt leaned close. "Then we could leave the body where General Kuno's patrols would find it."

"And if we hide *The Book of Counted Shadows*," Quinn added, "it will convince the emperor that he is on the right track. The harder it is to find, the more they will all be convinced that the book is the key."

"Meanwhile," Merritt said, lifting the Sword of Truth partway from its scabbard, "no one will ever suspect the true key."

"It all should work," Quinn said. "After all, no one knows much of anything about the power of Orden's origin. I'll obscure what's known about the star shift to better hide what is known. I won't have to worry about altering a lot of material, or contradicting a great deal of evidence of actual history, so it should be easier to create a credible diversion out of history."

"And look here." Merritt opened the journal he had in his hand and tapped a place on the page. "You wrote in your journal, 'The third attempt at forging the key failed today. The wives and children of the five men who died roam the halls, wailing in inconsolable anguish. How many men will die before we succeed, or until we abandon the attempt as impossible? The goal may be worthy, but the price is becoming terrible to bear.'"

"I see what you mean. That's the kind of thing that's too obvious in pointing people to the sword as the key. I know," Quinn said as he swiped a finger across the first words, making them disappear, "I'll change this part so that it says, 'The third attempt at forging a Sword of Truth failed today.' How's that sound? That way it disassociates the key from the sword and makes the sword look like a special object of its own."

Merritt smiled. "Perfect. That adds credibility to the sword being something other than the key."

"I'll add some real magic to the book," Quinn said, "so that it seems even more real. Some occult spells and spell-forms will make for a sinister book."

"You are a devious man, Quinn," Magda said with a grin.

Quinn arched an eyebrow. "If you think so now, wait until you see *The Book of Counted Shadows*."

Magda rushed into the sliph's room. Merritt followed close behind her.

Lord Rahl, leaning back against the low wall of the well, looked up when he heard them come through the doorway, and swept his long blond hair back off his face. He looked rather disoriented and euphoric after his journey in the sliph. It had that effect on a lot of people. Magda had to admit that it had had the same effect on her. Despite that, she still didn't like the sliph.

"I came as fast as I could." Lord Rahl gestured to Quinn. "Quinn filled me in on everything. Sounds like quite an eventful ordeal." He grinned at Magda. "Confessor, eh? Seems to fit." His gaze traveled the length of her white dress and back up again. "I must say, so does that dress. Quite well, in fact."

"Thank you," she said, not knowing exactly what to say.

"When I first got the message, I was pretty worried that for some crazy reason you were actually going to marry that pig of a prosecutor. I should have known better. Good job, Magda. Good job. You indeed did have a reason to stay at the Keep, as you told me the last time I saw you."

Merritt nodded his agreement. "Even though Magda uncovered the plot and brought Lothain's treason to light, I'm afraid that we still have a lot of work to do, and a difficult war ahead of us. Did Quinn tell you about the half people as well?"

Alric Rahl sighed as he nodded. "And these walking dead people things."

"We wanted you to know what your soldiers were facing," Merritt said. "They're going to be hard to fight. I haven't worked out a method, yet, to keep them away from us. I would suggest that you do something about any places the dead are buried, like the catacombs."

"I always worried about men with a weapon in their hand, or a gifted conjuring magic. I never thought I'd have to worry about the dead people."

"I can assure you, it's not a thought I like either," Quinn said from his writing desk.

A thought tickled at the back of Magda's mind, but she couldn't quite bring it forward.

"Say," Lord Rahl said, stretching his neck to look out the door to make sure no one was near. "I have to bring up something rather important. But it has to be kept a secret among just us in this room."

It seemed to Magda like a day of secrets. "What is it?"

Lord Rahl scratched his jaw as he searched for words. "We found something, something quite important."

"You 'found' it?" Merritt asked suspiciously. "Where did you 'find' this important something?"

Lord Rahl heaved a sigh. "It was on a man we killed. Well, actually, we killed a whole bunch of men until we finally killed this particular one. By how well he was being protected, we knew that he had to be an important person, or have something mighty important on him. It turned out to be the latter."

"So, what was it?" Magda asked.

Lord Rahl put his hands on the short stone wall of the sliph's well and leaned back to look up at them with blue eyes.

"It was covered in jewels."

Merritt was still looking suspicious. "You're telling us that you found important treasure?"

"You might say so. These jewels were covering a box." He gave them each a meaningful look.

"A box," Merritt repeated carefully. "What sort of box?"

Alric Rahl arched an eyebrow as he folded his arms. "A box as black as the Keeper's heart, and containing great power, if you catch my drift."

Magda glanced at Merritt before looking back at Lord Rahl. "And what makes you think that this box contains great power? Did you try to open it?"

He frowned indignantly. "Do you take me for a fool?"

"No," Magda said. "But you said that it contained great power. What do you know about this box?"

He shot her a look. "Are you forgetting that Baraccus and I were good friends? He told me about how the power of Orden was contained in three inky black boxes covered in jewels. The thing is, he said that the boxes had been sent away to the Temple of the Winds." He looked from Magda to Merritt and back again. "So if they're in the Temple of the Winds, what is one of them doing in this world in the possession of a dead man?"

"We'd better tell him," Merritt whispered to her.

Magda nodded as she let out a long sigh. "The boxes were stolen from the Temple of the Winds."

"Obviously. But who took them?"

Merritt shrugged. "I'd say Sulachan's people if I had to venture a guess."

"What about the other two?" Magda asked.

Lord Rahl, arms still folded, sighed unhappily. "Don't know. I only have the one. And you would have a hard time believing how many men we had to kill to get this one."

"I can only imagine," Merritt said. "But if it was Sulachan who had it, you had better believe that a lot more men than that are going to come to get it back."

"No doubt," Lord Rahl said.

"We have to hide it," Magda said to Merritt. "Trying to protect it is too risky. It must be hidden."

"That sounds well and good, but where?" Merritt asked. "I don't know a place safe enough that Emperor Sulachan couldn't get to it. After all, it was hidden—in the Temple of the Winds in the underworld—and he managed to get to it."

"Well," she said, "if he didn't know where to look he—"

Magda went silent as the thought tickling at the back of her mind suddenly became clear. She blinked. She wondered if it could work. She wondered if it was even possible.

She seized Merritt's shirtsleeve. "A gravity spell?"

Lord Rahl's face scrunched up into a frown. "A what?"

"A gravity spell," Merritt said, ignoring Lord Rahl, his attention focused on Magda because he realized from the look in her eyes that she was on to something important. "What about a gravity spell?"

"That little gravity spell you created and gave to me draws those little clay figures to it."

"Right," he said in a drawl as it started to dawn on him.

"What if you created a bigger gravity spell that would

draw the dead that Sulachan's forces have animated, and draw the half people to it as well? Naja helped create them. She knows how they function and how their spirits have been manipulated, so maybe she could give you information on the spells involved and then you could create a gravity spell specifically designed to draw them both in, right?"

"For someone born without the gift," Merritt said with a smile, "you sure have some pretty interesting ideas of how to use it. You make a pretty good maker's match."

Lord Rahl was looking from one face to the other and back again. "Draw them into where?"

Merritt ran his hand back over his neck. "That's the problem. It needs to be someplace where we could trap them. Once we draw them in, we would also have to keep them there."

Magda snapped her fingers. "Isidore's symbols."

Merritt was already nodding. "We could use Isidore's keeper spells to make a barrier to help prevent them from escaping."

Lord Rahl still had the serious scowl. "You mean that you think you could create a spell that would draw Sulachan's walking dead people and his half-dead people to it?" When Merritt smiled and nodded, Alric Rahl went on. "And then you would place a barrier spell to ensure that they were trapped?"

"That's exactly right," Merritt said. "If we could draw them in and trap them, then our forces wouldn't ever have to fight them. I was racking my brain trying to think of weapons and ways for us to fight these things, but if we trapped them somewhere instead, we wouldn't ever need to fight them. If we never had to fight an army of the dead and half dead, it could save the lives of untold numbers of our soldiers, to say nothing of the innocent people in places Sulachan invades."

"All we need is a place to put them," Magda said. "It has to be someplace remote that would provide physical barriers as well as the barrier spells, just to be sure. Maybe a blind canyon or something like that."

Lord Rahl's scowl was gone. His arms came unfolded as he stood. He looked suddenly intent and serious.

"The Dark Lands."

"The Dark Lands?" Merritt asked. "What are the Dark Lands?"

"A remote and inhospitable area in D'Hara. There is a place there, to the north in the Dark Lands, surrounded by mountains. There is only one way in and out. All around are impassable mountains. If you could draw them in with this spell of yours, you might be able to trap them in there. No one goes to that remote area in the Dark Lands. It's a dangerous place. Everyone already considers it demon ground."

"That's perfect," Magda said. She turned to Merritt. "As soon as you can come up with a gravity spell that works on Sulachan's dead and his half people, we can go there, set the spell, and draw them in."

"The barrier spells that I could make from what Isidore came up with wouldn't weaken for thousands of years.

"And," Merritt added with a smile as he leaned toward her with a sparkle in his eyes, "we could leave the box of Orden there as well. Then it, too, would be trapped there. After all, who is going to go on demon ground filled with the walking dead and with half people who want to rip you open and eat you alive?"

Magda put a hand to her chest and heaved a big sigh of relief. "We've just solved two problems with the same solution. As soon as you can create the spells, we can travel to the Dark Lands and set the trap."

"We?" He shook his head. "You're not going. The thing about a gravity spell is that it's distance-sensitive. If you were to take those little clay figures I gave you some distance away from the gravity spell, it wouldn't have enough power to draw them to it.

"So, I'm going to have to create this spell and then travel near the enemy forces so it has enough power to draw the dead out. When I get them all coming after me, I'll be able to lead them to the Dark Lands and into this remote place. I'll set the spell and as soon as they're all drawn in, I'll place the barrier spell to keep them in. Having them follow me in isn't what I would prefer, but it's the only way.

"It's too dangerous for you to come with me."

"Too dangerous?" Magda planted her fists on her hips. "Who is it that saved your hide by cutting down all those soldiers and setting you free?"

Lord Rahl lifted a hand. "Ah, is this a story I ought to know about? You cutting men down? What are you talking about?"

Merritt waved a hand irritably. "She had the sword."

"Ah, she had a sword. That explains it."

"Just because she killed a wizard and eight or ten of Lothain's soldiers all by herself, now she thinks she's qualified for such a fight."

Lord Rahl clasped his hands as he arched an eyebrow. "Sounds to me like maybe she is."

Merritt's mouth twisted, and then he gave in to a smile. "I suppose it does. It will take a little while to create the spells, but once they're ready, we can set the trap."

He smiled at Magda in a special, very private way. It made her grin.

I've found him," Naja said. Her voice sounded like it was coming from that far-distant world. She squeezed Magda's hand. "I've found him."

Magda swallowed. "Are you sure it's him?"

Naja, her eyes closed, slowly nodded. "I've found him. It's beautiful. His spirit is beautiful. I knew it would be."

A tear rolled down Magda's cheek. "Can we ... talk to him?"

Naja's smooth brow twitched slightly. "In a way. Like I told you before, if he permits it, in a way."

They were alone, the two of them. And yet, in a manner of speaking, they were among a whole underworld of spirits.

The room was dark except near them where it was lit by a dozen candles set all around them on the floor. It was the dead of the night and dead quiet. There was no light to leak in around the shutters. Magda and Naja were alone in the storage room of the First Wizard's apartment. It seemed the fitting place because Baraccus had spent so much time at his workbench there.

Both Naja and Magda sat cross-legged on a plush, round carpet set before Baraccus's workbench lined with candles. Beyond the candlelight, the rest of the room might as well have been the void of the underworld itself.

Magda wondered briefly if perhaps it was.

She hadn't told Merritt what she was going to try to do. She didn't know what he would think of the idea. She supposed that he would support whatever she wanted to do, but she didn't want to worry him. He was always incredibly respectful of Baraccus as her husband, and Magda's feelings about him.

But Baraccus was gone.

Magda was alone, now. She had people who cared about her, but she felt alone without Baraccus. It was a terrible feeling to miss him, and at the same time realize that he was gone and that he never could be in her life again. She didn't know how to find peace.

She thought that maybe if she knew why he had killed himself, that would help.

Merritt understood. As much as it stood unspoken between them, he understood. She wasn't sure that she did. Merritt, though, gave her respectful distance because of Baraccus.

In a way, she wished he wouldn't. But she didn't know how to get beyond what was lost.

It wasn't fair to Merritt, of course, but she couldn't help herself. She couldn't help her feelings.

She felt like one of the spirits of the half people, lost between worlds, not knowing where she belonged.

Naja had understood. She'd said that it was a common problem. Letting go, she'd said, was often hard. She said that people came to her because they had difficulty letting go. Naja seemed to understand Magda's conflicting emotions better than Magda did, and offered to help with a spirit reading so that her heart could find peace.

Shadow meowed softly as she materialized out of the darkness to rub against Naja's side. After letting her tail drag across the spirit woman, the cat carefully stepped into Magda's lap and curled up in a ball, where she promptly started her soft, steady purring.

The black cat seemed at peace among spirits.

"Can you ask him if he is at peace?"

Eyes still closed, Naja smiled. "I don't need to ask him that. I can feel that he is."

"He is? How is that possible? I mean, he's gone, he's alone . . . he's without me . . ."

"It's not that way for the spirits," Naja said. "The concerns of our world, the concerns of our hearts, are not the same as the concerns of the underworld."

"Can I talk to him?"

"As I told you before, in a way, and through me, if he will allow it. Ask."

Magda swallowed. "Baraccus, I miss you so much."

"He knows, Magda. He knows."

Magda felt funny trying to talk about such deep, personal feelings through someone other than Baraccus. She knew that she had to try, though, if she wanted to ask him why he would have killed himself. This was her one chance.

"But . . . even though I miss you, it's not the same anymore. You aren't here, alive, so I can't hold on to you in the way I want to."

"He knows that, too, Magda," Naja said in her gentle, soft voice.

"But I—"

"I know your heart Magda," Naja said in a suddenly strange, distant voice.

Magda looked, trying to see, but it seemed to have grown too dark to see the spiritist's lips moving. Shadows seemed to move in the blackness around them.

"I know your loyalty to me," the strange voice said. "But who I was, who you loved, no longer exists. I have passed on. In your world, only my memory can exist. Your loyalty to me because of that memory is a part of life, but it can become disloyalty to yourself if you hold it so closely that it crowds out the rest of life."

"Why did you leave me," she asked in a halting voice as a tear rolled down her cheek. "I thought you loved me more than anything. Why would you leave me all alone?"

The candles hissed for a time as she waited, not knowing if he would answer. Finally, the strange voice returned.

"I had to do as I did because I love the world of life."

Magda sucked back a sob. "Please, Baraccus, I don't understand."

"There are others who can do what I could do. There are others who can fight in the ways that I could fight. There are others who can serve our cause as I served it. In that way, as remarkable as you may have believed me to be, I wasn't. I was not essential.

"But you are unique, my rare flower. There has never been anyone exactly like you before, and there can never be anyone exactly like you again. We are each that way. Because of the exact way you are, there are no others who could have done the things you have done, when you did them, in the way you did them. There are no others who have had the particular experiences you've had that led you to the choices you made. What you did, and what you have become, no other could have done in your place.

"You were, and you continue to be, on a unique path.

"There were so many paths that would have taken the world into eternal darkness, but there was only one to take it safely through this perilous time. You took the world on that path when it was needed.

"Had I lived, you would not have made the choices that took you down that path.

"At the Temple of the Winds I saw the future. Not

merely one future, but many futures. I saw the future as it would be had I returned and lived. I saw the future without you. I saw the future in a thousand different ways, and then another thousand, and then another. I saw all the layers of possibilities and variation, all the choices, all branches and forks in prophecy.

"But I saw one future above all others that gave the world of life the best chance in the face of the approaching dark age. In that future I saw that if I let you go on to walk your own path, you would be what was needed.

"If I had lived, you would have been at my side. You would have had no reason to do more, to be more. The forks in prophecy would not have presented themselves in the same way. Doorways would have remained closed. Without you seeking out truth as you have done, our cause would have been lost because you would have never become a Confessor.

"There is so much more that I saw when I was there that brought me to my choice. Lothain lied. He did get into the Temple. He lied to hide his treason. Once in the Temple, he reinforced the damage done by his traitors on the Temple team, altered important things there, and damaged important elements flowing toward the world of life.

"Lothain choked off the gift from the world of life so that fewer and fewer will be born gifted, and since the Temple is in the world of the dead, he was especially successful at choking off Subtractive Magic. That was why the moon turned red. It turned red in warning because of the damage caused by Lothain."

Magda was not merely astonished to hear this, she was horrified. "You mean Lothain managed to break the Grace and end magic in this world?"

"Not entirely," Naja answered in the strange voice. "He tried, and while he did not succeed completely, he managed to do vast damage. He has doomed the world to begin down the path that Emperor Sulachan envisions, the path toward a world without magic. While he set the world on that path, I was at least able to keep it from being a certainty.

"That was my greatest purpose, what I could do that no other would have been able to do. But I was only able to do so much. I was able to get enough of the gift to flow along the lines of the Grace to ensure that, even as the gift in mankind dwindles, one day a pebble in the pond will be born with what is required to complete the restoration of the world of life, if he, too, makes the right choices at the right times.

"You remember the book I brought back and the mission I sent you on upon my return?"

Magda nodded. "Yes, you asked me to take the book, through the sliph, to your secret, private library. When I was gone, you killed yourself. How could I forget such a thing?"

"That journey you undertook was a portion of the part I was able to play in setting the future on a course that gives the world of life a chance in that future that you have now made possible because you took your path. Had you not undertaken that task for me, the world would have been doomed. Now, if the right choices are made by the right people for the right reasons at the right time, then mankind still has a chance to escape the fate that Sulachan and Lothain tried to impose.

"But until those others can be born, I had to let you save what we have. I could see that the only part I could play if I lived would be to keep you from blossoming. I saw that I had to die in order for you to undertake the journey you took to search for answers, fight the dream walkers, take up the oath, seek me in the underworld through a spiritist so that you could discover that the dead down in the catacombs were serving evil, then choose to find Merritt, help him find what he needed to create the key, and in the end come to understand why you would choose on your own to be altered to become a Confessor who was able to unmask the corruption in a way that all could see it.

"Had I lived, none of that would have happened. I had to let you take the path that would save the world for now. That allows you and others to live to fight another day.

"My death gave you the drive to find out why I sacrificed my life, which in turn opened your own truth. In that search for truth, you would expose what I could not, in a way I could not, to accomplish what I could not.

"You think of me as a great man, Magda. In your eyes I may be, but I was just a man. I had faults, I had weaknesses, I had limits. I couldn't do everything. But I like to think I had a noble mind, and with that reasoning mind what I saw when I was at the Temple was that what needed to be done, I could not do.

"But I also saw that you could.

"Merritt is similar to you in that he has a unique chance. There is no one else who has the knowledge, creativity, and skills that he has. No other ever envisioned what he first envisioned. No other ever would have. Only Merritt could have envisioned and created the Sword of Truth, and only Merritt could have envisioned and created a Confessor.

"The world needed you to be there to be that Confessor at that moment, and in moments to come.

"I know, Magda, your heart, and your loyalty to your love for me. But don't let that be the end of your ability to love. That love wouldn't harm me, or diminish me, or change what we had. It can only add to you and who you are. You need to embrace the reality of what is, not what was.

"What you and Merritt have is different from what you and I had. It can be more.

"You share more with Merritt than I could ever share with you. You share an understanding, a partnership of souls, in a way that you and I never could. You share the Sword of Truth with him, and you share the new beginning of becoming a Confessor with him. You have been reborn into that new life. Merritt made that possible.

"You did not see what I saw when Merritt pushed that sword through your heart. He did that not because he wanted to make you a Confessor, but because you wanted it. It was the choice you made. It was killing him inside, but he did it anyway.

"It was the hardest thing he had ever done in his life, and though it was killing him, though it was breaking his own heart, he did it because you wanted it. He wanted to give you what you wanted, no matter how much it hurt him."

Magda swallowed back her sobs. She tried to bring her voice forth, but she couldn't form words.

"Don't let what we had limit the even greater experience you can have with Merritt. Don't let a misguided loyalty to me limit your heart and what you can have in greater abundance for yourself.

"To love another, you must first love yourself. Love yourself, Magda, so that you can love him. Love yourself enough to let your memories of me ease away from closing your heart.

"Love yourself enough to know that you deserve happiness.

"Know that I have nothing but love for Merritt, as I have for you. You have walked the path that has taken you to the possibility of something wonderful. Don't lose sight of that path because you are looking back at a memory of me.

"I am no more. Let me go, Magda. I am at peace now, let me go deeper beyond the veil."

Tears ran down Magda's face as she sobbed.

"Thank you, Baraccus. You've given me so much. Thank you for my life. I won't waste it, I swear."

"I know you won't, Magda. I know you won't."

Magda stood in the center of the dais, before the half circle of the council's desk, before the council, in her white Confessor's dress. There were only three councilmen there, Sadler, Clay, and Hambrook, but they would soon add to those numbers so that they could do their work.

The center chair sat empty.

That center chair was hers, now.

She presided over the council, now.

She balanced the council, now, with a Confessor's voice.

Behind her, in the great council chambers, there were a limited number of people. It was not a council session opened to the general public. It was invited guests only.

General Grundwall was there, much chagrined that he had ever expressed faith in Lothain to her just because he thought that Magda had agreed to marry him. He had apologized countless times. Magda had to finally order him to never apologize to her about that again.

Tilly was there as well, healed, in good health, and in good cheer. She beamed with pride at seeing Magda in her white Confessor's dress, at seeing Magda having the important place at the Keep that Tilly always thought she should have.

Quinn, likewise all smiles, was there as well, as was Naja. Magda missed Baraccus and Isidore and all those like them who were no longer with them and were now with the good spirits, but she was thankful for the friends they did have with them.

Merritt stood beside her, looking as handsome as she had ever seen him look. The Sword of Truth, in its ornately worked gold and silver scabbard, gleamed against his dark outfit. Since she was to his left, she could see the word *Truth* standing out in gold letters on the hilt.

Councilman Sadler beamed with pride as he addressed them.

"Magda, Merritt, we at the Keep all owe you a tremendous debt of gratitude."

Magda's hand found Merritt's.

"Now," he said, "we must call upon you both to help the people not only of the Keep, but of the Midlands, D'Hara, and in fact all of the New World to stand against the threats we face.

"Merritt, we have taken your admonition under consideration and we agree that we should abide by your recommendation, and Magda's, that a Confessor's power is better suited to women than men. We agree that the Confessor's power should rightly only be invested in women.

"We need the ability of a Confessor to help us discover truth as we go forward in this struggle for our survival. We therefore ask that you create a new force in the world, the Confessors, a band of sisters who can stand for truth."

Merritt bowed his head as he squeezed Magda's hand. "I can do that."

"And Magda, we ask that you be their leader, the

Mother Confessor, and help make them as effective, as dedicated, as noble in fighting for truth as you have shown yourself to be."

Magda bowed her head as she squeezed Merritt's hand. "I can do that."

"And Merritt," Councilman Sadler said, "we have come to understand, as you have explained it, the particular vulnerabilities of a Confessor. Especially in the time following the use of her power, when she is weakened and less able to protect herself. Even more critically, because of the nature of the power that she possesses, she is going to be a prime target for a great many dangerous people.

"We therefore ask that you be permanently assigned to be protector to Magda, the Mother Confessor. Once the band of sister Confessors is created, they too will each need a wizard to be their protector and to help them in their duties.

"But for now, there are only you two, the Mother Confessor, and her wizard. That is, if you both agree, of course." He looked to each of them in turn. "Do you both agree to this?"

Magda smiled as she and Merritt shared a look.

Looking into her eyes, Merritt said, "Wizard Merritt agrees and promises to always protect Magda, the Mother Confessor."

Looking into Merritt's eyes, Magda said, "And Magda, the Mother Confessor, will always stand by her wizard, Merritt."

The people in the room erupted in cheering.

As the people were celebrating the news, Merritt leaned close. "You look positively stunning, Mother Confessor."

Magda's cheeks hurt from smiling.

"Oh, I forgot to tell you about your hair," he said in a private tone.

She smoothed her hair back, then pulled out the white confession flower she had placed there, the flower Baraccus had once given her that she had kept in her silver box of memories. She twirled the little flower in her fingers, thinking about the path she had taken.

"What about my hair?"

"You can't cut it."

Magda twitched a frown up at him. "I can if I want."

"No, actually, you can't."

"What are you talking about?"

He leaned a little closer, looking a bit guilty. "The power won't let a Confessor cut her hair."

Magda was truly puzzled. "Won't let me? What in the world are you talking about?"

"The length of a woman's hair denotes status in the Midlands. You are the Mother Confessor. There is no woman of higher status than the Mother Confessor. Cutting your hair would be lowering your status in the eyes of many, so the magic of a Confessor's power won't allow it."

"Won't allow it," she repeated in a flat tone.

"That's right, won't allow it."

"Well, what if it needs to be trimmed?"

"Someone else has to do it."

Magda's brow lifted. "Touchy, isn't it?"

"It can be when it comes to matters of power. It expects you to be respected."

"The length of my hair can't earn me respect."

Merritt shrugged. "I'm just warning you."

Magda leaned into him, smiling as she tucked her shoulder under his arm. "Thanks for the warning."

Merritt grinned as he put his arm around her. "Sure." He pointed. "Is that the confession flower from your box of memories?"

Magda nodded. "I wanted to wear it today. Baraccus

sacrificed his life so that this course for our future could come to be. He gave his life that we all might be standing here today and have this chance. I think he would be pleased."

"I think he would be, too," Merritt said.

Magda twirled the little white flower between her finger and thumb, watching it spin, thinking about all that had brought her to be the Mother Confessor.

As the flower was spinning in her fingers, it began to become transparent. She could see right through it.

And then, the flower vanished.

It was gone. Simply, gone.

"Did you see that?" Magda asked in astonishment.

"I sure did."

She looked up at Merritt's handsome features. "What do you think it could mean?"

"I think it means whatever you want it to mean."

Magda looked down at her empty fingers a moment.

"Everything," she finally said. "It means everything."